ASSEGAI

WILBUR SMITH was born in Central Africa in 1933. He was
educated at Michaelhouse and Rhodes University. He became
a full-time writer in 1964 after the successful publication of
When the Lion Feeds, and has written over thirty novels, all
meticulously researched on his numerous expeditions world-
wide. His books are now translated into twenty-six languages.

Find out more about Wilbur Smith by
looking at his own author website,
www.wilbursmithbooks.com

THE NOVELS OF WILBUR SMITH

THE COURTNEYS

When the Lion Feeds   The Sound of Thunder

A Sparrow Falls   Birds of Prey   Monsoon

Blue Horizon   The Triumph of the Sun

THE COURTNEYS OF AFRICA

The Burning Shore   Power of the Sword   Rage

A Time to Die   Golden Fox   Assegai

THE BALLANTYNE NOVELS

A Falcon Flies   Men of Men   The Angels Weep

The Leopard Hunts in Darkness

THE EGYPTIAN NOVELS

River God   The Seventh Scroll   Warlock

The Quest

Also

The Dark of the Sun   Shout at the Devil

Gold Mine   The Diamond Hunters

The Sunbird   Eagle in the Sky

The Eye of the Tiger   Cry Wolf

Hungry as the Sea   Wild Justice

Elephant Song

WILBUR SMITH

ASSEGAI

PAN BOOKS

First published 2009 by Macmillan

This edition published 2010 by Pan Books
an imprint of Pan Macmillan, a division of Macmillan Publishers Limited
Pan Macmillan, 20 New Wharf Road, London N1 9RR
Basingstoke and Oxford
Associated companies throughout the world
www.panmacmillan.com

ISBN 978-0-330-51106-3

Typeset by Set Systems Ltd, Saffron Walden, Essex
Printed in the UK by CPI Mackays, Chatham ME5 8TD

Visit www.panmacmillan.com to read more about all our books
and to buy them. You will also find features, author interviews and
news of any author events, and you can sign up for e-newsletters
so that you're always first to hear about our new releases.

This book is for my wife

MOKHINISO

who is the best thing
that has ever happened to me

AUGUST 9, 1906, was the fourth anniversary of the coronation of Edward VII, King of the United Kingdom and the British Dominions, and Emperor of India. Coincidentally it was also the nineteenth birthday of one of His Majesty's loyal subjects, Second Lieutenant Leon Courtney of C Company, 3rd Battalion, 1st Regiment, The King's African Rifles, or the KAR, as it was more familiarly known. Leon was spending his birthday hunting Nandi rebels along the escarpment of the Great Rift Valley in the far interior of that jewel of the Empire, British East Africa.

The Nandi were a belligerent people much given to insurrection against authority. They had been in sporadic rebellion for the last ten years, ever since their paramount witch doctor and diviner had prophesied that a great black snake would wind through their tribal lands belching fire and smoke and bringing death and disaster to the tribe. When the British colonial administration began laying the tracks for the railway, which was planned to reach from the port of Mombasa on the Indian Ocean to the shores of Lake Victoria almost six hundred miles inland, the Nandi saw the dread prophecy being fulfilled and the coals of smouldering insurrection flared up again. They burned brighter as the head of the railway reached Nairobi, then started westwards through the Rift Valley and the Nandi tribal lands down towards Lake Victoria.

When Colonel Penrod Ballantyne, the officer commanding the KAR regiment, received the despatch from the governor of the colony informing him that the tribe had risen again and were attacking isolated government outposts along the proposed route of the railway he remarked, with exasperation, 'Well, I suppose we shall just have to give them another good drubbing.' And he ordered his 3rd Battalion out of their barracks in Nairobi to do just that.

Offered the choice, Leon Courtney would have been otherwise occupied on that day. He knew a young lady whose husband had been killed quite recently by a rampaging lion on their coffee *shamba* in the Ngong Hills a few miles outside the colony's fledgling capital, Nairobi. As a fearless horseman and prodigious striker of the ball, Leon had been invited to play at number one on her husband's polo team. Of course, as a junior subaltern, he could not afford to run a string of ponies, but some of the more affluent club members were pleased to sponsor him. As a member of her deceased husband's team Leon had certain privileges, or so he had convinced himself. After a decent interval had passed, when the widow would have recovered from the sharpest pangs of her bereavement, he rode out to the *shamba* to offer his condolences and respect. He was gratified to discover that she had made a remarkable recovery from her loss. Even in her widow's weeds Leon found her more fetching than any other lady of his acquaintance.

When Verity O'Hearne, for that was the lady's name, looked up at the strapping lad in his best uniform, slouch hat, with the regimental lion and elephant tusk side badge, and burnished riding boots, she saw in his comely features and candid gaze an innocence and eagerness that roused some feminine instinct in her that at first she supposed was maternal. On the wide, shady veranda of the homestead she served him tea and sandwiches spread with The Gentleman's Relish. To begin with, Leon was awkward and shy in her presence, but she was gracious and drew him out skilfully, speaking in a soft Irish brogue that enchanted him. The hour passed with startling rapidity. When he rose to take his leave she walked with him to the front steps and offered her hand in farewell. 'Please call again, Lieutenant Courtney, if you are ever in the vicinity. At times I find loneliness a heavy burden.' Her voice was low and mellifluous and her little hand silky smooth.

Leon's duties, as the youngest officer in the battalion, were many and onerous so it was almost two weeks before he could avail himself of her invitation. Once the tea and sandwiches had been despatched she led him into the house to show him her husband's hunting rifles, which she wished to sell. 'My husband has left me short of funds so, sadly, I am forced to find a buyer for them. I hoped that you, as a military man, might give me some idea of their value.'

'I would be delighted to assist you in any possible way, Mrs O'Hearne.'

'You are so kind. I feel that you are my friend and that I can trust you completely.'

He could find no words to answer her. Instead he gazed abjectly into her large blue eyes for by this time he was deeply in her thrall.

'May I call you Leon?' she asked, and before he could answer she burst into violent sobs. 'Oh, Leon! I am desolate and so lonely,' she blurted, and fell into his arms.

He held her to his chest. It seemed the only way to comfort her. She was as light as a doll and laid her pretty head on his shoulder, returning his embrace with enthusiasm. Later he tried to re-create exactly what had happened next, but it was all an ecstatic blur. He could not remember how they had reached her room. The bed was a big brass-framed affair, and as they lay together on the feather mattress the young widow gave him a glimpse of Paradise and altered for ever the fulcrum on which Leon's existence turned.

Now these many months later, in the shimmering heat of the Rift Valley, as he led his detachment of seven *askari*, locally recruited tribal troops, in extended order with bayonets fixed, through the lush banana plantation that surrounded the buildings of the district commissioner's headquarters at Niombi, Leon was thinking not so much of his duties as of Verity O'Hearne's bosom.

Out on his left flank Sergeant Manyoro clicked his tongue against the roof of his mouth. Leon jerked back from Verity's boudoir to the present and froze at the soft warning. His mind had been wandering and he had been derelict in his duty.

Every nerve in his body came up taut as a fishing line struck by a heavy marlin deep in the blue waters of the Pemba Channel. He lifted his right hand in the command to halt and the line of *askaris* stopped on either side of him. He glanced from the corner of his eye at his sergeant.

Manyoro was a *morani* of the Masai. A fine member of that tribe, he stood at well over six feet, yet he was as slim and graceful as a bullfighter, wearing his khaki uniform and tasselled fez with panache, every inch the African warrior. When he felt Leon's eyes on him he lifted his chin.

Leon followed the gesture and saw the vultures. There were only two, turning wing-tip to wing-tip high above the rooftops of the *boma*, the government's district-administration station at Niombi.

'Shit and corruption!' Leon whispered softly. He had not been expecting trouble: the centre of the insurrection was reported seventy miles further west. This government outpost was outside the traditional boundaries of the Nandi tribal grounds. This was Masai territory. Leon's orders were merely to reinforce the government *boma* with his few men against any possibility that the insurrection might boil over the tribal borders. Now it appeared that that had happened.

The district commissioner at Niombi was Hugh Turvey. Leon had met him and his wife at the Settlers' Club ball in Nairobi the previous Christmas Eve. He was only four or five years older than Leon but he was in sole charge of a territory the size of Scotland. Already he had earned a reputation as a solid man, not one to let his *boma* be surprised by a bunch of rebels. But the circling birds were a sinister omen, harbingers of death.

Leon gave the hand signal to his *askari* to load, and the breech bolts snickered as the .303 rounds were cranked up into the chambers of the long-barrelled Lee-Enfields. Another hand signal and they went forward cautiously in skirmishing formation.

Only two birds, Leon thought. They might be strays. There

would have been more of them if . . . From directly ahead he heard the loud flapping of heavy wings and another vulture rose from beyond the screen of banana plants. Leon felt the chill of dread. If the brutes are settling that means there's meat lying out there, dead meat.

Again he signalled the halt. He stabbed a finger at Manyoro, then went forward alone, Manyoro backing him. Even though his approach was stealthy and silent he alarmed more of the huge carrion-eaters. Singly and in groups they rose on flogging wings into the blue sky to join the spiralling cloud of their fellows.

Leon stepped past the last banana plant and stopped again at the edge of the open parade-ground. Ahead, the mud-brick walls of the *boma* glared, with their coating of limewash. The front door of the main building stood wide open. The veranda and the baked-clay surface of the parade-ground were littered with broken furniture and official government documents. The *boma* had been ransacked.

Hugh Turvey and his wife, Helen, lay spreadeagled in the open. They were naked and the corpse of their five-year-old daughter lay just beyond them. She had been stabbed once through her chest with a broad-bladed Nandi *assegai*. Her tiny body had drained of blood through the massive wound, so her skin shone white as salt in the bright sunlight. Both her parents had been crucified. Sharpened wooden stakes had been driven through their feet and hands into the clay surface.

So the Nandi have learned something at last from the missionaries, Leon thought bitterly. He took a long, steady look around the border of the parade-ground, searching for any sign that the attackers might still be near by. When he was satisfied that they had gone, he went forward again, stepping carefully through the litter. As he drew closer to the bodies he saw that Hugh had been crudely emasculated and that Helen's breasts had been cut off. The vultures had enlarged the wounds. The jaws of both corpses had been wedged wide apart with wooden pegs. Leon stopped when he reached them and stared down at them. 'Why are their mouths prised open?' he asked, in Kiswahili, as his sergeant came up beside him.

'They drowned them,' Manyoro answered quietly, in the same language. Leon saw then that the clay beneath their heads was stained where some spilled liquid had dried. Then he noticed that their nostrils had been plugged with balls of clay – they must have been forced to draw their last breaths through their mouths.

'Drowned?' Leon shook his head in incomprehension. Then, suddenly, he became aware of the sharp ammonia stink of urine. 'No!'

'Yes,' said Manyoro. 'It is one of the things the Nandi do to their enemies. They piss in their open mouths until they drown. The Nandi are not men, they are baboons.' His contempt and tribal enmity were undisguised.

'I would like to find those who did this,' Leon muttered, disgust giving way to anger.

'I will find them. They have not gone far.'

Leon looked away from the sickening butchery to the heights of the escarpment that stood a thousand feet above them. He lifted his slouch hat and wiped the sweat from his brow with the back of the hand that held the Webley service revolver. With a visible effort he brought his emotions under control, then looked down again.

'First we must bury these people,' he told Manyoro. 'We cannot leave them for the birds.'

Cautiously they searched the buildings and found them deserted, with signs that the government staff had fled at the first hint of trouble. Then Leon sent Manyoro and three *askari* to search the banana plantation thoroughly and to secure the outside perimeter of the *boma*.

While they were busy, he went back to the Turveys' living quarters, a small cottage behind the office block. It had also been ransacked but he found a pile of sheets in a cupboard that had been overlooked by the looters. He gathered up an armful and took them outside. He pulled out the stakes with which the Turveys had been pegged to the ground, then removed the wedges from their mouths. Some of their teeth were broken and their lips had been crushed. Leon wetted his neckerchief with water from his canteen and wiped their faces clean of dried blood and urine. He tried to move their arms to their sides but rigor mortis had stiffened them. He wrapped their bodies in the sheets.

The earth in the banana plantation was soft and damp from recent rain. While he and some of the *askari* stood guard against another attack, four others went to work with their trenching tools to dig a single grave for the family.

O n the heights of the escarpment, just below the skyline and screened by a small patch of scrub from any watcher below, three men leaned on their war spears, balancing easily on one leg in the stork-like attitude of rest. Before them, the floor of the Rift Valley was a vast plain, brown grassland interspersed with stands of thorn, scrub and acacia trees. Despite its desiccated appearance the grasses made sweet grazing and were highly prized by the Masai, who ran their long-horned, hump-backed cattle on them. Since the most recent Nandi rebellion, though, they had driven their herds to a safer area much further to the south. The Nandi were famous cattle thieves.

This part of the valley had been left to the wild game, whose multitudes swarmed across the plain as far as the eye could see. At a distance the zebra were as grey as the dustclouds they raised when they galloped skittishly from any perceived danger, the kongoni, the gnu and the buffalo darker stains on the golden landscape. The long necks of the giraffe stood tall as telegraph poles above the flat tops of the acacia trees, while the antelope were insubstantial creamy specks that danced and shimmered in the heat. Here and there masses of what looked like black volcanic rock moved ponderously through the lesser animals, like ocean-going ships through shoals of sardines. These were the mighty pachyderms: rhinoceros and elephant.

It was a scene both primeval and awe-inspiring in its extent and abundance, but to the three watchers on the heights it was commonplace. Their interest was focused on the tiny cluster of buildings directly below them. A spring, which oozed from the foot of the escarpment wall, sustained the patch of greenery that surrounded the buildings of the government *boma*.

The oldest of the three men wore a kilt of leopard tails and a cap of the same black and gold speckled fur. This was the regalia of the paramount witch doctor of the Nandi tribe. His name was Arap Samoei and for ten years he had led the rebellion against the white invaders and their infernal machines, which threatened to desecrate the sacred tribal lands of his people. The faces and bodies of the men with him were painted for war: their eyes were circled with red ochre, a stripe was painted down their noses and their cheeks were slashed with the same colour. Their bare chests were dotted with burned lime in a pattern that simulated the plumage of the vulturine guinea fowl. Their kilts were made of gazelle skins and their headdresses of genet and monkey fur.

'The *mzungu* and his bastard Masai dogs are well into the trap,' said Arap Samoei. 'I had hoped for more, but seven Masai and one *mzungu* will make a good killing.'

'What are they doing?' asked the Nandi captain at his side, shading his eyes from the glare as he peered down the precipitous slope.

'They are digging a hole to bury the white filth we left for them,' said Samoei.

'Is it time to carry the spears down to them?' asked the third warrior.

'It is time,' answered the paramount witch doctor. 'But keep the *mzungu* for me. I want to cut off his balls with my own blade. From them I will make a powerful medicine.' He touched the hilt of the *panga* on his leopardskin belt. It was a knife with a short, heavy blade, the favoured close-quarters weapon of the Nandi. 'I want to hear him squeal, squeal like a warthog in the jaws of a leopard as I cut away his manhood. The louder he screams the more powerful will be the medicine.' He turned and strode back to the crest of the rugged rock wall, and looked down into the fold of dead ground behind it. His warriors squatted patiently in the short grass, rank upon rank of them. Samoei raised his clenched fist and the waiting *impi* sprang to its feet, making no sound that might carry to their quarry.

'The fruit is ripe!' called Samoei.

'It is ready for the blade!' his warriors agreed in unison.

'Let us go down to the harvest!'

The grave was ready, waiting to receive its bounty. Leon nodded at Manyoro, who gave a quiet order to his men. Two jumped down into the pit and the others passed the wrapped bundles down to them. They laid the two larger awkwardly shaped forms side by side on the floor of the grave with the tiny one wedged between them, a pathetic little group united for ever in death.

Leon removed his slouch hat and went down on one knee at the edge of the grave. Manyoro ordered the small detachment of men to fall in behind him with their rifles at the slope. Leon began to recite the Lord's Prayer. The *askari* did not understand the words, but they knew their significance for they had heard them uttered over many other graves.

'For thine is the kingdom, the power and the glory, for ever and ever, amen!' Leon ended and began to rise, but before he stood upright the oppressive silence of the hot African afternoon was shattered by a deafening hubbub of howls and screams. He dropped his hand to the butt of the Webley pistol holstered on his Sam Browne belt, and glanced around him swiftly.

Out of the dense foliage of the bananas swarmed a mass of sweat-shining bodies. They came from all sides, cavorting and prancing, brandishing their weapons. The sunlight sparkled on the blades of spear and *panga*. They drummed on their rawhide shields with their knobkerries, leaping high in the air as they raced towards the tiny group of soldiers.

'On me!' bellowed Leon. 'Form up on me! Load! Load! Load!' The *askari* reacted with trained precision, immediately forming a tight circle around him, rifles at the ready, bayonets pointing outwards. Appraising their situation swiftly, Leon saw that his party was completely surrounded except on the side nearest the *boma*'s main building. The Nandi formation must have split as it rounded it, leaving a narrow gap in their line.

'Commence firing!' Leon shouted, and the crash of the seven rifles was almost drowned in the uproar of shouting and drumming shields. He saw only one of the Nandi go down, a chieftain wearing kilts and headdress of Colobus monkey pelts. His head was snapped back by the heavy lead bullet, and bloody tissue erupted in a cloud from the back of his skull. Leon knew who had fired the shot: Manyoro was an expert marksman, and Leon had seen him single out his victim, then aim deliberately.

The charge faltered as the chief went down, but at a shriek of rage from a leopard-robed witch doctor in the rear, the attackers rallied and came on again. Leon realized that this witch doctor was probably the notorious leader of the insurrection, Arap Samoei himself. He fired two quick shots at him, but the distance was well over fifty paces and the short-barrelled Webley was a close-range weapon. Neither bullet had any effect.

'On me!' Leon shouted again. 'Close order! Follow me!' He led them at a run straight into the narrow gap in the Nandi line, making directly for the main building. The tiny band of khaki-clad figures was almost through before the Nandi surged forward again and headed them off. Both sides were instantly embroiled in a hand-to-hand mêlée.

'Take the bayonet to them!' Leon roared, and fired the

Webley into the grimacing face ahead of him. When the man dropped another appeared immediately behind him. Manyoro plunged his long silver bayonet full length into his chest and jumped over the body, plucking out the blade as he went. Leon followed closely and between them they killed three more with blade and bullet before they broke out of the ruck and reached the veranda steps. By now they were the only members of the detachment still on their feet. All the others had been speared.

Leon took the veranda steps three at a time and charged through the open door into the main room. Manyoro slammed the door behind them. Each ran to a window and blazed away at the Nandi as they came after them. Their fire was so witheringly accurate that within seconds the steps were cluttered with bodies. The rest drew back in dismay, then turned tail and scattered into the plantation.

Leon stood at the window reloading his pistol as he watched them go. 'How much ammunition do you have, Sergeant?' he called to Manyoro, at the other window.

The sleeve of Manyoro's tunic had been slashed by a Nandi *panga*, but there was little bleeding and Manyoro ignored the wound. He had the breech bolt of his rifle open and was loading bullets into the magazine. 'These are my last two clips, Bwana,' he answered, 'but there are many more lying out there.' He gestured through the window at the bandoliers of the fallen *askari* lying on the parade-ground, surrounded by the half-naked Nandi they had taken down with them.

'We will go out and pick them up before the Nandi can regroup,' Leon told him.

Manyoro slammed the breech bolt of the rifle closed and propped the weapon against the windowsill.

Leon slipped his pistol back into its holster and went to join him at the doorway. They stood side by side and gathered themselves for the effort. Manyoro was watching his face and Leon grinned at him. It was good to have the tall Masai at his side. They had been together ever since Leon had come out

11

from England to join the regiment. That was little more than a year ago, but the rapport they had established was strong. 'Are you ready, Sergeant?' he asked.

'I am, Bwana.'

'Up the Rifles!' Leon gave the regimental war-cry and threw open the door. They burst through it together. The steps were slippery with blood and cluttered with corpses so Leon hurdled the low retaining wall and landed on his feet running. He raced to the nearest dead *askari* and dropped to his knees. Quickly he unbuckled his webbing and slung the heavy bandoliers of ammunition over his shoulder. Then he jumped up and ran to the next man. Before he reached him a loud, angry hum rose from the edge of the banana plantation. Leon ignored it and dropped down beside the corpse. He did not look up again until he had another set of webbing slung over his shoulder. Then he leaped up as the Nandi swarmed back on to the parade-ground.

'Get back, and be quick about it!' he yelled at Manyoro, who was also draped with ammunition bandoliers. Leon paused just long enough to snatch up a dead *askari*'s rifle before he raced for the veranda wall. There he paused to glance back over his shoulder. Manyoro was a few yards behind him, while the leading Nandi warriors were fifty paces away and coming on swiftly.

'Cutting it a little fine,' Leon grunted. Then he saw one of the pursuers unsling the heavy bow from his shoulder. Leon recognized it as the weapon they used to hunt elephant. He felt a prickle of alarm at the back of his neck. The Nandi were expert archers. 'Run, damn it, run!' he shouted at Manyoro, as he saw the Nandi nock a long arrow, lift the bow and draw the fletching to his lips. Then he released the arrow, which shot upwards and fell in a silent arc. 'Look out!' Leon screamed, but the warning was futile, the arrow too swift. Helplessly he watched it plummet towards Manyoro's unprotected back.

'God!' said Leon softly. 'Please, God!' For a moment he thought the arrow would fall short, for it was dropping steeply, but then he realized it would find its mark. He took a step back towards Manyoro, then stopped to watch helplessly. The strike of the arrow was hidden from him by Manyoro's body but he heard the meaty *whunk* of the iron head piercing flesh and Manyoro spun around. The head of the arrow was buried deeply in the back of his upper thigh. He tried to take another pace but the wounded leg anchored him. Leon pulled the bandoliers from around his own neck and hurled them and the rifle he was carrying over the retaining wall and through the open door. Then he started back. Manyoro was hopping towards him on his unwounded leg, the other dangling, the shaft of the arrow flapping. Another arrow came towards them and Leon flinched as it hummed a hand's breadth past his ear, then clashed against the veranda wall.

He reached Manyoro and wrapped his right arm around his sergeant's torso beneath the armpit. He lifted him bodily and ran with him to the wall. Leon was surprised that although he was so tall the Masai was light. Leon was heavier by twenty pounds of solid muscle. At that moment every ounce of his powerful frame was charged with the strength of fear and desperation. He reached the wall and swung Manyoro over it, letting him tumble in a heap on the far side. Then he cleared the wall in a single bound. More arrows hummed and clattered around them but Leon ignored them, swept Manyoro into his arms, as though he was a child, and ran through the open door as the first of the pursuing Nandi reached the wall behind them.

He dropped Manyoro on the floor and picked up the rifle he had retrieved from the dead *askari*. As he turned back to the open doorway he levered a fresh cartridge into the breech and shot dead a Nandi as he was clambering over the wall. Swiftly he worked the bolt and fired again. When the magazine was empty he put down the rifle and slammed the door. It was made from heavy mahogany planks and the frame was deeply embedded in the thick walls. It shook as, on the other side, the Nandi hurled themselves against it. Leon drew his pistol and fired two shots through the panels. There was a

13

yelp of pain from the far side, then silence. Leon waited for them to come again. He could hear whispering, and the scuffle of feet. Suddenly a painted face appeared in one of the side windows. Leon aimed at it but a shot rang out from behind him before he could press the trigger. The head vanished.

Leon turned and saw that Manyoro had dragged himself across the floor to the rifle he had left propped beside the other window. Using the sill to steady himself he had pulled himself on to his good leg. He fired again through the window and Leon heard the solid thud of a bullet striking flesh, and then the sound of another body falling on the veranda. '*Morani!* Warrior!' he panted, and Manyoro grinned at the compliment.

'Do not leave all the work to me, Bwana. Take the other window!'

Leon stuffed the pistol into his holster, snatched up the empty rifle and ran with it to the open window, cramming clips of cartridges into the magazine – two clips, ten rounds. The Lee-Enfield was a lovely weapon. It felt good in his hands.

He reached the window and threw out a sheet of rapid fire. Between them they swept the parade-ground with a fusillade that sent the Nandi scampering for the cover of the plantation. Manyoro sank slowly down the wall and leaned against it, legs thrust out before him, the wounded one cocked over the other so that the arrow shaft did not touch the floor.

With one last glance across the parade-ground to confirm that none of the enemy was sneaking back, Leon left his window and went to his sergeant. He squatted in front of him and tentatively grasped the arrow shaft. Manyoro winced. Leon exerted a little more pressure, but the barbed iron head was immovable. Though Manyoro made no sound the sweat poured down his face and dripped on to the front of his tunic.

'I can't pull it out so I'm going to break off the shaft and strap it,' Leon said.

Manyoro looked at him without expression for a long moment, then smiled, his teeth showing large, even and white. His earlobes had been pierced in childhood, the holes stretched to hold ivory discs, which gave his face a mischievous, puckish aspect.

'Up the Rifles!' Manyoro said, and his lisping imitation of Leon's favourite expression was so startling in the circumstances that Leon guffawed and, at the same instant, snapped off the reed shaft of the arrow close to where it protruded from the oozing wound. Manyoro closed his eyes, but uttered no sound.

Leon found a field dressing in the webbing pouch he had taken from the *askari*, and bandaged the stump of the arrow shaft to stop it moving. Then he rocked back on his heels and studied his handiwork. He unhooked the water-bottle from his own webbing, unscrewed the stopper and took a long swallow, then handed it to Manyoro. The Masai hesitated delicately: an *askari* did not drink from an officer's bottle. Frowning, Leon thrust it into his hands. 'Drink, damn you,' he said. 'That's an order!'

Manyoro tilted back his head and held the bottle high. He poured the water directly into his mouth without touching the neck with his lips. His Adam's apple bobbed as he swallowed three times. Then he screwed on the stopper tightly and handed it back to Leon. 'Sweet as honey,' he said.

'We will move out as soon as it's dark,' Leon said.

Manyoro considered this statement for a moment. 'Which way will you go?'

'We will go the way we came.' Leon emphasized the plural pronoun. 'We must get back to the railway line.'

Manyoro chuckled.

'What makes you laugh, *Morani?*' Leon demanded.

'It is almost two days' march to the railway line,' Manyoro reminded him. He shook his head in amusement and touched his bandaged leg significantly. 'When you go, Bwana, you will go alone.'

'Are you thinking of deserting, Manyoro? You know that's a shooting offence—' He broke off as movement beyond the window caught his eye. He snatched up the rifle and fired three quick shots out across the parade-ground. A bullet must have thumped into living flesh because a cry of pain and anger followed. 'Baboons and sons of baboons,' Leon growled. In Kiswahili the insult had a satisfying ring. He laid the rifle across his lap to reload it. Without looking up he said, 'I will carry you.'

Manyoro gave his puckish smile and asked politely, 'For two days, Bwana, with half the Nandi tribe chasing after us, you will carry me? Is that what I heard you say?'

'Perhaps the wise and witty sergeant has a better plan,' Leon challenged him.

'Two days!' Manyoro marvelled. 'I should call you "Horse".'

They were silent for a while, and then Leon said, 'Speak, O wise one. Give me counsel.'

Manyoro paused, then said, 'This is not the land of the Nandi. These are the grazing lands of my people. These treacherous curs trespass on the lands of the Masai.'

Leon nodded. His field map showed no such boundaries: his orders had not made such divisions clear. His superiors were probably ignorant of the nuances of tribal territorial demarcations, but Leon had been with Manyoro on long foot patrols through these lands before this most recent outbreak of rebellion. 'This I know, for you have explained it to me. Now tell me your better plan, Manyoro.'

'If you go towards the railway—'

Leon interrupted: 'You mean if we go that way.'

Manyoro inclined his head slightly in acquiescence. 'If we go towards the railway we will be moving back into Nandi ground. They will grow bold and harry us, like a pack of hyenas. However, if we move down the valley . . .' Manyoro indicated south with his chin '. . . we will be moving into Masai territory. Each step they take in pursuit will fill the bowels of the Nandi with fear. They will not follow us far.'

Leon thought about this, then shook his head dubiously. 'There is nothing to the south but wilderness and I must get you to a doctor before the leg festers and has to be cut off.'

'Less than a day's easy march to the south lies the *manyatta* of my mother,' Manyoro told him.

Leon blinked with surprise. Somehow he had never thought of Manyoro as having a parent. Then he collected himself. 'You don't hear me. You need a doctor, somebody who can get that arrow out of your leg before it kills you.'

'My mother is the most famous doctor in all the land. Her fame as the paramount witch doctor is known from the ocean to the great lakes. She has saved a hundred of our *morani* who have been struck down by spear and arrow or savaged by lions. She has medicines that are not even dreamed of by your white doctors in Nairobi.' Manyoro sank back against the wall. By now his skin bore a greyish sheen and the smell of his sweat was rancid. They stared at each other for a moment, then Leon nodded.

'Very well. We will go south down the Rift. We will leave in the dark before the rise of the moon.'

But Manyoro sat up again and sniffed the sultry air, like a hunting dog picking up a distant scent. 'No, Bwana. If we go, we must go at once. Can you not smell it?'

'Smoke!' Leon whispered. 'The swine are going to flush us out with fire.' He glanced out of the window again. The parade-ground was empty, but he knew they would not come again from that direction: there were no windows in the rear wall of the building. That was the way they would come. He studied the leaves of the nearest banana plants. A light breeze was ruffling them. 'Wind from the east,' he murmured. 'That suits us.' He looked at Manyoro. 'We can carry little with us. Every extra ounce will make a difference. Leave the rifles and bandoliers. We will take a bayonet and one water-bottle each. That's all.' As he spoke, he reached for the pile of canvas webbing they had salvaged. He buckled three of the waist belts together to form a single loop, slipped it over his head and settled it on his right shoulder. It hung down just below his left hip. He held his water-bottle to his ear and shook it. 'Less than half.' He decanted the contents of the salvaged

17

bottles into his own, then topped up Manyoro's. 'What we can't carry we will drink here.' Between them they drained what was left in the others.

'Come on, Sergeant, get up.' Leon put a hand under Manyoro's armpit and hoisted him to his feet. The sergeant balanced on his good leg as he strapped his water-bottle and bayonet around his waist. At that moment something heavy thumped on the thatch above their heads.

'Torches!' Leon snapped. 'They've crept up to the back of the building and are throwing firebrands on to the roof.' There was another loud thump above them, and the smell of burning was stronger in the room.

'Time to go,' Leon muttered, as a tendril of dark smoke drifted across the window, then rolled with the breeze diagonally across the open parade-ground towards the trees. They heard the distant chanting and excited shouting of the Nandi as, for a moment, the curtain of smoke cleared, then poured down so densely that they could see no more than an arm's length in front of them. The crackle of flames had risen to a dull roar that drowned even the voices of the Nandi, and the smoke was hot and suffocating. Leon ripped the tail off his shirt and handed it to Manyoro. 'Cover your face!' he ordered, and knotted his neckerchief over his own nose and mouth. Then he hoisted Manyoro over the window sill and jumped out after him.

Manyoro leaned on his shoulder and hopped beside him as they crossed quickly to the retaining wall. Leon used it to orientate himself as they moved to the corner of the veranda. They dropped over it and paused to get their bearings in the dense smoke. Sparks from the roof swirled around them and stung the exposed skin of their arms and legs. They went forward again as quickly as Manyoro could move on one leg, Leon keeping the light breeze behind them. They were both choking in the smoke, their eyes burning and streaming tears. They fought the urge to cough, smothering the sound with the cloths that covered their mouths. Then, suddenly, they were among the first trees of the plantation.

The smoke was still thick, and they groped their way forward, bayonets at the ready, expecting at any moment to run into the enemy. Leon was aware that Manyoro was flagging already. Since they had left the *boma* he had set a furious pace that Manyoro, on one leg, could not sustain. He was already leaning most of his weight on Leon's shoulder.

'We daren't stop before we're well clear,' Leon whispered.

'On one leg I will go as far and as fast as you will on two,' Manyoro gasped.

'Will Manyoro, the great braggart, wager a hundred shillings on that?' But before the sergeant could respond Leon gripped his arm in silent warning. They stopped, peering ahead into the smoke and listening. They heard the sound again: someone coughed hoarsely not far ahead. Leon lifted Manyoro's hand from his shoulder and mouthed, 'Wait here.'

He went forward, crouching low with the bayonet in his right hand. He had never killed a man with a blade before, but in training the instructor had made them practise the motions. A human shape loomed directly in front of him. Leon leaped forward and used the hilt of the bayonet like a knuckle-duster, smashing it into the side of the man's head with such force that he fell to his knees. He threw an armlock around the Nandi's neck, choking any sound before it reached his lips. But the Nandi had coated his entire body with palm oil. He was as slippery as a fish and struggled violently. He almost managed to twist out of Leon's grasp but Leon reached around the wriggling body with the hand that held the bayonet and drove the point up under the Nandi's ribs, shocked by how easily the steel slipped in.

The Nandi redoubled his efforts and tried to scream, but Leon held the lock on his throat and the sounds he uttered were muffled. The dying man's violent struggles worked the blade around in his chest cavity as Leon twisted and sawed it. Suddenly the Nandi convulsed and dark red blood spouted from his mouth. It splattered over Leon's arm and droplets blew back into his face. The Nandi heaved once, then went slack in his grip.

Leon held him for a few seconds longer to make certain he was dead, then released the body, pushed it away and stumbled back to where he had left Manyoro. 'Come on,' he croaked, and they went forward again, Manyoro clinging to him, staggering and lurching.

Suddenly the ground gave way under them and they rolled down a steep mud bank into a shallow stream. There, the smoke was thinner. With a lift of relief Leon realized they had come in the right direction: they had reached the stream from the spring that ran to the south of the *boma*.

He knelt in the water and scooped handfuls into his face, washing his burning eyes and scrubbing the Nandi's blood off his hands. Then he drank greedily, Manyoro too. Leon gargled and spat out the last mouthful, his throat rough and raw from the smoke.

He left Manyoro and scrambled to the top of the bank to peer into the smoke. He heard voices but they were faint with distance. He waited a few minutes to regain his strength and reassure himself that no Nandi were close on their tracks, then slid down the bank to where Manyoro crouched in the shallow water.

'Let me look at your leg.' He sat beside the sergeant and took it across his lap. The field dressing was soaked and muddy. He unwrapped it and saw at once that the violent activity of the escape had done damage. Manyoro's thigh was massively swollen, the flesh around the wound torn and bruised where the shaft of the arrow had worked back and forth. Blood oozed out from around it. 'What a pretty sight,' he muttered, and felt gently behind the knee. Manyoro made no protest but his pupils dilated with pain as Leon touched something buried in his flesh.

Then Leon whistled softly. 'What do we have here?' In the lean muscle of Manyoro's thigh, just above the knee, a foreign body lay under the skin. He explored it with a forefinger and Manyoro flinched.

'It's the point of the arrow,' he exclaimed, in English, then switched back into Kiswahili. 'It's worked its way right through your leg from back to front.' It was hard to imagine the agony Manyoro was enduring, and Leon felt inadequate in the presence of such suffering. He looked up at the sky. The dense smoke was dissipating on the evening breeze and through it he could make out the western tops of the escarpment, touched with the fiery rays of the setting sun.

'I think we've given them the slip for now, and it will soon be dark,' he said, without looking into Manyoro's face. 'You can rest until then. You'll need your strength for the night ahead.' Leon's eyes were still burning with the effects of the smoke. He closed them and squeezed the lids tightly shut. But not many minutes passed before he opened them again. He had heard voices coming from the direction of the *boma*.

'They are following our spoor!' Manyoro murmured, and they shrank lower under the bank of the stream. In the banana plantation the Nandi called softly to each other, like trackers following blood, and Leon realized that his earlier optimism was groundless. The pursuers were following the prints of his boots: under their combined weight, they would have left a distinctive sign in the soft earth. There was nowhere for him and Manyoro to hide in the stream bed so Leon drew the bayonet from his belt and crawled up the bank until he lay just below the lip. If the searchers looked down into the stream and discovered them he would be close enough to spring out at them. Depending on how many there were he might be able to silence them before they raised a general alarm and brought the rest of the pack down on them. The voices drew closer until it seemed that they were on the very edge of the bank. Leon gathered himself, but at that moment there was a chorus of distant shouts from the direction of the *boma*. The men above exclaimed with excitement, and he heard them run back the way they had come.

He slid down the bank to Manyoro. 'That was very nearly the last chukka of the game,' he told him, as he rebandaged the leg.

'What made them turn back?'

'I think they found the body of the man I killed. But it won't delay them long. They'll be back.'

He heaved Manyoro upright, draped the other man's right arm over his shoulder and, half carrying and half dragging him, got him up to the top of the far bank of the stream.

The halt in the stream bed had not improved Manyoro's condition. Inactivity had stiffened the wound and the torn muscles around it. When Manyoro tried to put weight on it the limb buckled under him and he would have collapsed had Leon not caught him.

'From here you may indeed call me Horse.' He turned his back to Manyoro, then stooped and pulled him on to his back. Manyoro grunted with pain as his leg swung freely and bent at the knee, then controlled himself and uttered no further sound. Leon adjusted the webbing belts to form a sling seat for him, then straightened with Manyoro perched high on his back, legs sticking out, like a monkey on a pole. Leon took hold of them, as though they were the handles of a wheelbarrow, to prevent any unnecessary movement, then struck out for the foot of the escarpment. As they emerged from the irrigated plantation into the bush the smokescreen, which had concealed them thus far, blew away in pale grey streamers. However, by now the sun was low, balancing like a fireball on top of the escarpment, and the darkness was thickening around them.

'Fifteen minutes,' he whispered hoarsely. 'That's all we need.' By now he was into the bush along the foot of the escarpment wall. It was thick enough to afford them some cover, and there were folds and features in the terrain that were not obvious from afar. With the instincts and eyes of a hunter and a soldier, Leon picked them out and used them to screen their labouring progress. As darkness settled comfortingly over them and their immediate surroundings were swallowed in the gloom he felt a lift of optimism. It seemed they were clear of pursuit, but it was still too early to know for certain. He sank to the ground on his knees, then rolled gently on to his side to protect Manyoro from jolting. Neither spoke or moved for a while, then Leon sat up slowly and unbuckled the sling so that Manyoro could straighten his injured leg. He unscrewed the water-bottle's stopper and handed it to Manyoro. When they had both drunk, he stretched out full length. Every muscle and sinew in his back and legs seemed to scream aloud, begging for rest. 'This is just the start,' he cautioned himself grimly. 'By tomorrow morning we should really be enjoying ourselves.'

He closed his eyes, but opened them again as his calf muscle locked in an agonizing cramp. He sat up and massaged his leg vigorously.

Manyoro touched his arm. 'I praise you, Bwana. You are a man of iron, but you are not stupid and it would be a great stupidity for both of us to die here. Leave the pistol with me and go on. I will stay here and kill any Nandi who tries to follow you.'

'You whimpering bastard!' Leon snarled. 'What kind of woman are you? We haven't even started and you're ready to give up. Get on my back again before I spit on you where you lie.' He knew his anger was excessive, but he was afraid and in pain.

This time it took longer to get Manyoro settled in the loop of the sling. For the first hundred paces or so Leon thought his legs would let him down entirely. Silently he turned his insult to Manyoro on himself. Who is the whimpering bastard now, Courtney? With all the force of his mind and will he drove back the pain and felt the strength gradually trickle back into his legs. One step at a time. He exhorted his legs to keep moving. Just one more. That's it. Now one more. And another.

He knew that if he stopped to rest he would never start again, and went on until he saw the crescent moon appear above the high ground on the eastern side of the Rift Valley. He watched its splendid progress across the sky. It marked the passage of the hours for him as clearly as the tolling of a bell. On his back Manyoro was as quiescent as a dead man, but

Leon knew he was alive for he could feel the fever heat of his body against his own sweat-drenched skin.

As the moon started down towards the tall black wall of the western escarpment on his right, it threw weird shadows under the trees. Leon's mind began to play tricks on him. Once a black-maned lion reared up out of the grass directly in his path. He fumbled the Webley from its holster and aimed at the beast, but before he could take a fair sight over the short barrel the lion had become a termite mound. He laughed uncertainly. 'Stupid beggar! Next you'll be seeing elves and hobgoblins,' he said aloud.

He plodded on with the pistol in his right hand, phantoms appearing and dissolving before him. With the moon hanging halfway down the sky, the last grains of his strength slipped away, like water through cupped fingers. He reeled and almost went down. It took a mighty effort to brace his legs and recover his balance. He stood with legs wide apart, head hanging. He was finished and knew it.

He felt Manyoro stir on his back, and then, incredibly, the Masai began to sing. At first Leon could not recognize the words, for Manyoro's voice was a wispy breath, light as the dawn breeze in the savannah grass. Then his fatigue-dulled mind echoed the words of the Lion Song. Leon's grasp of Maa, the language of the Masai, was rudimentary – Manyoro had taught him the little he knew. It was a difficult language, subtle and complicated, unlike any other. However, Manyoro had been patient and Leon had a gift for languages.

The Lion Song was taught to the young Masai *morani* at his circumcision class. The initiates accompanied it with a stiff-legged dance, bounding high into the air, as effortlessly as a flock of birds taking flight, their red toga-like *shuka* cloaks spreading like wings around them.

> *We are the young lions.*
> *When we roar the earth shivers.*
> *Our spears are our fangs.*
> *Our spears are our claws.*

Fear us, O ye beasts.
Fear us, O ye strangers.
Turn your eyes away from our faces, you women.
You dare not look upon the beauty of our faces.
We are the brothers of the lion pride.
We are the young lions.
We are the Masai.

It was the song the Masai sang when they went out to plunder the cattle and women of lesser tribes. It was the song they sang when they went out to prove their valour by hunting the lion with nothing but the stabbing *assegai* in their hands. It was the song that gave them stomach for battle. It was the battle hymn of the Masai. Manyoro began the chorus again and this time Leon joined in, humming under his breath when he could not recall the words. Manyoro squeezed his shoulder and whispered in his ear, 'Sing! You are one of us. You have the heart of the lion and the strength of a great black mane. You have the stomach and heart of a Masai. Sing!'

They staggered on towards the south. Leon's legs kept moving, for the song's chorus was mesmerizing. His mind veered wildly between reality and fantasy. On his back he felt Manyoro slump into coma. He stumbled on but now he was not alone. Beloved and well-remembered faces appeared out of the darkness. His father and four brothers were there, egging him onwards, but as he drew closer to them they receded and their voices faded. Each slow, heavy pace reverberated through his skull, and sometimes that was the only sound. At others he heard myriad voices shouting and ululating, the music of drums and violins. He tried to ignore the cacophony, for it was pushing him to the edge of sanity.

He shouted to drive away the phantoms: 'Leave me alone. Let me pass!' They sank away, and he went onwards until the rim of the rising sun broke clear of the escarpment. Abruptly his legs went from under him and he collapsed as though he had been shot in the head.

The heat of the sun on the back of his shirt goaded him awake, but when he tried to lift his head he dissolved into vertigo, and could not remember where he was or how he had got there. His sense of smell and his hearing were tricking him now: he thought he could detect the odour of domestic cattle and their hoofs plodding over the hard ground, their mournful lowing. Then he heard voices – children's – calling shrilly to each other. When one laughed, the sound was too real to have been fantasy. He rolled away from Manyoro and, with a huge effort, raised himself on one elbow. He gazed around with bleary eyes, squinting in the glare of bright sunlight and dust.

He saw a large herd of multi-hued and humpbacked cattle with spreading horns. They were streaming past the spot where he and Manyoro lay. The children were real too: three naked boys, carrying only the sticks with which they were herding the cattle towards the waterhole. He saw that they were circumcised, so they were older than they appeared, probably between thirteen and fifteen. They were calling to each other in Maa, but he could not understand what they were saying. With another huge effort Leon forced his aching frame into a sitting position. The tallest boy saw that movement and stopped abruptly. He stared at Leon in consternation, clearly on the point of flight but controlling his fear as a Masai who was almost a *morani* was duty-bound to do.

'Who are you?' He brandished his stick in a threatening gesture but his voice quavered and broke.

Leon understood the simple words and the challenge. 'I am not an enemy,' he called back hoarsely. 'I am a friend who needs your help.'

The other two boys heard the strange voice and stopped to stare at the apparition that seemed to rise from the ground ahead of them. The eldest and bravest child took a few paces towards Leon, then stopped to regard him gravely. He asked another question in Maa, but Leon did not understand. In reply he reached down and helped Manyoro to sit up beside him. 'Brother!' he said. 'This man is your brother!'

The boy took a few quick paces towards them and peered at Manyoro. Then he turned to his companions and let fly a string of instructions accompanied by wide gestures that sent them racing across the savannah. The only word Leon had understood was 'Manyoro!'

The younger boys were heading towards a cluster of huts half a mile away. They were thatched in the traditional Masai fashion and surrounded by a fence of thorn bushes. It was a Masai *manyatta*, a village. The outer stockade of poles was the kraal in which the precious cattle herds were penned at night. The elder child approached Leon now and squatted in front of him. He pointed at Manyoro and said, in awe and amazement, 'Manyoro!'

'Yes, Manyoro,' Leon agreed, and his head spun giddily.

The child exclaimed with delight and made another excited speech. Leon recognized the word for 'uncle', but could not follow the rest. He closed his eyes and lay back with his arm over them to blot out the blazing sunlight. 'Tired,' he said. 'Very tired.'

He slipped away, and woke again to find himself surrounded by a small crowd of villagers. They were Masai, there was no mistaking that. The men were tall. In their pierced earlobes they wore large ornamental discs or carved horn snuffboxes. They were naked under their long red cloaks, their genitals proudly and ostentatiously exposed. The women were tall for their sex. Their skulls were shaven smooth as eggshells and they wore layers of intricately beaded necklaces that hung over their naked breasts. Their minuscule beaded aprons barely covered their pudenda.

Leon struggled to sit up and they watched him with interest. The younger women giggled and nudged each other to see such a strange creature among them. It was probable that none had ever seen a white man before. To command their attention he raised his voice to a shout: 'Manyoro!' He pointed at his companion. 'Mama? Manyoro mama?' he demanded. They stared at him in astonishment.

Then one of the youngest and prettiest girls understood

what he was trying to tell them. 'Lusima!' she cried, and pointed to the east, to the distant blue outline of the far wall of the escarpment. The others joined in shouting joyously, 'Lusima Mama!'

It was clearly Manyoro's mother's name. Everybody was delighted with their grasp of the situation. Leon mimed lifting and carrying Manyoro, then pointed to the east. 'Take Manyoro to Lusima.' This brought a pause in the self-congratulation and they stared at each other in bewilderment.

Again the pretty girl divined his meaning. She stamped her foot and harangued the men. When they hesitated she attacked the ferocious and dreaded warriors with her bare hands, slapping and pummelling them, even pulling one's elaborate plaited coiffure, until they went to do her bidding with shamefaced guffaws. Two ran back to the village and returned with a long, stout pole. To this they attached a hammock made from their leather cloaks knotted at the corners. This was a *mushila*, a litter. Within a short time they were settling Manyoro's unconscious body on it. Four picked it up, and the entire party set off towards the east at a trot, leaving Leon lying on the dusty plain. The singing of the men and the ululations of the women faded.

Leon closed his eyes, trying to summon sufficient reserves of strength to get to his feet and follow them. When he opened them again he found he was not alone. The three naked herd-boys who had discovered him were standing in a row, regarding him solemnly. The eldest said something and made an imperious gesture. Obediently Leon rolled on to his knees, then lurched to his feet. The child came to his side, took his hand and tugged at it possessively. 'Lusima,' he said.

His friend came and took Leon's other hand. He pulled at it and said, 'Lusima.'

'Very well. There seems to be no other option,' Leon conceded. 'Lusima it shall be.' He tapped the eldest child on the chest with a finger. 'Name? What is your name?' he asked, in Maa. It was one of the phrases Manyoro had taught him.

'Loikot!' the boy answered proudly.

'Loikot, we shall go to Lusima Mama. Show me the way.'

With Leon limping between them, they dragged him towards the far blue hills, following Manyoro's litter-bearers.

As they made their way across the valley Leon became aware of a single isolated mountain that rose abruptly from the wide floor of the plain. At first it seemed to be merely a buttress of the eastern escarpment and inconsequential in the immensity of the great valley, but as they came closer he saw that it stood alone and was not attached to the escarpment. It began to take on a grandeur that had been denied it by distance. It was higher and steeper than the Rift Valley wall behind it. The lower slopes were covered with groves of stately umbrella acacias, but at higher altitude these gave way to denser montane forest, which indicated that the summit was above the cloud, ringed by a sheer wall of grey rock, like the glacis of a man-made fortress.

As they approached this massive natural bastion Leon saw that the top of the mountain was covered with a mighty forest. Clearly its growth had been nurtured by the moisture from the swirling clouds. Even at this distance he could see that the outstretched upper branches of the trees were bedecked with old man's beard, and flowering tree orchids. The dense foliage of the tallest trees was starred with blooms as vivid as bridal bouquets. Eagles and other raptors had built their nests in the cliff below the summit and sailed on wide wings across the blue void of the sky.

It was the middle of the afternoon before Leon and his three companions reached the foot of the mountain. They had fallen far behind Manyoro and his party of litter-bearers, who were already halfway up the footpath that climbed the steep slope in a series of zigzags. Leon only managed the first two hundred feet of the climb before he subsided in the shade of an acacia beside the track. His feet could not carry him another step along the rocky path. He twisted one into his lap and fumbled with the boot laces. As he levered off his boot he groaned with pain. His woollen sock was stiff with dried black blood. Gingerly he peeled it off and stared in dismay at his foot. Thick slabs of skin had come away with the sock and his heel was flayed raw. Burst blisters hung in tatters from the sole and his toes might have been chewed by jackals. The three Masai boys squatted in a semi-circle, studying his wounds and discussing them with ghoulish relish.

Then Loikot took command again and barked a series of peremptory commands that sent the other two scampering into the bush, where a small herd of the long-horned Masai cattle were browsing on the grey-green scrub that grew under the acacias. Within minutes they returned with cupped hand-fuls of wet dung. When Leon discovered that it was intended as a poultice for his open blisters he made it clear that he would not submit to any more of Loikot's bullying. But the boys were persistent and kept importuning him while he tore the sleeves of his shirt into strips and wrapped his bleeding feet in them. Then he knotted the laces of his boots together and slung them around his neck. Loikot offered Leon his herding stick and Leon accepted it, then hobbled up the pathway. It grew steeper with every pace, and he began to falter again. Loikot turned on his comrades and issued another series of stern instructions, which sent them flying up the path on skinny legs.

Loikot and Leon followed them upwards at a dwindling pace, blood from Leon's bandaged feet daubing the stones of the path. Eventually he sagged once more on to a rock and stared up at the heights, which were clearly beyond his reach. Loikot sat beside him and began to tell him a long, compli-cated story. Leon understood a few words, but Loikot proved himself a skilled thespian: he leaped to his feet and mimed a warlike scene, which Leon guessed was an account of how he had defended his father's herds from marauding lions. It included much bloodcurdling roaring, leaping and stabbing of the air with his staff. After the trials of the last few days, the performance was a welcome distraction. Leon almost forgot his crippled feet, and laughed at the engaging lad's antics. It was almost dark when they heard voices on the path above them. Loikot shouted a challenge, which was answered by a party of half a dozen cloaked *morani*, coming down to them at a trot. They had brought with them the *mushila* on which they had carried Manyoro. At their bidding Leon climbed into it and as soon as he was settled four men lifted the pole between them and placed it on their shoulders. Then they took off at a run, back up the steep mountain path.

As they came over the edge of the cliff face on to the table top of the mountain, Leon saw the glow of fires under the gigantic trees not far ahead. The *mushila*-bearers carried him swiftly towards them and into a zareba of poles and thorn branches to a large open cattle pen. In a circle on open ground more than twenty large thatched huts were assembled around a tall, wide-spreading wild fig tree. The workmanship that had gone into their construction was superior to that of any others Leon had seen on his patrols through Masailand. The cattle in the pen were large and in fine condition: their hides shone in the flames and their horns were huge.

From the fires a number of men and women crowded forward to look at the stranger. The men's *shukas* were of fine quality, and the women's abundant jewellery and ornaments were beautifully made of the most expensive trade beads and ivory. There could be no doubt that this was an affluent community. Laughing and shouting questions at Leon, they gathered around his *mushila* and many younger women reached out to touch his face boldly and tug at his ragged uniform. Masai women seldom made any effort to disguise their predilection for the opposite sex.

Suddenly a hush fell over the noisy throng. A regal feminine figure was moving towards them from the huts. The villagers drew aside to leave an aisle and she came down it towards the *mushila*. Two servant girls followed her with burning torches, which cast a golden light upon the woman's tall and matronly figure as she glided towards Leon. The villagers bowed like a field of grass in the wind and made soft, purring sounds of respect and reverence as she passed between their ranks.

'Lusima!' they whispered, and clapped softly, averting their eyes from her dazzling beauty. Leon struggled up from the *mushila* and stood to meet her. She stopped in front of him and stared into his face with a dark, hypnotic gaze.

'I see you, Lusima,' he greeted her, but for a long moment she gave no sign of having heard him. She stood almost as tall as he did. Her skin was the colour of smoked honey, glossy and unlined in the torchlight. If she was indeed the mother of Manyoro she must have been much more than fifty, but she seemed at least twenty years younger. Her bare breasts were firm and rounded. Her tattooed belly bore no marks of age or childbearing. Her finely sculpted Nilotic features were striking and her dark eyes so penetrating that they seemed to reach effortlessly into the secret places of his mind.

'*Ndio*.' She nodded. 'Yes. I am Lusima. I have been expecting your coming. I was overlooking you and Manyoro on your night march from Niombi.' Leon was relieved that she spoke in Kiswahili, rather than Maa: communication between them would be easier. But her words made no sense. How could she know that they had come from Niombi? Unless, of course, Manyoro had regained consciousness and told her.

'Manyoro has not spoken since he came to me. He is still deep in the land of shadows,' Lusima assured him.

He started. She had responded to his unspoken question as though she had heard the words.

'I was with you, watching over you,' she repeated, and despite himself he believed her. 'I saw you rescue my son from certain death, and bring him back to me. With this deed you have become as another son to me.' She took his hand. Her grip was cool and hard as bone. 'Come. I must see to your feet.'

'Where is Manyoro?' Leon asked. 'You say that he is alive, but will he survive?'

'He is smitten and the devils are in his blood. It will be a hard fight, and the outcome is uncertain.'

'I must go to him,' Leon insisted.

'I will take you. But now he is sleeping. He must gather his strength for the trial ahead. I cannot remove the arrow until I have the light of day in which to work. Then I will need a strong man to help me. But you must rest also, for you have tried even your great strength to its limit. We will have need of it later.'

She led him to one of the huts and he stooped through the low entrance into the dim, smoky interior. Lusima indicated to him a pile of monkey-skin karosses against the far wall. He went to it and eased himself down onto the soft fur of one. She knelt in front of him and peeled the rags from his feet. While she was doing this, her servant girls prepared a brew of herbs in a three-legged black iron pot that stood over the cooking fire in the centre of the hut. Leon knew that they had probably been captured from a subservient tribe and were slaves in all but name: the Masai took whatever they wanted, cattle and women, and no other tribe dared defy them.

When the contents of the pot were ready the girls brought it to where Leon sat. Lusima tested the temperature and added cold but equally evil-smelling liquid from another gourd. Then she took his feet one at a time and immersed them in the mixture.

It took all his self-control to prevent himself crying out, for the liquid felt as though it was just off the boil, and the juices of the herbs were pungent and caustic. The three women watched his reaction carefully and exchanged approving glances when he managed an impassive expression and a stoic silence. Lusima lifted out his feet one at a time, then wrapped them in strips of trade cloth. 'Now you must eat and sleep,' she said, and nodded to one of the girls, who brought him a calabash and knelt respectfully to offer it to him with both hands. Leon caught a whiff of the contents. It was a Masai staple, which he dared not refuse: to do so would offend his hostess. He steeled himself and lifted the bowl to his lips.

'It is freshly made,' Lusima assured him. 'I mixed it with

my own hands. It will restore your strength and help to heal your wounded feet swiftly.'

He took a mouthful and his stomach heaved. It was warm but the fresh ox blood mixed with milk had taken on a slick jelly-like consistency that coated his throat. He kept swallowing until the gourd was empty. Then he lowered it and belched thunderously. The slave girls exclaimed with delight, and even Lusima smiled.

'The devils fly from your belly,' she told him approvingly. 'Now you must sleep.' She pushed him down on the kaross and spread another over him. A great weight bore down on his eyelids.

W hen he opened his eyes again, the morning sun was blazing through the doorway of the hut. Loikot was waiting for him at the door, squatting against the lintel, but he sprang to his feet as soon as Leon stirred. He came to him immediately and asked a question, pointing at his feet.

'Too early to tell,' Leon answered. Although every muscle in his body ached his head was clear. He sat up and unwrapped the bandages. He was amazed to see that most of the swelling and inflammation had subsided.

'Dr Lusima's snake oil.' He grinned. His mood was light, until he remembered Manyoro.

Quickly he rebandaged his feet, and hobbled to the large clay water pot that stood outside the door. He stripped off the remnants of his shirt and washed the dust and dried sweat from his face and hair. When he straightened up he found that half of the village women, both young and old, were sitting in a circle around him, watching his every move with avid attention.

'Ladies!' he addressed them. 'I am about to take a piss. You are not invited to observe the procedure.' Leaning on Loikot's shoulder he set off for the entrance to the cattle pen.

When he returned Lusima was waiting for him. 'Come,' she commanded. 'It is time to begin.' She led him to the hut that stood beside his. The interior was dark after the brilliant sunlight and it took his eyes a minute to adjust. The air was rank with woodsmoke from the fire and a more subtle odour, the sweet, nauseating smell of corrupting flesh. Manyoro lay face down on a leather kaross beside the fire. Leon went to him quickly and his spirits quailed. Manyoro lay like a dead man and his skin had lost its lustre. It was as dull as the soot that caked the bottom of the cooking pot on the fire. The lean muscles of his back seemed to have wasted. His head was twisted to one side and his eyes had receded into their sockets. Behind half-open lids they were as opaque as quartz pebbles from the riverbed. His leg above the knee was massively swollen, and the stench of the yellow pus that exuded from around the broken-off arrow filled the hut.

Lusima clapped her hands and four men crowded in. They picked up the corners of the litter on which Manyoro lay and carried him outside, across the open ground of the cattle pen to the single tall *mukuyu* tree in the centre. They laid him in the shade while Lusima shrugged off her cloak and stood bare-chested over him. She spoke softly to Leon: 'The arrowhead cannot come out the way it entered. I must draw it through. The wound is ripe. You can smell it. Even so, it will not give up the arrow easily.' One of the slave girls handed her a small knife with a rhino-horn handle, and the other brought a clay fire pot, swinging it around her head on its rope handle to fan the coals alight. When they glowed she placed the pot in front of her mistress. Lusima held the blade in the flames, turning it slowly until the metal glowed. Then she quenched it in another pot of liquid that smelled like the brew with which she had treated Leon's feet. It bubbled and steamed as the metal cooled.

With the knife in her hand Lusima squatted beside her son. The four *morani* who had carried him from the hut knelt with her, two at Manyoro's head and two at his feet. She looked up at Leon and spoke quietly: 'You will do thus and thus.' She explained in detail what she expected of him. 'Even though you are the strongest among us, it will take all your strength. The grip of the barbs in his flesh is strong.' She stared into his face. 'Do you understand, my son?'

'I understand, Mama.' She opened the leather bag that hung at her waist and took from it a hank of thin white twine. 'This is the rope you will use.' She handed it to him. 'I made it from the intestine of a leopard. It is tenacious. There is no stronger thread.' She reached into the bag again and found a thick strip of elephant hide. Gently she opened Manyoro's mouth. She placed the hide between his jaws and bound it in place with a short length of the catgut so that Manyoro could not spit it out.

'It will prevent him cracking his teeth when the pain reaches its zenith,' she explained.

Leon nodded, but he knew that the main reason for the gag was to prevent her son crying out and disgracing her.

'Turn him on to his back,' Lusima ordered the four *morani*, 'but do it gently.' As they rolled Manyoro over she guided the stump of the arrow shaft so that it did not catch in the kaross. Then she placed a block of wood on each side of it to keep it clear of the ground and to give the leg a firm platform. 'Hold him,' she ordered the *morani*.

She moved into position over the wounded leg and laid both her hands on it. Carefully she palpated the front of Manyoro's thigh, feeling for the point of the arrowhead under the skin of the hot, swollen flesh. Manyoro moved restlessly as her probing fingers descried the shape of the buried arrow-head. She brought the blade of the horn-handled knife down precisely on the spot and began to chant a spell in Maa. After a while Manyoro seemed to succumb to the monotonous refrain. His shrunken body relaxed and he snored softly around the leather gag.

Suddenly, without interrupting her chant, Lusima pressed the point of the blade down. With barely a check it sank into the dark flesh. Manyoro stiffened and every muscle stood proud. The blade grated on metal, and pus welled from the wound that the knife had opened. Lusima laid aside the knife and pressed down on either side of the cut. The sharp point of the arrowhead was forced out through the enlarged wound and the first row of barbs came into sight.

Leon had been able to examine a number of captured Nandi weapons during the campaign so he was not surprised to see that the arrowhead was of unconventional design. It had been forged from an iron pot-leg the thickness of Lusima's little finger. It was meant for deep penetration into the massive body of the elephant so it had no single large barb, such as appeared on the arrowhead medieval English bowmen had used against heavily armoured French knights. Instead there were row upon row of tiny jags, no larger than minnow scales, that would glide through flesh with little resistance. However, because of their large numbers and their back-facing angle it would be impossible to withdraw the arrowhead along its original entry channel.

'Quickly!' Lusima whispered to Leon. 'Tie it!'

He had the slip-knot in the catgut ready and looped it over the point of the arrow, just behind the first line of jags. 'I have it,' he told her, as he drew the loop tight.

'Hold him now. Do not let him move and twist the thread or it will be cut by the edges of the barbs,' Lusima warned the *morani*. Together they threw their combined weight across Manyoro's supine body.

'Pull,' Lusima urged Leon, 'with all your strength, my son. Draw this evil thing out of him.'

Leon took three turns of the catgut around his wrist and brought it up firmly. Lusima started chanting again as he applied all the strength of his right arm to the thin thread. He was careful not to jerk or twist it around the razor-sharp jags. Slowly he increased the pressure on the loop. He felt it stretch slightly, but the arrowhead remained lodged. He took an additional turn of the thread around his other wrist and moved until both shoulders were lined four-square with the angle at which the arrow had entered. He pulled again with both arms, ignoring the sharp pain of the thread cutting into his flesh. The muscles of his shoulders under the tattered shirt bunched and bulged. The cords stood out in his throat and his face darkened with effort.

'Pull,' Lusima whispered, 'and may Mkuba Mkuba, the greatest of the great gods, give strength to your arms.'

By now Manyoro was struggling so desperately that the four men could not hold him still. He was making a keening sound into the gag, and his eyes were wide, seeming to start out of the sunken sockets, bloodshot and wild. The trapped arrowhead raised his torn and swollen flesh into a peak, but still the barbs held firm.

'Pull!' Lusima urged Leon. 'Your strength surpasses that of the lion. It is the strength of M'bogo, the great buffalo bull.'

And the arrowhead moved. With a soft, ripping sound a second row of tiny jags appeared behind the first, then a third. At last two inches of dark-stained metal were protruding from the wound. Leon rested for a moment while he gathered himself for the final effort. Then he gritted his teeth until his jaw bulged and pulled again. Another inch of iron came reluctantly into sight. Then there was a rush of half-congealed black blood and purple pus. The stench made even Lusima gasp, but the fluids seemed to lubricate the arrow shaft, which slithered out of the wound now, like some evil foetus in the dreadful moment of its birth.

Leon fell back, panting, and stared in horror at the damage he had wrought. The wound gaped like a dark mouth, while blood and detritus streamed from the torn flesh. In his agony Manyoro had chewed through the elephant-hide gag and bitten into his lips. Fresh blood trickled down his chin. He was still struggling wildly, and the *morani* used all their strength and weight to hold him down.

'Keep the leg still, M'bogo,' Lusima called to Leon. One of her girls handed her a long thin horn of the klipspringer antelope, which had been carved into a crude funnel. She probed the sharp end deeply into the wound and Manyoro redoubled his struggles. The girl held a gourd to Lusima's lips and she filled her mouth with the liquid it contained. A few drops ran down her chin, and Leon caught its astringent odour. Lusima placed her lips around the flared end of the horn, like a trumpeter, and blew the substance down it and through the sharp end into the depths of the wound. Another mouthful followed the first. The liquid bubbled from the open wound, flushing out putrid blood and other matter.

'Turn him over,' she ordered the *morani*. Although Manyoro fought them they rolled him on to his stomach and Leon straddled his back, using all his weight to pin him down. Lusima worked the point of the horn into the entry wound at the back of the leg, then blew more of the infusion deep into the suppurating flesh.

'Enough,' she said at last. 'I have washed out the poisons.' She set aside the horn, placed pads of dried herbs over the wounds and bound them in place with long strips of trade cloth. Gradually Manyoro's struggles abated until at last he slumped back into a deathlike coma.

'It is done. There is nothing more I can do,' she said. 'Now it is a battle between the gods of his ancestors and the dark devils. Within three days we will know the outcome. Take him to his hut.' She looked up at Leon. 'You and I, M'bogo, must take turns to sit at his side and give him strength for the fight.'

Over the days that followed Manyoro hovered over the void. At times he lay in such a deep coma that Leon had to place his ear against his chest to listen for his breathing. At other times he gasped and writhed and shouted on his sleeping mat, sweating and grinding his teeth in fever. Lusima and Leon sat on each side of him, restraining him when he seemed in danger of injuring himself with his wild convulsions. The nights were long and neither slept. They talked quietly through the hours with the low fire between them.

'I sense you were not born on some far-away island over the sea, as most of your compatriots were but in this very Africa,' Lusima said. Leon was no longer surprised by her uncanny perception. He did not reply at once, and she went on, 'You were born far to the north on the banks of a great river.'

'Yes,' he said. 'You are right. The place is Cairo, and the river is the Nile.'

'You belong to this land and you will never leave it.'

'I had never thought to do so,' he answered. She reached across and took his hand, closed her eyes and was quiet for a while. 'I see your mother,' she said. 'She is a woman of great understanding. The two of you are close in spirit. She did not want you to leave her.'

Leon's eyes filled with the dark shadows of regret.

'I see your father also. It was because of him that you left.'

'He treated me like a child. He tried to force me to do things I did not want to do. I refused. We argued and made my mother unhappy.'

'What did he want you to do?' she asked, with the air of one who already knew the answer.

'My father grubs after money. There is nothing else in his life, neither his wife nor his children. He is a hard man, and we do not like each other. I suppose I respect him, but I do not admire him. He wanted me to work with him, doing the things he does. It was a bleak prospect.'

'So you ran away?'

'I did not run. I walked.'

'What was it you sought?' she asked.

He looked thoughtful. 'Truly, I do not know, Lusima Mama.'

'You have not found it?' she asked.

He shook his head uncertainly. Then he thought of Verity O'Hearne. 'Perhaps,' he said. 'Perhaps I have found someone.'

'No. Not the woman you are thinking of. She is just one woman among many others.'

The question was out before he could check himself: 'How

do you know about her?' Then he answered himself: 'Of course. You were there. And you know many things.'

She chuckled, and they were silent for a long while. It was a warm, comforting silence. He felt a strange bond with her, a closeness as though she were truly his mother.

'I do not like what I am doing with my life now,' he said at last. He had not thought about it until this moment, but as he said it, he knew it was the truth.

'Because you are a soldier you are not able to do what your heart tells you,' she agreed. 'You must do as the old men order.'

'You understand,' he said. 'I dislike hunting down and killing people I do not even know.'

'Do you want me to point the way for you, M'bogo?'

'I have come to trust you. I need your guidance.'

She was silent again for so long that he was about to speak. Then he saw that her eyes were wide open but rolled back in her head so that in the firelight only the whites were exposed. She was rocking rhythmically on her haunches and after a while she began to speak, but her voice had changed to a low, grating monotone. 'There are two men. Neither is your father, but both will be more than your father,' she said. 'There is another road. You must follow the road of the great grey men who are not men.' She drew a long, wheezing, asthmatic breath. 'Learn the secret ways of the wild creatures, and other men will honour you for that knowledge and understanding. You will walk with mighty men of power, and they will count you their equal. There will be many women, but only one woman who will be many women. She will come to you from the clouds. Like them she will show you many faces.' She broke off and made a strangling noise at the back of her throat. With supernatural chill he realized that she was in the struggles of divination. At last she shook herself violently and blinked. Her eyes rolled forward so that he could look into their dark centres as she focused on his face. 'Hearken to what I told you, my son,' she said softly. 'The time for you to choose will soon be upon you.'

41

'I did not understand what you were telling me.'

'In time it will become clear to you,' she assured him. 'When you need me I will always be here. I am not your mother, but I have become more than your mother.'

'You speak in riddles, Mama,' he said, and she smiled a fond but enigmatic smile.

I n the morning Manyoro regained consciousness but he was very weak and confused. He tried to sit up but did not have the strength to do so. He gazed at them blearily. 'What has happened? What place is this?' Then he recognized his mother. 'Mama, is it truly you? I thought it was a dream. I have been dreaming.'

'You are safe in my *manyatta* on Lonsonyo Mountain,' she told him. 'We removed the Nandi arrow from your leg.'

'The arrow? Yes, I remember . . . The Nandi?'

The slave girls brought him a bowl of ox blood and milk, which he drank greedily, spilling some down his chest. He lay back gasping. Then, for the first time, he noticed Leon squatting in the gloom of the hut. 'Bwana!' This time he managed to sit up. 'You are with me still?'

'I am here.' Leon went to him quietly.

'How long? How many days since we left Niombi?'

'Seven.'

'Headquarters in Nairobi will think you are dead or that you have deserted.' He gripped Leon's shirt and shook it agitatedly. 'You must report to Headquarters, Bwana. You must not neglect your duty for me.'

'We will go back to Nairobi when you are ready to march.'

'No, Bwana, no. You must go at once. You know that the major is not your friend. He will make trouble for you. You must go at once, and I will follow you when I am able.'

'Manyoro is right,' Lusima intervened. 'You can do no more here. You must go to your chief in Nairobi.' Leon had lost track of time, but now he realized with a guilty shock that it must be more than three weeks since he had had contact with his battalion headquarters. 'Loikot will guide you to the railway line. He knows that part of the country well. Go with him,' Lusima urged him.

'I will,' he agreed, and stood up. There were no preparations he needed to make for the journey. He had no weapons or baggage, and hardly any clothing other than his ragged khaki.

Lusima provided him with a Masai *shuka*. 'It is the best protection I can give you. It will shield you from sun and cold. The Nandi fear the red *shuka* – even the lions flee from it.'

'Lions also?' Leon suppressed a smile.

'You will see.' She returned his smile.

He and Loikot left within an hour of making the decision. During the rains of the previous season the boy had herded his father's cattle as far north as the railway and knew the land well.

Leon's feet had healed just sufficiently for him to lace on his boots. Limping gingerly he followed Loikot down the mountain towards the great plain below. At the foot he paused to relace his boots. When he straightened again he looked up and saw the tiny but unmistakable silhouette of Lusima standing on the lip of the cliff. He lifted one arm in farewell, but she did not acknowledge the gesture. Instead she turned and disappeared from his sight.

As his feet healed and hardened he was able to increase his speed and hurry after Loikot. The boy covered the ground with the long, flowing stride characteristic of his people. As he went he kept up a running commentary on everything that caught his attention. He missed nothing with the bright young eyes that could pick out the ethereal grey shape of a kudu bull standing deep in a thicket of thorn scrub three hundred yards distant.

The plain over which they were travelling abounded with

living creatures. Loikot ignored the herds of smaller antelope that skittered around them, but remarked on anything of more significance. By this time, with his sharp ear for language, Leon had picked up enough Maa to follow the boy's chatter with little difficulty.

They had carried no food with them when they left Lonsonyo Mountain and Leon had been puzzled as to how they would subsist, but he need not have worried: Loikot provided a strange variety of sustenance, which included small birds and their eggs, locusts and other insects, wild fruit and roots, a spurfowl, which he knocked out of the air with his staff as it flushed on noisy wings from under his feet, and a large monitor lizard that he pursued across the veld for half a mile before he beat it to death. The lizard's flesh tasted like chicken, and there was enough to feed them for three days, although by then the carcass had been colonized by swarms of iridescent blue flies and their fat white offspring.

Leon and Loikot slept each night beside a small fire, covered with their *shukas* against the chill, and started again while the morning star was still high and bright in the dawn sky. On the third morning the sun was still below the horizon and the light poor when Loikot stopped dead and pointed in the direction of a flat-topped acacia tree only fifty yards away. 'Ho, you killer of cattle, I greet you,' he cried.

'Who is it?' Leon demanded.

'Do you not see him? Open your eyes, M'bogo.' Loikot pointed with his staff. Only then did Leon make out two small black tufts in the brown grass between them and the tree. One flicked and the whole picture sprang into focus. Leon was staring at an enormous male lion, crouching flat in the grass and watching them with implacable yellow eyes. The tell-tale tufts were the black tips of its round ears.

'Sweet God!' Leon took a step back.

Loikot laughed. 'He knows I am Masai. He will run if I challenge him.' He brandished his staff. 'Hey, Old One, the day of my testing will soon come. I will meet you then, and we shall see which is the best of us.' He was referring to his

44

ritual trial of courage. Before he could be counted a man and have the right to plant his spear at the door of any woman who caught his fancy, the young *morani* must confront his lion face to face and kill him with his broad-bladed *assegai*.

'Fear me, you thief of cattle. Fear me, for I am your death!' Loikot raised his staff, held it like a stabbing spear and advanced on the lion with a lithe, dancing step. Leon was amazed when the lion leaped to its feet, curled its lip in a threatening growl, then slunk away into the grass.

'Did you see me, M'bogo?' Loikot crowed. 'Did you see how Simba fears me? Did you see him run from me? He knows I am a *morani*. He knows I am a Masai.'

'You crazy tyke!' Leon relaxed his clenched fists. 'You'll get us both eaten.' He laughed with relief. He remembered Lusima's words, and it occurred to him that, over the hundreds of years that the Masai had relentlessly hunted generation after generation of lions, their persecution had ingrained a deep memory in the beasts. They had come to recognize a tall red-cloaked figure as a mortal threat.

Loikot leaped in the air, pirouetted with triumph and led him on northwards. As they went, Loikot continued his instruction. Without slackening his pace he pointed out the spoor of large game as he came upon it, and described the animal that had made it. Leon was fascinated by the depth of his knowledge of the wild and its creatures. Of course, it was not difficult to understand how the child had become so adept: almost since he had taken his first step he had tended his tribe's herds. Manyoro had told him that even the youngest herd-boys could follow a lost beast for days over the most difficult terrain. But he was fascinated when Loikot came to a stop and, with the tip of his staff, traced the faint outline of an enormous round pad mark. The ground was baked hard by the sun, and covered with chips of shale and flint. Leon would never have picked out the track of a bull elephant without the boy's help, but Loikot could read every detail and nuance of it.

'I know this one. I have seen him often. His teeth are this

long . . .' He made a mark in the dust, then paced out three of
his longest strides and made a second mark. 'He is a great grey
chief of his tribe.'

Lusima had used the same description: 'Follow the great
grey men who are not men.' At the time it had puzzled Leon,
but now he realized she been speaking about elephant. He
pondered her advice as they went on into the north. He had
always been fascinated by the wild chase. From his father's
library he had read all the books written by the great hunters.
He had followed the adventures of Baker, Selous, Gordon-
Cumming, Cornwallis Harris and the rest. The lure of wild
sports was one of the most powerful reasons why he had
enlisted in the KAR rather than enter his father's business.
His father termed any activity not aimed specifically at the
accumulation of money as 'slacking'. But Leon had heard that
the army brass encouraged their young officers to indulge in
such manly pursuits as big-game hunting. Captain Cornwallis
Harris had been given a full year's leave of absence from his
regiment in India to travel to South Africa and hunt in the
unexplored wilderness. Leon longed to be able to emulate his
heroes but so far he had been disappointed.

Since he had joined the KAR he had applied on more
than one occasion for a few days' leave to indulge in his first
big-game hunt. Major Snell, his commanding officer, had
dismissed his requests out of hand. 'If you think you have
signed up for a glorified hunting safari then you are very much
mistaken, Courtney,' he said. 'Get back to your duties. I want
to hear no more of this nonsense.' So far his hunting had
been restricted to a few small antelope, Grant's and Thomson's gazelle – known to all as Tommies – which he had shot
to feed his *askari* while they were on patrol. But his heart
stirred when he watched the magnificent animals that flourished all around him. He longed for a chance to go after them.

He wondered if by counselling him to 'follow the great
grey men', Lusima was suggesting he should take to the life of
an ivory hunter. It was an intriguing prospect. He went on
more cheerfully behind Loikot. Life seemed good and full of

promise. He had comported himself honourably during his first military action. Manyoro was alive. A new career was opening ahead of him. Best of all, Verity O'Hearne was waiting for him in Nairobi. Yes, life was good, very good indeed.

Five days after they had left Lonsonyo Mountain, Loikot turned east and led him up the escarpment of the Great Rift Valley into the rolling forested hills of the uplands. They topped one and looked down into the shallow valley beyond. In the distance something glinted in the late-evening sunlight. Leon shaded his eyes. 'Yes, M'bogo,' Loikot told him. 'There is your iron snake.'

He saw the smoke of the locomotive spurting in regular puffs above the tops of the trees and heard the mournful blast of a steam whistle.

'I will leave you now. Even you cannot lose your way from here,' Loikot told him loftily. 'I must go back to care for the cattle.'

Leon watched him go regretfully. He had enjoyed the boy's lively company. Then he put it out of his mind and went down the hill.

The locomotive driver leaned out of the side window of his cab and spotted the tall figure beside the tracks far ahead. He saw at once from his ochre-red *shuka* that he was Masai. It was only as the engine puffed closer that the man swept open his cloak and the driver saw he was a white man in the ragged remnants of a khaki uniform. He reached for the brake lever and the wheels squealed on the steel rails as they drew to a halt in a cloud of steam.

M ajor Frederick Snell, officer commanding the 3rd
Battalion, 1st Regiment, The King's African Rifles,
did not look up from the document he was perusing
when Lieutenant Leon Courtney was marched under armed
escort into his office in Battalion Headquarters.

Snell was old for his command. He had fought without
particular distinction in the Sudan against the Mahdi, and
again in South Africa against the wily Boers. He was close to
retirement age, and dreading its arrival. On his army pension
he would be able to afford only a mean lodging in a town
such as Brighton or Bournemouth, which, for the remainder
of their days, would have to be home for both him and his
wife of forty years. Maggie Snell had spent a lifetime in army
quarters in tropical climes, which had yellowed her complexion, soured her disposition and sharpened her tongue.

Snell was a small man. His once bright ginger hair had
faded and fallen out until he was left with only a scraggly
white fringe around a freckled pate. His mouth was wide but
his lips were thin. His eyes were round, pale blue and protu-
berant, which justified his nickname: 'Freddie the Frog'.

He replaced his pipe between his lips and sucked at it,
making it gurgle noisily. He was frowning as he finished
reading the handwritten sheaf of paper. He still did not look
up, but removed the pipe from his mouth and flicked it against
the wall of his office, leaving a splatter of yellow nicotine
drops across the whitewash. He put it back in his mouth and
returned to the first page of the document. He read it again
with deliberation, then laid it neatly in front of him and at
last raised his head.

'Prisoner! Attention!' barked Sergeant Major M'fefe, who
commanded the guard detail. Leon stamped his battered boots
on the cement floor and stood erect.

Snell eyed him with distaste. Leon had been arrested three
days earlier when he had presented himself at the main gates

of Battalion Headquarters. Since then he had been held on Major Snell's orders in detention barracks. He had not been able to shave or change his uniform. The stubble on his jaw was dark and dense. What remained of his tunic was filthy and tattered. The sleeves had been ripped off. His bare arms and legs were criss-crossed with thorn scratches. But despite his present circumstances he still made Snell feel inadequate. Even in his rags Leon Courtney was tall and powerfully built, and he radiated an air of naïve self-confidence. Snell's wife, who seldom expressed approval of anyone or anything, had once remarked wistfully on how fetchingly handsome young Courtney was. 'He's set a few hearts fluttering hereabouts, I can tell you,' she had said to her husband.

Now Snell thought bitterly, No more fluttering hearts for a while. I shall see to that. Then at last he spoke aloud: 'Well, Courtney, this time you have outdone yourself.' He tapped the wad of papers in front of him. 'I have been reading your report with nothing less than wonder.'

'Sir!' Leon acknowledged.

'It defies belief.' Snell shook his head. 'Even for you the events you describe form a low watermark.' He sighed, but behind the disapproving expression he was elated. At last this bumptious young shaver had gone too far. He wanted to savour the moment. He had waited almost a year for it. 'I wonder what your uncle will make of this extraordinary account when he reads it.'

Leon's uncle was Colonel Penrod Ballantyne, the regimental commander. He was many years younger than Snell but he already outranked him by a wide margin. Snell knew that before he himself was forced into retirement Ballantyne would probably be promoted to general and given command of a full division in some pleasant part of the Empire. After that a knighthood would follow as a matter of course.

General Sir Penrod Bloody Ballantyne! Snell thought. He hated the man, and hated his bloody nephew, standing before him now. All his life he had been passed over while men like

Ballantyne had soared effortlessly over his head. Well, I can't do much about the old dog, he thought grimly, but this pup is a different matter entirely.

He scratched his head with the stem of his pipe. 'Tell me, Courtney, do you understand why I have had you detained since you arrived back in barracks?'

'Sir!' Leon stared at the wall above his head.

'In case that should mean, "No, sir", I would like to run through the events you describe in this report, and point out those that have given me concern. Do you have any objections?'

'Sir! No, sir.'

'Thank you, Lieutenant. On the sixteenth of July you were ordered to take under your command a detachment of seven men and to proceed immediately to the District Commissioner's headquarters at Niombi and take up guard duties to protect the station against possible forays by Nandi rebels. That is correct, is it not?'

'Sir! Yes, sir!'

'As ordered, you left these barracks on the sixteenth but you and your detachment did not reach Niombi until twelve days later, although you travelled by rail as far as Mashi siding. This left you a march of less than a hundred and twenty miles to Niombi. So it seems that you covered the distance at the rate of less than ten miles a day.' Snell looked up from the report. 'That could hardly be described as a forced march. Do you agree?'

'Sir, I have explained the reason in my report.' Leon was still standing to attention and staring at the nicotine-speckled wall above Snell's head.

'Ah, yes! You came across the tracks of a large war-party of Nandi rebels and decided in your infinite wisdom to disregard your orders to proceed to Niombi but rather to follow up and engage the rebels. I hope I have read your explanation correctly.'

'Yes, sir.'

'Please explain to me, Lieutenant, how you knew that these tracks were those of a war-party and not simply those of hunters from a tribe other than the Nandi or refugees fleeing from the area of the uprising.'

'Sir, I was advised by my sergeant that they were those of Nandi rebels.'

'You accepted his evaluation?'

'Yes, sir. Sergeant Manyoro is an expert tracker.'

'So you spent six days following up these mythical insurgents?'

'Sir, they were moving directly towards the mission station at Nakuru. It seemed they might be intent on attacking and destroying the settlement. I thought it my duty to prevent them doing so.'

'Your duty was to obey orders. Be that as it may, the fact is that you never managed to catch up.'

'Sir, the Nandi became aware that we were in pursuit, broke up into smaller parties and scattered into the bush. I turned back and proceeded to Niombi.'

'As you had been ordered?'

'Yes, sir.'

'Of course, Sergeant Manyoro is not in a position to corroborate your version of events. I have merely your word,' Snell went on.

'Sir!'

'So, to continue,' Snell glanced down at the report, 'you broke off the pursuit and at long last made for Niombi.'

'Sir!'

'When you reached the *boma* you discovered that while you had been wandering around the countryside the district commissioner and his family had been massacred. Immediately after this discovery you then realized you had led your detachment negligently into a Nandi ambush. You turned tail and ran, leaving your men to fend for themselves.'

'That is not what happened, sir!' Leon was unable to disguise his outrage.

'And that outburst was insubordination, Lieutenant.' Snell relished the word, rolling it around his mouth as though he was tasting a fine claret.

'I apologize, sir. It was not intended as such.'

'I assure you, Courtney, that it was taken thus. However, you disagree with my evaluation of the events at Niombi. Have you witnesses to support your version?'

'Sergeant Manyoro, sir.'

'Of course, I had forgotten how when you left Niombi you placed the sergeant on your back and, outrunning a rebel army, carried him southwards into Masailand.' Snell sneered luxuriously. 'It should be remarked at this point that you took him in the opposite direction from Nairobi, then left him with his mother. His mother forsooth!' Snell chuckled. 'How touching!' He lit his pipe and puffed at it. 'The relief party that reached the Niombi *boma* many days after the massacre found that all the corpses of your men had been so mutilated by the rebels that it was impossible to identify them with any certainty, especially as those who had not been decapitated had been largely devoured by vultures and hyena. I think you left your sergeant among those corpses, rather than with his mother as you avow. I believe that after you deserted the battlefield you skulked in the wilderness until you were able to recover your nerve sufficiently to return to Nairobi with this cock-and-bull story.'

'No, sir.' Leon was trembling with anger, and his fists were bunched at his sides so that the knuckles showed bone white.

'Since joining the battalion you have displayed a fine contempt for military discipline and authority. You have shown a much greater interest in such frivolous activity as polo and big-game hunting than in the duties of a junior subaltern. It is clear that you consider those duties beneath your dignity. Not only that, you have disregarded the decent demands of social convention. You have taken to yourself the role of a lascivious Lothario, outraging the decent folk of the colony.'

'Major, sir, I don't see how you can substantiate those accusations.'

'Substantiate? Very well, I will substantiate. You are probably unaware that during your prolonged absence in Masailand the governor of the colony has seen fit to repatriate a young widow to England to protect her from your depredations. The entire community of Nairobi is outraged by your behaviour. You are, sir, a confounded rogue, with respect for nothing and no one.'

'Repatriated!' Leon turned ashen under the filth and his tan. 'They have sent Verity home?'

'Ah, so you acknowledge the poor woman's identity. Yes, Mrs O'Hearne has gone back to England. She left a week ago.' Snell paused to let it sink in. He gloated at the knowledge that he himself had brought the sordid affair to the governor's attention. He had always found Verity O'Hearne devilishly attractive. After the death of her husband, he had often fantasized about comforting and protecting her in her bereavement. From a distance he had gazed at her longingly when she sat on the front lawn of the Settlers' Club taking tea with his wife and other members of the Women's Institute. She was so young, lovely and gay, and Maggie Snell, sitting beside her, so old, ugly and crabby. When he had heard whispers of her involvement with one of his subalterns he was devastated. Then he became extremely angry. Verity O'Hearne's virtue and reputation were in danger and it was his duty to protect her. He had gone to the governor.

'Well, Courtney, I do not intend to substantiate my allegations any further. All will be decided at your court-martial. Your dossier has been handed to Captain Roberts of Second Battalion. He has agreed to act as prosecuting officer.' Eddy Roberts was one of Snell's favourites. 'The charges against you will be desertion, cowardice, dereliction of duty and failing to obey the orders of a superior officer. Second Lieutenant Sampson of the same battalion has agreed to defend you. I know that the two of you are friendly, so I do not expect you to object to my choice. There has been some difficulty in finding three officers to make up the court. Naturally I am unable to sit on the panel, as I will be required to give evidence during the proceedings, and most officers are in the field against the last of the rebels. Fortunately a P&O liner docked in Mombasa over the weekend carrying a group on leave from India *en route* for Southampton. I have arranged that a colonel and two captains will travel up from Mombasa by train to Nairobi to make up a full panel of judges. They are due to arrive at eighteen hundred hours this evening. They will have to return to Mombasa by Friday to continue their voyage, so the proceedings must commence tomorrow morning. I will send Lieutenant Sampson to your quarters immediately to consult with you and to prepare your defence. You're in a sorry state, Courtney. I can smell you from where I sit. Go and get yourself cleaned up and be ready to appear before the court for arraignment first thing tomorrow morning. Until then you are confined to your quarters.'

'I request an interview with Colonel Ballantyne, sir. I need an extension of time to prepare my defence.'

'Unfortunately, Colonel Ballantyne is not in Nairobi at the moment. He is in the Nandi tribal lands with First Battalion making reprisals for the Niombi massacre and stamping out the last of the rebel resistance. It is unlikely that he will return to Nairobi for several weeks. When he does, I am certain he will take cognizance of your request.' Snell smiled coldly. 'That is all. Prisoner, dismiss!'

'Guard detail, attention!' barked Sergeant Major M'fefe. 'About turn! Quick march! Left, right, left . . .' Leon found himself out in the brilliant sunshine of the parade-ground, being marched at double time towards the officers' billets. Everything was moving so swiftly that he had difficulty in ordering his thoughts.

Leon's quarters were a rondavel, a single-roomed building with a circular mud-daub wall and a thatched roof. It stood in the centre of a row of identical huts. Each was occupied by an

ASSEGAI

unmarried officer. At his door, Sergeant Major M'fefe saluted
Leon smartly and said softly but awkwardly, in Kiswahili,
'I am sorry this has happened, Lieutenant. I know you are no
coward.' M'fefe had never, in twenty-five years of service,
been required to arrest and place under guard one of his own
officers. He felt ashamed and humiliated.

Even though most of Leon's company turned out to cheer
his performance in any cricket or polo match, and when they
saluted him it was always with a sparkling African grin, he
was only superficially aware of his popularity among the other
ranks so he was moved by the sergeant major's words.

M'fefe went on hurriedly to cover his embarrassment:
'After you left on patrol a lady came to the main gates and
left a box for you, Bwana. She told me to make sure you
received it. I put it in your room next to the bed.'

'Thank you, Sergeant Major.' Leon was equally embarrassed. He turned away and went into the sparsely furnished
hut. It contained an iron bedstead with a mosquito net
suspended over it from a rafter, a single shelf and a wardrobe
made from an old packing case. It was scrupulously clean and
tidy. The walls had been recently limewashed and the floor
gleamed with a coating of beeswax. His scant possessions were
arranged with geometrical precision on the shelf above his
bed. During his absence Ishmael, his manservant, had been as
meticulous as ever. The only item out of place was the long
leather case that was propped against the wall.

Leon crossed to the bed and sat down. He felt close to
despair. So many disasters had struck him at once. Almost
without conscious volition he reached out for the leather case
M'fefe had left for him, and laid it across his lap. It was made
of travel-scarred but expensive leather, covered with steamship labels, and fitted with three solid brass locks, whose keys
were attached by a thong to the handle. He unlocked it, lifted
the lid and stared in astonishment at the contents. Nestled in
the fitted green baize compartments were the components of
a heavy rifle with, in their own tailored slots, the ramrod, oil

can and other accessories. On the underside of the lid a large label bore the name of the gunmaker printed in ornate script:

HOLLAND & HOLLAND
Manufacturers of
Guns, Rifles, Pistols
and every description of breech loading firearms.
98 New Bond Street. London W.

With a sense of reverence Leon reassembled the rifle, fitting the barrels into the action and clamping them in position with the forestock. He stroked the oil-finished wood of the butt, the polished walnut silky smooth under his fingertips. He lifted the rifle and aimed it at a small gecko that hung upside-down on the far wall. The butt fitted perfectly into his shoulder and the barrels aligned themselves under his eye. He held the bead of the foresight in the wide V of the rear express sight rock-steady on the lizard's head.

'Bang, bang, you're dead,' he told it, and laughed for the first time since he had returned to barracks. He lowered the weapon and read the engraving on the barrels. *H&H Royal .470 Nitro Express.* Then the pure gold oval inlay let into the walnut of the butt caught his eye. It was engraved with the initials of the original owner: *PO'H.*

'Patrick O'Hearne,' he murmured. The magnificent weapon had belonged to Verity's dead husband. An envelope was pinned to the green baize of the lid beside the maker's label. He set down the rifle carefully on the pillow at the head of his bed and reached for it. He split the seal with his thumbnail and pulled out two folded sheets of paper. The first was a receipt dated 29 August 1906:

> *To whom it may concern: I have this day sold*
> *the H&H .470 rifle with serial number 1863 to*
> *Lieutenant Leon Courtney and have received from him*
> *the sum of twenty-five guineas in full and final payment.*
> *Signed: Verity Abigail O'Hearne.*

With this document Verity had transferred the rifle legally into his name so that nobody could contest his ownership. He folded the receipt and returned it to the envelope. Then he opened the other sheet of paper. It was undated and the handwriting was scrawled and uneven, unlike that on the receipt. Her pen had twice left splashes of ink on the page. It was obvious that she had been in a state of upheaval when she had written it.

> *Dearest, dearest Leon,*
>   *By the time you read this I will be on my way back to Ireland. I did not want to go, but I have been given little choice. Deep in my heart I know that the person who is sending me away is right and it is for the best. Next year I will be thirty years old, and you are just nineteen and a very junior subaltern. I am sure that one day you will be a famous general covered with medals and glory, but by then I will be an old maid. I have to go. This gift I leave you is an earnest of my affection for you. Go and forget me. Find happiness somewhere else. I will always hold you in my memory as I once held you in my arms.*

It was signed 'V'. His vision blurred and his breathing was uneven as he reread the letter.

Before he reached the last line there was a polite knock on the door of his rondavel. 'Who is it?' he called.

'It is me, Effendi.'

'Just a minute, Ishmael.'

Quickly he wiped his eyes on the back of his forearm, placed the letter under his pillow and packed the rifle back into its case. He pushed it under the bed and called, 'Come in, Beloved of the Prophet.'

Ishmael, who was a devout coastal Swahili, came in with a zinc bathtub balanced on his head. 'Welcome back, Effendi. You bring the sun into my heart.' He set the tub in the centre of the floor, then set about filling it with steaming buckets of water from the fireplace behind the hut. While the water cooled to a bearable temperature, Ishmael whipped a sheet around Leon's neck and then, with comb and scissors, took up position behind him and began to snip at Leon's sweat- and dust-caked hair. He worked with practised skill, and when he had finished he stood back and nodded, satisfied, then fetched the shaving mug and brush. He worked up a creamy lather over Leon's stubble, then stropped the long blade of the straight razor and handed it to his master. He held the small hand mirror while Leon scraped his jaw clean, then wiped away the last traces of soap.

'How does that look?' Leon asked.

'Your beauty would blind the houris of Paradise, Effendi,' Ishmael said solemnly, and tested the bathwater with one finger. 'It is ready.'

Leon stripped off his stinking rags and threw them against the far wall, then went to the steaming bath and lowered himself into it, with a sigh of pleasure. The bath was hardly large enough to accommodate him, and he sat with his knees under his chin. Ishmael gathered up his soiled clothing, holding it ostentatiously at arm's length, and carried it away. He left the door open behind him. Without knocking, Bobby Sampson ambled in.

'A thing of beauty is a joy for ever,' he said, with a diffident grin. Bobby was only a year older than Leon. He was a large, gawky but affable youth, and as the two most junior officers in the regiment, he and Leon had formed a friendship that had at its core the instinct for survival. They had sealed their friendship with the joint purchase of a dilapidated and road-beaten Vauxhall truck from a Hindu coffee-grower for the sum of three pounds ten shillings, almost their total combined savings. By working until all hours of the night they had restored it to an approximation of its former glory.

Bobby went to the bed and dropped on to it, placed his hands behind his head, crossed his ankles and contemplated the gecko, which had climbed into the rafters and now hung upside-down, above him. 'Well, old man, you seem to have got yourself into a bit of a pickle, what? I'm sure you know by now that Freddie the Frog is accusing you of all sorts of mischief and wrongdoing. Quite by chance, I happen to have with me a copy of the charge sheet.' He reached into the large side pocket of his uniform jacket and brought out a crumpled ball of papers. He smoothed them out on his chest, then waved them at Leon. 'Some pretty colourful stuff here. I'm impressed with your naughtiness. Trouble is, I've been ordered to defend you, what? What?'

'For God's sake, Bobby, stop saying "what". You know it drives me mad.'

Bobby put on an expression of contrition. 'Sorry, old boy. Truth is I haven't the faintest idea what I'm supposed to be doing.'

'Bobby, you are an idiot.'

'Can't help it, my old beauty. Mother must have dropped me on my head, don't you know? Anyway, back to the main item on the agenda. Have you any idea what I'm supposed to be doing?'

'You're supposed to bedazzle the judges with your wit and erudition.' Leon was beginning to feel more cheerful. He enjoyed the way Bobby hid his astute mind behind a bumbling façade.

'Bit depleted in the wit and erudition department, at the moment,' Bobby admitted. 'What else is there?'

Leon rose from the bath splashing soapy water over the floor. Bobby balled up the towel Ishmael had left on the end of the bed and threw it at his head.

'For a start, let's read through the charges together,' Leon suggested, as he towelled himself.

Bobby brightened. 'Brilliant idea. Always suspected you of being a genius.'

Leon pulled on a pair of khaki trousers. 'Bit short of seating in here,' he said. 'Move your fat arse.'

Bobby sat up, serious now. He made room for his friend on the bed, and Leon settled beside him. Together they pored over the charge sheet.

When the light in the hut faded, Ishmael brought in a

bullseye lamp and hung it on its hook. They worked on by its feeble yellow light, until at last Bobby rubbed his eyes and yawned, then pulled out his half-hunter and wound it vigorously. 'It's well past midnight and you and I have to be in court at nine o'clock. We'll have to call it a day. By the way, would you like to know what I think of your chances of acquittal?'

'Not really,' Leon answered.

'If you offered me odds of a thousand to one I wouldn't risk twopence ha'penny,' Bobby told him. 'If only we could find this sergeant of yours the story might have a different ending.'

'Fat chance of that happening before nine o'clock tomorrow. Manyoro's on top of a mountain in Masailand, hundreds of miles away.'

T he officers' mess had been converted into a courtroom to house the proceedings. The three judges were seated at the high table on the dais. There were two tables below them, one for the defence and the other for the prosecution. It was hot in the small room. On the outside veranda a punkah-wallah heaved regularly on the rope that disappeared into a hole in the ceiling above him, and from there over a series of pulleys to the fan hanging above the judges' table. Its blades whirred monotonously, stirring the languid air into an illusion of cool.

Sitting beside Bobby Sampson at the defence table, Leon studied the faces of his judges. Cowardice, desertion, dereliction of duty and failing to obey the orders of a superior officer: all of the crimes with which he was charged carried the maximum penalty of execution by firing squad. The skin of his forearms prickled. These men held over him the power of life and death.

'Look them in the eye and speak up,' Bobby whispered, holding up his notepad to conceal his lips. 'That's what my old daddy always told me.'

Not all of his judges looked human and compassionate. The senior man was the Indian Army colonel who had come by rail from Mombasa. It seemed that the journey had not agreed with him. His expression was sour and dyspeptic. He wore the flamboyant uniform of the 11th (The Prince of Wales' Own) Bengal Lancers. There were two rows of decoration ribbons on his chest, his riding boots gleamed and the tail of his multi-coloured silk turban was thrown back over one shoulder. His face was flushed by the sun and whisky, his eyes were as fierce as a leopard's, and the tips of his moustache were waxed into sharp points.

'He looks a right man-eater,' Bobby whispered. He had been following Leon's gaze. 'Believe me, he's the one we have to convince, and it's not going to be easy.'

'Gentlemen, are we ready to begin?' boomed the senior judge, and turned his cold, slightly bloodshot eyes on Eddy Roberts at the prosecution table.

'Yes, Colonel.' Roberts stood up respectfully to reply. He was Froggy Snell's favourite, which was why he had been selected.

The president looked at the defence table. 'What about you?' he demanded, and Bobby leaped to his feet with such alacrity that he sent his carefully arranged pile of papers cascading on to the floor. 'Oh, dearie me!' he stuttered and dropped to his knees to gather them up. 'I beg your pardon, sir.'

'Are you ready?' Colonel Wallace's voice was as loud as a foghorn in the confines of the small room.

'I am, sir. I am indeed.' Bobby peered up at him from the floor, clutching his papers to his chest. He was blushing rosily.

'We haven't got all week. Let's get on with it, young fellow.'

The adjutant, serving as clerk and court recorder, read the list of charges, then Eddy Roberts came to his feet to open the case for the prosecution. His manner was relaxed, and he spoke clearly and convincingly. The judges followed his address with attention.

'Damn me, but Eddy's rather good, what?' Bobby fretted.

After his preamble Eddy called Major Snell, his first witness, to the box. He led him through the charge sheet and had him confirm the details set out in the document. Then he questioned him on the accused's service record and the performance of his duties up to the time when he was sent to guard the *boma* at Niombi. Snell was too sly to let his evidence seem one-sided and prejudiced against Leon. However, he managed to make his qualified and lukewarm assessments seem like damning condemnation.

'I would reply to that question by saying that Lieutenant Courtney is a skilled polo player. He also evinces a passion for big-game hunting. These activities take up much of his time when he might be better employed elsewhere.'

'What about his other behaviour? Have you been made aware of any social scandal surrounding his name?'

Bobby jumped to his feet. 'Objection, Mr President!' he cried. 'That calls for conjecture and hearsay. My client's conduct when off duty has no bearing on the charges before the court.'

'What do you say to that?' Colonel Wallace turned his searching glare on Eddy Roberts.

'I believe that the accused's integrity and moral character have a direct bearing on this case, sir.'

'The objection is denied and the witness may reply to the question.'

'The question was . . .' Eddy pretended to consult his notes '. . . are you aware of any scandal surrounding the name of the accused?'

It was what Snell had been waiting for. 'As a matter of fact there has recently been an unfortunate incident. The accused became involved with a young gentlewoman, a widow. So blatantly scandalous was his behaviour that it brought the honour of the regiment into question, and enraged the local community. The governor of the colony, Sir Charles Eliot, had little option but to arrange for the lady in question to be repatriated.'

The heads of the three judges turned to Leon, their

expressions forbidding. It was only a few years since the death of the old queen, and despite the racy reputation of her son, the reigning sovereign, the older generations were still influenced by Victoria's strict mores.

Bobby scribbled on his notepad, then turned it so that Leon could read what he had written. 'I am not going to cross-examine on that issue, agreed?'

Leon nodded unhappily.

After a long pause to let the importance of that testimony register with the judges, Eddy Roberts picked up a thick book from the desk in front of him. 'Major Snell, do you recognize this book?'

'Of course I do. It's the battalion order book.'

Eddy opened it at a marked page and read aloud the extract that covered Leon's orders to take his detachment to Niombi *boma*. When he had finished he asked, 'Major Snell, were those your orders to the accused?'

'Yes.'

Eddy quoted once again from the open page of the order book: '"*You are ordered to proceed with utmost despatch . . .*"' He looked up at Snell. '*With utmost despatch*,' he repeated. 'Those were your precise instructions?'

'They were.'

'In the event the accused took eight days to make the journey. Would you consider that he acted "with utmost despatch"?'

'No, I would not.'

'The accused has given as his reason for his tardiness the fact that *en route* to Niombi he came across the tracks of a rebel war-party and felt it his duty to follow them up. Would you agree with him that it was his duty?'

'Certainly not! His duty was to proceed to Niombi and take up a guard position over the inhabitants, as he had been ordered to do.'

'Do you think that the accused would have been able to recognize with any certainty that the tracks he was following had been made by Nandi rebels?'

'I do not. I am strongly inclined to doubt the assertion that the tracks were left by humans. Given Lieutenant Courtney's predilection for *shikar* – hunting – it was more likely that the tracks of some animal, such as a bull elephant, excited his attention.'

'Objection, your honour!' wailed Bobby. 'That is merely conjecture on the part of the witness.'

Before the senior judge could make a ruling Eddy cut in smoothly: 'I withdraw the question, sir.' He was satisfied that he had placed the thought in the minds of the three judges. He led Snell on through Leon's report. 'The accused states that, with most of his men killed and his sergeant badly wounded, he fought a valiant defence against heavy odds and was only driven out of the Niombi *boma* when the rebels set fire to the building.' He tapped the page of the document. 'When that happened he placed the wounded man on his back and, using the smoke from the building as a screen, carried him away. Is this credible?'

Snell smiled knowingly. 'Sergeant Manyoro was a big man. He stood well over six feet.'

'I have a copy of his medical report. The man stood six feet three and a half inches with his feet bare. A very big man. You would agree?'

'Indeed.' Snell nodded. 'And the accused claims that he carried him something like thirty miles without being over-taken by the rebels.' He shook his head. 'I doubt that even such a powerful man as Lieutenant Courtney is capable of such a feat.'

'Then what do you think has happened to the sergeant?'

'I believe that the accused deserted him at Niombi with the rest of his detachment, and made his escape alone.'

'Objection.' Bobby jumped to his feet. 'Conjecture!'

'Objection sustained. The court recorder will strike the question and the witness's reply from the record,' said the turbaned colonel, but he glanced disapprovingly at Leon.

Eddy Roberts consulted his notes. 'We have heard evidence

that the relief column was unable to find the sergeant's body. How would you account for that?'

'I must correct you there, Captain Roberts. The evidence is that they were unable to identify the sergeant's body among the dead. That is a different matter. They found corpses in the burned-out building, but they were charred beyond recognition. The other bodies were either decapitated by the rebels or so badly mauled by vultures and hyena that they also were unrecognizable. Sergeant Manyoro could have been any one of those.'

Bobby cupped his face in his hands and said wearily, 'Objection. Supposition.'

'Sustained. Please stick to factual evidence, Major.' Snell and his favourite exchanged a smug glance.

Eddy went on in a businesslike tone: 'If Sergeant Manyoro had escaped from Niombi with the assistance of the accused, can you suggest where he is now?'

'No, I cannot.'

'At his family *manyatta*, perhaps? Visiting his mother, as the accused has stated in his report?'

'In my view that is highly unlikely,' Snell said. 'I doubt that we shall ever see the sergeant again.'

The judges adjourned for a lunch of cold roasted guinea fowl and champagne on the wide veranda of the officers' mess, and when they resumed Eddy Roberts continued his examination of Snell until the middle of the afternoon when he turned to the senior judge. 'No further questions, your honour. I have finished with this witness.' He was well satisfied and did not attempt to conceal it.

'Do you wish to cross-examine, Lieutenant?' The senior judge asked, as he consulted his pocket watch. 'I would like to conclude by tomorrow evening at the latest. We have a ship to catch in Mombasa on Friday evening.' He gave the impression that the verdict was already decided.

Bobby did his best to shake Snell's self-confident mien, but he had so little to work with that the man was able to turn aside his questions in an indulgent and condescending tone, as though he was speaking to a child. Once or twice he cast a conspiratorial glance at the three judges.

At last the colonel hauled out his gold watch again and announced, 'Gentlemen, that will do for the day. We will reconvene at nine in the morning.' He stood up and led his fellow judges to the bar at the back of the mess.

'I am afraid I didn't do very well,' Bobby confessed, as he and Leon went out on to the veranda. 'It will all be up to you when you give your evidence tomorrow.'

Ishmael brought their dinner and two bottles of beer from his lean-to kitchen at the back of Leon's rondavel. There was no chair in the hut, so the two men sprawled on the mud floor as they ate with little appetite and went despondently over their strategy for the morrow.

'I wonder if the Nairobi ladies will think you so dashing and handsome when you're standing against a brick wall wearing a blindfold,' Bobby said.

'Get out of here, you dismal johnny,' Leon ordered. 'I want to get some sleep.' But sleep would not come, and he turned, tossed and sweated until the early hours of the morning. At last he sat up and lit the bullseye lantern. Then, wearing only his underpants, he started for the door and the communal latrine at the end of the row of huts. As he stepped out on to his veranda he almost stumbled over a small group of men squatting at the door. Leon started back in alarm and held the lantern high. 'Who the hell are you?' he demanded loudly. Then he saw that there were five of them, all dressed in the ochre-red Masai *shukas*.

One rose to his feet. 'I see you, M'bogo,' he said, and his ivory earrings flashed in the lamplight almost as brilliantly as his teeth.

'Manyoro! What the hell are you doing here?' Leon almost shouted, with rising delight and relief.

'Lusima Mama sent me. She said you needed me.'

'What the devil took you so long?' Leon wanted to hug him.

'I came as swiftly as I could, with the help of these, my brothers.' He indicated the men behind him. 'We reached Naro Moru siding in two days' march from Lonsonyo Mountain. The driver of the train allowed us to sit on the roof and he brought us here at great speed.'

'Mama was right. I have great need of your help, my brother.'

'Lusima Mama is always right,' said Manyoro, flatly. 'What is this great trouble you are in? Are we going to war again?'

'Yes,' Leon answered. 'Big war!' All five Masai grinned with happy anticipation.

Ishmael had been alerted by their voices and he came staggering with sleep from the shack behind the rondavel to find the cause. 'Are these Masai infidels causing trouble, Effendi? Shall I send them away?' He had not recognized Sergeant Manyoro in his tribal dress.

'No, Ishmael. Run as fast as you can to Lieutenant Bobby and tell him to come at once. Something wonderful has happened. Our prayers have been answered.'

'Allah is great! His beneficence passes all understanding,' Ishmael intoned, then set off for Bobby's hut at a dignified jog.

'Call Sergeant Manyoro to the witness stand!' said Bobby Sampson confidently and loudly.

A stunned silence fell over the officers' mess. The judges looked up from their notes with immediate interest as Manyoro limped through the door on a crudely carved crutch. He wore his number-one dress uniform, with puttees neatly wound around his calves, but his feet were bare. The regimental badge on the front of his red fez and his belt buckle had been lovingly polished with Brasso until they gleamed like stars. Sergeant Major M'fefe marched behind him, trying unsuccessfully to stop himself grinning. The pair came to a halt in front of the high table, and saluted the judges with a flourish.

'Sergeant Major M'fefe will act as interpreter for those of us with limited Kiswahili,' Bobby explained. When the witness had been sworn in Bobby looked at the interpreter. 'Sergeant Major, please ask the witness to state his name and rank.'

'I am Sergeant Manyoro of C Company, 3rd Battalion, 1st Regiment, The King's African Rifles,' Manyoro announced proudly.

Major Snell's face crumpled with dismay. Until that moment he had not recognized Manyoro. Leon had heard him announce more than once at the mess bar when he was on his third or fourth whisky, 'These bloody wogs all look the same to me.' Such pejorative remarks were typical of Snell's overbearing disdainful attitude. No other officer would have used such a term to describe the men he commanded.

Have a good look at this bloody wog, Froggy, Leon thought happily. You won't forget his face in a hurry.

'Your honour,' Bobby addressed the senior judge, 'may the witness be allowed to give his evidence while seated? He has taken a Nandi arrow through his right leg. As you can see, it has not yet healed properly.'

All eyes in the room went down to Manyoro's thigh, which had been swathed in fresh bandages that morning by the regimental surgeon. A patch of fresh blood had oozed through the white gauze.

'Of course,' said the senior judge. 'Someone fetch him a chair.'

Everyone was leaning forward with anticipation. Major Snell and Eddy Roberts were exchanging agitated whispers. Eddy kept shaking his head.

'Sergeant, is this man your company officer?' Bobby indicated Leon at his side.

'Bwana Lieutenant, he is my officer.'

'Did you and your troop march with him to Niombi *boma?*'

'We did, Bwana Lieutenant.'

'Sergeant Manyoro, you need not keep calling me "Bwana Lieutenant",' Bobby protested, in fluent Kiswahili.

'*Ndio*, Bwana Lieutenant,' Manyoro agreed.

Bobby switched back into English for the benefit of the judges. 'On the march did you come across any suspicious tracks?'

'Yes. We found where a war-party of twenty-six Nandi warriors had come down the Rift Valley wall from the direction of Gelai Lumbwa.'

'Twenty-six? Are you sure?'

'Of course I am sure, Bwana Lieutenant.' Manyoro looked affronted at the fatuity of the question.

'How did you know for certain that it was a war-party?'

'They had no women or children with them.'

'How did you know they were Nandi and not Masai?'

'Their feet are smaller than ours, and they walk in a different way.'

'How different?'

'Short strides – they are midgets. They do not step first on to their heel and push off with their toe as a true warrior does. They slap their feet down like pregnant baboons.'

'So you could be certain that this was a Nandi war-party?'

'Only a fool or a small child could have doubted it.'

'Where were they headed?'

'Towards the mission station at Nakuru.'

'Was it your opinion that they were on their way to attack the mission?'

'I did not think that they were going to drink beer with the priests,' Manyoro replied loftily, and when the sergeant major had translated, the senior judge stifled a guffaw. The other judges smiled and nodded.

Eddy was looking glum now.

'You told all this to your lieutenant? You discussed it with him?'

'Of course.'

'He gave you orders to pursue this war-party?'

Manyoro nodded. 'We followed them for two days until we came so close that they realized we were after them.'

'How did they reach that conclusion?'

'The bush was open and even the Nandi have eyes in their heads,' Manyoro explained patiently.

'Then your officer ordered you to break off the pursuit and go to Niombi. Do you know why he decided not to engage the enemy?'

'Twenty-six Nandi went off in twenty-six directions. My lieutenant is not a fool. He knew we might catch one if we ran hard and were lucky. He also knew that we had frightened them off and they would not continue to Nakuru. My *bwana* had saved the mission from attack and he would not waste more time.'

'But you had lost almost four days?'

'*Ndio*, Bwana Lieutenant.'

'When you reached Niombi what did you find?'

'Another Nandi war-party had raided the *boma*. They had killed the district commissioner, his wife and child. They had speared the baby and drowned the man and woman by pissing in their mouths.'

The judges leaned forward attentively as Bobby led Manyoro through a description of the Nandi ambush and the desperate fighting that had followed. Without visible emotion Manyoro told of how the rest of the troop had been cut down, and how he and Leon had fought their way into the *boma* and beaten back the attackers.

'During the fight did your lieutenant behave like a man?'

'He fought like a warrior.'

'Did you see him kill any of the enemy?'

'I saw him kill eight Nandi, but there may have been more. I myself was occupied.'

'Then you received your wound. Tell us about that.'

'Our ammunition was almost finished. We went out to recover more from our dead *askari*, who were lying in the parade-ground.'

70

'Lieutenant Courtney went with you?'

'He led the way.'

'What happened then?'

'One of the Nandi dogs shot an arrow at me. It struck me here.' Manyoro drew up the leg of his khaki shorts and showed his bandaged leg.

'Were you able to run with that wound?'

'No.'

'How did you escape?'

'When he saw that I had been struck, Bwana Courtney turned back to fetch me. He carried me into the *boma*.'

'You are a big man. He carried you?'

'I am a big man because I am Masai. But Bwana Courtney is strong. His Masai name is Buffalo.'

'What happened next?'

Manyoro described in detail how they had held out until the Nandi set fire to the building, how they had been forced to abandon it and use the cover of the smoke from the burning roof to escape into the banana plantation.

'What did you do then?'

'When we reached the open ground beyond the plantation I asked my *bwana* to leave me with his pistol and go on alone.'

'Did you plan to kill yourself because you were crippled and you did not want the Nandi to catch and drown you as they had done to the district commissioner and his wife?'

'I would have killed myself rather than die the Nandi way, but not before I had taken a few of the jackals with me,' Manyoro agreed.

'Your officer refused to leave you?'

'He wanted to carry me on his back to the railway line. I told him it was four days' march through Nandi tribal lands and that we already knew the ground was swarming with their war-parties. I told him my mother's *manyatta* was only thirty miles distant and deep in Masailand where Nandi curs would never dare to follow. I told him that if he was determined to take me with him we should go that way.'

'He did as you suggested?'

'He did.'

'Thirty miles? He carried you on his back for thirty miles?'

'Perhaps a little further. He is a strong man.'

'When the two of you reached your mother's village, why did he not leave you there and return to Nairobi immediately?'

'His feet were ruined by the march from Niombi. He could not walk further on them. My mother is a famous healer of great power. She treated his feet with her medicine. Bwana Courtney left the *manyatta* as soon as he was able to walk.'

Bobby paused and looked at the three judges. Then he asked, 'Sergeant Manyoro, what are your feelings for Lieutenant Courtney?'

Manyoro answered, with quiet dignity, 'My *bwana* and I are brothers of the warrior blood.'

'Thank you, Sergeant. I have no further questions for you.'

For a long moment there was a hush of awe in the courtroom. Then Colonel Wallace roused himself. 'Lieutenant Roberts, do you wish to cross-examine this man?'

Eddy conferred hurriedly with Major Snell, then stood up reluctantly. 'No, sir, I have no questions for him.'

'Are there any more witnesses? Will you call your client to the stand, Lieutenant Sampson?' Colonel Wallace asked. He pulled out his watch and consulted it pointedly.

'With the court's indulgence, I shall call Lieutenant Courtney. However, I have almost finished and will not detain the court much longer.'

'I am relieved to hear that. You may proceed.'

When Leon took the stand Bobby handed him a sheaf of papers and asked, 'Lieutenant Courtney, is this your official report of the Niombi expedition, which you gave to your commanding officer?'

Leon thumbed through it quickly. 'Yes, this is my report.'

'Is there anything in it you wish to retract? Anything you wish to add to it?'

'No, there is not.'

'You affirm under oath that this report is true and correct in every detail?'

'I do.'

Bobby took the document from him and placed it before the judges. 'I wish this report to be entered into evidence.'

'It has already been entered,' said Colonel Wallace, testily. 'We have all read it. Ask your questions, Lieutenant, and let's have done with it.'

'I have no further questions, your honour. The defence rests.'

'Good.' The colonel was pleasurably surprised. He had not expected Bobby to be so quick. He scowled at Eddy Roberts. 'Are you going to cross-examine?'

'No, sir. I have no questions for the accused.'

'Excellent.' Wallace smiled for the first time. 'The witness may stand down, and the prosecution can get on with its summation.'

Eddy stood up, trying to portray the confidence he obviously lacked. 'May it please the court to direct its attention to both the written report of the accused, which he has affirmed under oath is correct in every detail, and to Sergeant Manyoro's corroborating evidence. They both confirm that the accused deliberately ignored his written orders to proceed with utmost despatch to Niombi station, and instead set off in pursuit of the Nandi war-party that he believed might be heading in the direction of Nakuru mission. I submit that the accused has admitted he was guilty of the charge of deliberately refusing to follow the orders of a superior officer in the face of the enemy. Absolutely no doubt about that.'

Eddy paused to gather himself. He took a deep breath as though he was about to dive into a pool of icy water. 'As for Sergeant Manyoro's slavish endorsement of the accused's actions thereafter, may I direct attention to his childlike and emotional statement that he and the accused are "brothers of the warrior blood".' Colonel Wallace frowned and his fellow judges stirred uneasily on their seats. It was not the reaction Eddy had hoped for, and he hurried on: 'I submit that the witness had been briefed by the defence and that he is completely in the thrall of the accused. I suggest to you that he would have parroted any words put into his mouth.'

'Captain Roberts, are you suggesting that the witness shot himself in the leg with an arrow to cover up his platoon commander's cowardice?' Colonel Wallace asked.

Eddy sat down as the courtroom exploded with laughter.

'Silence in court! Please, gentlemen, please!' the adjutant remonstrated.

'Is that your summation, Captain? Have you finished?' Wallace enquired.

'I have, your honour.'

'Lieutenant Sampson, do you care to refute the defence's summation?'

Bobby came to his feet. 'Your honour, we reject not only the entire substance of the summation but we take umbrage at the prosecution's slur on Sergeant Manyoro's honesty. We have full confidence that the court will accept the evidence of a truthful, valiant and loyal soldier, whose devotion to duty and respect for his officers is the very stuff that the British Army is made of.' He looked at each of the three judges in turn. 'Gentlemen, the defence rests.'

'The court will rise to consider its verdict. We will convene again at noon to give judgement.' Wallace stood up and said to the other two judges, in a clearly audible *sotto voce*, 'Well, chaps, it seems we might yet catch that ship.'

As they filed out of the courtroom Leon whispered to Bobby, '"*The very stuff that the British Army is made of*". That was masterly.'

'It was rather, wasn't it?'

'Buy you a beer?'

'Don't mind if you do.'

A n hour later Colonel Wallace sat at the high table and shuffled his papers. Then he cleared his throat juicily and began: 'Before I proceed with delivering the judgement, I wish to state that this court was impressed by the bearing and evidence of Sergeant Manyoro. We found him entirely credible, a truthful, loyal and valiant soldier.' Bobby beamed as he heard his own description repeated faithfully by Wallace. 'This statement should be appended to Sergeant Manyoro's service record.'

Wallace swivelled in his seat and glared at Leon. 'The judgement of this court is as follows. On the charges of cowardice, desertion and dereliction of duty we find the accused not guilty.' There were murmurs of relief from the defence. Bobby thumped Leon's knee under cover of the table. Wallace went on sternly, 'Although the court understood and sympathized with the accused's instinct to engage the enemy at every opportunity, in the tradition of the British Army, we find that when he took up the pursuit of the rebel war-party in defiance of his orders to proceed with utmost despatch to Niombi station he transgressed the Articles of War, which require strict obedience to the orders of a superior officer. We therefore have no alternative but to find him guilty of disobeying the written orders of his superior officer.'

Bobby and Leon stared at him with dismay and Snell folded his arms across his chest. He leaned back in his chair with a smirk on his wide mouth.

'I come now to the sentence. The accused will stand.' Leon came to his feet and snapped to rigid attention, staring at the wall behind Wallace's head. 'The verdict of guilty will be recorded in the service record of the accused. He will be detained until this court rises and immediately thereafter will be returned to duty with the full responsibility and privileges of his rank. God save the King!

'These proceedings are at an end.' Wallace stood, bowed to the men below him and led his fellow judges to the bar.

'There's time for a peg before the train leaves. I'll have a whisky. What about you chaps?'

As Leon and Bobby headed for the door of the courtroom, which had now reverted to its former role as the officers' mess, they drew level with the table at which Snell was still seated. He stood up and replaced his cap on his head, forcing them to come to attention and salute. His pale blue eyes bulged from their sockets and his lips were set in an expression that gave him the appearance not so much of a frog but of a venomous toad. After a deliberate pause he returned their salutes. 'I will have fresh orders for you tomorrow morning, Courtney. Be at my office at eight hundred hours sharp. In the meantime you may carry on,' he snapped.

'I doubt very much that you've made Froggy your friend for life,' Bobby muttered, as they went out on to the sunlit parade-ground. 'He'll make your life extremely interesting from now onwards. My guess is that his new orders will take you on foot patrol to Lake Natron or some other remote and God-forsaken place. We won't be seeing much of you for a month or so, but at least you'll be seeing more of the country.'

His *askari* thronged around Leon to congratulate him. '*Jambo*, Bwana. Welcome back.'

'At least you have some friends left,' Bobby consoled him. 'May I use the jalopy while you're sojourning in the outer wilderness?'

Many months later two horsemen rode stirrup to stirrup along the bank of the Athi river. The grooms followed at a distance, leading the spare horses. The riders wore wide-brimmed slouch hats and carried their lances at rest. Before them, the wide green expanse of the Athi plains stretched to the horizon. It was dotted with herds of zebra, ostriches, impala and wildebeest. A pair of giraffe stared down at them with great dark eyes as they rode past at a distance of only a hundred paces.

'Sir, I can't stand it much longer,' Leon told his favourite uncle. 'I'll have to put in for a transfer to another regiment.'

'I doubt any would have you, my boy. You have a large black mark on your service record,' said Colonel Penrod Ballantyne, commanding officer of the 1st Regiment, The King's African Rifles. 'What about India? I might put in a word for you with a few friends who were in South Africa with me.' Penrod was testing him.

'Thank you, sir, but I would never dream of leaving Africa,' Leon replied. 'When you were weaned on Nile water you can never break the shackles.'

Penrod nodded. It was the reply he had expected. He took a silver case from his top pocket and tapped out a Player's Gold Leaf. He put it between his lips and offered one to Leon.

'Thank you, sir, but I don't indulge.' Leon read the engraving on the inside of the lid before his uncle closed it. 'To Twopence, happy 50th birthday from your adoring wife, Amber.' Aunt Amber had a quirky sense of humour. Her nickname for Penrod had originally been Penny but after all their years of marriage she had decided his value had doubled.

'Well, sir, if no one else will have me I suppose I'll just have to put in my papers and resign my commission – I've already wasted nearly three years wandering in small circles in the wilderness, getting nowhere, at the behest of Major Snell. I can't take any more.'

Penrod considered this, but before he could decide on a suitable reply a movement further down the riverbank caught his eye. A warthog boar trotted out of a dense clump of riverine scrub. His curved white tusks almost met above his comically hideous face, which was decorated with the black wart-like protuberances that gave him his name. He carried his tufted tail straight as a ruler, pointing up at the sky. 'Here we go!' Penrod shouted. 'Tally ho and away!' He kicked his heels into his mare's flanks and she was off.

Leon raced after him, leaning along the neck of his polo pony as he couched his long pig spear. 'By God, this one's a huge brute. Look at those tusks! Up and at him, Uncle!'

Penrod's mare ran lightly, closing swiftly on the quarry, but Leon's bay gelding pushed up half a length behind her streaming tail. The warthog heard their hoofs thundering, stopped and looked back. He stared at the charging horses with astonishment, then whipped around and darted away across the plain kicking up puffs of dust with each beat of his sharp little hoofs, but he could not outrun the mare.

Penrod leaned out of the saddle and lined up the point of his spear, aiming at the patch of bald grey skin between the animal's humped shoulder-blades.

'Stick him, Twopence!' In his excitement Leon called the name reserved for exclusive use by his aunt. Penrod showed no sign of having heard. He carried home his charge, the point of his spear arrowing in towards the boar's withers. But at the last instant the warthog changed direction and doubled back under the mare's front legs. Even she, bred and trained to follow a bouncing polo ball adroitly, could not counter the manoeuvre and overran the quarry. The spearhead glanced off the boar's tough hide without drawing blood, and Penrod pulled the mare's head around steeply. She pranced and mouthed the bit, her eyes wild with the excitement of the chase.

'Come away, my darling! Full tilt and hell for leather!' Penrod exhorted her, and touched her ribs with blunted rowels. She came around again for the next run, but Leon cut across her line and his pony fastened on the warthog's hind-quarters as though he was attached to it by a leash. Horse and rider stayed with the pig as it twisted, turned and doubled desperately. They went around in a circle, Penrod laughing and shouting advice after them.

'Stay with him, sir. Watch out for the tusks – he nearly had you there!' The boar broke back on Leon's blind side and almost reached the cover of the dense scrub from which he had appeared, but Leon, rising high in his stirrups, switched his spear neatly to his left hand and drove the point between the warthog's shoulders. The animal took it cleanly through the heart. Leon let the shaft drop back as the gelding passed over the dying beast and the spearhead came free without jarring his wrist. The bright steel and two feet of the shaft behind it shone with the boar's heart blood. It squealed once and its front legs folded under it. It dropped, slid on its snout, then flopped on to its side, gave three kicks with its back legs and was dead.

'Oh, well done indeed, sir! A perfect kill!' Penrod reined in beside his nephew. They were both laughing breathlessly. 'What was that you called me a minute ago?'

'I do beg your pardon, Uncle. In the heat of the moment it just slipped out.'

'Well, slip it back in, you impudent puppy. No wonder Froggy Snell has it in for you. Deep down, I understand and sympathize with him.'

'It's been thirsty work. How about a cup of tea, sir?' Leon changed the subject smoothly.

As soon as Ishmael had seen they had killed, he had parked the tuck wagon in the shade and was already lighting the fire.

'That is the very least you can do to make amends. Twopence! What is the younger generation coming to?' Penrod grumbled.

By the time they dismounted the kettle was brewing. 'Three teaspoons of sugar, Ishmael, and a couple of your ginger snaps,' Penrod ordered, as he sat in one of the canvas camp chairs in the shade.

'Your honourable and esteemed lady wife would not like it, Effendi.'

'My honourable and esteemed lady wife is in Cairo. She will not be partaking,' Penrod reminded him, and reached for the biscuits as Ishmael placed the plate in front of him. He chewed with pleasure, washed down the crumbs with a swig of tea and smoothed his moustache. 'So, what do you intend after you've resigned your commission, if you won't go out to India?'

'It's Africa for me.' Leon sipped from his own mug, then said thoughtfully, 'I thought I might try my hand at elephant hunting.'

'Elephant hunting?' Penrod was incredulous. 'As a profession? As Selous and Bell once did?'

'Well, it's always fascinated me, ever since I read the books about their adventures.'

'Romantic nonsense! You're thirty years too late. Those old boys had the whole of Africa to themselves. They went where they liked and did as they wanted. This is the modern age. Things have changed. Now there are roads and railways all over the place. No country in Africa is still issuing unrestricted elephant licences that allow the holder to slaughter thousands of the great beasts. All that is over, and a damn good thing too. Anyway, it was a hard, bitter life, dangerous and lonely too, year after year of wandering alone in the wilderness without anyone to talk to in your own language. Put the notion out of your head.'

Leon was crestfallen. He stared into his mug while Penrod fished out and lit another cigarette. 'Well, I don't know what I'm going to do,' he admitted at last.

'Chin up, my boy.' Penrod's tone was kindly now. 'You want to be a hunter? Well, a few men are making a fine living doing just that. They hire themselves out to guide visitors from overseas on safari. There are rich men from Europe and America, royalty, aristocrats and millionaires, who are willing to pay a fortune for the chance to bag an elephant or two. These days, African big-game hunting is all the rage in high society.'

'White hunters? Like Tarlton and Cunninghame?' Leon's face was bright. 'What a wonderful life that must be.' His expression crumpled again. 'But how would I get started? I have no money, and I won't ask my father for help. He'd laugh at me anyway. And I don't know anybody. Why would dukes and princes and business tycoons want to come all the way from Europe to hunt with me?'

'I could take you to see a man I know. He might be willing to help you.'

'When can we go?'

'Tomorrow. His base camp is only a short ride out of Nairobi.'

'Major Snell has given me orders to take a patrol up to Lake Turkana. I have to scout out a location to build a fort up there.'

'Turkana!' Penrod snorted with laughter. 'Why would we need a fort up there?'

'It's his idea of fun. When I submit the reports he asks for, he sends them back to me with mocking comments scrawled in the margins.'

'I'll have a word with him, ask him to release you briefly for a special assignment.'

'Thank you, sir. Thank you very much.'

They rode out through the barracks gates and down the main street of Nairobi. Although it was early morning the wide, unsurfaced road was crowded and bustling like that of a gold-rush boom town. Sir Charles, the governor of the colony, encouraged settlers to come out from the old country by offering land grants of thousands of acres at a nominal fee and they flocked in. The road was almost blocked by their wagons, which were piled high with their scanty possessions and forlorn families as they journeyed on to take up their parcels of land in the wilderness. Hindu, Goanese and Jewish traders and storekeepers followed them. Their mud-brick shops lined the sides of the road, hand-printed boards on the fronts offering everything from champagne and dynamite to picks, shovels and shotgun cartridges.

Penrod and Leon picked their way through the ox wagons and mule teams until Penrod reined in before the Norfolk Hotel to greet a small man, in a solar topee, who was perched like an elf in the back of a buggy drawn by a pair of Burchell's zebra. 'Good morning, my lord.' Penrod saluted him.

The little man adjusted his steel-rimmed spectacles on the end of his nose. 'Ah, Colonel. Good to see you. Where are you headed?'

'We're riding out to visit Percy Phillips.'

'Dear old Percy.' He nodded. 'Great friend of mine. I hunted with him the first year I came out from home. We spent six months together, trekking up as far as the Northern Frontier district and on into the Sudan. He guided me to two enormous elephant. Lovely man. Taught me everything I know about hunting big game.'

'Which is a very great deal. Your feats with that .577 rifle of yours are almost as legendary as his.'

'Kind of you to say so, even though I detect a touch of hyperbole in that compliment.' He turned his bright, inquisitive eyes on Leon. 'And who is this young fellow?'

'May I present my nephew, Lieutenant Leon Courtney? Leon, this is Lord Delamere.'

'I'm honoured to make your acquaintance, my lord.'

'I know who you are.' His lordship's eyes twinkled with amusement.

Apparently he did not pretend the same high moral ethics as the rest of the local society. Leon guessed that his next remark would be some reference to Verity O'Hearne, so he added hastily, 'I am much taken with your carriage horses, my lord.'

'Caught and trained them with my own fair hands.' Delamere gave him a last piercing glance, then he turned away. Can understand why young Verity was so taken with him, he thought, and why all the old hens in the coop were cackling with jealous outrage. That young blade is the answer to a maiden's prayer.

He touched the brim of his helmet with his buggy whip. 'I wish you a very good day, Colonel. Give my compliments to Percy.' He whipped up the zebra and drove on.

'Lord Delamere was once a great *shikari*, but now he's become an ardent conservator of wild game,' Penrod said. 'He has an estate of more than a hundred thousand acres at

Soysambu on the west side of the Rift Valley which he's turning into a game sanctuary, mortgaging his family estates in England to the very hilt to do so. The finest hunters are all like that. When they tire of killing they become the most devoted protectors of their former quarry.'

They left the town and rode out along the Ngong Hills until they looked down on a sprawling encampment in the forest. Tents, grass huts and rondavels were spread out under the trees in no particular order.

'This is Percy's base, Tandala Camp.' '*Tandala*' was the Swahili name for the greater kudu. 'He brings his clients up from the coast by railway, and from here he can strike out into the blue on foot, on horseback or by ox wagon.' They rode on down the hill, but before they reached the main camp they came to the skinning sheds where the hunting trophies were prepared and preserved. There, the upper branches of the trees were filled with roosting vultures and the carnivorous marabou storks. The stench of drying skins and heads was rank and powerful.

They reined in the horses to watch two ancient Ndorobo working on the fresh skull of a bull elephant with their hand axes, chipping away the bone to expose the roots of the tusks. As they watched, one man drew a tusk free of its bony canal. The pair staggered away with it, their skinny legs buckling under the weight. They struggled unsuccessfully to lift the immense ivory shaft into a canvas sling suspended from the hook of a beam scale. Leon slipped out of the saddle and took their burden from them. Effortlessly he reached up and placed it in the sling. Under the weight of the tusk the needle revolved halfway around the scale's dial.

'Thanks for your help, young fellow.'

Leon turned. A tall man was standing behind his shoulder. He had the features of a Roman patrician. His short neat beard was silver grey and his bright blue eyes were steady. There could be no question as to who this was. Leon knew that Percy Phillips's Swahili name was Bwana Samawati, 'the man with eyes the colour of the sky'.

'Hello, Percy.' Penrod confirmed his identity as he rode up and dismounted.

'Penrod, you look fit.' They shook hands.

'So do you, Percy. Hardly a day older than when we last met.'

'You must be wanting a favour. Is this your nephew?' Percy did not wait for the reply. 'What do you think of that tusk, young man?'

'Magnificent, sir. I've never seen anything like it.'

'One hundred and twenty-two pounds.' Percy Phillips read the weight from the scale and smiled. 'The best piece of ivory I've taken in the last many years. Not too many of those around any more.' He nodded with satisfaction. 'Much too good for the miserable dago who shot it. Cheek of the man! He complained he'd been given short measure for his miserly five hundred pounds. Didn't want to pay up at the end of the safari. I had to talk to him very sternly indeed.' He blew softly on the scarred knuckles of his right fist, then turned back to Penrod. 'I had my cook bake a batch of ginger snaps for you. I remember your penchant for them.' He took Penrod's arm and, limping slightly, led him towards the large mess tent in the centre of the encampment.

'How did you hurt your leg, sir?' Leon asked, as he fell in with them.

Percy laughed. 'Big old bull buffalo jumped on it, but that was thirty years ago when I was still a greenhorn. Taught me a lesson I've never forgotten.'

Percy and Penrod settled in the folding chairs under the flap of the mess tent to exchange news of mutual acquaintances and bring each other up to date with goings-on in the colony. Meanwhile, Leon looked around the camp with interest. Despite its apparently haphazard layout it was obviously convenient and comfortable. The ground was swept clean. The huts were all in good repair. On the periphery of the main camp, on the slope of the hill above it, a small whitewashed and thatched bungalow was obviously Percy's home. There was only one exception to the camp's order, which caught Leon's attention.

A Vauxhall truck, of the same vintage as the vehicle he and Bobby owned, was parked behind a hut. It was in a terrible condition: one of the front wheels was missing, the windscreen was cracked and opaque with filth, the bonnet was propped open with a log and the engine had been removed to a crude workbench in the shade of a nearby tree. Somebody had started to strip it down, but seemed to have lost interest and abandoned it. Engine parts were scattered around or piled on the driver's seat. A flock of chickens had taken over the chassis as their roost and splashes of their white droppings almost obscured the original paintwork.

'Your uncle tells me you want to be a hunter. Is that right?'

Leon turned back to Percy Phillips when he realized he had been addressed. 'Yes, sir.' Percy stroked his silver beard and studied him thoughtfully. Leon did not look away, which Percy liked. Polite and respectful, but sure of himself, he thought. 'Have you ever shot an elephant?'

'No, sir.'

'Lion?'

'No, sir.'

'Rhino? Buffalo? Leopard?'

'Afraid not, sir.'

'What have you taken, then?'

'Just a few Tommies and Grant's for the pot, sir, but I can learn. That's why I've come to you.'

'At least you're honest. If you've never taken dangerous game, what *can* you do? Give me a good reason why I should offer you a job.'

'Well, sir, I can ride.'

'Are you talking about horses or human females?'

Leon flushed vividly. He opened his mouth to reply, but closed it again.

'Yes, young man, word gets around. Now, listen to me. Many of my clients bring their families with them on safari.

Wives and daughters. How do I know you won't try to rabbit them at the first opportunity?'

'Whatever you heard is not true, sir,' Leon protested. 'I'm not like that, at all.'

'You'll keep your fly buttoned around here,' Percy grunted. 'Other than ride, what else can you do?'

'I could mend that.' Leon pointed to the wreckage.

Percy showed immediate interest.

'I have one of the same make and model,' Leon went on. 'It was in similar condition to yours when I got it. I put it back together and now it runs like a Swiss watch.'

'Does it, by God? Damn motors are a complete mystery to me. All right, so you can ride and repair trucks. That's a start. What else? Can you shoot?'

'Yes, sir.'

'Leon won the Governor's Cup at the regimental rifle competition at the beginning of the year,' Penrod confirmed. 'He can shoot, I'll vouch for that.'

'Paper targets are not live animals. They don't bite you or jump on you if you miss,' Percy pointed out. 'If you want to be a hunter you'll need a rifle. I am not talking about a little service Enfield – a pea-shooter isn't much use in an argument with an angry buffalo. Have you got a real rifle?'

'Yes, sir.'

'What is it?'

'A Holland & Holland Royal .470 Nitro Express.'

Percy's blue eyes widened. 'Very well,' he conceded. 'That is a real rifle. They don't come better than that. But you'll also need a tracker. Can you find a good one?'

'Yes, sir.' He was thinking of Manyoro, but then he remembered Loikot. 'Actually, I have two.'

Percy gazed at a brilliant gold and green sunbird flitting about in the branches above the tent. Then he seemed to make up his mind. 'You're lucky. It just so happens that I am going to need help. I'm to lead a big safari early next year. The client is an extremely important person.'

'This client of yours, I wonder, could he be Theodore Roosevelt, the President of the United States of America?' Penrod asked innocently.

Percy was startled. 'In the name of all that's holy, Penrod, how on earth did you discover that?' he demanded. 'Nobody's supposed to know.'

'The US State Department sent a cable to the Commander in Chief of the British Army, Lord Kitchener, in London. They wanted to know more about you before the President hired you. I was on Kitchener's staff in South Africa during the war so he telegraphed me,' Penrod admitted.

Percy burst out laughing. 'You're a sly creature, Ballantyne. Here I was believing that Teddy Roosevelt's visit was a state secret. So you put in a good word for me. It seems I'm even deeper in your debt.' He turned back to Leon. 'Here's what I'll do with you. I'm going to make you prove yourself. First, I want you to put that heap of rubbish together and get it running.' He nodded at the dismembered truck. 'I want you to make good your boast. Do you understand?'

'Yes, sir.'

'When you've done that, you'll take your famous .470 and your two even more famous trackers, go out there into the blue and bag an elephant. I could never employ a hunter who's never hunted. When you've done that, I want you to bring back the tusks to prove it.'

'Yes, sir.' Leon grinned.

'Have you enough money to buy a game licence? It'll cost you ten pounds.'

'No, sir.'

'I'll lend it to you,' Percy offered, 'but the ivory will be mine.'

'Sir, lend me the money and you can have the pick of one tusk. I'll keep the other.'

Percy chuckled. The lad could fight his own corner. He was no pushover. He was beginning to enjoy him. 'Fair enough, boy.'

'If you take me on what will you pay me, sir?'

'Pay you? I'm doing your uncle a favour. You should pay me.'

'How about five shillings a day?' Leon suggested.

'How about one shilling?' Percy countered.

'Two?'

'You drive a hard bargain.' Percy shook his head sadly but stuck out his hand.

Leon shook it vigorously. 'You won't regret it, sir, I promise you.'

'**Y**ou've changed my life. I'll never be able to repay you for what you've done for me today.' Leon was elated as they rode back along the Ngong Hills towards Nairobi. 'You needn't worry too much about that. You don't think for one minute that I'm doing this because I'm your doting uncle?'

'I misjudged you, sir.'

'This is how you will repay me. First, I'm not going to accept your resignation from the regiment. Instead I shall transfer you to the reserves, then second you to military intelligence to work under my direct orders.'

Leon's face showed his dismay. A moment ago he had felt himself a free man. Now it seemed he was back in the smothering embrace of the army.

'Sir?' he responded cautiously.

'There are dangerous times ahead. Kaiser Wilhelm of Germany has more than doubled the strength of his standing army in the last ten years. He's no statesman or diplomat, but he is a military man, by training and instinct. He has spent his whole life training for war. All his advisers are army men. He has a boundless ambition towards imperial expansion. He has huge colonies in Africa, but they are not enough for him. I tell you, we shall have trouble with him. Think, German East Africa is right on our southern border.

Dar es Salaam is their port. They could have a warship there in very short order. They already have a full regiment of *askari* led by German regular officers stationed at Arusha. Von Lettow Vorbeck, the commanding officer, is a tough, cunning old soldier. In ten days' march he could be in Nairobi. I have pointed this out to the War Office in London, but they have concerns elsewhere, and don't wish to spend money reinforcing an unimportant backwater of the Empire.'

'This comes as a shock to me, sir. I have never looked at the situation in that way. The Germans down there have always been very friendly towards us. They have a great deal in common with our own settlers in Nairobi. They share the same problems.'

'Yes, there are some good fellows among them – and I like von Lettow Vorbeck. But his orders come from Berlin and the Kaiser.'

'The Kaiser is the grandson of Queen Victoria. Our present king is his uncle. The Kaiser is an honorary admiral in the Royal Navy. I cannot believe we would ever want to go to war with him,' Leon protested.

'Trust the instinct of an old warhorse.' Penrod smiled knowingly. 'Anyway, whatever happens I shall not be taken off-guard. I'm going to keep a sharp eye on our lovable southern neighbours.'

'How do I fit in?'

'At this stage our borders with German East Africa are wide open. There is no restriction of movement in either direction. The Masai and other tribes graze their herds north and south without the least concern for any boundaries laid out by our surveyors. I want you to set up a network of informers, tribesmen who move regularly in and out of German East Africa. You will play a clandestine role. Not even Percy Phillips must know what you're up to. Your cover story is convincing. As a hunter you'll have the perfect excuse to move freely through the country on both sides of the border. You will report directly to me. I want you to be my eyes along the border.'

'If there are questions I could let it be known that the informers are my game scouts, that I'm using them to keep an eye on the movements of the game herds, especially the elephant bulls, so that I know their exact position at any time and can take our clients straight to them,' Leon suggested. Now the game sounded as though it might be exciting and great fun.

Penrod nodded in agreement. 'That should satisfy Percy and anybody else who asks. Just don't mention my involvement or it will be all around the club the next time he has a few drinks. Percy is hardly the soul of discretion.'

A few weeks later Leon was spending almost every waking hour lying under Percy's truck, his arms coated to the elbows with black grease. He had seriously underestimated the enormity of the task, and the amount of damage Percy had wrought with his previous efforts at repair. There were few spare parts available in Nairobi and Leon was forced to consider cannibalizing the vehicle he and Bobby owned. Bobby stoutly resisted the idea, but in the end he agreed to sell his share of the vehicle to Leon for the sum of fifteen guineas, to be paid in instalments of a guinea a month. Leon immediately removed a front wheel, the carburettor and other parts, and carried them out to Tandala Camp.

He had been working on the engine for ten days when he woke one morning to find Sergeant Manyoro squatting outside his tent. He was not dressed in his khaki uniform and fez but in an ochre-red *shuka*, and carried a lion spear. 'I have come,' he announced.

'I see you have.' Leon had difficulty in hiding his delight. 'But why aren't you in barracks? They'll shoot you for desertion.'

'I have paper.' Manyoro brought out a crumpled envelope from under his *shuka*. Leon opened it and read the document quickly. Manyoro had at last been honourably discharged from the KAR on medical grounds. Although the leg wound had healed some time ago he had been left with a limp that rendered him unfit for military duty.

'Why have you come to me?' Leon asked. 'Why did you not return to your *manyatta*?'

'I am your man,' he said simply.

'I cannot pay you.'

'I did not ask you to,' Manyoro replied. 'What do you want me to do?'

'First, we are going to mend this *enchini*.' For a moment they contemplated the sorry spectacle. Manyoro had assisted with the restoration of the first vehicle so he knew what lay in store. 'Then we are going to kill an elephant,' Leon added.

'The killing will be easier than the mending,' was Manyoro's opinion.

Almost three weeks later Leon sat behind the steering-wheel while, with an air of resignation, Manyoro took up his position in front of the truck and stood to attention. He had lost all faith in the eventual success of the manoeuvres he had performed repeatedly over the last three days. On the first day Percy Phillips and the entire camp staff, including the cook and the ancient skinners, had formed an attentive audience. Gradually they had lost interest and drifted away, one by one, until only the skinners were left, squatting on their haunches and following every move with rapt attention.

'Retard the spark!' Leon began the incantations to the gods of the internal combustion engine.

The two old skinners chanted after him, 'Letaad de paak.' They were word perfect.

Leon moved the spark control lever on the left-hand side of the steering-wheel to the upright position. 'Throttle open.'

This one always tested the skinners' powers of enunciation to the limit. 'Frot le pen,' was as close as they could get.

'Handbrake on!' Leon pulled it on.

'Mixture rich!' He rotated the control knob until the indicator pointed straight ahead.

'Choke.' He jumped out, ran to the front of the vehicle

and pulled on the choke ring, then returned to the driver's seat.

'Manyoro, prime the carb!' Manyoro stooped and swung the crank handle twice. 'That's enough!' Leon warned him. 'Choke off!' He jumped out again, raced forward, pushed in the choke ring, then ran back to his seat.

'Two more turns!' Again Manyoro stooped and cranked the handle.

'Carb primed! Power on!' Leon turned the selector on the dashboard to 'battery' and looked to the heavens. 'Manyoro, hit her again!' Manyoro spat on his right palm, gripped the crank handle and swung it.

There was an explosion like a cannon shot and a spurt of blue smoke flew from the exhaust pipe. The crank handle kicked back viciously and knocked Manyoro off his feet. The two skinners were taken aback. They had not been expecting anything nearly as spectacular. They howled with fright and scuttled for the bushes beyond the camp. There was a shouted oath from Percy's thatched bungalow on the first slope of the hill at the perimeter of the camp and he stumbled out on to the stoep in his pyjama bottoms, beard in disarray, eyes unfocused with sleep. He stared in momentary confusion at Leon, who was beaming with triumph behind the steering-wheel. The engine rumbled, shook and backfired, then settled down into a loud, clattering beat.

Percy laughed. 'Let me get my trousers on, then you can drive me to the club. I'm going to buy you as much beer as you can drink. Then you can go out and find that elephant. I don't want you back in this camp until you have him.'

Leon stood below the familiar massif of Lonsonyo Mountain. He pushed his slouch hat to the back of his head and moved the heavy rifle from one shoulder to the other. He gazed up at the crest of the mountain. It took his sharp young eye to pick out the single lonely figure on the skyline. 'She's waiting for us,' he exclaimed in surprise. 'How did she know we were coming?'

'Lusima Mama knows everything,' Manyoro reminded him, and started up the steep path towards the summit. He carried the water-bottles, the canvas haversack, Leon's light .303 Lee-Enfield rifle and four bandoliers of ammunition. Leon followed him, and Ishmael brought up the rear, the skirts of his long white *kanza* flapping around his legs. An enormous bundle was balanced on his head. Before they had left Tandala Camp Leon had weighed it. It had come in at sixty-two pounds and contained Ishmael's kitchen supplies, everything from pots and pans to pepper, salt and his own secret mixture of spices. With Leon providing a daily supply of tender young Tommy buck chops and steaks and Ishmael's culinary skills they had eaten like princes since they had left the railway line at Naro Moru siding.

When they reached the mountaintop Lusima was waiting for them in the shade of a giant flowering seringa tree. She rose to her feet, tall and statuesque as a queen, and greeted them. 'I see you, my sons, and my eyes are gladdened.'

'Mama, we come for your blessing on our weapons and your guidance in our hunting,' Manyoro told her, as he knelt before her.

The next morning the entire village gathered in a circle around the wild fig tree, the council tree, in the cattle pen to witness the blessing of the weapons. Leon and Manyoro squatted with them. Ishmael had refused to join in such a pagan ritual, and he clattered his pots ostentatiously over the cooking fire behind the nearest hut. Leon's two rifles were laid side by side on a tanned lionskin. Beside them stood calabash gourds filled with fresh cow's blood and milk, and baked-clay bowls of salt, snuff and glittering glass trade beads. At last Lusima emerged from the low door of her hut. The congregation clapped and began to sing her praises.

'She is the great black cow who feeds us with the milk of her udders. She is the watcher who sees all things. She is the wise one who knows all things. She is the mother of the tribe.' Lusima wore her full ceremonial regalia. On her forehead hung an ivory pendant carved with mystical animal figures. Her *shuka* was thickly embroidered with a shimmering curtain of beads and cowrie shells. Heavy coils of bead necklace hung down to her chest. Her skin was oiled and polished with red ochre, shining in the sunlight, and she carried a fly switch made from the tail of a giraffe. Her steps were stately as she circled the display of rifles and sacrificial offerings.

'Let not the quarry escape the warrior who wields these weapons,' she intoned, as she sprinkled a pinch of snuff over them. 'Let blood flow copiously from the wounds they inflict.' She dipped the switch into the gourds and splashed blood and milk on to the rifles. Then she went to Leon and flicked the mixture over his head and shoulders. 'Give him strength and determination to follow the quarry. Make his hunter's eyes bright to see the quarry from great distance. Let no creature resist his power. Let the mightiest elephant fall to the voice of his *bunduki*, his rifle.'

The watchers clapped in rhythm and she continued her exhortations: 'Let him be the king among hunters. Grant him the power of the hunter.'

She began to dance in a tight circle, pirouetting faster and faster, until sweat and red ochre ran in a rivulet between her naked breasts. When she threw herself flat on the lionskin in front of Leon her eyes rolled back and white froth bubbled from the corners of her mouth. Her entire body began to tremble and twitch and her legs kicked spasmodically. She ground her teeth and her breath rasped painfully in her throat.

'The spirit has entered her body,' Manyoro whispered. 'She is ready to speak with its voice. Put the question to her.'

'Lusima, favourite of the Great Spirit, your sons seek a chief among the elephants. Where shall we find him? Show us the way to the great bull.'

Lusima's head rolled from side to side and her breathing became more laboured until at last she spoke through gritted teeth, in a hoarse unnatural voice: 'Follow the wind and listen for the voice of the sweet singer. He will point the way.' She gave a deep gasp and sat up. Her eyes cleared and refocused and she looked at Leon as though she was seeing him for the first time.

'Is that all?' he asked.

'There is no more,' she replied.

'I don't understand,' Leon persisted. 'Who is the sweet singer?'

'That is all the message I have for you,' she said. 'If the gods favour your hunt, then in time the meaning will become clear to you.'

Since Leon's arrival on the mountain Loikot had followed him around at a discreet distance. Now as he sat beside the campfire with a dozen of the village elders, Loikot was in the shadows behind him, listening attentively to the conversation, his head turning from face to face of the men who were speaking.

'I wish to know the movements of men and animals throughout Masailand and down the full length of the Rift Valley, even in the land beyond the great mountains of Kilimanjaro and Meru. I want this information gathered and sent to me as swiftly as possible.'

The village elders listened to his request, then discussed it animatedly among themselves, everyone coming up with a different opinion. Leon's grasp of the Maa language was not yet strong enough to follow the rapid fire of argument and counter-assertion. In a whisper Manyoro translated for him: 'There are many men in Masailand. Do you want to know about every single one of them?' the old men asked.

'I don't need to know about your people, the Masai. I want to know only about the strangers, the white men and especially the Bula Matari.' They were the Germans. The name meant 'breakers of rock', for the earliest German settlers had been geologists who chipped away at the surface mineral formations with their hammers. 'I want to know about the movements of the Bula Matari and their *askari* soldiers. I want to know where they build walls or dig ditches in which they place their *bunduki mkuba*, their great guns.'

The discussion went on late into the night with little decided. Finally the self-appointed spokesman of the group, a toothless ancient, closed the council with the fateful words, 'We will think on all these things.' They rose and filed away to their huts.

When they were gone a small voice piped out of the darkness at Leon's back, 'They will talk and then they will talk some more. All you will hear from them is the sound of their voices. It would be better to listen to the wind in the treetops.'

'That is great disrespect to your elders, Loikot,' Manyoro scolded him.

'I am a *morani*, and I choose carefully those to whom I give my respect.'

Leon understood that and laughed. 'Come out of the darkness, my fine warrior friend, and let us see your brave face.' Loikot came into the firelight and took his seat between Leon and Manyoro.

'Loikot, when we travelled together to the railway line you showed me the tracks of a big elephant.'

'I remember,' Loikot answered.

'Have you seen that elephant since then?'

'When the moon was full I saw him as he browsed among the trees close to where I was camped with my brothers.'

'Where was that?'

'We were herding the cattle near the smoking mountain of the gods, three full days' journey from here.'

'It has rained heavily since then,' Manyoro said. 'The tracks will have been washed away. Besides, many days have passed since the moon was full. By now that bull might be as far south as Lake Manyara.'

'Where should we begin the hunt if not at the place where Loikot last saw him?' Leon wondered.

'We should do as Lusima counsels. We should follow the wind,' said Manyoro.

The next morning, as they descended the pathway down the mountain, the breeze came from the west. It blew soft and warm down the Rift Valley wall and across the Masai savannah. High clouds sailed above, like a flotilla of great galleons with sails of shimmering white. When the party reached the valley floor they turned and went with the wind, moving swiftly through the open forest at a steady jog-trot. Manyoro and Loikot were in the van, picking over the myriad game tracks that dotted the earth, pausing to point out to Leon those that warranted special attention, then moving on again. Slowly Ishmael fell back under his enormous burden until he was far behind.

With the wind at their backs their scent was carried ahead and the grazing game herds threw up their heads as they caught the taint of man and stared at them. Then they opened their ranks and let the men pass at a safe distance.

Three times during the morning they cut the spoor of elephant. The wounds the beast had left on the trees where they had torn down large branches were white and weeping sap. Clouds of butterflies hung over massive mounds of fresh dung. The two trackers wasted little time on this sign. 'Two very young bulls,' Manyoro said. 'Of no account.'

They went on until Loikot picked out another sign. 'One very old cow,' he opined. 'So old that the pads of her feet are worn smooth.'

An hour later Manyoro pointed to fresh spoor. 'Here passed five breeding cows. Three have their unweaned calves at heel.'

Just before the sun reached its meridian Loikot, who was in the lead, stopped suddenly and pointed out a mountainous grey shape in a patch of sweet thorn forest far ahead. There was movement and Leon recognized the lazy flap of huge ears. His heartbeat quickened as they turned aside and worked their way out to get below the wind before they moved closer. They could tell by its bulk that it was a very large bull. He was feeding on a low bush and his back was turned to them so that they were unable to see his tusks. The wind held fair, and they came up softly behind him, closing in until Leon could count the wiry hairs in his worn tail and see the colonies of red ticks that hung like bunches of ripe grapes around his puckered anus. Manyoro signalled Leon to be ready. He slipped the big double rifle off his shoulder and held it with his thumb on the safety catch as they waited for the bull to move and allow them a sight of his tusks.

This was the closest Leon had ever been to an elephant, and he was awed by its sheer size. It seemed to blot out half the sky, as though he was standing beneath a cliff of grey rock. Suddenly the bull swung around and flared his ears wide. He stared directly at Leon from a distance of a dozen paces. Dense lashes surrounded small rheumy eyes and tears had left dark runnels down his cheeks. He was so close that Leon could see the light reflected in the irises as though they were two large beads of polished amber. Slowly he lifted the rifle to his shoulder, but Manyoro squeezed his shoulder, urging him to hold his fire.

One of the bull's tusks was broken off at the lip while the other was chipped and worn down to a blunt stump. Leon realized that Percy Phillips would cover him with scorn if he brought them back to Tandala Camp. Yet the bull seemed poised to charge and he might be forced to fire. Night after night over the past weeks, Percy had sat with him in the lamplight and lectured him on the skills required to kill one of these gigantic animals with a single bullet. They had pored together over his autobiography, which he had titled *Monsoon Clouds Over Africa*. He had devoted an entire chapter to shot placement, and illustrated it with his own lifelike sketches of African game animals.

'The elephant is a particularly difficult animal to tackle. Remember that the brain is a tiny target. You have to know exactly where it is from any angle. If he turns or lifts his head your aiming point changes. If he is facing you, broadside or angled away from you, the picture changes again. You must look beyond the grey curtain of his hide and see the vital organs hidden deep inside his massive head and body.'

Now Leon realized, with dismay, that it was not an illustration in a book that confronted him: it was a creature that could squash him to jelly and crush every bone in his body with a single blow of its trunk, and it would take only two long strides to reach him. If the bull came at him he would be forced to try to kill it. Percy's voice echoed in his head: 'If he is head on to you, take the line between his eyes and move down until you pick the top crease in his trunk. If he lifts his head or if he is very close you must go even lower. The mistake that gets the novice killed is that he shoots too high, and his bullet goes over the top of the brain.'

Leon stared hard at the base of the trunk. The lateral creases in the thick grey skin between the amber eyes were deeply etched. But he could not visualize what lay beyond. Was the bull too close? Must he shoot at the second or third crease rather than the first? He was uncertain.

Suddenly the bull shook his head so violently that his ears clapped thunderously against his shoulders, and raised a cloud of dust from the dry mud that coated his body. Leon swung the rifle to his shoulder, but the beast wheeled away and disappeared at a shambling run among the sweet thorn trees.

Leon's legs felt weak and his hands holding the rifle were trembling. Understanding of his own inadequacy had been thrust rudely upon him. He knew now why Percy had sent him out to be blooded. This was not a skill that could be learned from a book or even from hours of instruction. This was trial by the gun and failure was death. Manyoro came back to him and offered him one of the water-bottles. Only then did he realize that his mouth and throat were parched, and his tongue felt swollen with thirst. He had gulped down three mouthfuls before he noticed that the two Masai were studying his face. He lowered the water-bottle and smiled unconvincingly.

'Even the bravest of men is afraid the first time,' Manyoro said. 'But you did not run.'

They halted in the blazing noon and found shade under the spreading branches of a giraffe thorn tree while they waited for Ishmael to catch up and prepare the midday meal. He was still half a mile away across the plain and his form wavered in the heat mirage. Loikot squatted in front of Leon and frowned, which signalled that he had something of importance to impart and that this was a conversation between men.

'M'bogo, this is verily the truth that I will tell you,' he began.

'I am listening to you, Loikot. Speak and I will hear you,' Leon assured him, and assumed an earnest expression to encourage him.

'It is of no value to talk to those old men as you did two nights ago. Their minds are cooked to cassava porridge by the drinking of beer. They have forgotten how to track a beast. They hear nothing but the chatter of their wives. They see nothing beyond the walls of their *manyatta*. They can do nothing but count their cattle and fill their bellies.'

'Such is the way of old men.' Leon was acutely aware that, in Loikot's eyes, he himself was probably on the brink of dotage.

'If you want to know what is happening in all the world you must ask us.'

'Tell me, Loikot, who do you mean by "us"?'

'We are the guardians of the cattle, the *chungaji*. While the old men sit in the sun to drink beer and talk of mighty deeds from long ago, we the *chungaji* move through the land with the cattle. We see everything. We hear everything.'

'But tell me, Loikot, how do you know what the other *chungaji*, who are many days' march distant, see and hear?'

'They are my brothers of the knife. Many of us are of the same circumcision year. We shared the initiation ceremonies.'

'Is it possible that you are able to learn what the *chungaji* with their cattle on the plains beyond Kilimanjaro saw yesterday? They are ten days' march away.'

'It is possible,' Loikot confirmed. 'We speak to each other.'

Leon doubted this.

'At sunset this evening I will speak to my brothers and you will hear it,' Loikot offered, but before Leon could question him further they heard terrified screaming from out on the plain. Leon and Manyoro seized their rifles and jumped up. They stared out at Ishmael's distant figure. He was in full flight towards them, holding his bundle on his head with both hands. Close behind him came a gigantic cock ostrich. With its long pink legs it was gaining on him swiftly. Even from this distance Leon could see that it displayed its full breeding plumage. Its body was the deepest onyx black and the puffs of feathers on its tail and wing-tips were brilliant white. Now every feather was fluffed up in rage. Its legs and beak were flushed scarlet with sexual frenzy. It was determined to kill to protect its breeding territory from the white-robed invader.

Leon led the two Masai to the rescue. They shouted and waved their arms wildly to distract the bird, but it ignored them and bore down remorselessly on Ishmael. When it got within striking distance it stretched out its long neck and pecked the kitchen bundle so viciously that he was knocked off his feet. He went down, sprawling in a cloud of dust. His bundle burst open and his cooking pots and crockery clattered and bounced around him. The ostrich leaped on top of him, kicking and clawing with both feet. It lowered its head to peck his arms and legs, and Ishmael squealed as the blood flowed from the wounds it inflicted.

Nimble as a hare, Loikot outran the two older men,

shouting a challenge at the ostrich as he closed in. The bird jumped off Ishmael's prostrate form and advanced menacingly towards Loikot. Its stubby wings were spread and it began its threat dance, stepping high, lifting and lowering its head menacingly, cawing an angry challenge.

Loikot pulled up and spread the tails of his cloak as though they were wings. Then he began a perfect imitation of the ostrich's dance, using the same high steps and ritual head-bobbing. He was trying to provoke it to attack. Bird and boy circled each other.

The ostrich was being confronted on its own breeding ground and his outrage and affront at last overpowered even its instinct of survival. It rushed to the attack, head thrust out to the full reach of its long neck. It struck at Loikot's face, but Loikot knew exactly how to deal with it, and Leon realized he must have done this many times before. Fearlessly the boy jumped to meet the huge bird and locked both hands around its neck just behind the head. Then he lifted both feet off the ground and swung his full weight on the ostrich's neck, bearing its head down to the ground. The ostrich was pinned helplessly off-balance. It could not lift its head. It flopped around in a circle in an attempt to remain on its feet. Leon ran up and raised his rifle. He circled the mêlée to give himself a clear shot.

'No! Effendi, no! Do not shoot,' screamed Ishmael. 'Leave this son of the great *shaitan* to me.' On his hands and knees he was fumbling through the scattered debris of his kitchen utensils. At last he came to his feet clutching a gleaming carving knife in his right hand and raced to the struggling pair with his weapon held *en garde*.

'Twist its head over!' he shouted at Loikot. Now the bird's throat was exposed and, with the skill of a master butcher, Ishmael drew the edge of the razor-sharp blade across it, slitting it neatly from side to side and cutting down to the ostrich's vertebrae with a single stroke.

'Let him go!' Ishmael ordered, and Loikot released the bird. They jumped well clear of its flailing feet with their sharp talons. The ostrich bounded away but a long plume of blood shot high in the air from the open arteries in its throat. It lost direction and staggered in a circle, its long, scaly pink legs losing their driving force and its neck drooping like the stalk of a fading flower. It collapsed and lay struggling weakly to regain its feet, but regular jets of bright arterial blood continued to spurt on to the sun-baked earth.

'Allah is great!' Ishmael exulted, and pounced upon its still living carcass. 'There is no other God but God!' Neatly he slit open the bird's belly and cut out the liver. 'This creature is slain by my knife and I have sanctified its death in the name of God. I have drawn out its blood. I declare this meat halal.' He held the liver aloft. 'Behold the finest meat in all of creation. The liver of the ostrich taken from the living bird.'

They ate kebabs of ostrich liver and belly fat grilled over the coals of the camel-thorn acacia. Then, bellies filled, they slept for an hour in the shade. When they awoke the breeze, which had died away at noon, rose again and blew steadily across the wide steppe. They shouldered rifles and packs and went with the wind until the sun was no more than a hand's spread above the horizon.

'We must go to that hilltop,' Loikot told Leon, pointing to a pimple of volcanic rock that stood out directly in their path, highlighted in the ruddy glow of the setting sun. The boy scrambled ahead to the summit and stared down the valley. Shaded blue with distance three enormous bastions of rock thrust up towards the southern sky. 'Loolmassin, the mountain of the gods.' Loikot pointed out the most westerly peak as Leon came up beside him. Then he turned to the east and the two larger peaks. 'Meru and Kilimanjaro, the home of the clouds. Those mountains are in the land that the Bula Matari call their own but which has belonged to my people since the beginning time.' The peaks were more than a hundred miles on the far side of the border, deep inside German East Africa.

Awed into silence, Leon watched the sunlight sparkle on the snowfields of Kilimanjaro's rounded summit, then turned back to the long trail of smoke drifting from the volcanic crater of Loolmassin. He wondered if there was a more magnificent spectacle in all the world.

'Now I will speak to my brothers of the *chungaji*. Hear me!' Loikot announced. He filled his lungs, cupped his hands around his mouth and let out a high-pitched sing-song wail, startling Leon. The volume and pitch were so penetrating that, instinctively, he covered his ears. Three times Loikot called, then sat down beside Leon and wrapped his *shuka* around his shoulders. 'There is a *manyatta* beyond the river.' He pointed out the darker line of trees that marked the riverbed.

Leon calculated that it was several miles away. 'Will they hear you at such a distance?'

'You will see,' Loikot told him. 'The wind has dropped and the air is still and cool. When I call with my special voice it will carry that far and even further.' They waited. Below them, a small herd of kudu moved through the thorn scrub. Three graceful grey cows led the bull, with his fringed dewlap and spreading corkscrew horns. Their shapes were ethereal as drifts of smoke as they vanished silently into the scrub.

'Do you still think they heard you?' Leon asked.

The boy did not deign to answer immediately, but chewed for a while on the root of the tinga bush that the Masai used to whiten their teeth. Then he spat out the wad of pith and gave Leon a flash of his sparkling smile. 'They have heard me,' he said, 'but they are climbing to a high place from which to reply.' They lapsed into silence again.

At the foot of the hillock Ishmael had lit a small fire and was brewing tea in a small smoke-blackened kettle. Leon watched him thirstily.

'Listen!' said Loikot, and threw back his cloak as he sprang to his feet.

Leon heard it then, coming from the direction of the river. It sounded like a faint echo of Loikot's original call. Loikot cocked his head to follow it, then cupped his hands and sent his high, sing-song cry ringing back across the plain. He listened again to the reply, and the exchange went on until it was almost dark.

'It is finished. We have spoken,' he declared at last, and led the way down the hill to where Ishmael had set up camp for the night. He handed a large enamel mug of tea to Leon as he settled down beside the fire. While they ate their dinner of ostrich steaks and stiff cakes of yellow maize-meal porridge, Loikot relayed to Leon the gossip he had learned from his long conversation with the *chungaji* beyond the river.

'Two nights ago a lion killed one of their cattle, a fine black bull with good horns. This morning the *morani* followed the lion with their spears and surrounded it. When it charged, it chose Singidi as its victim and went for him. He killed it with a single thrust so has won great honour. Now he can place his spear outside the door of any woman in Masailand.' Loikot thought about this for a moment. 'One day I will do that, and then the girls will no longer laugh at me and call me baby,' he said wistfully.

'Bless your randy little dreams,' Leon said in English, then switched to Maa. 'What else did you hear?' Loikot began a recitation that went on for several minutes, a catalogue of births, marriages, lost cattle and other such matters. 'Did you ask if any white men are travelling at the moment in Masailand? Any Bula Matari soldiers with *askari*?'

'The German commissioner from Arusha is on tour with six *askari*. They are marching down the valley towards Monduli. There are no other soldiers in the valley.'

'Any other white men?'

'Two German hunters with their women and wagons are camped in the Meto Hills. They have killed many buffalo and dried their meat.'

The Meto Hills were at least eighty miles away, and Leon was amazed at how much information the boy had gathered from across such a wide area. He had read the old hunters' accounts of the Masai grapevine, but he had not set much store by them. This network must cover the entire Masai country. He smiled into his mug: Uncle Penrod now had his eyes along the border. 'What about elephant? Did you ask your brethren if they had seen any big bulls in this area?'

'There are many elephant, but mostly cows and calves. At this season the bulls are up in the mountains or over the escarpment in the craters of Ngorongoro and Empakaai. But that is common knowledge.'

'Are there are no bulls at all in the valley?'

'The *chungaji* saw one near Namanga, a very large bull, but that was many days ago and no one has seen him since. They think he might have gone into the Nyiri desert where there is no grazing for the cattle so none of my people are there.'

'We must follow the wind,' said Manyoro.

'Or you must learn to sing sweetly for us,' Leon suggested.

B efore dawn Leon woke and went to be alone behind the bole of a large tree, well away from where the others slept. He dropped his trousers, squatted and broke wind. His was the only wind that was blowing this morning, he thought. The wilderness around him was hushed and still. The leaves in the branches above him hung limp and motionless against the pale promise of dawn. As he returned to the camp he saw that Ishmael already had the kettle on the fire and the two Masai were stirring. He sat close enough to the flames to feel their warmth. There was a chill in the dawn. 'There is no wind,' he told Manyoro.

'Perhaps it will rise with the sun.'

'Should we go on without it?'

'Which way? We do not know,' Manyoro pointed out. 'We have come this far with my mother's wind. We must wait for it to come again to lead us on.'

Leon felt impatient and disgruntled. He had pandered long enough to Lusima's claptrap. He had a dull ache behind his eyes. During the night the cold had kept him awake and when he had slept he had been haunted by nightmares of Hugh

Turvey and his crucified wife. Ishmael handed him a mug of coffee but even that did not have its usual therapeutic effect. In the thicket beyond the campfire a robin began its melodious greeting to the dawn and from afar a lion roared, answered by another even further off. Then silence descended again.

Leon finished a second mug of coffee and at last felt its curative powers take effect. He was about to say something to Manyoro when he was distracted by a loud, rattling call, which sounded like a box of small pebbles being shaken vigorously. They all looked up with interest. Everyone knew which bird had made the sound. A honeyguide was inviting them to follow it to a wild beehive. When the men raided it they would be expected to share the spoils with the bird. They would take the honey, leaving the beeswax and the larvae for the honeyguide. It was a symbiotic arrangement that, down the ages, had been faithfully adhered to by man and bird. It was said that if anybody failed to pay the bird its due, the next time it would lead him to a venomous snake or a man-eating lion. Only a greedy fool would attempt to cheat it.

Leon stood up and the drab brown and yellow bird flashed from the top branches of the tree and began to display. Its wings hummed and resonated as it dived and pulled up, then dived again.

'Honey!' said Manyoro greedily. No African could resist that invitation.

'Honey, sweet honey!' Loikot shouted.

The last vestige of Leon's headache vanished miraculously, and he grabbed his rifle. 'Hurry! Let's go!' The honeyguide saw them following and darted away, whirring and rattling excitedly.

For the next hour Leon trotted steadily after the bird. He had said nothing of it to the others, but he could not shake off the haunting idea that the bird was Lusima Mama's sweet singer. However, his doubts were stronger than his faith and he steeled himself for disappointment. Manyoro was singing encouragement to the bird, and Loikot, skipping along at Leon's side, joined in with the chorus:

'Lead us to the hive of the little stingers,
And we will feast you on golden wax.
Can you not taste the sweet fat grubs?
Fly, little friend! Fly swiftly and we will follow.'

The little bird flitted on through the forest, darting from tree to tree, chirruping and dancing in the top branches until they caught up, then flashing away again. A little before noon they reached a dry riverbed. The forest along either bank was thicker and the trees taller, fed by subterranean waters. Before they reached the actual watercourse the honeyguide flew to the top of one of the tallest trees and waited for them there. As they came up, Manyoro cried out in delight and pointed at the tree-trunk. 'There it is!'

Like swift golden dust motes in the sunlight, Leon saw the flight of the bees homing in on the hive. Three-quarters of the way up, the trunk forked into two heavy branches and the crotch between them was split by a narrow, vertical cleft. A thin trickle of tree sap ran from the opening and congealed in translucent globules of gum on the bark around it. Into this opening the homecoming bees flitted, while those leaving the hive crawled out on to the lips of the opening and buzzed away. The image brought Verity O'Hearne to Leon's mind with sharp, lubricious nostalgia. It was the first time he had thought of her in several days.

The others laid aside their burdens to prepare for the harvest of the hive. Manyoro cut a square of bark from the trunk of another tree in the grove and rolled it into a tube, which he tied into shape with a strip of bark string. Then he fashioned a loop of bark into a handle. Ishmael had started a small fire and was feeding it with dry twigs. Loikot girded the tail of his *shuka* around his waist, leaving his legs and lower body bare, then went to the base of the tree and tested the texture of the bark and the girth of the trunk with his arms while he gazed up at the hive steeling himself mentally for the climb.

Ishmael fed chips of green wood into the fire and blew on

them until they glowed and emitted dense clouds of pungent white smoke. With the wide blade of his *panga*, Manyoro scooped the coals into the bark tube and took it to Loikot, who used the loop handle to sling the tube over his shoulder, then tucked the *panga* into the folds of his *shuka*. He spat on his palms and grinned at Leon. 'Watch me, M'bogo. No other can climb as I can.'

'It doesn't surprise me to learn that you are brother to the baboons,' Leon told him, and Loikot laughed before he sprang at the tree-trunk. Gripping alternately with his palms and the soles of his bare feet he shot up the trunk with amazing agility and reached the tree's high crotch without a pause. He climbed into the fork and stood upright, with a swarm of angry bees buzzing around his head. He took the bark tube from his shoulder and blew into one end, like a trumpeter. A jet of smoke poured from the opposite end. As it enveloped them the bees dispersed.

Loikot paused to pick a few stings from his arms and legs. Then he hefted the *panga* and, balancing easily, ignoring the dizzying drop below him, he stooped and swung the heavy blade at the cleft between his feet. With a dozen ringing blows he made white wood chips fly. Then he peered into the enlarged opening. 'I can smell the sweetness,' he shouted to the upturned faces below. He reached into the hive and brought out a large thick comb. He held it up for them to see. 'Thanks to the skills of Loikot, you will eat your fill today, my friends.' They laughed.

'Well done, little baboon!' Leon shouted.

Loikot brought out five more combs, each hexagonal cell filled to the brim with dark brown honey, and sealed with a lid of wax. He packed them gently into the folds of his *shuka*.

'Do not take it all,' Manyoro cautioned him. 'Leave half for our little winged friends or they will die.' Loikot had been taught that when he was still a child and did not reply. Now he was a *morani*, and wise in the lore of the wild. He dropped the smoke tube and the *panga* to the base of the tree and slithered down the trunk, jumping the last six feet to land lightly on his feet.

They sat in a circle and divided the combs. In the branches above, the honeyguide hopped and chirruped to remind them of his presence and the debt they owed him. Carefully Manyoro broke off the edges of the combs where the cells were filled with white bee larvae and laid the pieces on a large green leaf. He looked up at the hovering bird. 'Come, little brother, you have earned your reward.' He carried the larvae-filled pieces of honeycomb a short distance away, and placed them carefully in an opening in the scrub. As soon as he turned away, the bird flew down boldly to partake of the feast.

Now that custom and tradition had been observed, the men were free to taste the spoils. Sitting around the pile of golden combs they broke off pieces, and stuffed them into their mouths, murmuring with pleasure as they chewed the honey out of the cells, then spat out the wax and licked their sticky fingers.

Leon had never tasted honey like this dark, smoky variety garnered from the nectar of acacia flowers. It coated his tongue and the back of his throat with such intense sweetness that he gasped at the shock, and his eyes swam with tears. He closed them tightly. The rich wild perfume filled his head and almost overpowered him. His tongue tingled. When he breathed he felt the taste drawn down deep into his throat. He swallowed and exhaled as sharply as though he had gulped down a dram of highland whisky.

Half a comb was enough for him. He felt satiated with sweetness. He rocked back on his heels and watched the others for a while. At last he stood up and left them to their gluttony. They took no notice of his departure. He picked up his rifle and sauntered idly into the bush, heading for where he thought the riverbed might be. The vegetation became thicker as he went deeper into it until he pushed his way through the last screen of branches and found himself on the bank. It had been cut back by flood water into a sheer wall that dropped six feet to a bed of fine white sand a hundred paces wide, trampled by the paws and hoofs of the animals that had used it as a highway.

On the far bank a massive wild fig tree's roots had been exposed by the cutback. They twisted and writhed like mating serpents, and the branches that stretched out over the riverbed were laden with bunches of the small yellow figs. A flock of green pigeons had been gorging on the fruit and was startled into flight by Leon's sudden appearance. Their wingbeats clattered in the silence as they arrowed away along the watercourse.

Beneath the spreading wild fig branches the white sand had been heaped into large mounds. Scattered around them were several pyramids of elephant dung, which commanded Leon's attention. He held the rifle at arm's length in front of him and jumped from the top of the bank. The soft sand broke his landing and he sank into it to his ankles, but soon recovered his balance and set off across the riverbed. When he reached the mounds he realized that the elephant had been digging for water. With their forefeet they had kicked away the dry sand until they had reached a firmer damp layer. Then they had used their trunks to burrow until they had come to the subterranean water table. The prints of their pads where they had stood over the seep holes were clearly visible. They had sucked up the water with their trunks into spongy cavities in their massive skulls, and when these were full, they had lifted their heads, thrust their trunk tips into the back of their throats and squirted the water into their bellies.

There were eight open seep holes. He went to each in turn to examine the tracks left by thirsty animals. Having been instructed by three grand-masters of the trade – Percy Phillips, Manyoro and Loikot – he had learned enough bushcraft to read them accurately. The shape and size of the footprints that the elephant had left around the first four seeps proved them to have been cows.

When he came to the fifth there was only one set of tracks. They were so large that his first glimpse of them made him pause in mid-stride. He drew a quick breath, sharp with excitement, then hurried forward and dropped to his knees beside the prints of the front feet, which were deeply embedded on the lip of the hole where the beast must have stood for hours to suck up water.

Leon stared at them in disbelief. They were enormous. The animal that had made them must have been a massive old bull: the soles of his feet had worn smooth with age. One side of the print he was studying slipped away in a trickle of soft sand – which meant that the bull had left the riverbed only recently: the disturbed earth had not had time to settle. Perhaps the animal had been frightened off by the sound of Loikot chopping open the entrance to the beehive.

Leon laid the twin barrels of his rifle across the pad print to gauge its size, and whistled softly. His barrels were two feet long, and the diameter of the footprint was only two inches less. Applying the formula that Percy Phillips had propounded to him, he calculated that this bull must stand more than twelve feet high at the shoulder, a giant among a race of giants.

Leon jumped up and ran back across the riverbed. He scrambled up the bank and pushed his way through the undergrowth to where his three companions were huddled over the last scraps of honeycomb. 'Lusima Mama and her sweet singer have shown us the way,' he told them. 'I have found the spoor of a great bull elephant in the riverbed.' The trackers snatched up their kit and ran after him, but Ishmael scooped the remains of the honeycomb into one of his pots before he hoisted his bundle on to his head and followed.

'M'bogo, this is veritably the bull that I showed you the first time we travelled together,' Loikot exclaimed, as soon as he saw the spoor, and danced with excitement. 'I recognize him. This is a paramount chief of all the elephants.'

Manyoro shook his head. 'He is so old he must be ready to die. Surely his ivory is broken and worn away.'

'No! No!' Loikot denied it vehemently. 'With my own eyes I have seen his tusks. They are as long as you are, Manyoro, and thicker even than your head!' He made a circle with his arms.

Manyoro laughed. 'My poor little Loikot, you have been bitten by blow-flies, and they have filled your head with maggots. I will ask my mother to prepare for you a draught to loosen your bowels and clear these dreams from your eyes.'

Loikot bridled and glared at him. 'And perhaps it is not the elephant but you who has become old and senile. We should have left you on Lonsonyo Mountain, drinking beer with your decrepit cronies.'

'While you two exchange compliments the bull is walking away from us,' Leon intervened. 'Take the spoor, and let us settle this debate by looking upon his tusks and not merely upon the marks of his feet.'

As soon as they had followed the spoor out of the riverbed and into the open savannah it became obvious that the bull elephant had been thoroughly alarmed by the sound of axe blows and their voices as they had raided the beehive.

'He is in full flight.' Manyoro pointed out the length of the bull's strides. He had settled into the long swinging gait that covers the ground as fast as a man can run. They all knew that he could keep up that pace from dawn to dusk without pausing to rest.

'He is going east. It seems to me that he is heading for the Nyiri desert, that dry land where there are no men and only he knows where to dig for water,' Manyoro remarked after the first hour. 'If he keeps up this pace, by sunrise tomorrow he will be over the top of the escarpment and deep into the desert.'

'Do not listen to him, M'bogo,' Loikot advised. 'It is the habit of old men to be gloomy. They can smell shit in the perfume of the kigelia flower.'

After another hour they stopped for a swig from the water-bottles.

'The bull has not turned aside from his chosen path,' Manyoro observed. 'Not once has he paused to feed or even slowed his pace. Already he is many hours ahead of us.'

'Not only can this old man smell dung in the kigelia bloom, but he can smell it even in the flower between the thighs of the sweetest young virgin.' Loikot grinned cheekily at Leon. 'Pay him no heed, M'bogo. Follow me, and before sunset I will show you such tusks as will amaze your eyes and fill your heart with joy.'

But the spoor ran on straight and unwavering. Another hour, and even Loikot was beginning to wilt. When they stopped for a few minutes to drink and stretch out in the shade they were all quiet and subdued. Even though they had driven themselves hard since leaving the dry riverbed, they knew how far they had dropped behind the bull elephant. Leon screwed the stopper back on the water-bottle and stood up. Without a word the others came to their feet. They went on.

In the middle of the afternoon they stopped to rest again. 'If my mother was with us she would work such a spell as would turn the bull aside and make him start feeding,' said Manyoro, 'but, alas, she is not with us.'

'Perhaps she is watching over us, for she is a great magician,' said Loikot brightly. 'Perhaps she can hear me if I call to her.' He jumped to his feet and broke into a leaping praise dance, hopping high in the air on his long skinny legs. 'Hear me, Great Black Cow, hear me call to you.' Leon laughed and even Manyoro grinned and began to clap in time to the dance.

'Hear him, Mama! Hear our little baboon!'

'Hear me, Mother of the Tribe! You have shown us the marks of his feet, now do not let him walk away from us. Slow his great feet. Fill his belly with hunger. Make him stop to feed.'

'That's enough magic for one day. Surely the bull cannot

escape us now,' Leon intervened. 'On your feet, Manyoro. Let us go on.'

The spoor ran on. The bull was moving so fast that when it crossed areas of loose earth it kicked spurts of dust forward with each long stride. When Leon looked up at the sun his heart sank. There was no more than an hour of daylight left, no possibility of coming up with the elephant before darkness cloaked the spoor, forcing them to break off the pursuit until dawn on the morrow. By then he would be fifty miles ahead of them.

He was still gazing up at the sky so he bumped into Manyoro, who had stopped abruptly in his path. Both Masai were poring over the earth. They looked up at Leon and, with hand signals, urged him to remain silent. They were both grinning and their eyes shone. They had been revitalized and no longer showed any trace of fatigue. Manyoro indicated the altered spoor with an eloquent, graceful gesture.

Leon grasped that a little miracle had taken place. The bull had slowed, his pace had shortened, and he had turned aside from his determined flight towards the eastern escarpment of the valley. Manyoro pointed to a grove of *ngong* nut trees a quarter of a mile to their right. The tops of the trees were round in shape, taller and greener than the lesser trees surrounding them. He leaned over to Leon and placed his lips close to his ear. 'At this season the trees are in bearing. He has smelled the ripe nuts and cannot resist them. We will find him in the grove.' He took up a handful of earth and let it sift through his fingers. 'There is still no wind. We can move straight in towards him.' He looked back at Ishmael and signalled to him to stay where he was. Ishmael laid his bundle at his feet and lowered himself thankfully to the ground beside it.

With the two Masai still leading, they crept forward, moving from one patch of cover to the next, pausing to scan the forest ahead before going forward again. They reached the nearest *ngong* tree. The ground beneath it was littered with fallen nuts but the branches above were still thick with

115

bunches of half-ripe ones. The bull had stood under this tree for a long time, picking up the hard nuts with the fingers at the tip of his trunk and stuffing them into his mouth. Then he had moved on. They followed his huge pad marks to the next tree, where he had fed again, then moved on once more. This time he had headed towards a shallow depression, above which only the tops of the nut trees showed. They crept forward until they could look down into it.

At the same instant all three saw the enormous black mass of the bull elephant. He was three hundred paces away, standing in the shade of one of the largest nut trees, angled half away from them. He rocked gently from one forefoot to the other, ears fanning lazily, trunk draped nonchalantly over the curve of the only visible tusk. The other was hidden from view by his massive bulk, but Leon stared at the one he could see, hardly able to believe its length and girth. To him, it seemed the size of a marble column from a Greek temple.

'The wind?' he breathed to Manyoro. 'How is the wind?' Manyoro scooped up another handful of earth and dribbled it through his fingers. Then he dusted his hand on his leg and made a sign that was as clear as any words. 'No wind. Nothing.'

Leon broke open the barrels of his rifle and removed the fat brass cartridges from the breeches one at a time. He examined them for blemishes and polished them on his shirt before he slipped them back into place. He snapped the barrels shut and tucked the butt of the loaded rifle under his right armpit. Then he nodded to Manyoro, and as they moved forward, Leon took the lead. He angled towards the bull until the tree-trunk covered his approach, then turned straight towards it.

The tree blocked out the bull's head but his body protruded on one side of it, while the curve of the nearest tusk stuck out beyond the other. A shaft of sunlight pierced the canopy of leaves above his head and struck the ivory like the beam of a limelight. Closer still, and Leon heard the animal's belly rumble like distant thunder. He moved in steadily upon him, setting down each footstep with exaggerated care. Now he held the heavy rifle at the ready position across his chest.

The Holland was essentially a short-range weapon. He had fired several shots at a target before he had set out from Tandala Camp, and had discovered that the twin barrels were regulated to shoot to the same point of aim at precisely thirty yards. At any greater distance, the bullets would spread out unpredictably. He knew that to be completely certain of his shot he had to get closer than that. He wanted to reach the trunk of the nut tree and fire from behind its cover. Now he was so close that he could see the oxpeckers scrambling around on the elephant's wrinkled grey skin. There were five or six of the slender little yellow birds, balancing themselves with their tails as they foraged with their sharp red beaks in the creases of the skin for ticks, blind flies and other blood-sucking insects. One crept into the ear and the bull flapped loudly to warn it away from the sensitive parts deep inside. Other birds hung upside-down under his belly or in his crotch, pecking busily at the sagging folds of grey skin. Then, suddenly, they became aware of Leon's approach and ran up the bull's flanks to stand in a line along his spine, staring with glittering eyes at the intruder.

Manyoro tried to warn Leon of what was about to happen but he dared not speak, and Leon was so intent on his stalk that he did not see the desperate hand signals behind him. He was still a dozen paces from the bole of the ngong tree when the row of oxpeckers on the bull's back exploded into flight, uttered their frenzied twittering alarm call. It was a warning that the beast understood well, for the birds were not only his grooms but also his sentinels.

From comfortable somnolence he plunged forward, reaching his top speed in half a dozen strides. He had no idea where the danger lay, but he trusted the birds and simply ran in the direction he was facing. He was heading at a thirty-degree angle away from Leon. For a second Leon was stunned by the speed and agility of the massive creature. Then he raced forward in pursuit, aiming to get ahead of the bull before he could get clear away. For a short distance he gained ground, closing to just under the critical thirty-yard range. He fastened his eyes on the bull's head. The wide sails of the ears were cocked back so Leon could see the long, vertical slit of the earhole. But the head nodded violently and rolled from side to side with each stride. The oxpeckers were shrilling, and behind Leon, the two Masai shouted unintelligibly. All around there was movement and wild confusion and the bull pulled rapidly away. Within a few more strides he would be out of range.

Leon slammed to a halt. All his vision and attention were concentrated on the long slit of the earhole in the centre of the swinging and swaying head. The rifle came up to his shoulder and he looked over the barrels, hardly seeing them, so intense was his concentration. Time and movement seemed to slow into a dreamlike unreality. His vision was as sharp as a diamond drill. He saw beyond the moving wall of grey skin and the spreading ears. He saw the brain. It was an extraordinary sensation – Percy Phillips had called it the hunter's eye. With the hunter's eye he could see through skin and bone, and descry the exact position of the brain. It was the size of a football, set low behind the line of the earhole.

The rifle crashed, and even in the sunlight he saw the flame spurt from the muzzle. He was startled. He had not been aware of touching the trigger. He hardly felt the recoil of five thousand foot-pounds of energy kicking back into his shoulder. His vision was not deflected by it: he saw the bullet strike two inches behind the earhole, precisely where he knew it should go. He saw the bull's nearest eye blink shut, heard the heavy bullet strike bone with a sound like a woodman's axe swung against a hardwood tree. With his new gift of the hunter's eye he could imagine the bullet ploughing through bone and tissue, tearing into the brain.

The bull threw back his head, long tusks pointing for an instant at the sky. Then his front legs folded under him and he collapsed heavily into a kneeling position. The force of the impact sent up a cloud of dust and made the ground tremble beneath Leon's feet. The elephant lay on his folded front legs as though waiting to be mounted by a mahout, head supported by the curves of the tusks, sightless eyes wide open. The tail flicked once, then all was still. The echoes of gunfire rang in Leon's head, but all around was a deep hush.

'It's the dead elephant that kills you.' He heard Percy's warning in his memory. 'Always put in the *coup de grâce*.' Leon raised the rifle again and aimed for the crease in the bull's armpit. Again the rifle boomed. The beast never so much as twitched as the second bullet drove through its heart.

Leon walked forward slowly and reached out to touch the staring amber eye with a fingertip. It did not blink. His legs felt as soft and limp as boiled spaghetti. He sank down, leaned his back against the elephant's shoulder and closed his eyes. He felt nothing. He was empty inside. He felt no sense of triumph or elation, no remorse or sorrow for the death of such a magnificent creature. All that would come later. Now there was only the aching emptiness, as though he had just made love to a beautiful woman.

Leon sent Manyoro and Loikot off to some distant villages outside the boundaries of Masailand. Their task was to recruit porters to carry the ivory to the railway. They had to be from some tribe other than Masai, for the *morani* would not stoop to such menial employment. Leon and Ishmael camped for the following five days at a discreet distance upwind from the putrefying carcass, its belly swelling with gas. They guarded the tusks while they waited for them to loosen with rot in their bone canals.

The nights were raucous as the scavengers gathered. Jackals yipped and packs of hyena giggled, shrieked and squabbled among themselves. On the third night the lions arrived and added their imperial roaring to the general cacophony. Ishmael spent the hours of darkness perched in the top branches of one of the *ngong* trees, reciting verses from the Koran in

Kiswahili and calling on Allah for protection from these demons.

On the sixth day Manyoro and Loikot returned, followed by a gang of stalwart Luo porters whom Manyoro had hired for ten shillings.

'Ten shillings a day each?' Leon was aghast at such profligacy. Ten shillings was almost the sum of his worldly wealth.

'Nay, Bwana, for all of them.'

'Ten shillings a day for all six?' Leon was only slightly mollified.

'Nay, Bwana. It is for all six to carry the tusks to the railway, no matter how many days it takes.'

'Manyoro, your mother should be proud of you,' Leon told him with relief. 'I certainly am.' He led the porters to where the remains of the carcass lay. Only the great bones and the hide had not been dragged away and devoured by the scavengers. The head was still propped upright by the two curves of ivory. Leon looped a length of bark rope around one of the tusks and the Luo porters sang a work chant as they heaved on the line. The butt end of the tusk, which had been buried in the skull, slid out of its canal with little resistance. Until then almost half its length had been hidden and now the true dimensions were revealed for the first time. When they laid the two tusks side by side on a bed of fresh green leaves Leon was amazed by their length and lovely symmetry. Once again he used the barrels of his rifle as a gauge to measure them. The longer of the two was a hand's breadth over eleven feet and the lesser was almost exactly eleven feet.

Under Manyoro's direction the Luo cut two long poles of acacia wood and strapped each tusk to one. With a porter at each end they lifted the poles and started towards the railway, the remainder of the team trotting behind them, ready to spell them as they tired.

Leon was no longer entitled to a military travel pass, so on the steepest stretch of the railway, where it climbed up the escarpment from the floor of the Rift Valley, they waited for the night train from Lake Victoria. Here, even the double team of locomotives was reduced to walking speed. Under cover of darkness they ran alongside one of the goods trucks until they could catch hold of the steel ladder and clamber onto the roof. The Luo porters passed the tusks and Ishmael's bundle up to them. Leon tossed a canvas purse of shillings down to the headman and the porters shouted thanks and farewells until they were left in the darkness behind the guard's van. The locomotives puffed gamely to the top of the escarpment. The truck on which they were perched was filled with baskets of dried fish from the lake, but as the train picked up speed the stink was wafted away.

It was still dark when they dropped the tusks and their baggage over the side of the truck and jumped from the rolling train as it slowed before steaming into Nairobi station.

Percy Phillips was eating his breakfast in the mess tent when they staggered into Tandala Camp, bowed under the weight of the tusks.

'Upon my soul!' he spluttered into his coffee, and knocked over his chair as he sprang to his feet. 'Those aren't yours, are they?'

'One is.' Leon kept a straight face. 'Unfortunately, sir, the other is yours.'

'Take them to the beam scale. Let's see what we have here,' Percy ordered.

The entire staff of the camp trooped after them to the skinning shed and gathered around the scale as Leon lifted the smaller tusk into the sling.

'One hundred and twenty-eight pounds,' said Percy, non-committally. 'Now let's try the other.'

Leon hoisted the second into the sling and Percy blinked. 'One hundred and thirty-eight.' His voice cracked just a little. It was the largest tusk that had ever been brought into Tandala Camp. However, he could think of no good reason why the youngster should be told so. Don't want him to get too big for his boots, he thought, as he scratched his beard. Then he said to Manyoro, 'Put both tusks into the truck.' At last he looked at Leon and his eyes twinkled. 'All right, young fella, you can drive me in to the club. I'm about to buy you a drink.'

As the vehicle bounced and rattled over the track, Percy had to raise his voice to be heard above the racket of the engine. 'Righty-ho! Tell me all about it. Start at the beginning. Don't leave anything out. How many shots did it take you to put him down?'

'That isn't the beginning, sir,' Leon reminded him.

'It will do as a starting point. You can work backwards from there. How many shots?'

'One brain shot. And then I remembered your advice and put in a finisher when he was down.'

Percy nodded his approval. 'Now tell me the rest.' As he listened, Percy was impressed with Leon's account of the hunt. He made it sound fascinating, even to Percy who had lived it all a hundred times. One of the most important duties of a white hunter was to entertain his clients. They wanted more than simply to mow down a few animals: they were paying a fortune to take part in an unforgettable adventure and wanted to be taken out of their cosseted urban existence and led back to their primeval beginnings by someone they could trust and admire. Percy knew a number of fine men who were skilled in bushcraft and the lore of the wild but lacked charm and empathy. They were dour and taciturn. They understood the enchanted wilderness intimately but could not explain it to others. They never had a return client. Their names were not bandied around in the palaces of Europe or the exclusive clubs of London, New York and Berlin. No one clamoured for their services.

This lad did not fall into that category. He was willing and eager. He was modest, charming and tactful. He was articulate. He had a quirky, dry sense of humour. He was personable. People liked him. Percy smiled inwardly. Hell, even I like him.

When they reached the club Percy made him park directly in front of the main doors. He led Leon into the long bar where a dozen regulars, most of them living on remittances sent from their families in England, had already taken their seats. 'Gentlemen,' Percy addressed the congregation, 'I want you to meet my new apprentice, and then I'm going to take you outside and show you a pair of tusks. And I do mean a pair of tusks!'

When they trooped out to the front of the building they found that the news had already flashed through the town, and a small crowd was gathered around the truck. Percy invited them all into the bar.

By the time Hugh Delamere limped into the bar on the leg that had been chewed years ago by a lion, the proceedings were noisy. This was a state of affairs much to his lordship's liking. As was the case with so many English public-school boys, Delamere enjoyed boisterous games that resulted in broken furniture and other peripheral damage. This evening he was accompanied by Colonel Penrod Ballantyne. They congratulated Leon on his prowess as a hunter, and Delamere poured him a large Talisker whisky from his private stock, which he kept under the bar. Then he challenged uncle and nephew to a game of High Cockalorum, which involved a race around the large room without touching the floor. At one stage the shelves behind the bar were unable to bear his lordship's weight and collapsed in a crash of breaking bottles. Just before midnight one of the club residents came into the bar to complain of the noise. His lordship locked him into the wine cellar for the rest of the night.

A few hours later Percy was carried feet first into the billiard room and laid on the green baize of the table. Leon reached the front seat of the truck, where he passed what remained of the night.

He woke with an abominable headache.

'Good morning, Effendi.' Ishmael was standing beside the truck with a steaming mug of black coffee in his hand. 'I wish you a day perfumed with jasmine.' The coffee revived him sufficiently to call for Manyoro. Between them they were able to start the Vauxhall and drive down the main street to the headquarters of the Greater Lake Victoria Trading Company. Below the name on the board, some other script had recently been painted out by direct order of his excellency the governor. However, the writing was still legible under the single coat of paint intended to obliterate it: '*By appointment to His Majesty the King of England purveyor of fine, rare and precious items*'. The uncensored text read: '*Dealer in gold, diamonds, ivory carvings and curios, and all manner of natural produce. Sundry goods of every description for sale. Prop. Mr Goolam Vilabjhi Esq.*'

The proprietor hurried to meet Leon as he entered through the front door, carrying the lesser tusk. Mr Goolam Vilabjhi was a well-nourished little man with a beaming smile. 'By golly, Lieutenant Courtney, for me and my humble establishment this is a jolly great honour.'

'Good morning, Mr Vilabjhi, but I am no longer a lieutenant,' Leon told him, as he laid the tusk on the counter.

'But you are still the greatest polo player in Africa, and I have heard that you have become a mighty *shikari*. What is more, I see you bring proof of that.' He shouted to Mrs Vilabjhi in the back of the store, asking her to bring coffee and sweetmeats, then ushered Leon between rows of heavily laden shelves into his tiny cubby-hole office. A bookcase that occupied one entire wall was filled with all twenty-two volumes of the *Complete Oxford English Dictionary*, a full set of the *Encyclopaedia Britannica*, *Burke's Peerage and Gentry* and several dozen histories of the English kings, their people and language. Mr Vilabjhi was an ardent anglophile, royalist and proponent of the English language.

'Please be seated, kindest sir.' Mrs Vilabjhi bustled in with the coffee tray. She was even plumper than her husband and just as affable. When she had filled the glasses with the thick, sticky black liquid her husband shooed her away and turned back to Leon. 'Now, tell me, Sahib, what is your pleasure?'

'I want to sell you that tusk.'

Mr Vilabjhi thought about that for so long that Leon was

becoming restless. Eventually he said, 'Alack and alas, revered Sahib, I will not purchase that ivory from you.'

Leon was startled. 'Why the hell not?' he demanded. 'You're an ivory dealer, are you not?'

'Did I ever tell you, Sahib, that I was once a horse groom or, as we say in India, a syce, in the stables of the maharaja of Cooch Behar? I am the utmost admirer and connoisseur of the royal game of polo and the men who play it.'

'Is that why you won't buy my tusk?' Leon asked.

Mr Vilabjhi laughed. 'That is a fine jest, Sahib. No! The reason is that if I buy that tusk I will send it to England to be made into the keys of a piano or carved into pretty coloured billiard balls. Then you will hate me. One day when you are an old man you will think back on what I did with your trophy and you will say to yourself, "Ten thousand curses on the head of that infamous villain and flagitious scoundrel, Mr Goolam Vilabjhi Esquire!"'

'On the other hand, if you do not buy it I will call down a hundred thousand curses on your head right now,' Leon warned him. 'Mr Vilabjhi, I need the money and I need it badly.'

'Ah! Money, she is like the tide of the ocean. She comes in and she goes out. But a tusk like that you will never see again in all your existence.'

'At this moment my tide is so far out that it's over the horizon.'

'Then, Sahib, we have to find some ruse or, as we were wont to say in Cooch Behar, some stratagem to accommodate our diverse wishes.' He posed a moment longer in an attitude of deep thought, then raised one finger and touched his temple. 'Eureka! I have it. You will leave the tusk with me as security, and I will loan you the money you require. You will pay me interest at twenty per cent per annum. Then one day, when you are the most famous and renowned *shikari* in Africa you will come back to me and tell me, "My dear and trusted friend, Mr Goolam Vilabjhi Esquire, I have come to repay the debt I owe you." Then I will return your fine and magnificent tusk to you, and we will be lifelong friends until the day we die!'

'My dear and trusted friend, Mr Goolam Vilabjhi Esquire, I call down ten thousand blessings on your head.' Leon laughed. 'How much can you let me have?'

'I have heard tell that the weight of that tusk is one hundred and twenty-eight pounds avoirdupois.'

'My God! How did you know that?'

'Every living human creature in Nairobi knows it already.' Mr Vilabjhi cocked his head to one side. 'At fifteen shillings a pound I find that I am able to advance you the grand sum of ninety-six pounds sterling in gold sovereigns.' Leon blinked. That was the most money he had ever held in his hand at one time.

Before he left Mr Vilabjhi's shop he made his first purchase. On one of the shelves behind the counter he had noticed a small pile of red and yellow cardboard packets displaying the distinctive lion's head trademark of Kynoch, the pre-eminent manufacturer of cartridges in Britain. When he examined the boxes closely he was delighted to discover that they were marked 'H&H .470 Royal Nitro Express. 500 Grain. Solid'. Of the ten cartridges that Verity O'Hearne had left him as part of her gift, only three remained. He had fired five shots to check the sights on the rifle and two more to despatch the great bull.

'How much are those bullets, Mr Vilabjhi?' he enquired, with trepidation, and gulped at the reply.

'For you, Sahib, and for you only, I will make my very best and extra special price.' He gazed up at the ceiling as though seeking inspiration from Kali, Ganesh and all the other Hindu gods. Then he said, 'For you, Sahib, the price is five shillings for each bullet.'

There were ten packets, each containing five rounds. Leon did a quick mental calculation, and the result appalled him. Twelve pounds ten shillings! He touched the heavy bulge in his hip pocket. I can't afford it! he told himself. On the other hand, he answered, what kind of professional hunter goes out into the blue with only three cartridges in his belt? Reluctantly he reached into his pocket and brought out the canvas bank bag he had so recently deposited there.

The tide of his fortune had come in, all right, but just as rapidly it had started to ebb, as Mr Vilabjhi had warned him it would.

Manyoro and Ishmael were still waiting outside the front of the store. Leon paid them the wages he owed them. 'What are you going to do with all that money?' he asked Manyoro.

'I shall buy three cows. What else, Bwana?' Manyoro shook his head at such a foolish question. To a Masai, cattle were the only real wealth.

'What about you, Ishmael?'

'I am going to send it to my wives in Mombasa, Effendi.' Ishmael had six, the maximum that the Prophet allowed, and they were as voracious as a swarm of locusts.

Leon drove to the KAR barracks, with Ishmael and Manyoro. He found Bobby Sampson moping over a tankard of beer in the officers' mess. His friend brightened when he saw him and cheered up so much when Leon paid him the fifteen guineas he owed him for the Vauxhall that he bought him a beer.

From the barracks Leon drove out to the stock yards on the outskirts of the town. 'Manyoro, I wish to send a cow to Lusima Mama to thank her for her help in the matter of the elephant.'

'Such a gift is customary, Bwana,' Manyoro agreed.

'Nobody is a finer judge of cattle than you, Manyoro.'

'That is true, Bwana.'

'When you have chosen your own beasts, pick one out for Lusima Mama and strike a price with the seller.' That cost Leon another fifteen pounds, for Manyoro selected the best animal in the yard.

Before Manyoro set off to return to Lonsonyo Mountain, Leon gave him a canvas bag of silver shillings. 'This is for Loikot. If he keeps talking to his friends and brings the news to us there will be many more bags of shillings. Tell him to save all his money and soon he will have enough to buy himself a fine cow. Now go, Manyoro, and return swiftly. Bwana Samawati has much work for us to do.'

Driving the cows ahead of him, Manyoro took the rutted track that led down into the Rift Valley. When he reached the first bend he turned and shouted back to Leon, 'Wait for me, my brother, for I shall return in ten days' time.'

Leon drove back to the club to pick up Percy Phillips. He found him slumped in one of the armchairs on the wide stoep overlooking the sun-parched lawns. He was in a foul mood. His eyes were bloodshot, his beard was in disarray and his face as wrinkled as the khaki bush jacket in which he had passed the night. 'Where the hell have you been?' he growled at Leon and, without waiting for an answer, stumped down the steps to where the truck was rumbling and coughing blue exhaust smoke. His expression lightened a little when he saw the tusk on which Ishmael was sitting. 'Well, thank the Lord you've still got that. What happened to the other?'

'We sold it to the infidel Vilabjhi, Effendi.' Ishmael had got into the habit of referring to his master in the royal plural.

'That rogue! I bet he diddled you,' Percy said, and climbed into the front seat. He did not speak again until they were bumping down the final and worst section of the track into Tandala Camp.

'I managed to have a few words with your uncle Penrod last evening. He had received a cable from the American State Department. The former President of the United States of America and his entire entourage will be arriving in Mombasa in two months' time aboard the luxury German steamship Admiral to begin the grand safari. We must be ready for them.'

When they parked in front of the mess tent Percy shouted for tea to be brought. Two mugs of the brew restored his sense of well-being and good humour. 'Get out your pencil and notebook,' he ordered Leon.

'I don't possess either.'

'In future they will be your most essential items of equipment. Even more so than your rifle and quinine bottle. I have spares in my library. You can replace them when you next go into town.' He sent one of the servants to fetch them and soon Leon's pencil was poised over the first page.

'Now, here is a broad picture of what this safari will involve. Apart from the President there will be his son, a lad of about the same age as you, and his guests, Sir Alfred Pease, Lord Cranworth and Frederick Selous.'

'Selous!' Leon exclaimed. 'He's an African legend. I was weaned on his books. But he must be ancient.'

'Not at all,' Percy snapped. 'I doubt he's even sixty-five yet.'

Leon was about to point out that sixty-five was older than ancient when he saw Percy's forbidding gaze. He understood that, with Percy Phillips, age was a sensitive subject and retreated from the minefield into which he had been about to blunder. 'Oh, then he is still quite young,' he said hastily.

Percy nodded and went on: 'The President has taken on five white hunters other than myself. The ones I know well are Judd, Cunninghame and Tarlton, all fine fellows. I suppose they will have their apprentices with them. I understand from Penrod that there will be more than twenty naturalists and taxidermists from the Smithsonian Institute, the museum that is partially sponsoring the safari. I asked Penrod about journalists and other members of the press, but he tells me that the President has forbidden their presence. After two full terms in office, he has come to value his privacy.'

'So there will be no journalists?' Leon looked up from the notebook.

'Don't worry about that. No one of any note can ever get away from those cockroaches. American Associated Press is sending out a plague of them, but they will be in a separate safari that will shadow ours closely all the way, sending back copy to New York at every opportunity. A pox on all their houses.'

'That means our safari will be a party of more than thirty

people. There will be a small mountain of baggage, equipment and supplies to deal with.'

'Indeed,' Percy agreed sarcastically. 'The initial estimate from New York is that they will be shipping out about ninety-six tons. The rest will be purchased locally. That will include five tons of salt to preserve the specimens and trophies, and fodder for the horses. The shipment from America will be sent ahead of the main party, which will give us time to bring it up from the coast and have it broken down into sixty-pound packs for the porters.'

'How many mounts will they need?' Leon asked, with interest.

'They intend to do much of the hunting on horseback. The President wants a string of at least thirty,' Percy answered. 'That is one of your fields of expertise, so among your other duties I am putting you in charge of the horse lines. You will have to recruit a team of reliable syces to take care of them.' He paused. 'And, of course, the two trucks will also be your responsibility. I want to use them for resupply of small items to where the President is camped at any time.'

'Two motors? You have only one.'

'I am commandeering the other vehicle from you for the duration of the safari. You had better make sure that both are in good running order.' Percy made no mention of remuneration for the use of Leon's truck, or for the cost of repairs to get it back on four wheels and induce them to turn.

'Lord Delamere is lending us his chef from the Norfolk Hotel. There will be four or five sous-chefs. I will sign on your man Ishmael to work in the camp kitchens. Oh, by the way, Cunninghame will be recruiting around a thousand native porters to carry the baggage and provisions for the safari. I told him last night that you were fluent in Kiswahili and that you would be happy to help him with the job.'

'Did you mention that I would also be pleased to help him with the actual hunting?' Leon asked innocently.

Percy raised one beetling grey eyebrow. 'Would you now? Given your vast experience, I am sure the President would be honoured to have you as a guide. However, you will have many more important duties to keep you entertained, young fella.' That particular form of address was beginning to irritate Leon, but he had decided that that was why Percy employed it so frequently.

'You are absolutely right, sir. I hadn't thought of that.' And he gave Percy his most winning smile.

Percy had difficulty preventing himself smiling back. He liked it more and more that the lad could take what he handed out without whining. He relented. 'There will be well over a thousand mouths to feed. Under the game laws of the colony, buffalo are classed as vermin. There is no limit on the numbers that can be shot. One of your jobs will be to keep the safari in meat. You will have all the hunting your heart could desire. That I promise.'

Two months and six days later the German passenger liner SS *Admiral* steamed into Kilindini lagoon, the deep-water harbour that served as a port for the coastal town of Mombasa. The ship's rigging was blazing with coloured bunting. At her mainmast head she flew Old Glory and at her foremast the black eagles of the Kaiser's Germany. On the foredeck the band blared out 'The Star Spangled Banner' and 'God Save the King'. The beach was crowded with spectators and government dignitaries, headed by the governor of the territory and the commander of His Britannic Majesty's forces in British East Africa, all in full dress uniform, complete with feathers in their cocked hats and swords on their hips.

Lying out in the deep water, a flotilla of barges and surfboats waited to ferry the passengers to the beach. Former President Colonel Teddy Roosevelt and his son were first to climb down into one of the waiting boats. As the distinguished visitors took their seats on the thwarts and the oarsmen pulled in towards the beach, the dark rainclouds lowering over the lagoon opened their bellies and, with a barrage of thunder and fork lightning, loosed a torrential downpour on the scene. Roosevelt arrived on the beach, having been carried through the shallows on the back of a muscular half-naked porter. His bush jacket was soaked and he was roaring with laughter. It was just the type of adventure he relished.

The governor hurried forward to meet him, clutching with one hand the plume of white ostrich feathers on his cocked hat, and with the other, trying to disentangle his sword from between his legs. He had placed his private train at the disposal of the President and his entourage. As soon as they were all safely aboard, the clouds rolled aside and brilliant sunshine sparkled on the choppy waters of the lagoon. The large crowd burst into a chorus of 'For He's A Jolly Good Fellow'. Teddy Roosevelt stood plump and beaming on the balcony of the leading carriage and acknowledged the cheers as the driver blew his whistle and the train pulled away at the start of the journey up-country to Nairobi.

One hundred miles inland the train halted at Voi siding, the southernmost extent of the vast plains that lay between the Tsavo and Athi rivers. A wooden bench had been built as a viewing platform over the cowcatcher at the front of the locomotive. The President and Frederick Selous climbed up and settled themselves on the bench. Selous was the most revered of all the African hunters, the author of many books on travel and adventure, and a naturalist who had devoted his life to studying and cherishing the animals of the great continent. Renowned for his strength and determination, it was said of him that 'When all the others fall by the way-side Selous keeps on to the end of the road.' His physique was robust, his beard steely grey, his eyes were steady and far-seeing and his expression was mild and saintly. Selous and Roosevelt, although so different in appearance, were kindred spirits of the wild open spaces.

While the train puffed across the plains of Tsavo, teeming to the horizon with herds of antelope, the two great men huddled together in conversation, discussing the wonders that lay all around them. As darkness fell they retired to the comfort of the governor's carriage. When the train pulled into Nairobi station early the following morning the entire population was on the platform to catch a glimpse of the former President.

Over the following days a programme of receptions, balls and sporting events, including polo and horse-racing, had been arranged for his entertainment. It was a week before Roosevelt had performed his social obligations and the safari was ready to depart. Again they travelled by train as far as the remote bush siding of Kapiti Plains. When they arrived the safari was drawn up like a small army to meet them.

The next morning, when the march began, the President, with Selous and his son on either hand, rode at the head of the column. Behind them, carried by a uniformed *askari*, Old Glory spread in the breeze. Next came the KAR marching band, giving an approximate rendition of 'Dixie'. The rest of the thousand-strong group straggled back two miles over the veld.

Leon Courtney was not one of this multitude. For the last six weeks he had been setting up supply dumps at waterholes along the safari's intended route.

Reluctantly, Percy Phillips had given Leon an assistant. At first Leon had been horrified. 'Hennie du Rand?' he protested. 'I know him. He's an Afrikaner Boer from South Africa. The fellow fought against us in the war. He rode with the commando of the notorious Koos de la Rey. God alone knows how many Englishmen Hennie du Rand has shot.'

'The Boer War ended several years ago,' Percy pointed out. 'Hennie may be a tough character, but at heart he's a good fellow. Like most Boers he's a true bushman, and he has shot more elephant and buffalo than any other man I know. He's a good mechanic too. He can help you maintain the trucks and drive one. You'll need somebody to help you shoot enough buffalo to keep the safari supplied with fresh meat, and there's nobody better. You can learn a hell of a lot from him, if you listen. But his greatest recommendation is that he will work for his grub and a few shillings a day.'

'But—' said Leon.

'No more ifs or buts. Hennie's your assistant, and you'd better get used to the fact, young fella.'

In just the first few weeks, Leon discovered that not only was Hennie an indefatigable worker but he knew a great deal more about motor maintenance and bushcraft than Leon did, and was happy to share this knowledge with him. His relations with the staff were excellent. He had lived with African tribesmen all his life and understood their ways and customs. He treated them with humour and respect. Even Manyoro and Ishmael liked him. Leon found him good company around the campfire in the evenings and he was a fascinating raconteur. He was over forty, lean and sinewy. His beard was grizzled, and his face and arms were darkly sunburned. He spoke with a strong Afrikaans accent. '*Ja, my jong Boet*,' he told Leon, after they had run down a herd of buffalo on foot and killed eight fat young heifers with as many shots. 'Yes, my young friend. It seems we're going to make a hunter of you yet.'

With Manyoro and four other men they skinned, gutted and quartered the carcasses, then loaded them into the two trucks and delivered them to within half a mile of the great sprawling main camp of the presidential safari. This was as close as Percy would allow the vehicles to approach. He did not want the President and Selous to be disturbed by the sound of engines. Another team of porters came out from the camp to carry in the carcasses.

When they were alone Leon and Hennie parked the older Vauxhall under a pod mahogany tree and rigged a block and tackle from the main branch. They hoisted the truck's rear and between them removed the differential, which had been emitting an alarming grinding sound. They began to strip down the offending part and lay out the pieces on a tattered square of tarpaulin. They looked up at the sound of approaching hoofbeats. The rider was a young man in jodhpurs and a wide-brimmed hat. He dismounted and hitched his horse, then sauntered up to where they were working.

'Hello there. What are you up to?' he drawled, with an unmistakable American twang.

Before he replied Leon looked him up and down. His riding boots were expensive and his khakis were freshly washed and ironed. His face was pleasant, but not striking. When he removed his hat, his hair was a nondescript mousy colour, but his smile was friendly. It struck Leon that the two of them were almost the same age: the other was no more than twenty-two at most.

'We're having a spot of bother with this old bus,' Leon told him, and the stranger grinned.

'"Having a spot of bother with this old bus",' he repeated. 'God, I love that Limey accent. I could listen to it all day.'

'What accent?' Leon mimicked him. 'I ain't got no accent. Now you, you got a funny accent.' They burst out laughing.

The stranger held out his hand. 'My name's Kermit.' Leon looked down at his own palm, which was smeared with black grease. 'That don't matter,' Kermit assured him. 'I love to tinker with autos. I've got a Cadillac back home.'

Leon wiped his hand on the seat of his pants and took the other's. 'I'm Leon, and this ragamuffin is Hennie.'

'Mind if I sit awhile?'

'If you're a famous mechanic you can lend a hand. How about pulling out that rack and pinion? Grab a spanner.'

They all worked in silent concentration for a few minutes, but both Leon and Hennie were watching the newcomer surreptitiously. At last Hennie gave his *sotto voce* opinion: '*Hy weet wat hy doen.*'

'What language is that, and what did Hennie say?'

'It's Afrikaans, an African version of Dutch, and he said you know what you're up to.'

'So do you, pal.'

They worked on for a while, then Leon asked, 'Are you part of the great Barnum and Bailey circus?'

Kermit laughed delightedly. 'Yeah, I suppose I am.'

'What's your job? Are you from the Smithsonian Institute?'

'In a manner of speaking, but mostly I just sit around and listen to a bunch of old men talking a load of bulldust about how things were much better in their day,' Kermit replied.

'Sounds like great fun.'

'Did you guys shoot that load of buffalo that was brought into camp this morning?'

'It's part of our job to keep the camp in meat.'

'Now that really sounds like fun. Mind if I tag along next time you go out?'

Leon and Hennie exchanged a glance. Then Leon asked carefully, 'What calibre of a rifle is it that you have?'

Kermit went to his horse and drew the weapon out of its boot under the saddle flap. He came back and handed it to Leon, who worked the lever action to check that the breech was empty then lifted it to his shoulder. '.405 Winchester. I hear it's a good buffalo rifle but that it kicks like Bob Fitzsimmons punches,' he said. 'Can you shoot it worth a damn?'

'I reckon.' Kermit took the weapon back. 'I call it Big Medicine.'

'All right. Meet us here at four o'clock on the morning of the day after tomorrow.'

'Why don't you pick me up in the main camp?'

'Forbidden,' Leon said. 'We lower forms of animal life are not allowed to disturb the great and the mighty.'

At four in the morning it was still dark when he and Hennie drove up to the rendezvous in the two vehicles, with the skinners and trackers, but Kermit was waiting for them. Leon was impressed. He had doubted that he would show up. They followed a game trail through the remaining hours of darkness, Manyoro loping ahead to warn of stumps and holes. It was cold and Kermit huddled under a sheet of tarpaulin to shelter from the wind. When the trail reached a dry riverbed which presented an impassable obstacle to the trucks they parked under a tree and climbed out. When they took out the rifles, Kermit looked hard at Leon's. 'That piece has had a long life.'

'It's seen some action,' Leon agreed. Percy had lent him a beaten-up old .404 Jeffreys from his own battery of firearms because its ammunition was less than a quarter of the price and in more plentiful supply than that for the .470 Holland. Despite its appearance the weapon was accurate and reliable, but Leon was not proud of it.

'Can you shoot it worth a damn?' Kermit mocked him lightly.

'On a good day.'

'Let's hope that today's a good day,' Kermit needled.

'We shall see.'

'Where are we heading?' Kermit changed the subject.

'Late yesterday Manyoro picked up a large herd that was heading this way. He's leading us to it.'

They went down into the riverbed and crossed below a large green pool whose waters had not yet dried up from the previous wet season. The edges had been heavily trampled by the many animals, including herds of buffalo, who were regularly drinking from it. They went up the far bank into an area of flowering acacia and open glades covered with fresh green grass.

The dawn came up in splendour, the air cool and sweet. The denizens of the forest were coming to life: the men paused for a few minutes at a clearing to watch a troop of baboons foraging for insects and roots. They were led by the young males, vigilant and alert to danger. Following them came the breeding females, holding their tails high to display their naked pink posteriors and pudenda, advertising their maturity and availability. Some carried infants perched on their backs like jockeys. The older youngsters frolicked and chased each other rambunctiously about the glade. As a rearguard, the large dog males moved with a swaggering arrogance, ready to rush forward to confront any threat that the younger males in the vanguard discovered. A small herd of bushbuck, delicately built antelope with spiral horns and creamy stripes across their shoulders, kept pace with the troop. They were using the screen of vigilant apes as sentries and lookouts for leopards and other predators.

When the parade of animals had passed the men went on, but stopped again behind Manyoro as he pointed with his spear at the soft earth of the far side of the glade that had been churned by the passage of great hoofs. 'This is the herd.'

'How many, Manyoro?'

'Two hundred, perhaps three.'

'When?'

Manyoro pointed out a short arc of the dawn sky.

'Less than an hour.' Leon translated for Kermit. 'They're feeding slowly towards thicker cover below the hills where they will lie up during the heat of midday. Remember now what I told you. We shoot only the three- and four-year-old females.'

'Why can't we shoot the big bulls?' Kermit demurred.

'Because the meat is as tough as motor tyres, and tastes a hell of a lot worse. Even a hungry Ndorobo wouldn't touch it.' Kermit nodded unhappily.

Leon looked back at Manyoro. 'Take the spoor,' he said.

They had not gone more than a mile before the open bush became much denser. Within a short space it was so thick that they could not see through it for more than a few yards. Suddenly Manyoro held up his hand and they stopped to listen. From ahead came the crackle of many large bodies moving through the undergrowth, and then they heard the plaintive bellow of a weaning calf pleading with its dam for the udder.

Leon leaned towards Kermit and whispered, 'Right! Here we go. Don't shoot until one of us does. We have to get in close enough to make certain of brain shots. Don't shoot for the body. We don't want to damage the meat, and it won't be very good for our health to have to follow a wounded buffalo through this thick stuff.' He nodded to Manyoro and they went on.

They came into an area of second growth where, the previous dry season, a bushfire had burned through. The scrub was low enough to expose hundreds of dark bovine backs, but high enough to cover the rest of their bodies. The herd was browsing as they moved so their heads were down. Then one came up and gazed directly at them. The base of the horns met on top of its head in a rounded boss, and the tips curled down on each side to give the beast a mournful appearance. They froze immediately and the buffalo seemed not to recognize them as human. It was chewing a mouthful of coarse grass, and after a while it snorted and lowered its head to continue feeding.

'Manyoro, this is too thick,' Leon whispered, 'but they've changed direction. It looks like they don't intend to lie up until much later in the day. Now they're moving back towards the river we crossed earlier this morning. I think they're going to drink at the pool.'

'*Ndio*, Bwana. They have led us in a circle. The river runs just this side of that little hill.' Manyoro pointed at a rocky kopje not more than a mile ahead.

'Get ahead of the herd and we'll lie in wait for them above the pool,' Leon ordered.

In single file Manyoro led them at a trot, circling the slowly moving herd, keeping below the breeze. Once they were ahead they broke into a run and sprinted for the river. When they reached it they kept on across the wide, sandy bed, and took up positions among the trees on the far side.

They did not have too long to wait before the leading buffalo came down the bank in a pack. Snorting and lowing with thirst they stampeded into the pool, and when the leading animals were belly deep they lowered their heads and sucked up water thirstily. The noise they were making was loud enough to drown Leon's whisper to Kermit.

'Pick out a cow on the side of the herd nearest to you. The

range is thirty yards. Remember, go for the head. If you miss I'll know to back up your shot.'

'I won't miss,' Kermit whispered back at him and raised the Winchester. With alarm Leon saw that the American was shaking. The muzzle of his rifle wavered erratically.

Buck fever! He had recognized the symptoms of uncontrollable excitement that can overpower a novice when first presented with dangerous big game. He opened his mouth to order him to hold his fire, but the Winchester roared and the barrel jumped high in the air. Leon saw the bullet nick the hump on the back of a very large bull at the edge of the pool and fly on to strike the cow standing directly behind him in the rump. He realized that the heavy recoil of the Winchester had thrown Kermit off-balance and for the moment he was unsighted. Before he could recover, Leon fired two quick shots, smoothly recycling the bolt of the Jeffreys without lowering the butt from his shoulder. His first bullet hit the wounded bull just below the boss of his horns and the animal dropped, dead before he hit the ground. The second caught the wounded cow just as she was gathering herself to rush back up the bank. It struck the base of the skull at the juncture with the spinal column. The beast flopped nose first into the white sand and lay still.

On Leon's left side Hennie was working with machine-like rapidity, firing into the herd of milling, panic-stricken animals. At each shot one went down. Kermit recovered from the recoil of the Winchester and saw that the bull he had fired at was dead, as was the cow behind it. He let out a wild cowboy yell. 'Yee-ha! I got two with one shot.'

He raised his rifle again, but Leon shouted, 'That's enough! Don't shoot.' Kermit didn't seem to hear him. He fired again. Leon spun around to mark the strike of his bullet, ready to finish off any animal he wounded. However, this time Kermit had pulled off a perfect brain shot and another bull buffalo crashed down.

'Enough!' Leon shouted. 'Stop firing!' He pushed down the barrel of the rifle as Kermit tried to raise it again. Below them the herd thundered up the far bank of the riverbed and crashed away into the bush, leaving nine dead buffalo lying around the pool.

Kermit was still shaking with excitement. 'Hell's bells!' he panted. 'That was the best fun I ever had. I got three buffalo with two shots! Must be some kind of record.'

Leon was amused by his childlike jubilation. He could not bring himself to tell him what had really happened and spoil it for him. Instead he laughed with him. 'Well done, Kermit!' He punched his shoulder. 'That was some shooting. I've never seen anything like it.' Kermit grinned at him ecstatically. Not for a moment did Leon realize that with a tiny white lie his life had changed for ever.

By the time they had butchered the enormous carcasses darkness had fallen. Rather than risk a night drive back along the game tracks, which were filled with old tree stumps and antbear holes that could smash the trucks' suspension, they camped on the riverbank. Ishmael prepared fresh buffalo tongue for their dinner, and afterwards they sipped their coffee around the fire and listened to the hyenas, who had been attracted by the smell of buffalo blood and guts, sobbing and shrieking in the dark bush around their camp. Hennie fossicked in his haversack and brought out a bottle, pulled the cork and offered it to Kermit, who held it up to the firelight. It was less than half full with a pale brown liquid.

'The President don't allow hard liquor in the camp. I haven't taken a real drink in a month. What kind of poison is this?' he asked cautiously.

'My aunty in Malmesbury down in the Cape makes it from peaches. Its called Mampoer. It'll put hair on your chest and load your fun-gun with buckshot.'

Kermit took a swig. His eyes opened wide as he swallowed. 'You can call it Mam-whatever. I call it a hundred-per-cent-proof moonshine.' He wiped his mouth with the back of his hand and passed the bottle to Leon. 'Have a blast of that, pardner!' He was still euphoric, and Leon was even happier that he had allowed him to claim the buffalo kills. The bottle went around the fire twice before it was empty and all three were in expansive mood.

'So, Hennie, you're from South Africa. Were you there during the war?' Kermit asked.

Hennie considered his reply for a minute. '*Ja*, I was there.'

'We read a lot about it in the States. The newspapers say it was something like our own war against the South. Damn hard and bitter.'

'For some of us it was worse than that.'

'Sounds like you were mixed up in the fighting.'

'I rode with de la Rey.'

'I read about him,' Kermit said. 'He was the greatest commando leader of them all. Tell us about it.'

The Mampoer had loosened the tongue of the usually taciturn Boer. He became almost eloquent as he described the fighting in the veld, where thirty thousand Boer farmers had stretched the military might of the greatest empire the world had ever seen almost to its limits.

'They would never have forced us to surrender if that bloody butcher Kitchener had not turned on the women and children we had left on our farms. He burned the farms and shot the cattle. He herded all the women and children into his concentration camps and put fish-hooks into their food so they coughed up blood before they died.' A single tear ran down one of his weathered brown cheeks. He wiped it away and excused himself brokenly. 'Ag! I am sorry. It's the Mampoer, but they are bad memories. My wife, Annetjie, died in the camps.' He stood up. 'I'm going to turn in. Good night.' He picked up his blanket roll and walked away into the darkness. After he had gone Kermit and Leon sat quietly for a while, their mood sombre now.

Leon spoke softly: 'It wasn't fish-hooks. It was diphtheria that killed them. Hennie can't understand that on our side it wasn't deliberate, but the Boer women had always lived out on the open veld. When they were crowded together they had no idea of hygiene. They didn't know how to keep the camps clean. They became filthy plague holes.' He sighed. 'Since the war the British Government has tried to make compensation. They have poured millions of pounds into the country to rebuild the farms. Last year they allowed free elections. Now a government under the two Boer generals, Louis Botha and Jannie Smuts, runs the country. Never has a victor treated the vanquished with such generosity and magnanimity as Britain has shown.'

'But I understand how Hennie feels,' Kermit said. 'There are many people in the south of our country who, even after forty years, have not been able to forget and forgive.'

The following morning Hennie behaved as though the conversation had not taken place. After they had breakfasted on coffee and the remains of the cold tongue, they climbed into the heavily laden trucks. The trackers and skinners sat on the bloody buffalo joints. Kermit cajoled Leon into letting him drive one truck and Hennie followed in the second.

Once again Kermit's mood was gay and carefree. Leon found him a pleasant companion. They had so much in common. They were both passionate about horses, motor-cars and hunting and had much to talk about. Although Kermit did not elaborate, he hinted that he had a father who was rich and powerful and dominated his life.

'My father was just the same,' Leon told him.

'So what did you do?'

'I said, "I respect you, Dad, but I cannot live under your rules." Then I left home and joined the army. That was four years ago. I haven't been back since.'

'Son of a gun! That must have taken some guts. I often wish I could do that, but I know I never will.'

Leon found that the better he came to know Kermit the

143

more he liked him. What the hell? he thought. He shoots like a crazy maniac, but no one's perfect. During the conversation he discovered that Kermit was a keen naturalist and ornithologist. He would be if he's at the Smithsonian, Leon reasoned, and told Kermit to stop the truck whenever he spotted some interesting insect, bird or small animal to show him. Hennie kept going and disappeared into the distance ahead.

They were not far from the spot where Kermit had left his horse the previous day, only a few miles from the presidential camp, when suddenly and unexpectedly two white men stepped out of the bush into the track in front of them. They were dressed in safari clothing but neither carried a rifle. However, one was armed with a large camera and tripod.

'Damn it to hell! The gentlemen of the fourth estate,' Kermit muttered. 'Just can't get away from them.' He braked to a halt. 'I guess we just have to be nice and polite to them or they'll cook our goose for us.'

The taller of the two strangers hurried to the driver's side. 'Excuse me, gentlemen,' he smiled ingratiatingly. 'May I trespass on your good nature and ask you a few questions? Are you connected to President Roosevelt's safari, by any chance?'

'Mr Andrew Fagan of the Associated Press, I presume, to paraphrase the deathless words of Dr David Livingstone.' Kermit pushed his hat back and returned his smile.

The journalist recoiled in astonishment, then peered more closely at him. 'Mr Roosevelt Junior!' he exclaimed. 'Please forgive me. I didn't recognize you in that get-up.' He was staring at Kermit's filthy, blood-stained clothing.

'Mr Who Junior?' Leon demanded.

Kermit looked embarrassed, but Fagan hastened to reply. 'Don't you know who you're riding with? This is Mr Kermit Roosevelt, the son of the President of the United States.'

Leon turned accusingly to his new friend. 'You didn't tell me!'

'You didn't ask.'

'You might have mentioned it,' Leon insisted.

'It would have changed things between us. It always does.'

'Who is this young friend of yours, Mr Roosevelt?' Andrew Fagan asked, and whipped his notepad out of his back pocket.

'This is my hunter, Mr Leon Courtney.'

'He looks very young,' Fagan observed dubiously.

'You don't have to grow a long grey beard to be one of the greatest hunters in Africa,' Kermit told him.

'. . . greatest hunters in Africa!' Fagan scribbled shorthand on his pad. 'How do you spell your name, Mr Courtney? With one *e* or two?'

'Just one.' Leon felt uncomfortable and glared at Kermit. 'Now see what you've got me into.'

'I guess you've been out hunting.' Fagan pointed at the head of the bull buffalo in the back of the truck. 'Who shot that creature?'

'Mr Roosevelt did.'

'What is it?'

'It's a Cape buffalo, *Syncerus caffer*.'

'My God, it's huge! Can we have some photographs, please, Mr Roosevelt?'

'Only if you give us a couple of copies. One for Leon and one for me.'

'Of course. Bring your guns. Let's have one of you on each side of the horns.' The photographer set up his tripod and arranged the pose. Kermit looked composed and debonair, Leon as though he was facing a firing squad. The flash powder exploded in a cloud of smoke, much to the consternation of the skinners and camp staff.

'Okay! Great! Now can we have that tribesman in the red robe in the picture? Tell him to hold his spear higher. Like this. What is he? Some kind of chief?'

'He's the king of the Masai.'

'No kidding! Tell him to look fierce.'

'This mad fool thinks you're dressed like a woman,' Leon told Manyoro in Maa, and he scowled murderously at the photographer.

'Great! God, that's so great!'

It was another half an hour before they were able to drive on.

'Does that happen all the time?' Leon asked.

'You get used to it. You have to be nice to them or they write all sorts of garbage about you.'

'I still think you should have told me that your father was the ruddy President.'

'Can we hunt together again? They've given me an old fellow called Mellow as my hunter. He lectures me as though I'm a schoolboy, and tries to stop me shooting.'

Leon thought about it. 'In two days' time the main camp is moving on up to the Ewaso Ng'iro river. I have to ferry the tents and heavy equipment up there ahead of it. But I'd like to hunt again with you if my boss gives me a chance. You're not a bad fellow, despite your lowly antecedents.'

'Who's your boss?'

'An old gentleman called Percy Phillips, though you'd better not call him old to his face.'

'I know him. He often dines with my father and Mr Selous. I'll do what I can. I don't think I can take much more of Mr Mellow.'

Fate played into Kermit's hands. Two nights after the grand safari moved into the camp on the south bank of the Ewaso Ng'iro river, the chef Lord Delamere had loaned to the President prepared a banquet to celebrate American Thanksgiving Day. There was no turkey so the President himself shot a giant Kori bustard. The chef roasted the bird and concocted a stuffing that contained spiced buffalo liver.

The next morning half the men in camp were struck down by virulent diarrhoea – the buffalo liver had apparently deteriorated in the heat. Even Roosevelt, he of the iron constitution, was affected. Frank Mellow, who had been appointed as Kermit's hunter, was one of the worst stricken, and the camp doctor ordered him to the hospital in Nairobi.

Kermit, who had not eaten the stuffing, seized his advantage: he negotiated the appointment of his replacement hunter with his father through the door of the long-drop outhouse to which the President was confined by his indisposition. Roosevelt put up only token resistance to his son's proposal, and Kermit could go to Percy Phillips as the bearer of the presidential decree. That evening Leon found himself hailed into Percy's tent.

'I don't know what you've been up to, but all hell's broken out. Kermit Roosevelt wants you to have the job as his hunter to replace Frank Mellow and has talked his father into allowing it. They didn't consult me so I have no choice but to agree.' He glared at Leon. 'You aren't yet dry behind the ears. You haven't dealt with lion, leopard or rhino yet, and I told the President so. But he's sick and didn't want to listen. Kermit Roosevelt is a wild and reckless young rascal, just like you. If you get him hurt, you and I are finished. I'll never have another client, and I'll strangle you slowly with my bare hands. Do you understand?'

'Yes, sir, I understand very well.'

'All right, go ahead. I can't stop you.'

'Thank you, sir.' Leon began to leave, but Percy stopped him.

'Leon!'

He turned back in surprise. Percy had never before called him by his first name. Then, with even greater surprise, he saw that Percy was smiling. 'This is your big chance. You'll never have another like it. If you're lucky and clever, you'll be on your way to the top. Good luck.'

1

The next day Leon and Kermit rode out at large, not seeking any particular quarry animal but ready to take on whatever the day brought forward.

'If we found a lion, a big black-maned old male, that would be my dream come true. Not even my father has taken one of those.'

'You may have to wait until we leave Masailand,' Leon told him. 'This country's extremely unhealthy for big black-maned lions.'

'How's that?' Kermit looked intrigued.

'Every young *morani* longs for a chance to kill his lion and prove his manhood. All the *morani* of the same circumcision year go out in a war-party. They hunt down a lion and surround it. When the lion realizes he cannot escape he picks one of the men and charges him. The *morani* must stand and meet the charge with his shield and *assegai*. When he kills he is allowed to make a war-bonnet from the mane and wear it with honour. He can also choose any girl in the tribe. The custom thins out the lion population somewhat.'

'I reckon I'd take the girl before the fur bonnet.' Kermit laughed. 'But you have to admire that kind of courage. They're a magnificent people. Look at your man, Manyoro. He moves with all the grace of a panther.'

Manyoro was trotting ahead of the horses but at that moment he pulled up and leaned on his spear, waiting for the horsemen to come up. He pointed across the open plain ahead at the huge dark shape that stood on the edge of a clump of bush. It was almost a mile away, its outline insubstantial through the shimmer of heat haze.

'Rhino. From here it looks like a big bull.' Leon fished out of his saddle bags the pair of Carl Zeiss binoculars that Percy had given him in recognition of his promotion from apprentice to fully fledged hunter. He focused the lenses and studied the distant shape. 'It's a rhino, all right, and the biggest one I've ever seen. That horn is unbelievable!'

'Bigger than the one my father shot five days ago?'

'I'd say much, much bigger.'

'I want it,' said Kermit, vehemently.

'So do I,' Leon agreed. 'We'll circle out under the wind and stalk him from those bushes. We should be able to get a clean shot for you from thirty or forty yards.'

'You sound just like Frank Mellow. You want me crawling around on my hands and knees, or wriggling along on my belly like a rattlesnake. I've had enough of that.' Kermit was already trembling with excitement at the prospect of the hunt. 'I'm going to show you how the old frontiersmen used to hunt bison back out west. Follow me, pardner.' With that, he clapped his heels into the flanks of his mare and bounded away across the plain, galloping straight at the distant animal.

'Kermit, wait!' Leon shouted after him. 'Don't be a fool.' But Kermit did not glance back. He drew Big Medicine from the rifle boot under his knee and brandished it on high.

'Percy's right. You're a wild and reckless rascal,' Leon lamented, as he urged his own horse in pursuit.

The rhino heard them coming but his eyesight was so weak that he could not place them immediately. He switched his whole massive body from side to side, kicking up dust and snorting ferociously, peering about with myopic piggy eyes.

'Yee-ha!' Kermit let out a cowboy yell.

Guided by the sound, the rhino focused on the shape of horse and rider and instantly burst into a charge, coming directly at them. Kermit stood high in the stirrups, raised his rifle and fired from the back of the galloping horse. His first bullet flew high over the rhino's back and kicked up dust from the plain two hundred yards behind it. He reloaded with a quick pump of the lever and fired again. Leon heard the meaty thump of the bullet slapping into the beast's body but could not see where it had hit. The rhino did not even flinch from the shot but tore in to meet the horse.

Kermit's next wild shot missed again, and Leon saw the dust fly between the rhino's front feet. Kermit fired once more, and Leon heard this shot tell on the baggy grey hide. The bull bucked in agony and tossed his horn high, then lowered it to gore the horse as they came together.

But Kermit was too quick for him. With the skill of an expert polo player, he used his knees to turn his horse across the line of the charge. Horse and rhino passed each other in opposite directions, and although the latter hooked at Kermit with his long horn, the point flashed a hand's breadth past his knee. At the same time Kermit leaned out from the saddle and fired with the muzzle almost touching the grey hide between the bull's plunging shoulders. As the rhino received the bullet he hunched his shoulders and bucked. He swung around to chase after the horse, but now his gait was short and hampered. Bloody froth dribbled from his open mouth. Kermit reined in his horse while he reloaded his rifle, then fired twice more. When the rhino took these last bullets his body convulsed and he slowed to a walk. The great head hung low, and he staggered unevenly from side to side.

Coming up at a gallop, Leon was appalled by the brutal display. It ran contrary to every concept he had of the fair chase and the humane kill. Up to this moment he had been unable to intervene in the butchery for fear of hitting Kermit or his mount, but now his field of fire was clear. The wounded rhino was less than thirty paces away, and Kermit was well out on the flank reloading his rifle. Leon dragged his horse back on its haunches and it skidded to a halt. He kicked his feet out of the stirrups and sprang to the ground, bringing up the Holland as he landed. He aimed for the point where the rhino's spine joined the skull, and his bullet cleaved the vertebrae like the blade of an executioner's axe.

Kermit rode up to the carcass and dismounted. His face was flushed and his eyes sparkled. 'Thanks for your help, pardner.' He laughed. 'By God! That was really exciting! How did you like the Wild West style of hunting? Grand, isn't it?' He showed not the least guilt or remorse for what had just happened.

Leon had to take a breath to keep his temper. 'It was wild, I'll give you that. I am not so sure about the grand bit,' he said, his voice level. 'I dropped my hat.' He swung up into his saddle and rode back for it.

What do I do now? he wondered. Do I have a showdown with him? Do I tell him to find himself another hunter? He saw the hat on the ground ahead, rode up to it and dismounted. He picked it up and dusted it against his leg. Then he jammed it on his head. Be sensible, Courtney! If you walk away, you're finished. You might as well go back to Egypt and take the job with your father.

He mounted up and rode slowly back to where Kermit stood beside the dead rhino, stroking the long black horn. He looked up at Leon as he dismounted, his expression thoughtful. 'Something bothering you?' he asked quietly.

'I was worrying about how the President's going to feel when he sees that horn. It must be damn nigh five feet long. I hope he won't turn bright green.' Leon succeeded in keeping his smile natural. He knew those words were a perfect peace-offering.

Kermit relaxed visibly. 'That colour might suit him well enough. I can't wait to show it to him.'

Leon glanced up at the sun. 'It's late. We won't be able to get back to the main camp this evening. We'll stay here tonight.'

Ishmael had been following them on one mule and leading another, which carried the cooking pots and other necessities. As soon as he came up he set about putting together a rudimentary fly camp.

Before it was fully dark he brought their dinner to them. They leaned back against their saddles with the enamel plates balanced on their laps and tucked into the yellow rice and Tommy buck stew.

'Ishmael's a magician,' Kermit said, his mouth full. 'I've had worse grub at restaurants in New York City. Tell him that, will you?'

Ishmael acknowledged the compliment gravely.

Leon scraped his plate clean and put the last spoonful into his mouth. Still chewing, he reached into his saddle bag and brought out a bottle. He showed the label to Kermit. 'Bunnahabhain single malt whisky.' Kermit smiled happily. 'Where on earth did you find that?'

'Compliments of Percy. Although he's unaware of his own generosity.'

'My God, Courtney, it's you who's the real magician.'

Leon poured a dram into their enamel mugs, and they sipped, sighing with pleasure.

'Let's suppose for the moment that I am your fairy godmother,' Leon suggested, 'and that I can grant you any wish. What would it be?'

'Apart from a beautiful and willing girl?'

'Apart from that.'

They both chuckled, and Kermit pondered for only a few seconds. 'How big was that elephant my father got a few days ago?'

'Ninety-four and ninety-eight. Didn't quite make the magic number of one hundred.'

'I want to do better.'

'You worry a lot about doing better than him. Is this meant to be a competition?'

'My father has always succeeded in everything he turns his hand to. Hell, he was a war hero, a state governor, a hunter and sportsman all before he turned forty, and as if that wasn't enough, he became the youngest and most successful President of America ever. He respects winners and despises losers.' He took a sip. 'From what you've told me, you and I have lived through the same situation. You should understand.'

'You think your father despises you?'

'No. He loves me but he doesn't respect me. I want his respect more than anything else in the world.'

'You've just taken a bigger rhino than he has.'

They looked across at the enormous carcass, the horn glinting in the firelight.

'That's a start.' Kermit nodded. 'However, knowing my father, he'd put much more value on an elephant or a lion. Find one of those for me, Fairy Godmother.'

Manyoro was sitting at the other fire with Ishmael, and Leon called across to him, 'Come to me, my brother. There is something of importance we must discuss.' Manyoro got up and came to squat across the fire from him. 'We need to find a big elephant for this *bwana*.'

'We have given him a Swahili name,' Manyoro said. 'We have named him Bwana Popoo Hima.'

Leon laughed.

'What's so funny?' Kermit asked.

'You have been honoured,' Leon told him. 'Manyoro at least respects you. He has given you a Swahili name.'

'What is it?' Kermit demanded.

'Bwana Popoo Hima.'

'That sounds disgusting,' Kermit said, suspicious.

'It means "Sir Quick Bullet".'

'Popoo Hima! Hey! Tell him I like that!' Kermit was pleased. 'Why did they choose that name?'

'They're very impressed by the way you shoot.' Leon turned back to Manyoro. 'Bwana Popoo Hima wants a very big elephant.'

'Every white man wants a very big elephant. But we must go to Lonsonyo Mountain to seek the counsel of our mother.'

'Kermit, the advice I have from Manyoro is that we go to a Masai lady witch doctor on a mountaintop. She will tell us where to find your elephant.'

'Do you really believe in that sort of thing?' Kermit asked.

'Yes, I do.'

'Well, it just so happens that so do I.' Kermit nodded seriously. 'In the hills to the north of our ranch in the badlands of Dakota there lives an old Indian shaman. I never hunt without going to see him first. Every real hunter has his little superstitions, even my father, who's the hardest-nosed guy you'll ever meet. He always carries a rabbit's foot when he goes out into the field.'

'It pays to give Lady Luck a wink and a nod,' Leon agreed. 'This lady I'm taking you to meet is her twin sister. She's also my adopted mother.'

'Then I reckon we can trust her. When can we leave?'

'We're more than twenty miles from the main camp. We'll lose a couple of days if we take the rhino head back there first. I plan to cache it here and Manyoro will pick it up later. That way we can leave at once for the mountain.'

'How far?'

'Two days, if we push along.'

The next morning they hoisted the rhino head into the high branches of a pod mahogany tree and wedged it in a fork where it was well out of the reach of hyenas and other scavengers. Then they headed east, and camped only when it was too dark to see the ground ahead. Leon did not want to risk one of the horses breaking a leg in an antbear hole. During the night he woke and lay for a minute listening for what had disturbed him. One of the horses whickered and stamped.

Lions! he thought. After the horses. He threw off his blanket and reached for his rifle as he sat up. Then he saw an alien figure sitting at the smouldering ashes of the fire. It was shrouded in an ochre-red *shuka*.

'Who is it?' he demanded.

'It is me, Loikot. I have come.'

He stood up and Leon recognized him at once, although he was several inches taller than he had been when they had last met only six months before. In the same period his voice had broken and he had become fully a man. 'How did you find us, Loikot?'

'Lusima Mama told me where you were. She sent me to welcome you.'

Their voices had roused Kermit. He sat up and asked sleepily, 'What's going on? Who's this skinny kid?'

'He's a messenger from the lady we're going to visit. She sent him to find us and bring us to the mountain.'

'How the hell did she know we were on our way? We didn't know ourselves until last night.'

'Wake up, Bwana Popoo Hima. Think about it. The lady

is a sorcerer. She keeps her eye on the road and her foot on the gas. You wouldn't want to play poker with her.'

In the middle of the morning they raised the flat top of Lonsonyo Mountain above the dreaming blue horizon ahead, but it was late in the day when they stood under its towering mass, and dark before they rode into the *manyatta* and dismounted in front of Lusima's hut. She had heard the horses and stood tall in the doorway with the firelight behind her. She was naked except for the string of beads around her waist. Her skin had been freshly anointed with fat and ochre, and polished until it gleamed.

Leon walked across to her and went down on one knee. 'Give me your blessing, Mama,' he asked.

'You have it, my son.' She touched his head. 'My motherly love is yours also.'

'I have brought another petitioner to you.' Leon stood up and beckoned Kermit forward. 'His Swahili name is Bwana Popoo Hima.'

'So this is the prince, the son of a great white king.' Lusima looked closely into Kermit's face. 'He is a twig of the mighty tree, but he will never grow as tall as the tree from which he sprang. There is always one tree in the forest that grows taller than any other, one eagle that flies higher than any other bird.' She smiled kindly at Kermit. 'All these things he knows in his heart, and it makes him feel small and unhappy.'

Even Leon was amazed at her insight. 'He longs desperately to earn his father's respect,' he agreed.

'So he comes to me to find him an elephant.' She nodded. 'In the morning I will bless his *bunduki* and point the way of the hunter for him. But now you will feast with me. I have killed a young goat for you and this *mzungu*, who does not drink blood and milk, and prefers cooked meat.'

They gathered at noon the next day under the council tree

155

in the cattle pen. Big Medicine lay on the tanned lionskin. The blued metal was freshly oiled and her woodwork shone. The sacrificial offering of fresh cow's blood and milk, salt, snuff and glass trade beads had been set out. Leon and Kermit squatted side by side at the head of the lionskin with Manyoro and Loikot behind them.

Lusima emerged from her hut, magnificent in her finery. She came to the council tree with her regal stride, her slave girls attending her closely. The men clapped with respect and called her praises: 'She is the great black cow who feeds us with the milk of her udders. She is the watcher who sees all things. She is the mother of the tribe. She is the wise one who knows all things on this earth. Pray for us, Lusima Mama.'

She squatted in front of the men and asked the ritual questions: 'Why do you come to my mountain? What is it you seek from me?'

'We beg you to bless our weapons,' Leon replied. 'We importune you to divine the path that the great grey men take through the wilderness.'

Lusima rose and sprinkled the rifle with blood and milk, snuff and salt. 'Make this weapon as the dreadful eye of the hunter that it may slay whatever he looks upon. May his *popoo* fly straight as the bee returning to the hive.'

Then she went to Kermit and, with the giraffe-tail switch, sprinkled the blood and milk on his bowed head. 'The game will never escape him, for he has the heart of the hunter. Let him follow his quarry unerringly. May it never escape his hunter's eye.'

Leon whispered the translation to Kermit, and after each sentence she spoke, they clapped and said the refrain to her prayer: 'Even as the great black cow speaks, let it be so.'

Lusima began to dance, whirling in a tight circle, her bare feet like those of a young girl, her sweat mingled with the oil and ochre until she glowed like a carving of precious amber. At last she collapsed on the lionskin and her face contorted. She bit her lips until blood ran down her chin. Her whole body juddered and shook, her breath sawing and rasping in her throat, froth coating her lips and mingling pinkly with the blood. When she spoke her voice was as thick and hoarse as a man's: 'The hunter makes his way homewards. The clever hunter listens to the cheeping of the small black birds in the dawn,' she grated. 'If he waits on the hilltop the hunter will be thrice blessed.' She gasped and shook herself as a hunting spaniel does when it clambers from the water on to the river-bank.

'**W**ell, your mama's clues were fairly cryptic,' Kermit remarked drily, as they ate the dinner of roasted porcupine, as tender and juicy as a sucking pig, that Ishmael had provided. 'Was she telling me to give it up and go home, do you think?'

'Didn't your Indian shaman teach you that when you're dealing with occult prediction you have to consider every word for its possible associations? You cannot take anything literally. To give you an example, last time I asked for her help, Lusima told me to follow the sweet singer. This turned out to be the bird called a honeyguide.'

'She seems to be something of an ornithologist, but she gave us black birds instead of honeyguides.'

'Let's start at the beginning. Did she tell you to go home or to go homewards?'

'Homewards! My home is in New York, USA.'

'Well, that would give us a bearing of north-west by north and a touch north, I reckon.'

'In the absence of any other suggestions we'll have to give that a go,' Kermit agreed.

Leon navigated on the army-issue compass he had liberated when he left the KAR, and they camped that first night under the lee of a small rocky kopje. Just before dawn they were drinking coffee while they waited for the sun. Suddenly Loikot cocked his head and held up his hand for silence. They stopped talking and listened. The sound was so faint that it was only fitfully audible when the morning breeze dropped a little or veered favourably.

'What is it, Loikot?'

'The *chungaji* are calling to each other.' He stood and picked up his spear. 'I must go up the hill so I can hear what they are saying.' He slipped away into the darkness, while they listened to the distant sounds.

'They don't sound like human voices,' Kermit said, 'more like the piping of sparrows.'

'Or the cheeping of little black birds?' Leon asked. 'Lusima Mama's little black birds?'

They burst out laughing.

'I think you have it. Loikot will have news for us when he comes down the hill.'

They heard him calling, closer and clearer than the other voices, and the exchange of news on the Masai grapevine continued until after the sun was well clear of the horizon. Then, at last, there was silence as the wind and rising heat made further discourse unintelligible. Soon after this Loikot returned. He was puffed with self-importance. It was clear that he was not going to speak until someone pleaded with him to do so.

Leon humoured him. 'Tell me, Loikot, what did you and your brothers of the circumcision knife speak about?'

'There was much talk about the safari of ten thousand porters and many *wazungu* camped on the Ewaso Ng'iro river and the great killing of animals by the king of a land called Emelika.'

'After this what did you speak about?'

'There has been an outbreak of red-water disease among the cattle near Arusha. Ten have died.'

'Is it possible that you also discussed the movement of elephant in the Rift Valley?'

'Yes, we spoke of that,' Loikot replied. 'We all agreed that this is the season when the big bulls come down into the Rift. In recent days the *chungaji* have seen many in the land between Maralal and Kamnoro. There was talk of three travelling eastwards in one herd, all very big.' Then, at last, he broke into a smile, and his voice took on an urgent cadence. 'If we are to catch them, M'bogo, we must go quickly north-wards to cut them off before they move on into Samburuland and Turkana.'

Manyoro and Loikot ran ahead of the horses with the long loping stride they referred to as 'gobbling up the earth greed-ily'. The two horsemen trotted behind them, then Ishmael, further back, riding one mule and leading the other on which were loaded all his pots, pans and supplies.

Kermit was in his usual irrepressible mood. 'A good horse between your legs, a rifle in your hand and the promise of game ahead! Son of a gun, this is the life for a man.'

'I can't think of anything I'd rather be doing,' Leon agreed.

Kermit reined in suddenly and shaded his eyes with his hat to look out to one side at a patch of grey thorn scrub. 'That's a big kudu bull over there,' he said. 'Bigger than any that Mellow got for me.'

'Do you want another kudu, or do you want a cracking hundred-pounder jumbo? Make up your mind, chum. You can't have both.'

'Why not?' Kermit demanded.

'The big bull elephant with your name branded on his backside may be just over the next rise. You fire a shot here and he'll take off at a rate of knots. He won't stop running until he gets across the Nile.'

'Spoilsport! You're as bad as goddamned Frank Mellow.' Kermit kicked his horse into a canter to catch up with the two Masai, who had pulled well ahead.

In the middle of the afternoon a line of low hills pushed their crests over the flat horizon, resembling the knuckles of a clenched fist. They camped that night below the tallest. Before dawn the next morning they drank coffee around the fire, then left Ishmael with the horses to break camp and pack his mule while they climbed to the summit of the hill. When they reached it Loikot sang out across the valley. He was answered almost immediately by a similar but distant cry coming out of the remaining shreds of the night. The exchange went on for some time before he turned to Leon. 'That one I was speaking to is not Masai. This is the border between our land and the Samburu,' Loikot told him. 'He is half a Samburu, the tribe who are our bastard cousins. They speak Maa but not as we do. They speak it in a funny way, like this.' He rolled his eyes and made an idiotic hee-hawing sound, like a demented donkey. Manyoro thought this was hilarious and staggered around in a circle, slapping his cheeks and repeating the imitation of a Samburu speaking Maa.

'Now that you two clowns have had your little joke, will you tell us what your bastard cousin the Samburu had to say?'

Still gasping and hiccuping with merriment, Loikot answered, 'The Samburu donkey says that last evening as they were driving the cattle into the *manyatta* they saw the three bulls. He says that every one of them has very long white teeth.'

'Which way were they heading?' Leon demanded eagerly.

'They were coming straight up this valley, towards where we are now.' Quickly Leon translated this news to Kermit, and watched his eyes light up. 'So if I'd let you shoot that kudu yesterday you would have blown away any chance we ever had of catching them.'

'I'm covered with shame and remorse. In future I promise to listen to the words of the Great One who knows all.' Kermit gave him a sardonic salute.

'Go to hell, Roosevelt!' Leon grinned. 'I'm sending Manyoro and Loikot down into the valley to check that they didn't pass during the night. However, it's new moon at the moment, so I doubt they would have kept moving after dark. I'd bet good money that they rested during the darkest hours and that they're only now starting to move again.' They sat and watched the two Masai go down the hillside and disappear among the trees in the gut of the valley.

'So far we've followed Lusima's advice about little black birds cheeping in the dawn. What was her next suggestion?' Kermit asked suddenly.

'She spoke of the hunter who waits on the hilltop being thrice blessed. Here we are on the hilltop. Let's see if your three blessings are on the way.'

As soon as the sun poked its fiery head above the horizon Leon unslung the strap of the binoculars from his shoulder, and settled with his back against a tree-trunk. Slowly he panned the lenses across the valley below. Within an hour he picked out the figures of Manyoro and Loikot coming back up the hill, but they were walking at a leisurely pace and chatting to each other. He lowered the binoculars. 'They're in no hurry, which means they've had no luck. The bulls haven't passed this way. Not yet anyway.' The two Masai came up and squatted close by. Leon looked a question at Manyoro, but he shook his head.

'*Hapana*. Nothing.' He took out his snuffbox and offered Loikot a pinch before he helped himself. They sniffed and sneezed, closing their eyes, then whispered quietly together so that their voices would not carry down into the valley. Kermit stretched out on the stony ground, pulled the brim of his hat over his eyes and, within minutes, was snoring gently. Leon kept the binoculars moving over the valley, lowering them every once in a while to rest his eyes and polish the lenses on his shirt tail.

Over the ages a number of large round boulders had become dislodged from the hillside and had rolled down on to the valley floor. Some resembled the backs of elephant, and more than once Leon's heart tripped as he picked up a massive grey shape in the field of the binoculars, until he realized it was a grey rock and not elephant hide he was seeing. Once more he lowered the binoculars and spoke softly to Manyoro: 'How long should we wait here?'

'Until the sun reaches there.' Manyoro pointed to the zenith. 'If they do not come by then it is possible they have turned aside. If so, we must go down to the horses and ride to the *manyatta* where the Samburu saw them yesterday. There we can pick up the spoor and follow it until we catch up with them.'

Kermit lifted his hat off his eyes and asked, 'What did Manyoro say?' Leon told him and he sat up. 'I'm getting bored,' he announced. 'This is a game of hurry up and wait.'

Leon did not bother to reply. He lifted the binoculars and resumed the search.

Half a mile down the valley there was a patch of greener growth that he had noticed earlier. He knew by the colour and density of the foliage that it was a grove of monkey-berry trees. The fruits were purple and bitter to human taste but attracted all varieties of wild game, large and small. In the centre of the grove lay one of the huge rolling boulders, its rounded top showing above the monkey berry. He picked it out again and was about to pass on when his nerves jumped taut. The rock seemed to have changed its outline and grown larger. He stared at it until his eyes swam. Then it changed shape again. He caught his breath. An elephant was standing behind the boulder, half hidden by it, so that only its rump and the curve of its spine were exposed. How the animal had reached that position without any of them seeing it was another demonstration to him of how silently and stealthily such a large creature could move. He felt his chest closing until he was breathing asthmatically. He kept staring at the elephant but it did not move again. There's only one, so it can't be the herd we're looking for. Probably it's a stray cow or a young bull. He tried to fortify himself against disappointment.

Then his eyes flicked to the right as he picked up another movement. The head of a second elephant pushed through the screen of monkey-berry branches. He gasped again. This was a bull: his head was huge, the forehead bulged impressively and the ears were spread like the sails of a schooner. The dangling trunk was framed by a pair of long, curved tusks, the ivory thick and bright.

'Manyoro!' Leon whispered urgently.

'I see him, M'bogo!'

Leon glanced at him and saw that both Masai were on

their feet, staring down at the monkey-berry grove. 'How many?' he asked.

'Three,' Loikot answered. 'One is behind the rock. The second is facing us, and the third is standing between them but hidden behind the trees. I can see only his legs.'

Kermit sat up quickly, alerted by the restrained tension in their voices. 'What is it? What have you seen?'

'Nothing much.' Leon was trembling. 'Just a hundred-pounder, maybe two or even three. But I suppose you're too bored to give a damn.'

Kermit scrambled to his feet, still half dazed with sleep. 'Where? Where?'

Leon pointed. Then Kermit saw them. 'Well, I'll be—' he blurted. 'Kick me in the head! Shake me awake! This isn't true, is it? Tell me I'm not dreaming. Tell me those tusks are real.'

'You know what, chum? From here they look real to me.'

'Get your rifle! Let's go after them.' Kermit's voice cracked.

'What a good plan, Mr Roosevelt. I can find no vice in it.' Even as they watched, the three elephant ambled out of the monkey-berry grove and came down the valley towards them. In single file they followed a broad game path that passed close to the base of the hill on which they stood.

'How many elephant do I have on my licence?' Kermit demanded. 'Is it three?'

'You know damn well it is. Are you thinking of taking all of them? Greedy boy.'

'Which one has the biggest tusks?' Kermit was stuffing cartridges into the magazine of the Winchester.

'Hard to tell from here. All three are big. We'll have to get in a lot closer to pick the largest. But we'd better crack on speed. They're moving fast.'

They scrambled down the hillside, loose stones rolling under their boots. The trees and the intervening bulge of the slope impeded their view, and they lost sight of the bulls. They reached the valley floor with Leon in the lead. He turned left along the base of the hill, running hard to get into a position from which they could intercept the elephants.

He reached the game trail, which was wide and beaten smooth over the aeons by the passage of hoofs, pads and feet, and turned on to it. Kermit was on his heels and the two Masai were only a few strides further back. Leon saw that the trail ahead was cut by a shallow gully that ran down from the hillside. It had been washed out by the run-off of storm water. Before they reached it a number of things happened almost simultaneously. Leon saw the leading bull emerge from the trees on the far side of the gully four or five hundred yards ahead, followed closely by the other two, all moving in single file directly towards them.

Then a booming cry echoed off the hilltop on their left flank: the alarm call of a sentinel baboon warning the troop of danger. He had spotted the men in the valley below his post. Immediately the cry was taken up by the rest. The clamour of harsh barks rang out across the valley. The three elephant stopped abruptly. They stood in a close group, swaying uncertainly, lifting their trunks to test the air for the scent of danger, swinging their heads from side to side, ears spread to listen.

'Stand dead still!' Leon cautioned the others. 'They'll pick up any movement.' He stood and watched them intently. Which way would they run? he wondered. His heart was hammering against his ribcage from the exertion of the race down the hill and with excitement: all three elephant carried at least a hundred pounds of ivory on each side of their heads.

Which way must we go? Then he made up his mind. 'We have to get into the gully before they spot us,' he panted, and started forward again. They reached the gully without the elephant locating them and plunged down the steep bank into the middle of a herd of impala, which were browsing on the low branches of the bush that choked the dry watercourse. The herd exploded into a panic-stricken rush of leaping and snorting animals, bounded up the far side of the gully and stampeded down the game trail, towards the three great bulls.

The leader saw them tearing towards him, spun around and ran straight at the steep hillside. The other two followed.

Leon looked over the top of the bank and saw what was taking place. 'Damn those bloody impala to hell and back!' he gritted. The three elephant were running up the first incline at the base of the hill, heading diagonally away from him, making for the crest of the hills. 'Come on, Kermit,' he yelled frantically. 'If we can't cut them off before they get to the top we'll never see them again.'

They ran across the narrow strip of level ground and reached the base of the hill. By now they were two hundred yards behind the elephant. Leon went straight at the slope, taking long strides, jumping over the smaller rocks in his path.

The elephant were unable to tackle such a steep slope head-on. The leader turned across it and began a series of climbing dog-leg turns. Meanwhile Leon and Kermit continued to move straight up, cutting across each of the loops that the bulls were forced to make. On each leg they gained on their gigantic quarry.

'I don't think I can keep this up,' Kermit gasped. 'I'm about done in.'

'Keep going, chum.' Leon reached back and seized his wrist. 'Come on! We're nearly there.' He dragged him upwards. 'We're ahead of them now. Not much further to go.'

At last they staggered out on to the summit of the hill and Kermit leaned against a tree-trunk. His shirt was soaked with sweat, his chest heaved and the air whistled in his throat. His legs were shaking under him, like those of a man in palsy. Leon looked back down the slope. The leading bull was a hundred feet below their level, but he was coming up swiftly, taking each turn along the contour. Leon judged he would pass less than thirty yards from where they stood on the skyline, but he seemed unaware of their presence. 'Get ready, chum. Down on your backside. Give yourself a steady shot. Quickly now. They'll be on us in a few seconds,' he hissed at Kermit. 'They'll only give you one chance. Take the leader.

Shoot him in his armpit, just behind the shoulder. Go for his heart. Don't try the brain shot.'

Suddenly the leading bull saw the figures crouching on the skyline above him and stopped again, swinging his trunk uncertainly. He began to turn away down the hillside, but Manyoro and Loikot were coming up behind him. They screamed and waved their arms, trying to turn him back towards the hunters on the crest.

The bull hesitated again, swinging his head from side to side. His companions pressed up close behind him. The two Masai raced towards them, howling like demons and flapping their *shukas*. By contrast the men on the ridge waited silent and motionless. To the leading bull they seemed the lesser threat. He turned back again, and kept on up the slope directly towards where Leon and Kermit were. The other two followed his lead.

'Here they come. Get ready,' Leon said softly.

Kermit was sitting flat on his buttocks, elbows braced on his knees. But he was still panting and, with consternation, Leon saw that the barrel of his Winchester was wavering. He dreaded that Kermit was about to put on one of his eccentric displays of marksmanship, but the moment had come. He drew a breath and snapped, 'Now, Kermit! Take him!'

He raised the Holland, ready to back up when Kermit missed, as he surely must. The Winchester crashed and leaped in Kermit's grip. Leon gaped and lowered his rifle. The bullet had hit the leading bull not on the shoulder but cleanly in the earhole. The elephant flopped to his knees, killed instantly. Leon jumped as the Winchester crashed again. The second bull, coming up behind the fallen leader, dropped lifelessly to another perfect brain shot. But he fell on the steep slope and began to roll down it. The carcass gathered momentum, and thundered downwards, raising an avalanche of loose rock and rubble. Manyoro and Loikot were almost caught up in it. At the last moment they threw themselves aside and the carcass slithered past.

The third bull stood on the open slope below the summit,

cornered between the two groups of men. Manyoro jumped to his feet and ran towards him, shouting and waving his *shuka*. The bull's nerve broke and he turned for the crest. Leon and Kermit were standing in his line of escape. The beast's flight turned into a full-blooded charge: he cocked his ears half back and rushed straight at them, squealing with rage.

'Again!' Leon yelled. 'Do it again! Shoot him!' He swung up the Holland, but before he could fire the Winchester crashed for the third time. This elephant was below Kermit's level, but head-on to him, so the aiming point was deceptively higher. Nevertheless he had judged it perfectly and his aim was dead true. The last bull threw his trunk over his head and died as swiftly and painlessly as his companions. He also rolled away down the slope, sliding the last few hundred feet until his body came to rest against the trunk of one of the larger trees near the base of the hill. From the first shot to the last, only a minute or two had passed. Leon had not fired once.

The echoes of gunfire died away against the hills on the far side of the valley and a deep silence descended on the land. No bird sang and no ape barked. All of nature seemed to hold its breath and listen.

At last Leon broke the hush. 'When I say shoot him in the head you shoot him in the body. When I say shoot him in the body you shoot him in the head. When I give you an easy shot you botch it. When I give you an impossible shot you hit it right on the button. What the hell, Roosevelt? I really don't know why you need me here.'

Kermit did not seem to hear him. He sat staring at the rifle in his lap with a stunned look on his sweat-streaked face. 'God love me!' he whispered. 'I've never shot that good before.' He raised his head and gazed down at the three massive bodies. Slowly he stood up and walked to the nearest elephant. He stooped and laid his right hand reverentially on one of the long, gleaming tusks. 'I can't believe what happened. Big Medicine just seemed to take over from me. It was as though I was standing outside myself, and watching it all happen from a distance.' He raised the Winchester to his lips

167

like a communion chalice and kissed the blued metal breech block. 'Hey there, Big Medicine, Lusima Mama put one hell of a spell on you, didn't she?'

It was six days before the tusks could be pulled from the decomposing flesh, and by then Manyoro had assembled a gang of porters from the nearby Samburu villages to take them back to the base encampment on the Ewaso Ng'iro river. On the return march they made a detour to pick up the cached rhino head. The long file of porters was carrying an impressive array of big-game trophies as they approached the camp. They were still several miles short of the river when they saw a small group of horsemen riding towards them from the direction of the camp.

'I bet this is my dad coming to find out what I've been doing.' Kermit was grinning in anticipation. 'I can't wait to see his face when he lays eyes on this lot.'

While they reined in to wait for the approaching riders to come up, Leon brought up his binoculars and studied them. 'Hold on! That isn't your father.' He stared a few moments longer. 'It's that newspaper fellow and his cameraman. How the hell did they know where to find us?'

'I reckon they must have an informer in our camp. Apart from that, they have eyes like circling vultures,' Kermit commented. 'They don't miss anything. Anyway, we can't avoid talking to them.'

Andrew Fagan rode up and lifted his hat. 'Good afternoon, Mr Roosevelt,' he called. 'Are those elephant tusks that your men are carrying? I had no idea they grew so large. Those are gigantic. You're having a wonderfully successful safari. I offer you my heartiest congratulations. May I have a closer look at your trophies?'

Leon called to the porters to lay down their burdens. Fagan dismounted and went to inspect them, exclaiming with amazement. 'I'd love to listen to your account of the hunt, Mr

Roosevelt,' he said, 'if you could spare me the time. And, of course, I'd be extremely grateful if you and Mr Courtney would be good enough to pose for a couple more photographs. My readers would be fascinated to hear of your adventures. As you know, my articles are syndicated to almost every newspaper in the civilized world from Moscow to Manhattan.' An hour later Fagan and his cameraman had finished. Fagan had half filled his notebook with shorthand scribbles, and his photographer had exposed several dozen flash plates of the hunters and their trophies. Fagan was eager to get back to his typewriter. He intended to send a galloper to the telegraph office in Nairobi with his copy and instructions that it was to be sent urgent rate to his editor in New York. As they all shook hands Kermit unexpectedly asked Fagan, 'Have you met my father?'

'No, sir, I have not, though I must add that I am one of his most ardent admirers.'

'Come to see me tomorrow at the main camp,' Kermit told him. 'I'll introduce you.'

Fagan was flabbergasted by the invitation, and as he rode away he was still calling his thanks.

'What came over you, chum?' Leon asked. 'I thought you hated the fourth estate.'

'I do, but they're better as friends than enemies. One day Fagan may be a useful man to know. Now he owes me a big marker.'

Leon and Kermit rode into the main camp on the river in the late afternoon. Nobody was expecting them. With his robust constitution, the President had completely recovered from the effects of his Thanksgiving dinner. He was sitting under a tree outside his tent, reading his leatherbound copy of Dickens's *The Pickwick Papers*, one of his perennial favourites. With a bemused air he regarded the uproar that his son's arrival had created. The entire personnel of the camp, almost a thousand strong, was hastening from every direction to greet the returning hunters. They crowded around them, craning for a closer look at the tusks and the rhino head.

Teddy Roosevelt laid aside his book, adjusted his steel-rimmed spectacles on his nose, stood up from his chair, tucked in his shirt over the bulge of his belly and came to find the cause of the commotion. The crowd parted deferentially to allow him through. Kermit jumped from the saddle to greet his father. They shook hands warmly and the President took his son's arm. 'Well, my boy, you have been away for almost three weeks. I was starting to worry about you. Now you'd better show your old man what you've brought home.' The two went to where the porters had laid out their bundles for inspection. Leon was still mounted and close enough to the President to have a clear view of his face over the heads of the crowd. He was able to watch every nuance of his expressions.

He saw mild, indulgent interest give way to astonishment as Roosevelt counted the tusks lying on the ground. Then astonishment gave way to dismay as he took in the size of the ivory shafts. He dropped Kermit's arm and walked slowly down the line of trophies. His back was turned to his son, but Leon saw dismay harden to envy and outrage. He realized that for the President to have reached his position of utmost eminence he must be one of the most competitive men on earth. He was accustomed to excelling in any endeavour and ranking first and foremost in any company. Now he was being forced to come to terms with the fact that, for once, he had been outshone by his son.

The President stopped at the end of the line and stood with his hands clasped behind his back. He chewed the ends of his moustache and frowned heavily. Then his expression cleared and he was smiling as he turned to Kermit. Leon was filled with admiration for how swiftly he had controlled his emotions.

'Splendid!' said Roosevelt. 'These tusks beat anything we already have, and almost certainly anything we'll get before the end of the expedition.' He seized Kermit's hand again. 'I'm proud of you, really and truly proud. How many shots did you have to make to get these extraordinary trophies?'

'You'd better ask my hunter that, Father.'

Still clasping Kermit's right hand, the President looked at Leon. 'Well, Mr Courtney, how many was it? Ten, twenty or more? Tell us all, please.'

'Your son killed the three bulls with three consecutive bullets,' Leon replied. 'Three perfect brain shots.'

Roosevelt stared into Kermit's face for a moment, then pulled him roughly into the circle of his muscular arms and embraced him fiercely. 'I'm proud of you, Kermit. I couldn't be prouder than I am at this moment.'

Over the President's shoulder, Leon could see Kermit's face. It glowed. Now it was Leon's turn to suffer mixed emotions: he rejoiced for his friend, but for himself he felt tearing agony. If only my father could bring himself to say that to me one day, he thought, but I know he never will.

The President broke the embrace at last and held Kermit at arms' length, beaming into his face with his head cocked on one side. 'I'll be damned if I haven't sired a champion,' he said. 'I want to hear all about it at dinner. But my nose detects that you need a bath before we eat. Go and get cleaned up now.' Then he looked across at Leon. 'I'd be pleased if you'd join us for dinner as well, Mr Courtney. Shall we say seven thirty for eight?'

While Leon used his straight razor on the dark and dense stubble that covered his jaws, Ishmael filled the galvanized-iron bath almost to the brim with hot water that smelled of woodsmoke from the fire. When Leon stepped out of it, his body glowing pinkly, Ishmael had a large towel ready for him, which he had warmed beforehand at the fire. A set of crisply ironed khakis lay on Leon's bed and beneath it stood a pair of mosquito boots, polished to a gloss.

A short time later, his hair combed and pomaded, Leon set off towards the circus-sized mess tent. Determined not to be late for the President's dinner, he was half an hour early. As he passed Percy Phillips's tent the familiar voice hailed him. 'Leon, come in here for a minute.'

He stooped through the fly to find Percy sitting with a glass

171

in his hand. He waved it to indicate the empty chair across the floor from where he sat. 'Take a pew. The President keeps a dry table. The strongest brew you'll be offered tonight is likely to be cranberry syrup.' He made a small *moue* of distaste and pointed at the bottle on the table beside Leon's chair. 'You'd better fortify yourself.'

Leon poured himself two fingers of single malt Bunnahabhain whisky and topped it up with river water that had been boiled, then cooled in a porous canvas waterbag. He tasted it. 'Elixir! I could get addicted to this stuff.'

'You can't afford it. Not yet anyway.' Percy held out his own glass. 'You'd better refresh me while you're about it.' When his glass was recharged he raised it to Leon. 'Mud in your eye!' he said.

'Up the Rifles!' Leon returned. They drank and savoured the fragrant liquor.

Then Percy said, 'By the way, did I congratulate you on your recent spectacular successes?'

'I cannot recall you doing so, sir.'

'Damn me, I could have sworn I did. I must be getting old.' His eyes twinkled. They were bright blue and clear in the wrinkled, sun-baked face. 'All right, then, listen well. I'm only going to say this once. You earned your spurs today. I'm damned proud of you.'

'Thank you, sir.' Leon was more deeply moved than he had expected to be.

'In future you can drop the "sir", and make it Percy.'

'Thank you, sir.'

'Percy, just plain Percy.'

'Thank you, Plain Percy.'

They drank in companionable silence for a while. Then Percy went on, 'I suppose you know I'll turn sixty-five next month?'

'I'd never have thought it.'

'The hell you wouldn't. You probably thought I was well over ninety.' Leon opened his mouth to protest politely, but Percy waved him to silence.

'This is probably not the time to bring up the subject, but I feel myself slowing down. The old legs are not what they once were. Nowadays every mile I walk feels like five. Two days ago I clean missed a Tommy buck at a hundred yards, a dead sitter. I need some help around here. I was thinking of taking on a partner. A junior partner. In fact, a very junior partner.'

Leon nodded cautiously, waiting to hear more.

Percy took the silver hunter watch from his pocket and snapped open the engraved lid, studied the dial, closed the lid, drained his glass and stood up. 'It would never do to keep the former President of the United States of America waiting for his dinner. He enjoys his food. Pity he doesn't feel the same way about wine. However, I've no doubt that we'll survive.'

There were ten for dinner in the big tent. Freddie Selous and Kermit had the seats of honour on each side of the President. Leon was placed at the foot of the table, in the chair furthest from his host. Teddy Roosevelt was a born raconteur. His tongue was silver, his knowledge encyclopedic, his intellect monumental, his enthusiasm infectious and his charm irresistible. He held the company spellbound as he carried them with him from one subject to another, from politics and religion to ornithology and philosophy, tropical medicine to African anthropology. Leon let the eland steak on his plate grow cold as he listened with rapt attention to the President evaluating the present international tensions in Europe. This was a subject that Penrod Ballantyne had expounded in great depth with his nephew as they had sat around the campfire on their pig-sticking forays into the veld, so it was familiar ground.

Suddenly the President singled him out. 'What is your opinion, Mr Courtney?'

Leon was dismayed as every head turned to him expectantly. His first instinct was to escape by replying that he had little interest in the subject and that he did not feel qualified to express an opinion, but then he rallied himself. 'Well, sir, you will excuse me for looking at this from a British point of view. I believe that the danger lies in the imperial aspirations of Germany and Austria. This, with the proliferation of exclusive treaties between numerous states that is now taking place across Europe. These alliances are complex but they all make provision for mutual protection and support in the event of conflict with an outsider. That could trigger a domino effect if the junior partner in such an alliance blundered into confrontation with its neighbour and called upon its more powerful ally to intervene.'

Roosevelt blinked. He had not expected such a weighty response. 'Examples, please,' he snapped.

'We believe that the British Empire can only be held together by a powerful Royal Navy. Kaiser Wilhelm the Second has made no secret of his intention to build the German Navy into the most powerful force in the world. Our empire is threatened by this. We have been forced into concluding treaties with other nations in Europe, such as Belgium, France and Serbia. Germany has treaties with Austria and Turkey, a Muslim nation. In 1905 when tension rose between Morocco and France, our new strategic partner, it precipitated a crisis across all of North Africa. Because of its alliance with Turkey, Germany was obliged to intervene against France. France is our ally, therefore we were obliged to intervene on her behalf. It was a chain effect. Only intense diplomatic negotiation and a mountain of luck averted war.'

Leon saw the expressions on the faces of his audience turning to respect, and was encouraged to continue. He made a deprecatory gesture. 'It seems to me that the world is teetering on the brink of the abyss. There are wheels within wheels, and countless threads in the web, as I know you, Mr President, of all people, will be aware.'

Roosevelt folded his arms across his chest. 'A wise head on young shoulders. You must dine with us again tomorrow evening. I would like your views on racial divisions and tensions in Africa. But now to more important affairs. My son likes to hunt with you. He tells me that the two of you have made plans to build upon your recent triumphs with elephant and rhinoceros.'

'I am delighted that Kermit wishes to continue hunting with me, sir. I enjoy his company immensely.'

'What is your next quarry to be?'

'My head tracker has discovered the lair of a very large crocodile. Would a specimen like that be of interest to the Smithsonian?'

'By all means. But that shouldn't take too long, if you know where the croc's holed up. After that what are your plans?'

'Kermit wants to take a good lion.'

'Cheeky young devil!' He punched Kermit's shoulder play-fully. 'Not content with beating me at jumbo and rhino, now you want to make it three in a row!' The company laughed with him and Teddy Roosevelt went on, 'Okay, buddy, you're on! Shall we have ten dollars on it?' The two of them shook hands to seal the bet and then the President said, 'If it's to be lions, we are fortunate to have the world's leading expert on the subject right here with us.' He turned from his son to the handsome greybeard at his other side. 'Perhaps, Selous, you would be good enough to give us some hints on how to go about it. In particular I'm interested in hearing you talk about the warning signals a lion gives the hunter before it charges. Can you describe them for us, and tell us what it's like to face such a charge?'

Selous laid down his knife and fork. 'Colonel, I have the greatest respect and admiration for the lion. Apart from his regal bearing, his strength is such that he can carry the carcass of a bullock in his jaws as he leaps over the six-foot fence of a cattle pen. His jaws are so formidable that they can crush the hardest bone as though it were chalk. He is swift as death. When he attacks, his first burst of speed covers the ground at forty miles an hour.'

With his soft but authoritative voice Selous kept them

enthralled for almost an hour until the President interrupted him. 'Thank you. I want to make an early start tomorrow, so if you gentlemen will excuse me, I'm off to bed.'

Leon walked with Percy as they made their way back to their tents. 'I'm impressed, Leon, with your political acumen, although I detected tones of your uncle Penrod in what you had to say tonight. I think Teddy Roosevelt was also impressed. It seems to me that you've managed to set both feet securely on the ladder to the stars. Just as long as you don't get his son bitten by a lion. Remember Frederick Selous's advice. They're devilishly dangerous creatures. When the lion lays back his ears and flicks his tail straight up it's the signal that he's going to charge, and you'd better be ready to shoot straight.' They had reached Percy's tent. 'Good night,' Percy said, stooped through the fly and let the canvas flap drop.

Leon and Kermit lay side by side on the riverbank behind a thin screen of reeds that Manyoro and Loikot had built the previous afternoon. The two Masai trackers lay close behind them. They had been waiting since dawn for Manyoro's crocodile to show itself. There were peep holes in the screen through which they had a view over the algae-green pool. It was almost two hundred yards to the far bank, which was shaded by a forest of tall pod mahogany trees, their branches festooned with serpentine lianas and hung with the nests of bright yellow weaver birds. The males hung upside-down under the nests they had woven, vibrating their wings and chittering excitedly to attract a watching female to fly down and take up residence. Watching their antics passed the time for Leon, but Kermit was already beginning to fidget.

Manyoro had positioned the hide on top of the steep bank directly above the game trail that ran down through the reed beds to the water's edge. There were few places around the pool that afforded such easy access to the water. The hunters had moved into the hide while it was still dark, and as the light strengthened, Manyoro pointed out to Leon where the crocodile had hidden under the bank by burrowing into the soft mud below the surface. It had wriggled and squirmed until it had stirred the bottom ooze into a porridge, then lain motionless and allowed the fine mud to settle again over its head and back. The only trace of its presence was the regular chicken-wire outline in the mud that adumbrated its scaly back. Leon could barely make out the shape of its head and the two prominent projections in the skull that held its eyes.

It had taken both himself and Manyoro some time to point out the indistinct shape of the great body to Kermit. When at last he located it Kermit, with his usual impetuosity, had decided to fire immediately at the hazy outline of the head. It had taken many minutes of whispered argument before Leon was able to persuade him that even the Winchester, despite Lusima's blessing, would not be able to drive a soft-nosed bullet through three feet of water without being stopped dead, as if by a brick wall.

It was now almost noon, and in the heat, herds of antelope and zebra had come to drink at the three other watering points around the pool, but nothing had approached the one that the crocodile had staked out. Kermit was becoming more restless by the minute: he was on the point of rebellion and would soon demand to shoot, Leon thought.

Leon's luck held. He spotted movement on their left flank. He touched Kermit's arm and pointed with his chin at the small group of Grevy's zebra emerging from the trees and making their way timidly down the game path towards the waterhole. Kermit perked up. 'Perhaps we're going to see some action at last,' he murmured, and touched Big Medicine's stock.

The Grevy's is the largest member of the horse family, larger even than a Percheron carthorse. With good reason its alternative name is the Imperial Zebra. The stallion that led them stood five feet high at the shoulder and probably weighed close to a thousand pounds. The herd moved with the utmost caution, as do all prey animals when they are aware that predators may be guarding the water. They took only a few paces before stopping to search all around for any sign of danger, then coming on a few more paces.

Kermit watched their approach with eager anticipation. Big Medicine was loaded and lay in front of him propped on a saddle bag that gave him a steady rest. At last the leading stallion stepped gingerly on to the pathway that had been cut into the bank by the hoofs of the thousands of thirsty animals that had come before him, and went down it to the narrow beach. He stood at the water's edge and made another long scrutiny of the banks around him. At last he made the fateful decision: he lowered his head and sank his velvety black muzzle into the water. As soon as he began to drink the rest of the herd followed him down the path, jostling each other in their eagerness to reach the water.

That was the moment the crocodile had waited for so patiently. He used his tail to propel himself upwards, bursting out of the mud and through the surface of the pool in a sparkling cloud of spray. The men on the bank recoiled instinctively, shocked by the size of the monstrous reptile, the speed and violence of the attack.

'God, he must be twenty feet long!' Kermit gasped.

The stallion was heavy, but this brute was four or five times heavier. Despite this difference the zebra's hoofs were anchored on solid ground and all his power was in his legs. The crocodile's were small, bent and weak. All its strength was in its tail. In a straight tug-of-war the zebra would have the advantage. The croc had to get him into deeper water where his hoofs would find no purchase. There, the croc's massive tail would give it an overwhelming advantage.

It did not attempt to seize the stallion in its jaws and try to drag it in, but swung its head like a battle club. With all that weight and power behind the blow it was so fast that the eye could barely follow it. The hideous horny skull crashed into the side of the zebra's head, breaking bone and stunning him. He fell on his side in four feet of water, legs kicking convulsively above the surface, thrashing head from side to side as he started to drown. Now the croc surged forward, seized the zebra's muzzle in its jaws and dragged him into the deep water. It began a series of barrel rolls, churning the water to foam, wringing the zebra's neck as though he were a chicken, at the same time disorientating and drowning him. The crocodile kept rolling until the last glimmer of life had been extinguished in the striped body, then released its grip and backed away.

Twenty yards offshore, it hung on the surface, watching the body of the dead zebra for any last signs of life. The body floated almost completely submerged, with only one back leg sticking above the surface, pointing skywards. The crocodile was fully broadside to the hunters, with only the top of its back and the upper half of its head exposed. The head was rendered all the more hideous by its fixed, sardonic grin.

Kermit was stretched prone behind the saddle bag with the rifle tucked into his shoulder, and his cheek pressed to the stock's comb. His left eye was tight shut and the right was narrowed with concentration, levelled behind the gun sights.

Leon leaned closer to him. 'Aim for the corner of his smile, exactly at water level, under the eye.' The last words were still on his lips when the Winchester roared. Watching through the binoculars Leon saw the tiny splash as the bullet flicked the surface directly under the wicked little eye, then went on to smash into the croc's head.

'Perfect!' Leon shouted, as he jumped to his feet.

'*Piga!*' Manyoro sang out. 'He is hit!'

'*Ngwenya kufa!* The crocodile is dead!' Loikot shrieked with laughter as he sprang to his feet and launched into a wild, leaping dance. The crocodile hurled its entire body high out of the water, thrashing the surface with its tail in a series of gigantic convulsions. It snapped its jaws, then again leaped high out of the water and fell back with a mighty splash, spinning over and over, its tail kicking up waves that broke heavily against the beach.

'*Ngwenya kufa!*' the men on the bank exulted, as the crocodile's death frenzy reached a crescendo.

Abruptly the massive body froze, the tail arched and went rigid, and the crocodile lay motionless on the surface for a moment, then sank, disappearing beneath the green waters.

'We're going to lose him!' Kermit shouted anxiously, and hopped on one leg as he pulled off his boots.

'What the hell do you think you're doing?' Leon grabbed him.

'I'm going to pull him out.'

Kermit struggled to free himself, but Leon held him easily. 'Listen, you idiot, you go into that water and the croc's grandpapa will be waiting to meet you.'

'But we're going to lose him! I have to fish him out!'

'No, you don't! Manyoro and Loikot will wait here until tomorrow when the croc will have blown up with gas and floated to the surface. Then you and I will come back and put ropes on it.'

Kermit quietened down a little. 'He's going to be washed away downstream.'

'The river is no longer flowing. This is a blind pool. Your croc ain't going anywhere, chum.'

It was late afternoon, and they were sitting under the fly of Leon's tent, drinking tea and endlessly going over the details of the crocodile hunt, when there was an excited stir and a hubbub ran through the encampment, indicating the imminent return of the President. Kermit jumped up. 'Come on!' he said to Leon. 'Let's go see what my old man's bagged.' He strode away, but turned back. 'Don't say anything about the croc. He won't believe it until he sees it.'

Teddy Roosevelt rode into camp, and they were there to greet him when he dismounted and tossed the reins to a syce. He smiled when he saw Kermit, and there was a triumphant twinkle in the eyes behind the steel-rimmed spectacles.

'Hi, Dad,' Kermit called. 'Did you have a good day?'

'Not bad. I opened the lion account.'

Kermit's face fell. 'You got a lion?'

'Yep!' the President affirmed, still smiling. He jerked his thumb over his shoulder. Kermit saw a party of bearers coming down the trail through the trees. They were carrying a tan body slung on a pole between them. They dumped their burden next to the taxidermy tent, and three of the Smithsonian scientists came out to view the day's bag. They cut the ropes that bound the paws of the lion to the pole, and stretched the carcass on the ground to measure and photograph it.

Kermit laughed with relief. Even he, who knew little about them, could see that this was an immature lioness. 'Hey, Dad!' He chuckled as he turned to his father. 'If you call that a real lion, I might as well call myself the President of the United States of America. She's a baby.'

'You're right, son,' his father agreed, still smiling smugly. 'Poor little sweetheart, I had to shoot her. She wouldn't let us get close to the body of her mate. She guarded it ferociously. At least we can have her mounted as part of a family group in one of the showcases in the African Hall at the museum. What do you think?' He directed the question at George Lemmon, the chief of the team of scientists.

'We're delighted to have her, sir. She's a fine specimen. Her hide is unblemished, it still has the immature spotting of a cub, and her teeth are perfect.'

The President looked back over his shoulder and remarked comfortably, 'Oh, good! They're bringing the male in now.' Another team of bearers was just emerging from the forest. Four were staggering under the weight of the huge body they were carrying.

'Good gracious! That looks like a very fine lion to me.' Frederick Selous had come from his tent in his shirtsleeves, carrying his sketchpad. 'We must make sure that those fellows handle it carefully. It would never do to have the skin abraded or damaged.'

The bearers came up with the lion swinging on the pole to the rhythm of their trot. They lowered it gently to the ground beside the lioness. Sammy Edwards, the head taxidermist, stretched it out carefully and ran his measuring tape from the tip of its onyx-black nose to the black tuft at the end of its tail. 'Nine feet one inch.' He looked up at the President. 'That's a great lion, sir, the largest I've ever had a tape on.'

After dinner that evening Kermit came to Leon's tent. He brought with him a silver hip flask of Jack Daniel's whiskey. They turned the lamp low, sat in the canvas chairs under the mosquito net and kept their voices to a whisper.

'Andrew Fagan was the guest of honour this evening,' Kermit told Leon. In response to Kermit's invitation Fagan had arrived in camp during the afternoon. 'He got on well with my father. The old man enjoyed having a new audience.'

They were silent for a few minutes, then Kermit went on, 'I don't grudge it to my father. He's as keen as any of us to get good trophies, and he works like a man half his age. You weren't there, of course, but I can tell you that he did rather overdo it at dinner tonight. He didn't actually boast or gloat over me but he came damned close. Of course Fagan was lapping it all up.'

Leon studied the amber liquid in his glass and murmured sympathetically in agreement.

'I mean it was a good lion, a fine lion, but it wasn't the best lion anyone in Africa has ever taken, was it?' Kermit asked earnestly.

'You're absolutely right. It was a very big-bodied lion, but its mane was a ruff. It wasn't much bigger than a lady's ostrich-feather boa,' Leon assured him, and Kermit burst out laughing, then checked himself with a hand over his mouth. They were more than a hundred yards from the President's tent, but the great man expected silence in camp after lights out.

'A lady's boa,' Kermit repeated delightedly, then made an attempt at a feminine falsetto, 'Are we off to the ballet, my darlings?' They savoured the joke for a while and pulled at the Jack Daniel's.

Then Kermit said, 'Sometimes I almost hate my father. Does that make me evil?'

'No, it makes you human.'

'Tell me honestly, Leon, what did you really think of that lion?'

'We can beat it.'

'Do you think so? Do you honestly think so?'

'Your father's lion hasn't a single black hair in its boa. Not one,' he said, and Kermit had to smother another burst of laughter at the word 'boa'. The Jack Daniel's was warming his belly and lifting his spirits.

When his friend had controlled his mirth, Leon repeated, 'We can beat it. We can get a bigger and blacker lion. Manyoro and Loikot are Masai. They have a special affinity with the big cats. They say we can do better, and I believe them.'

'Tell me how we're going to do it.' Kermit gazed solemnly into his face.

'We'll make up a flying column and ride ahead of the main safari into the country beyond Masailand, where the lions haven't been picked over for the last thousand years by the *morani*. We can move many times faster than the rest of them because they're limited to the pace of the porters. In a few days we can have a lead of a hundred miles or more. When does the President plan to move on north, do you know?'

'My father told us at dinner tonight that he plans to stay here for a while. It seems that a few days ago the local guides led him and Mr Selous to a large swamp about twenty miles east of here. Near it they found a set of tracks that Mr Selous believes may be those of a male sitatunga antelope, but they were larger than the species he himself discovered in 1881 in the Okavango delta. That one is named after him, *Limnotragus selousi*. He's convinced my father that this may be an entirely new sub-species. To my father the opportunity of discovering a species previously unknown to science is irresistible. He dreams of a sitatunga named *Limnotragus roosevelti*. He would sacrifice his first-born for that.' He grinned. 'I expect he'll want to hang around here until he finds this buck or convinces himself it doesn't exist.'

'I can understand his interest. What do you know about the sitatunga?'

'Not much,' Kermit admitted.

'It's a fascinating creature, very rare and elusive. It's the only truly aquatic antelope. Its hoofs are so long and splayed that on land it can barely walk, but in deep mud or water it's as agile as a catfish. When threatened it ducks under the surface and can remain submerged for hours with only the tips of its nostrils above the water.'

'Hell, I'd love to get one of those,' Kermit said.

'You can't have everything, chum. Lion or sitatunga, it's your choice.' Leon did not wait for a reply. 'The President's plans suit us well enough. We can leave them to it and ride on the day after tomorrow. Now, do you suppose there may be another noggin lingering at the bottom of that flask of yours? If there is, I don't think we should let it go to waste, do you?'

They spent the following day hastily assembling the personnel and equipment for their flying column. They picked out a string of six ponies, and three pack mules. Then, with the high spirits of schoolboys escaping the surveillance of their headmaster, they rode northwards.

In the late afternoon of the third day they were following the course of a small unnamed river when there was a shout from the Masai trackers, who were a hundred yards ahead.

They gesticulated and pointed at a swift feline shape that had broken out of a patch of scrub and was darting away across the open floodplain, heading for the cover of the thicker forest beyond.

'What is it?' Kermit rose in his stirrups and shaded his eyes with his hat.

'Leopard,' Leon told him. 'A big tom.'

'It has no spots,' Kermit protested.

'You can't see them at this distance.'

'Can I ride him down?'

'Gunfire won't disturb any lions that hear it,' Leon assured him, 'not like elephant. They have the curiosity of cats. A few shots might even attract them.' Kermit needed to hear no more. He let out a wild cowboy yell and, with his hat, urged his mount into a mad gallop, at the same time drawing Big Medicine from her boot under his right knee and brandishing it over his head.

'Here we go again, folks.' Leon laughed. 'Another stealthy, carefully planned stalk with Sir Quick Bullet.' He kicked his own horse into a gallop, and raced in pursuit. The leopard heard the commotion, stopped and sat on his haunches, gazing back in astonishment. Then he realized how precarious his situation was, whipped around and raced away, stretching out with each bound, long, sleek and graceful.

'Yee-ha! Up and at him!' Kermit howled, and even Leon was infected by the excitement of the headlong charge.

'View halloo! Gone away!' He gave the old fox-hunting cry and lay flat along his pony's neck, pushing him hard, both hands on the reins. The rush of the wind in his face was intoxicating. Abandoning all restraint they raced each other across the plain.

The nose of Leon's pony was creeping up to the level of Kermit's boot. He looked back under his own armpit, saw Leon gaining, slapped his hat against his mount's neck and banged his heels into its flanks. 'Let's move!' he urged it. 'Come on, baby. Get the lead out!' At that moment his horse stepped in a suricate hole. Its right fore snapped, with a sound like a whiplash, and it went down as though it had been shot through the brain. Kermit was thrown high and clear. He hit the ground with his shoulder and the side of his face. His rifle flew from his hand and he rolled like a ball under the pounding hoofs of Leon's horse. Leon pulled the mare's head around and they just managed to avoid stepping on Kermit. She responded to the pressure of reins, bit and spur, tossing her head violently. They rode back to the downed rider. Kermit's horse was struggling to rise but its foreleg was fractured clean through just above the fetlock joint, the hoof dangling loosely. Kermit was lying still, stretched out on the hard earth.

He's killed himself. God! What am I going to tell the President? Leon agonized, as he kicked his feet out of the stirrups. He threw his right leg over his horse's neck and dropped to the ground. He ran to Kermit, but by the time he reached him his friend was sitting up groggily. The skin had been scoured from the left side of his face, his eyebrow was torn half off, and hung over his eye in a loose flap, and the eye itself was bunged up with dust.

'Mistake!' he mumbled, and spat out a mouthful of blood and mud. 'That was a big mistake!'

Leon laughed with relief. 'You trying to tell me it wasn't deliberate? I thought you did it just to impress me.'

Kermit ran his tongue around the inside of his mouth. 'No teeth missing,' he announced, speaking as though his palate was cleft.

'Luckily you fell on your head or you might have damaged yourself.' Leon knelt beside him, took his head between both hands and turned it from side to side, examining the eye. 'Try not to blink like that, or grit will scratch the eyeball.'

'Easily enough said. How about "try not to breathe" as your next stupid instruction?'

Ishmael galloped up on his mule and handed Leon a waterbag.

'Hold his eye open, Ishmael,' Leon ordered, then poured water into it, sluicing out most of the mud. Then he handed

the bag to Kermit. 'Rinse your mouth and wash your face.'
The two Masai were squatting close at hand where they could
have a good view of the proceedings, which they were discussing with relish. 'Will you two hyenas stop gloating, and set up
the pup tent, then lay out Popoo Hima's blanket roll. I want
to get him out of the sun.'

While they helped Kermit into the little tent, Leon drew
the big Holland from its boot on his saddle and shot the
maimed horse. He made it seem cold and clinical, but his
empathy with horses was intense, and even though it was a
mercy killing, it tore at his conscience.

'Get the saddle and tack off that poor creature,' he told
Manyoro, as he ejected the empty brass cartridge case and
slipped the rifle back into its sheath. He hurried to the little
tent and stooped through the entrance. 'Where's Big Medicine?' Kermit demanded, and tried to get up.

Leon pushed him down. 'I'll send Manyoro to find it.' He
raised his voice: 'Manyoro! Bring the bwana's bunduki.'
Then he held a finger in front of Kermit's eyes. 'Watch it.'
He moved it slowly from side to side, then nodded, satisfied.
'Despite your best efforts, it doesn't seem that you've managed
to concuss yourself, thank God. Now let's take a look at the
place where your left eyebrow was once attached to your face.'
He examined the damage closely. 'I'm going to have to put in
a few stitches.'

Kermit looked alarmed. 'What do you know about stitching
people up?'

'I've stitched up plenty of horses and dogs.'

'I ain't no horse or dog.'

'No, those animals are pretty smart.' To Ishmael he said,
'Fetch your sewing kit.'

At that moment Manyoro appeared in the entrance, his
expression mournful. He held a separate piece of the Winchester in each hand. 'She is broken,' he said in Kiswahili.

Kermit grabbed the shattered pieces from him. 'Oh, hell
and damnation!' he moaned. The butt stock had snapped
at the neck of the pistol grip and the front sight had been

knocked off. It was obvious that the rifle could not be fired. Kermit cradled it as though it were a sick child. 'What am I going to do?' He looked at Leon pitifully. 'Can you repair it?'

'Yes, but not until we get back to camp and I can find my tool-kit. I'll have to bind that butt with the green skin of an elephant's ear. When it dries, it'll be hard as iron and better than new.'

'What about the front sight?'

'If we can't find the original, I'll hand-file one from a piece of metal and solder it in place.'

'How long will all that take?'

'A week or so.' He saw Kermit's stricken expression and tried to pull the punch a little. 'Maybe a bit less. Depends how soon we can find a fresh elephant ear and how quickly it dries. Now, keep still while I sew you up.'

Kermit was in such distress that he seemed inured to the primitive surgery Leon inflicted. First he washed the wound with a diluted solution of iodine, then got busy with needle and thread. Either procedure was more than enough to make a strong man weep, but Kermit seemed more concerned with Big Medicine than his own suffering.

'What am I going to shoot with in the meantime?' he lamented, still holding the rifle.

'Luckily I brought my old service .303 Enfield as a back-up.' Leon ran the needle through a flap of skin.

Kermit grimaced but clung to the subject doggedly. 'That's a pop gun.' He sounded affronted. 'It may be fine for Tommy, impala or even human beings, but it's much too light for lion!'

'If you get in close and put the bullet in the right place, it'll do the job.'

'Close? I know what that means to you! You want me to stick the barrel in the bloody cat's earhole.'

'Very well, you go ahead in your usual style and blaze away at half a mile. But I don't think that'll work.'

Kermit thought about it for a while, but he didn't seem overjoyed with the idea. 'How about you lend me that big old Holland of yours?'

'I love you like my own brother, but I'd rather lend you my little sister for the night.'

'Have you got a little sister?' Kermit asked, with sudden interest. 'Is she pretty?'

'I don't have a sister,' Leon lied, anxious to protect his siblings from Kermit's attentions, 'and I'm not going to lend you my rifle.'

'Well, I don't want your pathetic little .303,' Kermit said petulantly.

'Good! Then I suggest you ask Manyoro to lend you his spear.'

Manyoro grinned expectantly at the mention of his name.

Kermit shook his head and gave him the sum total of his Kiswahili: '*Mazuri sana*, Manyoro. *Hakuna matata!* Very good, Manyoro. Don't worry.' The Masai looked disappointed, and Kermit turned back to Leon. 'Okay, pal. I'll try a few shots with your pop gun.'

I n the morning Kermit's eye was swollen and closed, and his torso was decorated with a few spectacular bruises. Fortunately the damage was to his left eye, so his shooting eye was still clear. Leon blazed the bark of a fever tree to give him a target at sixty paces, then handed him the .303. 'At that range she'll throw an inch high, so hold the pip of the foresight just a touch under,' he advised. Kermit fired two shots, and they bracketed the mark, a finger's breadth apart.

'Wow! Not bad for a beginner.' Kermit had impressed himself. He cheered up visibly.

'Pretty darned good even for a marksman like Popoo Hima,' Leon agreed. 'But just remember, don't shoot at anything that's over the horizon.'

Kermit did not acknowledge the pleasantry. 'Let's go find a lion,' he said.

They camped that evening beside a small waterhole, which still contained water from the last rains. They rolled into their blankets as soon as they had eaten, and both men were asleep within minutes.

In the wee hours Leon shook Kermit awake. He sat up groggily. 'What's happening? What time is it?'

'Don't worry about the time, just listen,' Leon told him.

Kermit looked around and saw that the two Masai and Ishmael were sitting by the fire. They had fed it with wood chips and the flames danced brightly. Their faces were intent and rapt. They were listening. The silence drew out for many minutes.

'What are we waiting for?' Kermit demanded.

'Patience! Just keep your ears open,' Leon chided him. Suddenly the night was filled with sound, a mighty bass booming, rising and falling, like waves driven by a hurricane. It made the skin tingle and the hair rise along the forearms and up the back of the neck. Kermit threw aside his blanket and sprang to his feet. The sound died away in a series of sobbing grunts. The silence afterwards seemed to grip every man and beast in creation.

'What the hell was that?' Kermit gasped.

'A lion. A big dominant male lion proclaiming his kingdom,' Leon told him quietly. Manyoro added something in Maa, then he and Loikot laughed at the joke.

'What did he say?' Kermit demanded.

'He said that even the bravest man is twice frightened by a lion. The first time when he hears his roar, the second and last time when he meets the beast face to face.'

'He's right about the first time,' Kermit admitted. 'It's an incredible sound. But how do you know it's a big male and not a lioness?'

'How would I know the voice of Enrico Caruso from Dame Nellie Melba's?'

'Let's go shoot him.'

'Good plan, chum. I'll hold the candle and you fire. It should be easy.'

'Then what are we going to do?'

'I, for one, am going to climb under my blanket and try to

get some sleep. You should do the same. Tomorrow is going to be a busy day.' Once again they stretched out beside the fire, but they were both far from sleep when another thunderous roar echoed through the night.

'Listen to him!' Kermit murmured. 'The son of a gun's inviting me out to play. How can I sleep with that racket going on?' The last sawing grunts died into silence, and then came another sound, almost a distant echo of the first roar, far away and faint. They shot upright, and the Masai exclaimed.

'What the hell was that?' Kermit asked. 'It sounded like another lion.'

'That's exactly what it was,' Leon assured him.

'Is it a brother of the first?'

'Anything but. It's the first lion's rival and enemy to the death.' Kermit was about to ask another question, but Leon stopped him. 'Let me talk to the Masai.' The discussion was in quick-fire Maa, and at the end Leon turned back to Kermit. 'All right, this is what's going on out there. The first lion is the older and dominant male. This is his territory and he almost certainly has a large harem of females and their cubs. But he's getting old now and his powers are fading. The second male is young and strong, in his prime. He feels ready to challenge for the territory and the harem. He's prowling the boundary and getting up courage for the death battle. The old man's trying to frighten him off.'

'Manyoro could tell all that from listening to a few roars?'

'Both Manyoro and Loikot speak lion language fluently,' Leon told him, with a straight face.

'Tonight I'll believe anything you tell me. So we've got not one but two big lions?'

'Yes, and they won't be moving far. The old man dare not leave the door open, and the youngster can smell those ladies. He won't be going anywhere either.'

After this, there was no question of anyone sleeping. They sat at the fire, planning the hunt with the Masai and drinking Ishmael's number-one very best coffee until the first rays of the sun gilded the treetops. Then they ate breakfast of Ishmael's renowned ostrich-egg omelettes and a batch of his equally famous scones, hot from the pot. One ostrich egg was the equivalent of two dozen large chicken eggs, but there were no leftovers. While they mopped up the last drops of grease from the pan with pieces of scone, Ishmael and the Masai broke camp and loaded the mules. The air was still sweet and cool when they rode out to see what the day would bring.

A mile down the riverbank they surprised a herd of several hundred buffalo returning from the water. Leon dropped two with consecutive shots from the left and right barrels of the Holland. They sliced open the paunches so that the smell of carrion would be broadcast on the sultry breeze, then the mules dragged them into the most favourable positions, with open ground around them and no thick cover close at hand into which a wounded lion could escape. While they were positioning the bait, the porters cut bundles of green branches and covered the carcasses so that vultures and hyena would have difficulty reaching them. On the other hand such a flimsy covering would not deter a big lion for more than a moment.

They rode on down the river, and into the area where the lions had been roaring during the night. Every mile or two Leon shot whatever large mammal offered itself: giraffe, rhino or buffalo. By sunset they had laid down, over a stretch of ten miles, a string of highly attractive lion bait.

That night they were again deprived of a full night's sleep by the roaring and counter-roaring of the two antagonists. At one time the older lion was so close to where they lay that the ground trembled under their blanket rolls with the imperious power of his voice, but this time there was no answer from his challenger.

'The young lion has found one of our baits.' Manyoro interpreted his silence. 'He is feeding on it.'

'I thought lions never ate carrion,' said Kermit.

'Don't you believe it. They're as lazy as domestic tabbies. They'll eat a hand-out for preference, never mind how stinking rotten it may be. They only go to the trouble of making their own kills when all else fails.'

Two hours after midnight the old lion had stopped roaring, and the darkness was still.

'Now he's found a bait for himself,' Manyoro observed. 'We'll have them both tomorrow.'

'How many lions am I allowed on my licence?' Kermit asked.

'Enough to satisfy even you,' Leon told him. 'Lions are vermin in British East Africa. You may shoot all you wish.'

'Good! I want both these big guys. I want to take them home to show my father.'

'So do I,' Leon agreed fervently. 'So do I.'

As soon as it was light enough for the trackers to read the sign, they started back along the chain of bait. Leon and Kermit wore heavy jackets, for the morning was chilly, and perfumed like a fine Chablis.

The first three baits they visited were untouched, although the vultures brooded dark, hunch-backed and morose as undertakers in the treetops around them. When they came to the fourth, Leon halted a few hundred yards from it and, with the binoculars, carefully glassed the pile of branches that covered it.

'You're wasting time, pal. There ain't nothing there,' Kermit told him.

'On the contrary,' Leon said softly, without lowering the glasses.

'What do you mean?' Kermit's interest quickened.

'I mean there's a big male lion right there.'

'No!' Kermit protested. 'I don't see a damned thing.'

'Here.' Leon handed him the glasses. 'Use these.'

Kermit focused the lenses and stared through them for a minute. 'I still don't see a lion.'

'Look where the branches have been pulled open. You can see the striped haunches of the zebra in the gap . . .'

'Yeah! I've got that.'

'Now look just over the top of the zebra. Do you see two small dark lumps on the far side?'

'Yup, but that's not a lion.'

'Those are the tops of his ears. He's lying flat behind the zebra watching us.'

'My God! You're right! I saw an ear flick,' he exclaimed. 'Which lion is it? The young or the old one?'

Leon conferred quickly with Manyoro, Loikot interjecting his own learned opinions every few sentences. At last he turned back to Kermit. 'Take a deep breath, chum. I have news for you. It's the big one. Manyoro calls him the lion of all lions.'

'What do we do now? Do we ride him down?'

'No, we walk him up.' Leon was already swinging down from the saddle and drawing the big Holland from its boot. He opened the action, drew the brass cartridges from the breeches and exchanged them for a fresh pair from his bandolier. Kermit followed his example with the little Lee-Enfield. The syces came forward and took the reins of their mounts and led them to the rear, then laid down their waterbags, and squatted to take a little snuff. Soon they jumped up, hefted their lion spears and stabbed the air with bloodthirsty grunts, prancing high with each thrust of the long bright blades, priming themselves for battle.

As soon as all the hunters were ready, Leon gave Kermit his instructions. 'You'll take the lead. I'll be three paces behind you so I don't block your field of fire. Walk slowly and steadily, but not directly towards him. Make it seem that you're going to pass about twenty paces on his right. Don't look directly at him. Keep your eyes on the ground ahead of you. If you stare at him you'll spook him into running or charging prematurely. At about fifty paces he'll give you a warning growl. You'll see his tail start to thrash. Don't stop and don't hurry. Keep walking. At about thirty paces he'll stand up and confront you head-on. At this point an average lion will either run or charge. This one is different. Sparring with the young pretender has put him in a belligerent, reckless mood. His blood is up. He'll charge. He'll give you three or four seconds, then come. You must hit him before he starts to move or before you can blink he'll be doing forty miles an hour straight at you. When I call the shot, take him just under the chin in the centre of his chest. These cats are soft. Even the .303 will put him down. However, you must keep shooting as long as he's on his feet.'

'You're not going to fire, are you?'

'Not until he starts chewing your head off, chummy. Now, walk!' They moved out in open order, Kermit leading, Leon a few paces back and the two Masai coming up behind him, marching shoulder to shoulder with their *assegais* presented.

'Excellent,' Leon encouraged Kermit softly. 'Keep up that speed and direction. You're doing fine.' Within another fifty paces Leon saw the lion lift his head a few inches. The dome of his skull was now visible and he raised his mane in a threatening gesture. It was like a small haystack, dense and black as Hades. Kermit hesitated in mid-stride.

'Steady, steady. Keep moving!' Leon cautioned him. They walked on, and now they could see the lion's eyes under the great bush of the mane. They were cold, yellow and inexorable. Another ten slow paces and the lion growled. It was a low, deep, infinitely menacing sound, like distant summer thunder. It stopped Kermit in his tracks and he turned to face the beast head-on, at the same time starting to bring up the long rifle. That movement, and Kermit's direct stare, triggered the lion.

'Look out! He's going to come,' Leon said sharply, but the lion was already in full charge, rushing at Kermit, grunting in short staccato bursts like the steam pistons on a speeding locomotive, black mane fully erect with rage, long tail swinging from side to side. He was enormous, and growing bigger as he closed the gap between them with every stride.

'Shoot him!' Leon's voice was lost in the sharp crack of

the .303. The bullet, hastily aimed, flew over the lion's back, and kicked up a spurt of dust two hundred yards behind him. Kermit was quick on the reload. His next shot was low and struck the ground between the beast's forelegs. The lion kept boring straight in, a yellow blur of speed, grunting with heart-stopping fury, kicking up dust and slashing his tail.

Sweet Christ! Leon thought. It's going to get him down! He swung up the Holland focusing all his mental and physical powers on the great maned head and the open grunting jaws. He was only barely conscious of his forefinger tightening on the front trigger. The instant before the lion crashed his full 550-pound body weight into Kermit's chest at forty miles an hour, Kermit fired his third shot.

The muzzle of the .303 Lee-Enfield was almost touching the shiny black button of the lion's nose. The light bullet struck the very tip of the snout and lanced through into the brain. The tan body turned slack and flabby as a sack of chaff. Kermit hurled himself aside at the last instant and the lion piled up in a heap on the spot where he had been standing. He stared down at it, his hands shaking, breath sobbing in his throat. Sweat trickled into his eyes.

'Shoot him again,' Leon shouted, but Kermit's legs gave way under him and he sat down. Leon ran up and stood over the lion. At point-blank range he shot him through the heart. Then he turned back to where Kermit was sitting with his head between his knees. 'Are you okay, chum?' he asked, with deep concern.

Slowly Kermit raised his head and stared at him as though he was a stranger. He shook his head in confusion. Leon sat beside him and put a muscular arm around his shoulders. 'Easy does it, chum. You did a great job. You stood to the charge. You never broke. You stood there and shot him down like a hero. If your daddy had been here he would have been proud of you.'

Kermit's eyes cleared. He took a deep breath and then he said huskily, 'Do you think so?'

'I damn well know so,' Leon said, with utter conviction.

'You didn't shoot, did you?' Kermit was still as unsteady as a long-distance runner regaining his breath after a hard race.

'No, I didn't. You killed him yourself, without any help from me,' Leon assured him.

Kermit did not speak again but sat staring quietly at the magnificent body of the lion. Leon remained at his side. Manyoro and Loikot started to circle them in a shuffling, stiff-legged, hopping and leaping dance.

'They're about to perform the lion dance in your honour,' Leon explained.

Manyoro began to sing. His voice was powerful and true.

> *'We are the young lions.*
> *When we roar the earth shivers.*
> *Our spears are our fangs.*
> *Our spears are our claws . . .'*

After each line they sprang high with the ease of birds taking to flight and Loikot came in with the refrain. When the song ended they went to the dead lion and dipped their fingers in his blood. Then they came back to where Kermit still sat. Manyoro stooped over him and smeared a streak of blood down his forehead.

> *'You are Masai.*
> *You are morani.*
> *You are a lion warrior.*
> *You are my brother.'*

He stepped back and Loikot took his place in front of Kermit. He also anointed Kermit's face, painting red stripes down each cheek, then intoned,

> *'You are Masai.*
> *You are morani.*
> *You are a lion warrior.*
> *You are my brother.'*

They squatted in front of him and clapped their hands rhythmically.

'They are making you a Masai and a blood brother. It is the highest honour they can offer you. You should acknowledge it.'

'You also are my brothers,' Kermit said. 'Even when we are divided by great waters, I shall remember you all the days of my life.'

Leon translated for him and the Masai murmured with pleasure.

'Tell Popoo Hima that he does us great honour,' said Manyoro.

Kermit stood up and went to the body of the lion. He knelt in front of it as though at a shrine. He did not touch it immediately, but his face shone with a particular radiance as he studied the enormous head. The mane started two inches above the opaque yellow eyes and ran back, wave after wave of dense black hair, over the skull and neck, over the massive shoulders, under the chest, and only ended halfway down the broad back.

'Leave him be,' Manyoro told Leon. 'Popoo Hima is taking the spirit of his lion into his own heart. It is right and fitting. It is the way of the true warrior.'

The sun had set before Kermit left the lion and came to the small fire where Leon sat alone. Ishmael had placed a log at each side to act as seats and another, up-ended, on which he had set two mugs and a bottle. As Kermit sat down facing Leon he glanced at the bottle. 'Bunnahabhain whisky. Thirty years old,' Leon told him. 'I begged it from Percy this time in case something like this happened and we were forced to celebrate. Sadly, he only let me have half a bottle. Said it's really too good for the likes of you.' Leon poured it into the mugs, then reached across to hand one to Kermit.

'I feel different,' Kermit said, and took a sip.

'I understand,' Leon said. 'Today was your baptism by fire.'

'Yes!' Kermit answered vehemently. 'That's it exactly. It was a mystic, almost religious experience. Something strange and wonderful has happened to me. I feel as though I'm somebody else, not the old me, somebody better than I ever was before.' He groped for words. 'I feel as though I've been reborn. The other me was afraid and uncertain. This one is no longer afraid. Now I know I can meet the world on my own terms.'

'I understand,' Leon said. 'Rite of passage.'

'Has it happened to you?' Kermit asked.

Leon's eyes narrowed with pain as he remembered the pale naked bodies lying crucified on the baked earth, heard again the flitting of Nandi arrows and remembered the weight of Manyoro on his back. 'Yes . . . but it was nothing like today.'

'Tell me about it.'

Leon shook his head. 'These are things we should not talk about too much. Words can only sully and belittle their significance.'

'Of course. It's something very private.'

'Exactly,' Leon said, and raised his mug. 'We don't have to labour it. We know it in our hearts. The Masai have a description for this shared truth. They say simply, "brothers of the warrior blood".'

They sat for a long time in companionable silence, then Kermit said, 'I don't think I'll be able to sleep tonight.'

'I'll keep vigil with you,' Leon replied.

After a while they began to recall and discuss the tiniest details of the day's hunt, how the first growl had sounded, how big the lion had appeared as he rose to his full height, how swiftly he came. But they skirted the emotional aspects. The whisky level sank slowly in the bottle.

A little before midnight they were startled to hear horses approaching the camp in the darkness, and voices speaking English. Kermit started up. 'Who the hell can that be?'

'I think I can guess.' Leon chuckled as a figure in riding breeches and a slouch hat came into the firelight. 'Good evening, Mr Roosevelt, Mr Courtney. I was just passing and thought I'd drop in to say howdy.'

'Mr Andrew Fagan, I hope you don't mind if I call you a

bloody liar. You've been shadowing us night and day for almost two weeks. My trackers have picked up your spoor on most days.'

'Come, come, Mr Courtney.' Fagan laughed. 'Shadowing is too strong a word. But it's true that I have a more than passing interest in what the two of you have been up to, as has the rest of the world.' He removed his hat. 'May we visit with you for a spell?'

'I'm afraid you've come a little late,' Kermit said. 'As you can see, the bottle is well-nigh empty.'

'By some remarkable twist of fate, I have a spare in my pack.' Fagan called to his photographer, 'Carl, will you please find that bottle of Jack Daniel's for us, then come join the party?' When they had all settled down in the firelight and taken the first taste from their mugs, Fagan asked, 'Anything interesting happen today? We heard some shooting from your direction.'

'Tell him, Leon!' Kermit was bubbling over, but he didn't want to appear a braggart.

'Well, now that you mention it, this afternoon Mr Roosevelt managed to shoot the lion we've been looking for since the start of our safari.'

'A lion!' Fagan spilled a few drops of whisky. 'Now that's real news. How does it compare with the one taken a week or so ago by the President?'

'You'll have to judge that for yourself,' Leon said.

'May we see it?'

'Come this way,' Kermit told him eagerly and, picking up a burning brand from the fire, he led them to where the lion lay. Up to now it had been hidden by the night. He held the flame high to illuminate the scene.

'Well, damn me to hell, that's a monster!' said Fagan, and turned quickly to his photographer. 'Carl, get your camera.' For almost another hour he persuaded Kermit and Leon to pose with the trophy, although Kermit needed little persuasion. Their vision was starred with the multiple explosions of flash powder when finally they returned to the fire and took up their mugs again. Fagan pulled out his notepad. 'So, tell us, Mr Roosevelt, how does it feel to have done what you did today?'

Kermit thought about that for a while. 'Mr Fagan, are you a hunter? It will make it easier to explain if you are.'

'No, sir. I'm a golfer, not a hunter.'

'Okay. For me this lion was like you shooting a hole-in-one in the Open Championship, during a playoff with Willie Anderson for the title.'

'Wonderful description! You have a gift with words, sir.' Fagan wrote swiftly. 'Now tell me the whole story, blow by blow, from when you first saw that huge beast to the moment of the kill.' Kermit was still wrought up with excitement and whiskey. He left nothing out, and did not stint on the use of hyperbole. He appealed regularly to Leon for confirmation of the finer details. 'Isn't that so? Isn't that exactly what happened?' And Leon backed him up loyally, as a hunter is duty-bound to do for his client. At last, when the story was told, they sat in silence digesting the details. Leon was about to suggest that it was time for everybody to turn in when a thunderous roar came from the darkness.

'What was that?' Andrew Fagan was alarmed. 'What in God's name was that?'

'That's the lion we're going to hunt tomorrow,' said Kermit, off-handedly.

'Another lion? Tomorrow?'

'Yup.'

'Mind if we tag along?' Fagan asked, and Leon opened his mouth to refuse, but Kermit beat him to it.

'Sure. Why not? You're welcome, Mr Fagan.'

E arly the next morning the skinners began work on the lion, and coated the wet skin with a thick layer of rock salt.

'Wait here when you've finished,' Leon told them. 'I'll send Loikot to fetch you.'

As the light came up out of the east he watched the treeline across the glade. As soon as he could make out individual leaves against the dawn sky, he said, 'Shooting light! Mount up, please, gentlemen.' When they were all in the saddle, he gave a hand signal to Manyoro. With the two Masai trackers leading they moved out in close order. Gradually Leon eased his pony back into the column until he was riding stirrup to stirrup with Fagan. He spoke softly but firmly. 'Mr Roosevelt was very generous to allow you to join the hunt. If it had been up to me I would have refused. However, you may have underestimated the danger involved. If things go wrong somebody could get badly hurt. I'm going to insist that you keep well back, and safely out of the way.'

'Of course, Mr Courtney. Anything you say.'

'By "well back", I mean at least two hundred yards. I will be taking care of my client. I won't be able to look after you as well.'

'I understand. Two hundred yards away and as quiet as a mouse it shall be, sir. You won't even know we're there.'

Manyoro led them two miles to the next lion bait. As they approached the bloated carcass of the old giraffe, a large colony of vultures that had been feeding on it launched into flight and a clan of a dozen or more hyenas fled in grotesque panic, their tails twisted over their backs, giggling shrilly, blood and offal smearing their grinning jaws.

'Hapana.' Manyoro shrugged. 'Nothing.'

'There are three more baits. He's bound to be on one of them. Don't waste time, Manyoro, lead us on,' Leon ordered. The second carcass lay in the centre of an open glade of freshly burned black stubble surrounded on three sides by green Kusaka-saka bush, whose dense foliage hung close to the ground and afforded a safe retreat for a fleeing animal. But Leon had seen to it that there was a wide area of open ground around the carcass. Space enough for them to work in.

The first thing that struck Leon and tautened his nerves was that the upper branches of the trees were loaded with a huge colony of vultures and a small group of four hyena was standing at the edge of the Kusaka-saka. Both vultures and hyena were keeping well away from the dead buffalo cow in the middle of the clearing. There must be something there that they did not like. Then Manyoro, who was well in the lead, stopped and made a discreet gesture that warned Leon as clearly as if he had spoken.

Leon reined in. 'Be careful. He's here,' he said to Kermit. 'Wait. Manyoro's getting hot. Let him work it out for us.' Fagan and his party rode up. 'You will stay here,' Leon told them. 'Don't come any closer until I give you the signal. You will have a good view of the proceedings from here, but you must keep well out of harm's way.' They watched Manyoro test the wind. It was light and warm, but blowing directly from them to the bait. Manyoro shook his head and made another gesture.

'Right, chummy, the lion's on the kill,' Leon told Kermit. 'We're going in. Same drill as last time. Steady. Don't hurry. But whatever you do, don't stare at the bloody lion this time.'

'Okay, boss.' Kermit was grinning with nervous excitement and his hand was trembling as he reached down for the rifle in its boot. Leon hoped that the slow walk-in would give him time to get a grip on himself.

They dismounted.

'Check your piece. Make sure you have a bullet up the spout.' Kermit did as he was told and Leon saw with relief that his hands had steadied. He signalled to Manyoro to take up his position behind them and they started the long slow march across the open burned area. Little puffs of fine ash rose from each step they took. They were still two hundred and fifty yards from the carcass when the lion stood up from behind it. He was very big, every bit as big as the old lion. His mane was full but ginger, touched only lightly with sooty black at the tips. He was in beautiful condition, his hide sleek and glossy, with no ugly scars. When he snarled his fangs were shiny white, long and perfect. But he was young, and therefore unpredictable.

'Don't look at him!' Leon warned, in a whisper. 'Keep walking but, for God's sake, don't look at him. We must get closer. Much closer.' When they were still a hundred and fifty yards from him the lion snarled again and his tail twitched uncertainly. He turned his great maned head and glanced behind him.

Oh, shit! No! Leon lamented silently. He's lost his nerve. He's not going to hold his ground. He's going to break.

The lion looked back at them, and snarled for the third time, but the sound lacked murderous intensity. Then, abruptly, he swung away and bounded across the open ground towards the safety of the Kusaka-saka thicket.

'He's getting away!' Kermit shouted, and ran forward three quick paces, then stopped dead. He lifted the Lee-Enfield.

'No!' Leon shouted urgently. 'Don't shoot.' The range was far too long, and the lion was a fast-moving target. Leon ran forward to restrain Kermit, but the Lee-Enfield cracked sharply and the muzzle jumped. The lion's long lean muscles played beneath the glossy hide like those of an athlete in his prime. Leon saw the bullet strike. At the point of impact the skin jumped and rippled, as though a stone had been tossed into a still, deep pond. It was two hands' span behind the last rib in the lion's flank, and low of the central line of the body.

'Gut shot!' Leon moaned. 'Much too far back.' The lion grunted as he took the bullet and burst into a dead run. In the time it took Leon to get the rifle to his shoulder the beast had almost reached the safety of the Kusaka-saka. It was far beyond the accurate range of the Holland. Nonetheless Leon was forced to fire. The lion was wounded. It was his moral duty to try to finish it, no matter how remote the chances of success. He cut loose with the first barrel, only to see the heavy bullet drop too sharply and throw up dust under the lion's chest. The report of his second shot blended with the first, but he did not see the strike before the lion disappeared into the bush. He looked back quickly at Manyoro, who touched his left leg.

'Broken his bloody back leg,' Leon said angrily. 'That won't slow him down much.' He ejected the spent cartridges and reloaded the Holland.

'Don't just stand there with an empty rifle admiring the view,' he snapped at Kermit. 'Reload the damned thing.'

'I'm sorry,' Kermit said, shamefaced.

'So am I,' Leon retorted grimly.

'He was getting away,' he tried to explain.

'Well, now he's well and truly got away, with your bullet in his belly.' Leon beckoned Manyoro to join him, and the two squatted, heads close together, talking seriously. After a while Manyoro went back to join Loikot, and the two Masai took snuff together. Leon sat down on the bare earth with the Holland across his lap. Kermit was sitting a little way off, watching Leon's expression. Leon ignored him.

'What do we do now?' Kermit asked at last.

'We wait.'

'What for?'

'For the poor beggar to bleed out, and for his wounds to stiffen up.'

'And then?'

'Then Manyoro and I go in there and flush him out.'

'I'll go with you.'

'No, you bloody well won't. You've had enough fun for the day.'

'You could get hurt.'

'That's a distinct possibility.' Leon chuckled bitterly.

'Give me another chance, Leon,' Kermit asked pathetically.

Leon turned his head and looked directly at him for the first time, his eyes hard and cold. 'Tell me why I should.'

'Because that magnificent animal is dying a slow and agonizing death in there, and I am the one who hurt him. I owe it to God, the lion and my sacred honour as a man to go in there and put him out of his misery. Do you understand that?'

'Yes,' said Leon, and his expression softened. 'I understand very well, and I salute you for it. We'll go in together and I'll count it an honour to have you beside me.'

He was about to say more, but he glanced across the clearing and his expression crumbled into horror. He scrambled to his feet. 'What does that blithering idiot think he's playing at?' Andrew Fagan was riding slowly along the very edge of the Kusaka-saka, directly towards the spot where the wounded lion had disappeared. Leon broke into a run to try to head him off.

'Go back, you bloody fool! Get back!' he bellowed, at the top of his lungs. Fagan did not even look around. He rode on slowly into mortal danger. Leon was running hard, covering the ground swiftly, and did not shout again. He was saving his breath for the terrible moment he knew was coming. Now he was so close that Fagan must hear him: 'Fagan, you idiot! Come away from there!' he yelled, and waved the rifle above his head. This time Fagan looked around and waved his riding crop cheerily, but he did not check his horse.

'Come back here immediately!' Leon's voice was high with desperation.

This time Fagan stopped the horse and his smile evaporated. He turned towards Leon, and at that moment the lion erupted from the dense screen of Kusaka-saka at full charge, grunting with fury. Mane erect and yellow eyes blazing, he rushed towards Fagan.

His horse threw up its head, then reared wildly on its back legs. Fagan lost one stirrup and was thrown on to his mount's neck. The horse bolted, and Fagan clung to it with both arms. Over the short distance the lion was faster than horse and rider so he overtook them swiftly. Leaping up, he hooked the long yellow claws of both front paws deeply into the horse's croup.

The horse whinnied with agony and bucked violently in

an attempt to free itself from the cruel grip. Fagan lost his seat and hit the ground with a thump like a sack of charcoal thrown from the back of a coal dray, but his foot caught in a stirrup and he was towed behind the struggling horse, under the back legs of the lion. The horse squealed and kicked savagely, trying to dislodge its attacker. Its hoofs flashed around Fagan's head. As one of the lion's back legs was broken, he could not get enough purchase to pull the horse down. The struggle was almost obscured by clouds of ash kicked up from the burned grass. Unsighted by the dustcloud, Leon dared not shoot for fear of hitting the man rather than the lion. Then Fagan's stirrup leather snapped under the strain and he rolled clear of the mêlée.

'Fagan, come to me!' Leon roared. This time Fagan responded with alacrity. He came to his feet with the stirrup steel still on his right foot and stumbled towards him. Behind him the lion and the horse were still struggling, the horse kicking with both back legs, dragging the lion in a circle, the lion roaring, holding on with his front paws and trying to bite into the horse's heaving rump.

The horse kicked again and this time landed both hoofs solidly on the lion's chest. The blow was so heavy that he was thrown backwards and his claws tore free of the horse's flesh. He rolled onto his back but in the same movement sprang to his feet. The horse broke away at a wild gallop, blood spraying from the deep wounds in its croup, and the lion started after it, but the running figure of Fagan diverted his attention. He changed direction swiftly and came after Fagan. Fagan glanced back and wailed pitifully.

'Come to me!' Leon was running to meet him, but the lion was faster. He was still unable to fire because Fagan was directly between him and the beast. In a second it would have him.

'Get down!' Leon screamed. 'Fall flat and give me a clear shot.'

Perhaps in obedience, but more likely because his legs simply gave way under him in a paralysis of fear, Fagan collapsed and, like an armadillo, rolled himself into a ball on the bare earth, knees drawn up to his chest and both hands clasped to the back of his head. His eyes were screwed tightly shut in a face that was a blanched mask of terror. It was almost too late. The lion rushed in as silently as death, no longer grunting in the last fatal moments of the charge, jaws agape, fangs bared. He stretched out his neck to bite into Fagan's helpless body.

Leon let drive with his first barrel and the bullet smashed through the lion's lower jaw. White chips of teeth flew like gaming dice from a cup. Then the expanded bullet drove on with immense power through the full length of the great tawny body, from breast to anus. It hurled the lion backwards, end over end, in an untidy somersault. He rolled back on to his feet and stood, swaying unsteadily, head hanging, blood dribbling from open jaws. Leon's second shot crashed into his shoulder, shattering bone and ripping through the heart. The lion fell back in a loose-limbed tangle, eyes tightly closed. His broken, bloody jaws mouthed the air fruitlessly.

Leon had two more fat brass cartridges held ready between the fingers of his left hand. With a flick of his thumb on the top lever and a snap of his wrist the action of the Holland sprang open, and when the spent cartridge cases had pinged away he replaced them with one deft movement, swiftly as a card-sharp palming an ace. The Holland leaped back to his shoulder. He fired the insurance shot into the lion's chest, and the unbroken back leg kicked spasmodically in the final death throes, then stilled.

'Thank you for your co-operation, Mr Fagan. You may stand up now,' Leon said politely. Fagan opened his eyes and looked around as if he expected to find himself lying before the pearly portals of Paradise. He climbed painfully to his feet.

His face was as white as a Kabuki mask, but glossy with sweat. His body was powdered with ash. However, the front of his twenty-dollar Brooks Brothers riding breeches was sopping wet. When he took a hesitant pace towards Leon his boots squelched.

Andrew Fagan Esquire, stalwart of the fourth estate, doyen of the American Associated Press, committee member of the New York Racquets Club, and eight-handicap captain of the Pennsylvania Golf Club, had just pissed his pants copiously.

'Tell me truly, sir, did you not find that a lot more invigorating than eighteen holes of golf?' Leon asked mildly.

Eventually the great presidential safari left the banks of the Ewaso Ng'iro river and trundled on ponderously towards the north-east through the wildly beautiful hinterland. Kermit and Leon made the most of the dwindling days that remained to them. They rode afar and hunted hard, more often than not with marked success. Once Leon had repaired Big Medicine, Kermit never missed another shot. Was it Lusima's spell, Leon wondered, or simply that he had instilled into Kermit his own code of ethics, understanding and respect for the quarry they pursued together? The true magic was not in any spell: it was that Kermit had matured into a highly skilled and responsible hunter, a man of poise and self-confidence. Their friendship, tried and tested, took on a steely, durable character.

Four months after leaving the Ewaso Ng'iro the safari came upon the mighty flow of the Victoria Nile at a place called Jinja at the head of that vast body of fresh water, Lake Victoria. Here they had reached the parting of the ways.

Percy Phillips's contract ended at the river. On the eastern bank of the Nile they could see another vast encampment: Quentin Grogan was waiting to take over from Percy, and conduct President Roosevelt northwards through Uganda, the Sudan and Egypt to Alexandria on the Mediterranean. From there he and his party would take ship for New York.

Roosevelt ordered a farewell luncheon on the bank of the Nile. Although he did not partake himself, he allowed champagne to be served to his guests. It was a convivial gathering, which ended with a speech by the President. One by one he picked out each of his guests and regaled the others with some amusing or touching anecdote regarding the person he was addressing. There were cries of 'Hear, hear!' and 'For he's a jolly good fellow!'

At last he came to Leon. He recounted details of the lion hunt and the rescue of Andrew Fagan. His audience was hugely delighted when he referred to that unfortunate gentleman as the Piddling Press. Fagan was not present, having given up his pursuit of the safari shortly after the incident with the lion. Shaken, he had returned to Nairobi.

'That reminds me – I almost forgot. Didn't I make a bet with you, Kermit? Something about the biggest lion, wasn't it?' President Roosevelt went on, amid laughter from the guests.

'Indeed you did, Father, and indeed it was!'

'We wagered five dollars, as I recall?'

'No, Father, it was ten.'

'Gentlemen!' Roosevelt appealed to the rest of the table. 'Was it five or ten?'

There were amused cries of 'Ten it was! Pay up, sir! A bet is a bet!'

He sighed and reached for his wallet, selected a green banknote and passed it down the length of the table to where Kermit sat. 'Paid in full,' he said. 'You are all my witnesses.' Then he turned back to his guests. 'Few of you know that my son was made an honorary member of the Masai tribe by his two trackers after he shot that winning lion.'

More cries of 'Bravo! Kermit's a jolly good fellow!'

The President held up a hand for silence. 'I think it is only fitting that I should repay the honour.' He looked at Leon. 'Will you call Manyoro and Loikot, please?' Earlier Leon had warned the pair that they would be summoned by Bwana Tumbo; President Roosevelt's Swahili name meant Sir Mighty Stomach.

Manyoro and Loikot were waiting at the back of the tent and came swiftly. They were resplendent in their flowing red *shukas*, their hair braids dressed with red ochre and fat. They carried their lion *assegais*.

'Leon, please translate for these fine fellows what I want to tell them,' the President said. 'You have given to my son, Bwana Popoo Hima, the great honour of your tribe. You have named him a *morani* of the Masai. Now I name you both warriors of my nation, America. These are the papers that prove you have become Americans. You may come at any time to my country and I will personally welcome you. You are Masai but you are now also American.' He turned to his secretary, who stood behind his chair and took from him the citizenship certificate scrolls tied with red ribbons. He handed them to the Masai, then shook hands with each man. Spontaneously Manyoro and Loikot launched into the lion dance around the lunch table. Kermit jumped to his feet and joined them, leaping, shuffling and miming. The company clapped and cheered, and Roosevelt rocked in his chair with laughter. When the dance ended, Manyoro and Loikot stalked with great dignity from the tent.

The President rose to his feet again. 'Now, for the friends who are leaving us today, I have a few souvenirs of the time we have spent so pleasurably together.' His secretary entered the tent again, carrying a pile of sketchpads. The President took them from him and walked around the table handing them out to his guests. When Leon opened his pad he found it dedicated to him personally,

> *To my good friend and Nimrod, Leon Courtney, To remind you of happy days spent with Kermit and me in the Elysian fields of Africa, Teddy Roosevelt*

The pad contained dozens of hand-drawn cartoons. Each was a depiction of an incident that had taken place over the last months. One showed Kermit being thrown from his horse, titled '*Aff. Son and Heir takes a tumble and hilarious emotions of Mighty Nimrod on witnessing said performance.*' Another was of Leon finishing off the lion, which Roosevelt had annotated,

211

'*Prominent journalist saved from becoming lion dinner by Mighty Nimrod and joyful emotions of aff. Son and Heir on witnessing prowess of aforesaid Mighty Nimrod.*' Leon was amazed and humbled by the gift, which he knew was priceless, every line drawn by the hand of the mighty man himself.

Too soon the luncheon drew to a close: the boats were waiting on the bank to ferry the presidential party across the river. Leon and Kermit walked together down the bank in silence. Neither was able to think of words to say that would not sound maudlin or trite.

'Would you take a gift to Lusima from me, pardner?' Kermit broke the silence as they came to the edge of the water. He handed Leon a small roll of green banknotes. 'It's only a hundred dollars. She deserves a lot more. Tell her my *bunduki* shot real fine, thanks to her.'

'It's a generous gift. It will buy her ten good cows. There is nothing more desirable to a Masai than that,' Leon said.

'So long, pardner. In Limey terminology, it was all jolly good fun,' Kermit said.

'In Americanese, it was super awesome. Goodbye and God speed, chum.' Leon offered his right hand.

Kermit shook it. 'I'll write you.'

'I bet that's what you tell all the girls.'

'You'll see,' Kermit said, and went down into the waiting boat. It pulled away from the bank and out across the swift, wide waters of the Nile. When it was almost beyond earshot Kermit stood up in the stern and shouted something. Leon just made out the words above the roaring of the waters in the falls downstream. 'Brothers of the warrior blood!'

Leon laughed, waved his hat and bellowed back, 'Up the Rifles!'

'And now, my fine-feathered friend, it's time to come back down to earth. For you the fun is over. You've work to do. First, you must see to the horses and make sure they're taken back safely to Nairobi. Then you will gather up the trophies we left at the camps along the way. Make sure they're well dried and salted, pack them up and get them to the railway at Kapiti Plains. They have to be shipped to the Smithsonian in America as soon as possible, yesterday for preference. You must service all the equipment and the vehicles, including all five ox-wagons and the two trucks. Everything has been on the road for the better part of a year, and some of it is in ruinous condition. Then you must get it back to Tandala Camp so that it can be made ready for our next clients. I've several booked and then there's Lord East-mont – it's two years since he arranged his safari with me. Of course, you'll have Hennie du Rand to help you, but even so it'll keep you out of mischief for quite a while. Not much time for the Nairobi ladies, I'm afraid.'

Percy winked at him. 'As for me, I'm going to leave you to it. I'm heading back to Nairobi. My old buffalo leg is hurting like blue blazes and Doc Thompson's the only man who can fix it.'

Several months later Leon drove one of the trucks with assorted kit into Tandala, followed closely by the second with Hennie du Rand at the wheel. Since dawn that day they had come almost two hundred miles over rutted and dusty roads. Leon switched off the engine, which stuttered to a halt. He climbed down stiffly from the driver's seat, took off his hat and slapped it against his leg, then coughed in the resulting cloud of talcum-fine dust.

'Where the hell have you been?' Percy came out of his tent. 'I'd just about given you up for dead. I want to speak to you, sharpish.'

'Where's the fire?' Leon asked. 'I've been driving since

three this morning. I need a bath and a shave before I utter another word, and I'm in no mood to take bullshit from anyone, not even you, Percy.'

'Whoa now!' Percy grinned. 'You have your bath. You sure as hell need it. Then I'd like a few minutes of your precious time.'

An hour later Leon came into the mess tent, where Percy was sitting at the long table with his wire-rimmed reading glasses on the end of his nose. On the table in front of him was a pile of unanswered letters, accounts, cash books and other documents. His writing fingers were black with ink.

'I'm sorry, Percy. I shouldn't have gone for you like that.' Leon was contrite.

'Think nothing of it.' Percy replaced his pen in the inkwell and waved him to the chair on the opposite side of the table. 'Famous man like you has the right to be uppity sometimes.'

'Sarcasm is the lowest form of wit.' Leon bridled again. 'All I am around here is a famous dogsbody.'

'Here!' Percy pushed a pile of newsprint across the table. 'You'd better read these. Give your sagging morale a boost.'

Mystified at first, Leon began to make his way through the sheaf. He found that the clippings had been taken from dozens of newspapers and magazines from across North America and Europe, publications as diverse as the *Los Angeles Times* and *Deutsche Allgemeine Zeitung* from Berlin. There were more articles in German than there were in English, which surprised him. However, his schoolboy German was sufficient to enable him to follow their gist. He studied one that read: 'Greatest White Hunter in Africa. So says the son of the President of America.' Below it was a photograph of Leon, looking heroic and dashing. He laid it aside and picked up the next, which had a photograph of him shaking hands with a beaming Teddy Roosevelt. The headline under it read, 'Give me a lucky hunter rather than a clever one. Col. Roosevelt congratulates Leon Courtney on taking a huge man-eating lion.'

The next featured Leon holding a pair of long, curved elephant tusks so that they formed an archway high above his head, the caption beneath it declaring, 'The greatest hunter in Africa with a pair of record elephant tusks'. Other articles pictured Leon aiming a rifle at an imaginary beast out of frame, or galloping a horse across the savannah among herds of wild game, always rakish and debonair. There were hundreds of column inches of text. Leon counted forty-seven separate articles. The last was headlined, 'The man who saved my life. Did you not find that a lot more invigorating than eighteen holes of golf? Byline Andrew Fagan, Senior Contributing Editor, American Associated Press.'

When he had skimmed through them, Leon stacked the cuttings neatly and slid them back across the table to Percy, who immediately shoved them back to him. 'I don't want them. Not only are they nonsense but they're a bit too sickly and sycophantic for my stomach. You can burn them or give them back to your uncle Penrod. It was he who collected them. By the way, he wants to see you, but more of that later. First I want you to read this other mail. It's much more interesting.' Percy passed a stack of envelopes across the table.

Leon took it from him and shuffled through them. He saw that nearly all of the letters were written on expensive vellum or heavy linen paper, with ornately embossed headings. Most were hand-penned but a few had been typed on cheaper paper. They were addressed in such varying styles as, 'Herr Courtney, Glücklicher Jäger, Nairobi, Afrika,' or 'M. Courtney, Chasseur Extraordinaire, Nairobi, Afrique de l'Est,' or, more simply, 'The greatest hunter in Africa, Nairobi, Africa'.

Leon looked up at Percy. 'What's this?'

'Enquiries from people who have read Andrew Fagan's articles and want to come hunting with you, poor benighted souls. They know not what they do,' Percy explained briefly.

'They're addressed to me but you opened them!' Leon accused him sternly.

'I thought you'd want me to. They might have contained something that needed an urgent reply,' Percy answered, with an innocent air and an apologetic shrug.

'A gentleman does not open mail addressed to another.' Leon looked him straight in the eye.

'I'm not a gentleman, I'm your boss, and don't you forget it, sonny boy.'

'I can change that as quick as a flash of lightning.' Leon had sensed the new authority and status that the letters in his hand had given him.

'Now, now, my dear Leon, let us not be hasty. You are correct. I should not have opened your letters and I apologize. Dreadfully uncouth of me.'

'My dear Percy, your very decent apology is accepted unconditionally.'

They were quiet as Leon skimmed through the last of his correspondence.

'There's one from a German princess, Isabella von Hoherberg something or other.' Percy broke the silence.

'I saw it.'

'She attached her photograph,' Percy added helpfully. 'Not at all bad. Suit a man my age. But you like them mature, don't you?'

'Do shut up, Percy.' At last Leon looked up. 'I'll read the rest later.'

'Do you think this might be the time to talk about my offer of a partnership?'

'Percy, I'm deeply moved. I didn't think for one moment you were serious about that.'

'I am.'

'All right. Let's talk.'

It was almost evening before they had thrashed out the framework of their new financial arrangement.

'One last thing, Leon. You must pay for your private use of the motor. I'm not going to sponsor your amorous forays into Nairobi.'

'That's fair enough, Percy, but if you're going to make such a stipulation, I want to make two of my own.'

Percy looked suspicious and uneasy. 'Let's hear what they are.'

'The name of the new firm—'

'It's Phillips and Courtney Safaris, of course,' Percy cut in hurriedly.

'That's not alphabetical, Percy. Shouldn't it be Courtney and Phillips or more simply C and P Safaris?'

'It's my show. It should be P and C Safaris,' Percy protested.

'Not any more is it your show. It's our show now.'

'Cocky little bugger. I'll spin you for it.' He groped in his pocket and brought out a silver shilling. 'Heads or tails?'

'Heads!' said Leon.

Percy spun the coin high and caught it on the back of his left hand as it fell. He covered it with the right. 'Are you sure you really want heads?'

'Come on, Percy. Let's have a look.'

Percy peeped under his hand and sighed. 'This is what happens to the old lion when the young one starts feeling his oats,' he said unhappily.

'Lions don't eat oats. Let's have a look at what you're hiding.'

Percy showed him the coin. 'Very well, you win,' he capitulated. 'It's C and P Safaris. What's your second demand?'

'I want our partnership contract backdated to the first day of the Roosevelt safari.'

'Ouch, and shiver my timbers! You really are rubbing my nose in it! You want me to pay you full commission for your hunt with Kermit Roosevelt!' Percy pantomimed disbelief and deep distress.

'Stop it, Percy, you're breaking my heart.' Leon smiled.

'Be reasonable, Leon. That'll amount to almost two hundred pounds!'

'Two hundred and fifteen, to be precise.'

'You're taking advantage of a sick old man.'

'You look hale and hearty to me. Are we in agreement?'

'I suppose I have no other option, you heartless boy.'

'May I take that as yes?'

Percy nodded reluctantly, then smiled and held out his hand. They shook and Percy grinned triumphantly. 'I would have gone up to thirty per cent on your commission if you'd pressed me, rather than the piddling twenty-five you settled on.'

'And I would have agreed to twenty if you'd held out a little longer.' Leon's smile was equally smug.

'Welcome aboard, partner. I think we're going to get along together rather well. I suppose you want your two hundred and fifteen pounds right this minute? You don't want to wait until the end of the month, by any chance, do you?'

'You suppose right. I want it now and would rather not wait till the end of the month. One other thing. It's almost a year since I had a moment to myself. I'm taking some time off, and I'll be needing a motor. I have business to attend to in Nairobi, and possibly even further afield.'

'Give the lady, whoever she may be, my fond greetings.'

'Percy, I should warn you that your fly buttons are undone and your mind is hanging out.'

L eon's first stop in Nairobi was at the headquarters of the Greater Lake Victoria Trading Company in the main street. The Vauxhall's engine was still stuttering and backfiring in preparation for final shutdown when Mr Goolam Vilabjhi Esquire rushed out of his emporium to greet him. He was followed closely by Mrs Vilabjhi and a horde of small caramel-hued cherubs with raven hair and enormous liquid dark eyes, all clad in brilliant saris and chittering like starlings.

Mr Vilabjhi seized Leon's hand before he had alighted from the truck and shook it vigorously. 'You are a thousand and one times welcome, honoured Sahib. Since your last visit to us, my eyes have alighted on no finer vista than that afforded by your pleasing visage.' He led Leon into the store without releasing his grip on his right hand. With the other he swatted at the circling swarm of children. 'Away with you! Be gone! Bad children. Wicked and uncivilized female personages!' he cried, and they took not the least notice, except to keep just out of range. 'Please forgive and forget them, Sahib. Alas and alack! Mrs Vilabjhi produces only female personages despite my most dedicated endeavours to the contrary.'

'They are all extremely pretty,' said Leon gallantly. This encouraged the smallest cherub to sidle in under her father's ineffectually swinging hand and reach up on tiptoe to take Leon's. She helped her father to lead him.

'Enter! Enter! I beg of you, Sahib. You are ten thousand times welcome.' Mr Vilabjhi and the cherub led him to the back wall of the store. The colourful religious icons of the green-faced, multi-armed goddess Kali and the elephant-headed god Ganesh had been moved to the far ends of the wall to make way for the most recent addition to the gallery. This was a large gold picture frame with a wooden plaque, ornately carved and painted with gold leaf. It bore the legend,

Respectfully dedicated to Sahib Leon Courtney Esquire.

World-renowned polo player and shikari.

Esteemed and deeply beloved friend and boon companion of Colonel

Theodore Roosevelt, President of the United States of America

and of

Mr Goolam Vilabjhi Esquire.

Behind the glass of the frame were pasted a number of the English-language newspaper clippings originating from American Associated Press.

'My family and I are very much hoping and praying that you will sign one of these splendid publications to be the jewel in the crown of my collection of cherished memorabilia of our friendship.'

'Nothing would give me greater pleasure, Mr Vilabjhi.' Despite himself Leon was deeply touched. The Vilabjhi girls crowded around him as he signed a photograph of himself: '*To my good friend and benefactor, Mr Goolam Vilabjhi Esq. Sincerely, Leon Courtney.*'

Blowing on the damp ink, Mr Vilabjhi assured him, 'I will treasure this personally handwritten autograph for the rest of my days and as long as I shall live.' Then he sighed. 'I suppose that now you wish to speak about redeeming your genuine elephant ivory tusk, which I still have in my possession.'

When Manyoro and Loikot carried the tusk out to the truck Leon followed them with small girls hanging from both his hands and others firmly clutching the legs of his khaki trousers. Only with difficulty was he able to dislodge them and climb into the driver's seat. He drove on to the new Muthaiga Country Club, whose pink-painted brick and plaster walls had replaced the old Settlers' Club's whitewashed mud-daub on a site far beyond the teeming bustle of Main Street.

His uncle Penrod was waiting for him in the members' bar. The first thing Leon noticed as the colonel rose to greet him was that he had put on a bit more flesh, especially around the belt. Since their last meeting more than a year ago Penrod had moved up from the category of well covered to distinctly portly. There was also a little more grey in his moustache. As soon as they had shaken hands Penrod suggested, 'Shall we go to lunch? Today Chefie's serving steak and kidney pie. It's one of my favourites. I don't want the riff-raff to get at it ahead of me. We can talk as we eat.' He led Leon to a table on the terrace under the pergola of purple bougainvillaea, set discreetly out of earshot of other diners. As he tucked the white napkin into the front of his collar Penrod asked, 'I suppose Percy's shown you the articles written by that Yankee Andrew Fagan, and the letters from prominent people that they have evoked?'

'Yes, I have them, sir,' Leon replied. 'As a matter of fact, I found them rather embarrassing. People seem to be making such an awful fuss. I'm certainly not the greatest hunter in Africa. That was Kermit Roosevelt's idea of a joke, which Fagan took seriously. Actually I'm still a greenhorn.'

'Never admit it, Leon. Let them think what they want to. Anyway, from what I hear, you're learning fast.' Penrod smiled comfortably. 'As a matter of fact, I had a small hand in the whole subterfuge. Rather neat, I thought, little stroke of genius.'

'How are you involved, Uncle?' Leon was startled.

'I was in London when the first articles appeared. They gave me a bit of a brainwave. I cabled the military attaché at our embassy in Berlin and asked him to tout the articles to the German press, especially the sporting and hunting publications that are read by the upper crust. It's a stereotype that most of that type of German, like their English counterparts, are enthusiastic sportsmen and have their own hunting estates. My plan was to lure the notables among them here to go on safari with you. This will give you the opportunity to gather all kinds of intelligence, which will certainly prove invaluable when the time comes that we have to fight them.'

'Why would they want to confide in me, Uncle?'

'Leon, my lad, I cannot believe you're completely unaware of your winning ways. People seem to like you, especially the Fräuleins and the mademoiselles. Safari life, being close to Mother Nature and her creatures, has a way of inducing even the most reticent to relax, lower their guard and speak more freely. Not to mention the way it also loosens the strings of female corsets and drawers. And why would a senior figure in the Kaiser's Germany, a major arms manufacturer or one of their consorts, suspect a fresh-faced innocent like you of being a nefarious secret agent?' Penrod lifted a finger in the direction of the head waiter, who hovered nearby in his flowing white ankle-length *kanza*, scarlet sash and tasselled fez. 'Malonzi! Please bring us a bottle of the 1879 Château Margaux from my private bin.'

Malonzi returned bearing the lightly dusted claret bottle in white-gloved hands with the reverence it deserved. Penrod watched him go through the solemn ritual of drawing the cork, sniffing it, then decanting the glowing red wine. He poured the first few drops into a crystal glass. Penrod swirled it around and sniffed the bouquet. 'Perfect! I think you'll enjoy this, Leon. Count Pillet-Will was awarded the Premier Grand Cru Class Appellation for this particular vintage.'

After Leon had paid respect to the noble claret, Penrod

waved for Malonzi to bring on the steaming platters of steak and kidney pie, with a golden crust. Then he fell to with a will, and spoke through a mouthful, 'I took the liberty of going through your mail, especially that from Germany. I just couldn't wait to see what fish we had in our net. Hope you don't mind?'

'Not at all, Uncle. Please feel free.'

'I picked out six letters as especially worthy of our attention, then cabled the military attaché at the embassy in Berlin who sent me political appraisals of the selected subjects.'

Leon nodded cautiously.

'Four are especially important and influential persons in either the social, political or military sphere. They would be privy to all affairs of state and, if not actually members of his council, certainly they are confidants of Kaiser Bill. They will have intimate knowledge of his intentions and preparations regarding the rest of Europe, together with Britain and our empire.' Leon nodded again, and Penrod went on, 'I have discussed this with Percy Phillips and told him that you are, over and above all your other responsibilities, a serving officer in British Military Intelligence. He has agreed to co-operate with us in all ways possible.'

'I understand, sir.'

'The one prospective client we have picked out in preference to the others is the Princess Isabella Madeleine Hoherberg von Preussen von und zu Hohenzollern. She is a cousin of the Kaiser and her husband is Field Marshal Walter Augustus von Hoherberg, of the German High Command.'

Leon looked suitably impressed.

'By the way, how is your German, Leon?'

'It was once fair to middling, but is now more than a little rusty, Uncle. I took both German and French at school.'

'I saw that in your service record. Seems languages were your top subjects. You must have an ear for them. Percy tells me you speak Kiswahili and Maa like a native. But have you had much contact with German-speakers?'

'I went on a walking tour of the Black Forest during one

222

holiday with groups of other scholars. I met a number of locals with whom I rubbed along rather well. One was a girl called Ulrike.'

'Best place to learn a language,' Penrod remarked, 'under the bedcovers.'

'We never got around to that, sir, more's the pity.'

'I should hope not, well-bred young gentleman like you.' Penrod smiled. 'Anyway, you'd better brush up. You're going to spend a great deal of time in the company of Germans soon, much of which might in fact be under the bedcovers, given the predilections of upper-class Fräuleins. Does this possibility offend your high moral standards?'

'I shall try to come to terms with it, Uncle.' Leon could scarcely refrain from smiling.

'Good man! Never forget that it's all for King and country.'

'When duty calls, who are we to forbear?' Leon asked.

'Exactly. Couldn't have phrased it better myself. And fear not, I've already found a language tutor for you. His name is Max Rosenthal. He was an engineer at the Meerbach Motor Works in Weiskirchen before he came out to German East Africa. For some years after his arrival he ran a hotel in Dar es Salaam. There, he developed an over-intimate relationship with the cognac bottle, which lost him the job. However, he's only a periodic drunk. When he's sober he's a first-rate worker. I persuaded Percy to employ him to manage your safari camps and to sharpen up your use of the lingo.'

When they parted on the front steps of the club, Penrod took Leon's arm in a conspiratorial grip and told him seriously, 'I know you're new to the business of spying so I offer a word of advice. Write nothing down. Keep no notes of what you observe. Rather, record it all in your head and report it to me when next we meet.'

W hen Leon met Max Rosenthal at Tandala Camp he proved to be a powerfully built Bavarian, with huge hands and feet and a bluff, jovial manner. Leon liked him on first sight.

'Greetings.' They shook hands. 'We'll be working together. I'm sure we'll get to know each other well,' Leon said.

Max let out a fruity chuckle that shook his belly. 'Ah, so! You speak a little German. That's very good.'

'Not so very good,' Leon corrected him, 'but you will help me to improve it.'

Almost immediately Max proved invaluable, a gifted teacher, and a hard, efficient worker, who relieved Leon of much of the mundane work of camp organization and arranging catering supplies. He and Hennie du Rand made a good team of workhorses and freed Leon to learn the organizational and economic skills that the safari business demanded. Leon made it a rule to communicate with Max only in German and, in consequence, as the months passed, his grip on the language strengthened with surprising rapidity.

Lord Eastmont was only weeks away from arriving for his safari when Leon received a cable from Berlin to the effect that the Princess Isabella Madeleine Hoherberg von Preussen von und zu Hohenzollern had decided to come out to Africa on the next sailing of the German liner SS *Admiral* from Bremerhaven. Her royal duties were such that she could only afford six weeks in Africa before she must return to Germany. She demanded that all be ready for her on her arrival.

This peremptory communication threw Tandala into turmoil. Percy raged through the camp, hindering rather than helping the frantic efforts of Leon and his staff to change the elaborate arrangements already in place for Eastmont. They now had two major safaris to run simultaneously, which they had never attempted previously. In the end the only circumstance that saved the day was that the princess would stay just six weeks, while Lord Eastmont had arranged a four-month

adventure. Leon was able to reassure Percy that on the day
the princess sailed for Germany he would rush with his staff
to assist Percy with the remainder of his expedition.

Accordingly, when the princess arrived in Kilindini lagoon
on board the *Admiral*, Leon went out from the beach in a
launch to welcome her. He waited on the deck for almost an
hour before she deigned to leave her stateroom. When finally
she ascended the companionway to the main deck she was
escorted by the ship's captain and four of his senior officers,
all fawning on her obsequiously. The rest of her entourage,
including her secretary and two plump, pretty handmaidens,
trailed behind her.

The princess cut a striking figure as she stepped into the
sunshine. Leon had seen photographs of her but he was still
unprepared for her in the flesh. His first impression was of her
towering height and her contrastingly lean body. She was
almost as tall as him, but he could easily have encircled her
waist with his hands. Her bust was boyish and her carriage
imperious. Her eye was steely, and as penetrating as a rapier,
and her features were hard and as sharp as a whipsaw. She
wore a green loden ankle-length riding habit of superb cut.
The toes of her boots, which showed under the skirts, glowed
with the lustre of expensive leather. Surprisingly she carried a
9mm Luger pistol in a holster on her belt, and a wide-brimmed
safari hat in her left hand. Her ash-blonde hair was braided
into two thick ropes and looped on top of her head. Leon
knew from Penrod that she was fifty-two, but she looked
thirty.

'Your Royal Highness, I am your servant.'

She did not bother to acknowledge his bow but continued
to regard him as though he had just let off a particularly
obnoxious fart. At last she spoke, her tone icy. 'You are very
young.'

'Your Royal Highness, this is a regrettable circumstance for
which I must apologize. In time I hope to correct it.'

The princess did not smile. 'I said you were young. I did
not say you were too young.' She held out her right hand.

When he took it in his he found it as hard and cold as her expression. He kissed the air an inch short of her bony white knuckles. The crêpe of tiny wrinkles across the back tittle-tattled her age.

'The governor of the territory of British East Africa has placed his private railway coach at your disposal for the journey to Nairobi,' Leon told her.

'*Ja!* This is fitting and anticipated,' she agreed.

'His excellency also begs your presence as guest of honour at a special dinner at Government House to be arranged at any time convenient to you, Princess.'

'I did not come to Africa to eat in the company of junior civil servants. I came here to kill animals. Many animals.'

Leon bowed again. 'Immediately, ma'am. Does Your Royal Highness have any particular preference for the animals she wishes to kill?'

'Lions!' she answered. 'And pigs.'

'How about a few elephants and buffalo?'

'No! Only big lions and pigs with long tusks.'

B efore they set off into the blue, the princess tried out every mount in the string of thoroughbreds that Leon had assembled for her. She rode astride like a man. As Leon watched her appraise the first horse with her disdainful expression, walking around it twice before she swung up gracefully into the saddle and bent the animal to her will, he realized that she was a superb horsewoman. In fact, he had seldom seen another woman who came close to her.

When they rode out from Tandala and were among the game herds, she forgot her original demand for lions and pigs and became a great deal less selective. She had a beautiful little 9.3 x 74 Mannlicher rifle made by Joseph Just of Ferlach, inlaid with gold by Wilhelm Röder with sylvan scenes of fauns and naked nymphs cavorting riotously together. When she bowled over three running Grant's gazelle at a range of three hundred yards in three consecutive shots without dismounting, Leon decided she was probably the most deadly shot, man or woman, he had ever met.

'Yes, I want to kill many animals,' she remarked, as she reloaded the Mannlicher. She was smiling warmly for the first time since she had arrived in Africa.

When he took the princess up Lonsonyo Mountain to meet Lusima, Leon was unprepared for the way the two women reacted instantly to each other. Figuratively, they arched their backs and spat like two cats. 'M'bogo, this is one with many deep, dark passions. No man will fathom her. She is as deadly as a mamba. She is not the one I promised you. Be on your guard,' Lusima told Leon.

'What did the black bitch say?' the princess demanded. The hostility between the two women crackled in the air like static electricity.

'That you are a lady of immense power, Princess.'

'Tell the great cow not to forget that either.'

When it came to the ceremony of blessing the rifles under the council tree, Lusima emerged from her hut in her ceremonial finery, but when she was still ten paces from where the Mannlicher lay on the lionskin she stopped. Her face changed to the colour of dried mud.

'What troubles you, Mama?' Leon asked quietly.

'That *bunduki* is a thing of evil. The white-haired woman is as powerful a sorcerer as I am. She has placed a spell on her own *bunduki* that frightens me.' She turned back towards her hut. 'I will not leave my hut until that witch departs from Lonsonyo Mountain,' she vowed.

'Lusima has been taken ill. She must go to her hut to rest,' Leon translated.

'*Ja*, I know very well what troubles her.' The princess gave one of her rare, thin-lipped smiles.

T wenty days later, in country that Manyoro and Loikot had declared totally devoid of lions, they rode out of camp at dawn for the princess to continue her slaughter of warthogs – she had already accounted for more than fifty, including three boars with incredibly long tusks. They had not ventured more than half a mile from the camp when they came across an enormous solitary black-maned lion standing in the middle of an open grassy *vlei*. Without a moment's hesitation, and without dismounting, the princess brought up the little Mannlicher and, with a surgeon's precision, put a bullet through the lion's brain.

The two Masai should have been delighted with this performance but they were strangely subdued as they began to skin the carcass. It was left to Leon to tender his congratulations, which the princess ignored. He heard Loikot mutter to Manyoro, 'This lion should never have been here. Where did he come from?'

'Nywele Mweupe summoned him,' Manyoro said sulkily. They had given the princess the Swahili name 'White Hair'. Manyoro had not combined it with either of the titles of respect, 'Memsahib' or 'Beibi'.

'Manyoro, even from you that is an enormous stupidity,' Leon snapped at him. 'That lion came to the smell of all those warthog carcasses.' He sensed mutiny in the air. Lusima had obviously had a word or two with Manyoro.

'The *bwana* knows best,' Manyoro conceded, with ostentatious courtesy, but he neither looked at Leon nor smiled. When they had finished the skinning, the two Masai did not perform the lion dance for the princess. Instead they sat apart and took snuff together. When Leon remarked on the omission Manyoro did not respond, but Loikot muttered, 'We are too tired to dance and sing.'

When he shouldered the bundled green skin and started back for camp, Manyoro's limp on the leg that had received the Nandi arrow, usually barely noticeable, became heavily pronounced. This was his way of expressing protest or disapproval.

When they rode into camp the princess sprang down from the saddle and strode into the mess tent where she dropped into a canvas chair. She threw her riding whip on to the table, removed her hat and sailed it across the tent, then shook out her braids and commanded, 'Courtney, tell that useless cook of yours to bring me a cup of coffee.'

Leon relayed the order to the kitchen tent, and minutes later Ishmael hurried in with a steaming porcelain coffee pot on a silver tray. He set it down, poured a cup of the brew and placed it in front of her. Then he stood to attention behind her chair, waiting to be dismissed.

The princess raised the cup to her lips and sipped. She pulled a face of utter disgust and hurled the cup with its contents at the far wall of the tent. 'Do you think I am a sow that you place such pig swill before me?' she screamed. She seized her riding whip from the table and leaped to her feet. 'I will teach you to show me more respect, savage.' She drew back her whip arm to strike at Ishmael's face. He made no effort to protect himself but stared at her in terrified astonishment.

Behind her, Leon sprang from his chair and grabbed her wrist before she could launch the blow. He swung her around to face him. 'Your Royal Highness, there are no savages among my people. If you want this safari to continue you should bear that firmly in mind.' He held her easily until she stopped struggling. Then he went on, 'You should go to your tent now and rest until dinner time. You are clearly overwrought by the excitement of the lion hunt.'

He released her and she stormed from the tent. She did not reappear when Ishmael rang the dinner gong and Leon dined alone. Before he retired he checked her tent surreptitiously and saw that her lantern was still burning. He went to his own quarters and filled in his game book. He was about to add a comment about the incident in the mess, but as he started to write he remembered Penrod's caution. Instead of relieving his feelings he wrote, 'Today the princess proved once more that she is a remarkable horsewoman and rifle shot. The cool manner in which she despatched the magnificent lion was extraordinary. The more I see of her, the more I admire her skills as a huntress.'

He blotted the page, put the game book back in his campaign bureau and locked the drawer. Then, for half an hour, he read the book his uncle Penrod had written on his experiences during the Boer War, entitled *With Kitchener to Pretoria*. When his eyelids drooped he set it aside, undressed and climbed under the mosquito net. He blew out the lantern and settled down contentedly to enjoy a good night's rest.

He had barely closed his eyes before he was startled awake by the loud report of a pistol shot coming from the direction of the princess's tent. His first thought was that some dangerous animal, lion or leopard, had broken into it. He fought his way out of the folds of the mosquito net and grabbed the big Holland, which stood fully loaded beside the bed, ready for just such an emergency. Clad only in his pyjama bottoms he ran to her tent. He saw that her lantern was still burning.

'Your Royal Highness, are you all right?' he called. When he received no reply he pulled open the canvas fly and ducked inside, rifle at the ready. Then he stopped in amazement. The princess stood facing him in the middle of the floor. Her silver hair cascaded over her shoulders and down to her waist. She wore an almost transparent rose pink nightdress. The lantern was behind her so every line of her long lean body was revealed. Her feet were bare but surprisingly small and shapely. She held the riding whip in one hand and the 9mm Luger pistol in the other. The smell of burned nitro powder still hung in the air. Her face was blanched with fury and her eyes blazed like cut sapphires as she glowered at him. She lifted the Luger and fired a second shot through the canvas roof. Then she tossed the pistol on to the enormous bed that filled half the floor space.

'You swine! Do you think you can treat me like rubbish in front of all your servants?' she demanded, as she took a step towards him, swinging the whip menacingly. 'You are no better than the creatures who work for you.'

'Kindly control yourself, ma'am,' he warned her.

'How dare you address me thus? I am a royal princess of the House of Hohenzollern. And you are a commoner of a mongrel race.' Her English was perfectly enunciated. She smiled icily. 'Ah, so! Now at last you grow angry, serf! You want to fight back but you dare not. Your bowels are too soft. You do not have the courage. You hate me but you must suffer any humiliation I might choose to heap on you.'

She threw the whip at his feet. 'Put away that rifle. You cannot use it to bolster your flabby manhood. Pick up the whip!' Leon laid the Holland on the groundsheet below the entrance wall of the tent and scooped up the whip. He was quivering with rage. Her insults had raked him cruelly and brought him to the brink of abandoning all restraint. He was not certain what to do with the whip, but it felt good in his right hand.

'M'bogo, is all well? We heard shots. Is there trouble?' Manyoro called softly through the canvas wall, and the princess drew back a few paces.

'Go, Manyoro, and take the others with you. None of you must return until I call you,' Leon shouted back.

'*Ndio*, Bwana.'

He heard their soft steps retreating, and the princess laughed in his face. 'You should have asked them to help you. You do not have the courage to stand up to me on your own.' She laughed. '*Ja*, now you grow angry again. That is good. You want to strike me but you dare not do so.' She leaned towards him until their faces were only inches apart.

'You have a whip in your hand. Why do you not use it? You hate me, but you are afraid of me.' Suddenly and unexpectedly she spat in his face. Instinctively he lashed out at her and the whiplash snapped across her cheek. She reeled back, clutching the red weal, and wailed piteously, 'Yes! I deserved that. You're so masterful when you're angry.' She flung herself at his feet, and clung to his knees. He was

231

trembling with disgust at himself and threw the whip across the tent.

'I wish you good night, Your Royal Highness.' He tried to turn away to the door but, with surprising strength, she tripped him. The instant he was off-balance she landed on his back with all her weight and he fell across the bed, the princess on top of him. 'Are you mad?' he demanded.

'Yes!' she replied. 'I am crazy for you.'

It was only an hour short of dawn when she allowed him to leave her tent. On the way to his own bed he noticed that the tents of her staff, her secretary and handmaidens, were in darkness – despite the cries of the princess, which had made the long night clamorous. It seemed that all of them must have become inured long ago to the princess's peccadilloes.

T he next morning at breakfast she acted as though nothing had changed. She snapped shrewishly at her handmaidens, was cruelly sarcastic to her secretary, and ignored Leon, not even acknowledging his polite greeting until she had finished her second cup of coffee. Then she stood up and announced, 'Courtney, today I have a great desire to kill pigs.'

Leon had devised a series of small game drives, which gave the princess endless pleasure. He and the trackers would corner a sounder of warthog in a patch of thick scrub, then place the princess in a commanding position over the open ground beyond the thicket, and beat the pigs towards her. As soon as they broke from cover she would wade into them with the Mannlicher. She had trained Heidi, the prettier of her handmaidens, to reload the spare magazines. Each held six rounds, and the princess could change an empty one in an instant. She pressed the release catch and let it drop. Heidi caught it as it fell and reloaded it with her deft pink fingers, trained by relentless needlework since childhood. Then the princess would slip a fully charged magazine into the breech and keep shooting with barely a pause. Her rate of fire was almost as staggering as her accuracy. She could get off twelve shots in as many seconds. Often the warthog would not co-operate with the beaters: they might break from cover in an unexpected direction or double back through the line of beaters, not offering Her Royal Highness a single shot. When this happened she either flew into a coldly furious rage, railing at Leon and his team, or retreated into an icy silence from which she could only be drawn by the prospect of spilling more blood.

Late that afternoon Leon and his beaters, their ranks strengthened by the inclusion of Max Rosenthal, Ishmael and the skinners, managed to pull off their most spectacular *battue* of the safari. They drove twenty-three warthogs, boars, sows and piglets, past the princess and her loader. She managed to kill twenty-two. The one that escaped was a lean old sow that changed direction just as she fired. The bullet flew wide and the sow doubled back between the princess's legs when she was least expecting it, sending her flying. She sat up with her skirts above her knees and her hat over her eyes. 'You dirty little cheat!' she screamed, as the sow disappeared into the thicket, tail held high and straight as a pennant.

That evening at dinner she was almost genial and expansive, but not entirely so. She urged Leon to take another glass of the excellent Krug, and peeled a grape with her long white fingers before placing it between plump Heidi's lips.

'Eat, my darling! You did fine work today,' she urged. But immediately afterwards she shrieked at her secretary and ordered him to leave the table for his ill manners in taking up a warthog chop in his fingers without excusing himself to her. When she had finished, she stood up without another word and stalked away to her tent.

It had been a long, hot, hard day and Leon was hoping for

a full night's sleep. He had just finished scrubbing his teeth and was buttoning his pyjama jacket when he heard the dreaded pistol shot.

'For King and country!' he grumbled, as he went to her tent, but he was intrigued to discover what entertainment the princess had planned for the evening.

The princess was stretched out languidly on the big bed. However, she was not alone. Her maid, Heidi, knelt in the middle of the floor. She was stark naked except for a miniature saddle on her back and a gold bit in her mouth. The tiny golden bells on the reins tinkled as she tossed her head and whinnied.

'Your steed awaits you, Courtney,' said the princess. 'Would you like to take her for a little trot?'

When she had exhausted her imagination, she sent Heidi away, but when Leon started to follow the girl the princess stopped him. 'I did not say you could leave, Courtney.' She moved over on the bed and patted the mattress beside her. 'Stay awhile, and I will tell you interesting stories of the wicked and wonderful things that I do with my friends in Berlin.'

The goosedown mattress was wondrously soft and warm. Leon stretched out on it. At first he listened idly to her anecdotes. They seemed so far-fetched that they must be fairy-tales, the kind that the devils of hell must spin to their offspring. They were about witchcraft and Satan worship, obscene and sacrilegious rituals.

Then, with a creepy sensation that made the hair at the back of his neck rise, he began to realize that she was naming well-known personages from the upper reaches of the German aristocracy and military. What she was relating as amusing titbits of scandal was political cordite – and sweating, unstable cordite at that. What would Penrod make of such volatile information? Would he believe a single word of it?

The following evening, as he filled in his game book after a hard day's hunting, he tried to recall every name the princess had mentioned. He started recording them on one of the back pages. There were sixteen on his list when he had completed it. He was about to lock away the book when he became uneasy.

Nobody, except Penrod, will ever read this, he thought. But the niggling doubt remained at the back of his mind as he prepared for bed. Finally he unlocked the bureau and took up his straight razor. He spread open the game book and carefully cut out the incriminating page. He held it over the lantern flame and let it burn to a black crisp. Then he crushed the ashes to dust, and climbed into bed to await the summons of his client. However, that night no pistol shot sounded before he fell asleep.

He woke with the dawn light creeping into his tent, feeling fresh and bright after a full seven hours' sleep.

Before the company had finished breakfast Manyoro came to the mess tent and squatted outside the opening where only Leon could see him. As soon as they made eye contact Manyoro rose to his feet and slipped away. Leon excused himself and followed him. Manyoro was waiting for him in the servants' compound.

'What ails you, brother?' Leon asked him.

'Swalu has been bitten by a snake.'

Swalu was the head skinner. 'Did he see what manner of snake it was?' Leon asked, with consternation.

'It was *futa*, M'bogo.'

'Are you sure?' Leon clutched at the faint hope that it had not been a black mamba, the most venomous serpent in Africa.

'It came into his bed. After it had bitten him three times

235

he killed it with his skinning knife. I have seen the snake. It is *futa*.'

'Is Swalu yet dead?'

'No, M'bogo. He waits for your blessing before he goes to his ancestors.'

'Take me to him swiftly.' They hurried to one of the grass huts in the compound and Leon stooped through the low doorway. Swalu lay on his sleeping mat. The other three skinners sat in a circle around him. The body of the snake lay close by. Its head had been hacked off, but a single glance confirmed Manyoro's identification. It was a black mamba, not a particularly large specimen, only about four feet long, but its single bite would have contained sufficient venom to kill twenty men. Swalu had been bitten thrice.

Swalu lay on his back, naked except for his loincloth. His head was supported by a carved wooden pillow. There were two double fang punctures on his chest, and one on his cheek. His eyes were wide, but glazed and sightless. White froth bubbled out of his mouth and nostrils.

Leon knelt beside him and took his hand. It was cold, but the fingers twitched. 'Go in peace, Swalu,' Leon whispered in his ear. 'Your ancestors wait to welcome you.' Barely perceptibly Swalu's cold fingers squeezed his hand. Then Swalu smiled faintly and died. Leon sat with him awhile, then leaned forward and closed his staring eyes.

'Dig his grave deep,' Leon told the other skinners. 'Place rocks above him so that the hyena cannot reach him.'

'Why would she wish to kill Swalu?' Manyoro asked, of nobody in particular. The skinners stirred uneasily.

'No more of that!' Leon snapped as he stood up. 'The *futa* was a *futa* and nothing else. It was not a witch's thing!'

'As the *bwana* says,' Manyoro agreed, with studied politesse, but he did not look at Leon.

Leon went back to the mess tent. The princess was finishing a cup of coffee. She greeted him coldly. 'Ah, so! You have made time to take care of your client's needs. I am gratified.'

'Forgive me, Your Royal Highness, a small matter demanded my attention. What can I do for you?'

'I have lost one of my gold lockets. It contains a strand of my mother's hair. It is of paramount importance to me.'

'We will find it,' he assured her. 'When and where do you remember last having seen it?'

'After the pig *battue* yesterday. I sat under that tree while I waited for you and your men to butcher the animals. I remember rubbing the locket between my fingers. I must have dropped it there.'

'I will go to recover it immediately.' Leon bowed to her. 'I shall return before noon.' She waved him away and he strode from the tent, calling to the syce to bring his horse.

When Leon and the trackers reached the area of the warthog drive they found a large and splendidly dappled tom leopard feeding on the remains of the carcasses. It raced away and disappeared into the tall grass. Leon and the trackers went to where the princess had sat and searched the entire surrounding area.

'*Hapana.*' Manyoro admitted defeat at last. 'There is nothing.' They returned to the camp.

The princess's handmaidens were sitting in the mess tent, working on their embroidery frames, drinking coffee, whispering and giggling together.

'Where is your mistress?' Leon asked, and they exchanged a glance, giggled a little more and shrugged, but did not reply. He left them and went to his own tent, ducked in through the fly and found the princess sitting on his bed. His campaign bureau was open and the contents were spread around her. His game book was open on her lap.

'Princess.' He bowed stiffly. 'I regret we were unable to find your jewel.'

She touched the locket, which now hung at her throat. The single large diamond set in the lid glinted in the subdued light. 'No matter,' she said. 'One of my maids found it under my bed. I must have dropped it there.'

'I am relieved to hear that.' He looked pointedly at the

game book. 'Is there anything in particular Your Royal Highness was looking for?'

'No, nothing, really. I was bored in your absence so I was passing the time. I was diverted by your accounts of my prowess . . .' she paused significantly and stared into his eyes '. . . in the chase.' She closed the book and stood up. 'So Courtney, how are you going to amuse me today? What is there for me to kill?'

'I have found a formidable leopard for you.'

'Take me to it!'

T he leopard was in its prime, beautiful even in death. The fur on its back was burned gold alloyed with copper that shaded to fluffy cream under the belly. It was dappled with clusters of starkest black as though it had been touched repeatedly by the bunched fingertips of Diana, the goddess of the hunt. The whiskers were stiff and glassy white, the fangs and claws perfect. There was very little blood. The princess's single shot had struck the heart squarely as it ran from one of the warthog carcasses. As they loaded it on to the back of a mule, Manyoro whispered to Loikot, just loudly enough for Leon to hear, 'Will she send the mate of the *futa* tonight to visit one of us?'

Leon ignored him, pretending not to have heard. Manyoro followed the mule with a dramatically exaggerated limp.

That night at dinner the princess commanded Leon to open a bottle of 1903 Louis Roederer Cristal vintage champagne from her store. Twice during the meal she touched him intimately beneath the table, something she had never done before. Against his will his body responded to the skill of her fingers. When she felt it, she smiled and released him. Then she whispered something to Heidi that he could not catch, but both her handmaidens dissolved into unbridled fits of giggles.

Later that evening the Luger shot through the roof of the royal tent summoned Leon before he had completed the entry in his game book for the leopard hunt. As he set it aside he felt himself succumbing to the perverse arousal she was able to evoke in him so readily. 'She could corrupt St Peter and all the angels of heaven,' he told himself, as he went to do her bidding.

The following morning when they rode out to continue the chase for warthogs she spurred up alongside Leon's horse and chatted as gaily as a young girl. Once more Leon was disconcerted by the mercurial change in her mood and wondered what it foreshadowed. He did not have to wait long to find out.

'Oh, how I love to kill pigs,' she remarked, 'and these African ones are amusing, but they do not match up to our German wild boar.'

'We have other pigs that are bigger and more dangerous,' Leon protested. 'The giant forest hog that live in the bamboo forests of the Aberdare mountains can weigh more than a thousand pounds.'

'Poof!' She dismissed his statement with a wave of her hand. 'There is only one variety of game that truly thrills me beyond all others.'

'Which is it? Is it a very rare species?' he asked, with interest, and she laughed lightly.

'Not at all. In the Polynesian islands they call them "long pigs".' He stared at her in disbelief. 'Ah, so! Now at last you understand.' She laughed again. 'I have killed many, but the thrill never palls. Shall I tell you of my first one, Courtney?'

'If you so wish.' His voice was hoarse with horror.

'He was a young gamekeeper on one of the royal estates. I was thirteen. Although I was still a virgin, I wanted him, but he was married and he loved his wife. He laughed at me. When I was alone with him in the forest hunting capercaillie, I sent him forward to pick up a bird I had shot. When he had gone ten paces I shot him in the back of his legs with both barrels of my shotgun. The blast tore away the bone and his legs were held by only strings and tatters of flesh. There was much blood. I sat beside him and talked to him as he lay bleeding to death. I explained why I had had to kill him. He pleaded for mercy, not for himself, he said, but for his slattern of a wife and the miserable brat she carried in her belly. He wept and begged me to fetch a doctor to save him. I laughed at him, as he had once dared to laugh at me. He took almost an hour to die.' Her expression was dreamy. They rode on in silence for a while, and then she asked innocently, 'You would never disappoint me as the gamekeeper did, would you, Courtney?'

'I hope not, ma'am.'

'So do I, Courtney. So, now that we understand each other so well, I want you to find me two-legged pigs to hunt. Will you do that for me?'

Leon felt his gorge rising, and his voice was shaky when he replied, 'Your Royal Highness, this is something I never expected. You must give me a little time to think about it. You do know that you are asking me to commit a capital offence?'

'I am a princess. I will protect you from retribution. Nobody has ever questioned me about the gamekeeper or any of the others. I am not one of the common people. I possess the divine right of royalty. I will be your shield. The disappearance of a few savages will not even be remarked.' She leaned across from her horse and stroked his muscular forearm. With an effort he resisted the urge to pull it back and punch her in the face. Her voice was low and seductive. 'Courtney, until you experience it you cannot imagine the pleasure of this special type of hunting.'

Leon drew a deep breath to steady himself, but his senses were reeling with this recital of insensate lust and brutality. He found it difficult to think clearly. He had an almost overwhelming compulsion to put both his hands around her throat and destroy her. Then he realized that his instinctive response was diametrically opposed to his duty, which was to glean every last grain of information from her at any cost to himself and others around him. After that he must use her influence to obtain access to others of her ilk and do the same to them. She was the key to the upper hierarchy of German society that had been fortuitously placed in his hands. He was not the judge and executioner. He was merely a tiny cog in the great machinery of British Military Intelligence.

In the end duty prevailed. With a huge effort of will he managed to control his hands. Instead of taking her by the throat he took her hands and squeezed them. Then he smiled and whispered, 'Of course, Your Royal Highness. I will do as you ask. However, you must give me time to make the arrangements.'

'This safari ends in sixteen days' time. After that I must return to Germany. I shall be angry if you disappoint me . . . very angry.' There was cold menace in her tone, and the thought of the young German gamekeeper came back into his mind.

I t was still early when they returned to camp. The princess went to her tent to bathe, and Leon hurried to his own and scribbled a hasty note to Penrod in his game book:

Uncle, I have such stories to tell you of my new friend and her old friends in the highest places as will turn your hair white. However, I am now in the coils of this monster. She demands that I commit an unspeakably foul act for her amusement. Both my own conscience and the law forbid me to give in to her. If I am forced to refuse her outright, she will take great offence. She will shut down the conduit of information from Germany that you are so carefully nurturing. I implore you to devise some means of diplomatically removing her from British East Africa before this happens. Your aff. nephew.

He tore the page from the book, folded it and buttoned it into the breast pocket of his bush jacket. He left his tent and went back towards the mess tent, passing close enough to the royal tent to hear the princess furiously haranguing Heidi and the maid's muffled sobs. He walked on down to the servants' compound where he found Manyoro and Loikot sitting outside their hut, taking snuff. They fell silent as they saw him approaching.

With a quick glance around to make certain they were not watched, he handed the folded note to Manyoro. 'Take Loikot with you. Go to Nairobi at once with all speed. Give this paper to my uncle, Colonel Ballantyne, at KAR Headquarters. Do not dawdle along the way. Leave now. Speak to nobody of this business except my uncle.'

They stood up immediately and reached for their spears, which were planted in the earth on each side of the hut doorway.

Leon took Manyoro's shoulders to reinforce his orders. 'My brother,' he said softly, 'run fast and the witch will soon be gone.'

'*Ndio*, M'bogo.' Manyoro smiled for the first time in weeks, and he was not limping when he and Loikot trotted out of the camp and set off in the direction of Nairobi.

T hat evening when she summoned him to her tent he was able to assure the princess that 'I have despatched both my trackers to make the arrangements for us to hunt long pigs. They know of an Arab whose dhows ply the length and breadth of Lake Victoria. His main business is in ivory and hides, but clandestinely he deals in other goods.'

'That *is* exciting. I knew I could rely on you, Courtney.' The princess fidgeted, crossing and recrossing her long legs, wriggling her bottom on the canvas seat of her chair as though she was scratching an itch. 'The very thought excites me. When do you think your people will return?'

'I would expect them here in five or six days, leaving plenty of time for you to introduce me to this new sport before you leave.'

'Until then we must amuse ourselves as best we can.' She lay back in the chair and lifted the skirts of her riding habit to her knees. 'I am sure you can find something to entertain me.'

F our evenings later Leon brought the princess back to camp after a day of pursuing warthogs. She was in a black, furious mood. He had orchestrated four drives for her, and none had succeeded. Each time, the quarry had flushed from cover unexpectedly and caught them unprepared. The princess had not fired a single shot all day at her favoured quarry. On the homeward ride she had worked off some of her ire on a troop of baboons, shooting five out of the treetops before the survivors escaped in shrieking panic.

Approaching the outskirts of the camp Leon was surprised

to see two Ford motor-cars, painted in drab military brown, parked beside the skinning shed. As they rode past, a handful of *askari* in the uniforms of the KAR fell smartly into line, sloped their rifles and saluted. Leon recognized the sergeant and his troopers. They were members of the regimental head-quarters guard. His spirits soared as he acknowledged them. 'At ease, Sergeant Miomani.'

The NCO grinned with delight that Leon remembered him and snapped his arm down smartly. He shouted at his men, 'Order arms! Stand at ease! Fall out. One, two, three!'

They rode on into the camp.

'Who are those people, and what are they doing here, Courtney?' the princess demanded.

'They are British soldiers, Your Royal Highness, that much I can tell you. But as to why they are here I have no idea,' he lied smoothly. 'I expect we shall be enlightened soon enough.' But he held the thought that Loikot and Manyoro must have run like gazelle and Penrod Ballantyne driven like a fury to get here a day earlier than he had anticipated.

Leon and the princess dismounted outside the mess tent and Leon shouted to the kitchen for Ishmael to bring coffee – 'and make sure it's hot!' Then he ushered the princess into the cool gloom of the tent.

Penrod rose from one of the camp chairs and quickly forestalled any remark that Leon could make. 'I expect you are surprised to see me.' He seized Leon's right hand and shook it, then turned to the princess. 'Would you be so kind as to present me to Her Royal Highness?'

'Your Royal Highness, may I present Colonel Penrod Ballantyne?' he said, then noticed the crown and the trio of stars on Penrod's epaulettes. His uncle's promotion must have come through since their last meeting, and he corrected himself quickly: 'I beg your pardon, Princess. I should have said Brigadier General Penrod Ballantyne, the officer com-manding His Britannic Majesty's forces in British East Africa.' Penrod saluted, then took three smart paces forward and offered her his right hand.

The princess ignored it and studied his face coldly, 'Ah, so!' she said, walked past him and seated herself in her usual chair at the table. 'Courtney, tell your cook to hurry with my coffee. I am thirsty.' She had spoken in German. Then she looked at Penrod again. 'What do you want here? This is a private safari. You are disturbing my pleasure.' Her English was flawless.

Penrod went to the chair facing hers across the table. As he lowered himself into it he said, 'Your Royal Highness, I apologize for my intrusion but I am here on behalf of His Excellency the Governor of British East Africa.'

'I did not invite you to be seated,' the princess told him, and Penrod stood up abruptly.

His face turned puce but his voice remained level. 'I beg your pardon, ma'am.'

'They have no manners, these English.' She spoke to the air above his head. 'Ja, so? What does this governor of yours want from me?'

'He has sent me to inform you that a severe epidemic of Rift Valley rabies has broken out and is sweeping through the territory. Already more than a thousand local people have succumbed to the disease, and more are dying each day. The latest reported deaths are from villages not far from here. Your Royal Highness, you are in mortal danger.'

The princess's lofty expression changed dramatically. She stared at Penrod in horror. 'What is this Rift Valley rabies?'

'I believe the German translation is *Tollwut*, ma'am.'

'*Tollwut? Mein Gott!*'

'Indeed, Your Royal Highness. And this is a particularly virulent and infectious form. It inflicts a horribly cruel and inevitable death, with the victim writhing in convulsions, screaming for water and finally drowning in his own foaming saliva.'

'*Mein Gott!*' she repeated softly.

'The governor feels strongly that he should not allow you to remain in danger of contracting the disease, but before making any decision he cabled Berlin. The secretary to His

Imperial Majesty has relayed the Kaiser's instructions order-ing you to terminate your stay here and return at once to Germany. Accordingly, His Excellency has reserved a state-room on board the Italian liner *Roma* for you. It sails from Kilindini lagoon on the fifteenth of the month for the port of Genoa. From there you will be able to take the overnight express to Berlin. I have come to accompany you to the *Roma*, which will dock at Kilindini in five days' time. We must hurry to make the sailing.'

'When do you wish to depart?' the princess asked, and stood up.

'Can you be ready within the hour, ma'am?'

'*Jawohl!*' She fled, screaming for her maids. 'Heidi! Brun-hilde! Pack my travelling bags! Do not bother with the cabin trunks. We leave within the hour!' As soon as she had gone Penrod and Leon grinned at each other like schoolboys who had just pulled off a spectacular bit of mischief.

'Rift Valley rabies, indeed! How did you dream up that one, Perfidious Albion?'

'Absolutely deadly disease!' Penrod winked almost imper-ceptibly. 'Just so happens that this is the first outbreak in medical history.'

'How do you like Her Royal Highness?'

'Charming,' he replied. 'Bloody charming! I wanted to turn her over my knee and give her six of the very best.'

'If you had, she would probably have fallen deeply in love with you.'

'Like that, is it?' Penrod stopped smiling. 'You must have interesting tales to tell.'

'Tales that will set your hair on fire, believe me. You ain't heard nothing like them. But not here, not now.'

Penrod nodded. 'You're learning the game fast. As soon as I've packed the lovely princess into the boat at Kilindini, I will be back to listen to your stories and to stand you lunch at the Muthaiga Club.'

'With a bottle of the '79 Margaux to go with it?' Leon suggested.

'Two, if you're man enough!' Penrod promised.

'You're an absolute brick, Uncle.'

'Think nothing of it, dear boy.'

Long before the appointed hour the princess appeared from her tent with her secretary and maids following close behind her, their arms full of her coats and silk dresses. Penrod had the motor-cars standing by, the engines popping and rumbling. Leon offered the princess his hand as she stepped up into the first. She brushed his groin with her fingertips as she sat down, and dropped her voice so that only he could hear her. 'Give my fond farewell to my big friend.'

'Thank you, ma'am. His head droops to think of you gone.'

'Impudent boy!' She pinched his tender flesh so viciously that he gasped and his eyes watered. 'Do not be familiar. You must remember your place.'

'Please forgive my presumption, Your Royal Highness. I am desolate. But tell me, what shall I do with all the equipment you are leaving, the furniture, rifles and champagne? Shall I pack it and forward it to you?'

'*Nein!* I do not want it. You can keep it or burn it.'

'You are very generous. But will you ever return to hunt with me?'

'Never!' she said vehemently. 'Rabies? No, thank you!'

'Will you send your friends to hunt with me, Princess?'

'Only the ones I truly hate.' She saw his expression and relented slightly. 'But do not worry, Courtney. The friends I truly hate are more numerous than the ones I truly like.' She turned to Penrod in the seat behind her. 'Tell your driver to take me away from this dreadful rabies-infested place.'

'*Auf wiedersehen*, Princess!' Leon doffed his hat and waved, but she did not bother to turn as the vehicles bumped away along the rutted track.

T wo weeks later Penrod rode out to Tandala Camp on his grey stallion, and Ishmael had a pot of freshly brewed Lapsang Souchong tea and a plate of ginger snaps ready to welcome him. Ishmael did not serve his ginger snaps to just anyone but reserved them for especially favoured guests. After Penrod had fortified himself, he and Leon mounted up and set out on the eight-mile return ride to Muthaiga.

'I was really looking forward to a bit of a canter,' Penrod said. 'Never seem able to get away from my desk, these days.' He glanced at Leon. 'On the other hand, you look to be in fine fettle, dear boy.'

'The princess kept me hard at it. Did she tell you she mowed down more than a hundred warthogs, not to mention a monstrous black-maned lion and a fine leopard?'

'That gracious lady and I exchanged barely a dozen words on the entire journey to the coast. I rely on you to bring me up to date. That's why I came to fetch you. Out here we can talk without fear of eavesdroppers.' He waved a hand at the surrounding forest and the rolling green hills. 'Not many big ears and eyes out here. So now, Leon, tell your indulgent uncle everything.'

'You had better fasten the chin-strap of your helmet, sir, or it will likely be blown sky-high by my revelations.'

'Start at the beginning, and leave nothing out.' The leisurely ride to the Muthaiga Country Club took almost an hour and a half, just long enough for Leon to make his report. Penrod did not interrupt except to confirm a name or to ask him to enlarge on some detail. More than once he drew a sharp breath, his features registering extreme disapproval. They were riding up the driveway to the club before Leon was able to say, 'That's about it, Uncle.'

'Enough and more than enough,' Penrod replied grimly. 'Coming from anybody but you I would have had reservations. Some of it is so bizarre as to be almost beyond the grasp of a rational mind. You have accomplished more than I could possibly have hoped for.'

'Do you want me to write all this down, sir?'

'No. If you had done so previously she would have tumbled to you when she searched your tent. I'll remember it, probably never forget it for the rest of my days.' Penrod was silent until they reached the end of the driveway and pulled up their horses in front of the clubhouse. Then he said quietly, 'A remarkable lady, this princess of yours, Leon.'

'Not mine, sir, I assure you. As far as I'm concerned the hyenas can have her.'

'Come, let's go to lunch. Chefie has marrow bones and corned-beef hot-pot on the menu today. I hope your grisly tales haven't spoiled my appetite.'

'Nothing could do that, sir.'

'Careful, my lad. Show some respect for my grey hairs and the stars on my shoulders.'

'Forgive me, General. I meant no offence. I was simply implying that you are a connoisseur of impeccable taste.'

Once Penrod had greeted most of the other diners in the room, stopping for a moment at each table, they finally reached the terrace and settled into their chairs under the bougainvillaeas. Malonzi opened and poured the wine, then served the hors d'oeuvre of marrow bones on toast and withdrew discreetly.

'Let me bring you up to date with everything that has been happening in the wider world while you've been cavorting with royalty and warthogs in the wilderness.' Penrod scooped a large greasy lump of marrow out of the bone on to his toast, as he began a short résumé of events in Europe. 'The most startling item of gossip is that in the recent elections the Social Democratic Party has, for the first time in history, become the largest party in the German Reichstag. It has more than doubled its seat total from the 1907 election. Big trouble brewing there. The German military ruling élite will have to do something spectacular to reassert themselves. Anyone for a nice little war?' He popped the marrow toast into his mouth and chewed with gusto. 'And Serbia will surely want to wade into Austria. How about another little war? Talking of which, the one in Turkey rumbles on. The Turks have thrown the Bulgarians back from the gates of Constantinople, but it cost them twenty thousand casualties . . .' He devoured the rest of the marrow and washed it down with a glass of Margaux.

While he waited for Malonzi to serve the hot-pot he went on, 'Now, closer to home you have a large accumulation of mail, which includes a dozen or more enquiries for your services as a hunter. I picked them up from the post office and read them to save you the trouble.'

'I've said it before but I'll say it again. Uncle, you're a brick!'

Penrod acknowledged the compliment with a gracious wave of his fork.

'Most of these communications were from nobodies – I discarded those. However, three show great promise, all from our favourite country, Deutschland. One is from a conservative minister of government, the second from a Count Bauer, an adviser to the Imperial Chancellor, Theobald von Bethmann-Hollweg, and the third from a captain of industry who is the largest single contractor to the military. Naturally we wish to cultivate all three. However, the most attractive from our point of view is the industrialist. His name is Graf Otto Kurt Thomas von Meerbach. He is the head of the Meerbach Motor Works.'

'I know of them.' Leon was impressed. 'They developed the Meerbach rotary engine for aeroplanes. They're in competition with Count Zeppelin working on dirigible airships. Hell's bells and buckets of blood! I'd love to meet the fellow. I'm fascinated by the idea of taking to the skies, but to date I've never even laid eyes on one of the incredible new flying machines, let alone had a chance to go up in one.'

Penrod smiled at his boyish enthusiasm. 'If all goes as planned, you might soon have your chance. With Percy's blessing I have replied by urgent-rate cable to von Meerbach in your name. I gave him full details of what you have to offer, including available dates and your standard rates. But, in the meantime, you haven't tasted the hot-pot. It's jolly good. Oh, and by the way, there's also a letter from your pal Kermit Roosevelt.'

'Which you opened to save me the trouble?'

'Good Lord, no.' Penrod was horrified. 'Wouldn't dream of it. That's your private mail.'

'As opposed to all my other correspondence, which is public, Uncle?' Leon asked, and Penrod smiled comfortably.

'Line of duty, my dear boy.' Then he changed the subject. 'So, I understand that, with the princess out of your hair, you're charging off hot-foot to assist your partner, Percy, with the Eastmont safari.'

'That's correct. I leave first thing tomorrow. Percy's hunting on the west bank of Lake Manyara down in German territory. He left a note for me at Tandala. He says that Lord Eastmont is keen to get at least a fifty-inch buffalo and Manyara's the best place to find one.'

'Percy introduced me to Eastmont when he was passing through Nairobi. We had dinner together here, Percy, me and their two lordships, Eastmont and Delamere.'

'What did you make of Eastmont, if I might ask, sir?'

'You might indeed. In fact, I was about to tell all – you and Percy need to know. From our very first meeting I thought he was an odd fish. Something about him troubled me. It was only after he and Percy had left for Manyara that it all came back to me with a rush and a roar, if you'll pardon the poetic licence.'

'Pardon granted, sir. Please continue. I'm all ears.'

'I remembered there had been a nasty little incident in the South African campaign back in '99. A young captain of the Middlesex Regiment of Yeomanry Cavalry named Bertie Cochrane was in command of a forward reconnaissance platoon at a place called Slang Nek when they ran into a strong Boer contingent. At the first shots young Cochrane ran. He left his sergeant to try to fight off the Boers and ran for home and Mother. It was a massacre. The platoon took fifteen casualties from a strength of twenty before they could extricate themselves. Cochrane was court-martialled for cowardice in the face of the enemy, found guilty and cashiered. He might have been given a blindfold and a .303 bullet if not for his friends in high places. When I remembered all this I sent a cable to somebody I know at the War Office to check my memory of the incident. The reply came back affirmative. Cochrane and Eastmont are one and the same fellow, but there were a few more snippets of information. After his dishonourable discharge, young Bertie Cochrane married an extremely wealthy American oil heiress. Less than two years later, the new Mrs Cochrane drowned in a boating mishap on Ullswater in the Lake District of Cumberland. Cochrane was tried at the Middlesex Assizes for the murder of his wife, but acquitted for lack of evidence. He inherited her fortune, and two years later, on the death of his uncle, he became Earl of Eastmont, with an estate of more than ten thousand acres near Appleby in Westmorland. Thus plain old Bertie Cochrane became Bertram, Earl of Eastmont.'

'Dear God! Does Percy know this?'

'Not yet, but I rely on you to give him the glad tidings.'

Leon was in pensive mood when he rode home to Tandala. When he got there Manyoro and Loikot were waiting for him. He gave them instructions for an early start the next morning on the journey to join Percy's hunting camp on the banks of Lake Manyara, then went to his tent to read his mail.

There were three of his mother's marvellously fond and entertaining letters. Each was more than twenty pages long, and they were dated a month apart but had arrived at the Nairobi post office together. He learned that his father was well and prosperous, as always. His mother's latest book was titled *African Reflections* and it had been accepted for publication by Macmillan of London. Leon's eldest sister, Penelope, was to marry her childhood sweetheart in May, which was six weeks ago. He would have to send her a belated wedding gift. He laid the three maternal letters aside for reply, then slit open the letter with the New York postmark and Kermit's red wax seal on the flap.

Kermit had kept his word. His letter was breezy and chatty. He described the last months of the great safari with Quentin Grogan up the Nile and through the Sudan and Egypt. Big Medicine had continued to wreak havoc among the game herds. On the voyage from Alexandria to New York he had fallen in love again, but the girl was already engaged. He seemed to have taken this rejection in good part. Then he went on to describe a dinner party at the home of Andrew Carnegie, the steel multi-millionaire who had financed the great presidential safari. One of the other guests had been a German industrialist from Weiskirchen in Bavaria. His name was Otto von Meerbach. Kermit had been seated across the dinner table from him and they had taken to each other immediately. After dinner, when the ladies had withdrawn, they had lingered over the port and cigars.

> Otto is an extraordinary character, straight out of the
> pages of a lurid novel, complete with duelling scar and all.
> He is a great mountain of a man, booming with energy
> and self-assurance, and even if one does not like him, one
> has to admire him. He is the proprietor of the Meerbach
> Motor Works. I am sure that you have heard of it. In
> fact, I think I remember you and I discussing it. It's one
> of the biggest and most successful enterprises in all of
> Europe, employing more than thirty thousand workers.
> MMW developed the rotary engine for flying machines
> and dirigible airships. It also makes motor-cars and trucks
> for the German Army and airplanes for their air force.
> But the really interesting thing about Otto is that he is
> an avid hunter. He has huge estates in Bavaria where he
> hunts stags and wild boar. In winter he hosts hunting
> parties at his Schloss, which are famous. It is nothing out

*of the the ordinary for the guns to shoot more than two
hundred wild boar in a day. He has invited me to join him
as one of his guests the next time I am in Europe. I told
him about our safari, and he was very interested. He told
me he has been thinking about an African safari for many
years. He asked me for your address and of course I gave
it to him. I hope you do not mind?*

'So that's how von Meerbach found out where to get hold
of me,' Leon said aloud. 'Thank you, Kermit.' The letter
continued for a few more pages.

*Otto's wife, or maybe she is his mistress, I am not
entirely certain of the relationship, is truly one of the
most beautiful ladies I have ever laid eyes upon. Her
name is Eva von Wellberg. She is very refined and quiet
but, my sweet Lord, when she turned those eyes on me
my heart melted like butter in a skillet. I would readily
have fought a duel with Otto for her favours, even
though he is reputed to be one of the most accomplished
swordsmen in Europe. That's how strongly I feel about
this lovely consort of his.*

Leon laughed. The hyperbole was so typical of Kermit. He
interpreted his description to mean that Eva was probably
fair-to-middling attractive. Kermit ended by exhorting Leon
to reply soon, letting him have all the news of his own
activities and of the many friends Kermit had made in British
East Africa, particularly Manyoro and Loikot. It concluded,
'*salaams and Weidmanns Heil (Otto taught me this, it means
Hunters' Salute) from your BWB*'. It took a moment for Leon
to work out what the letters stood for. He smiled again. 'And
all the best to you, too, Kermit Roosevelt, my brother of the
warrior blood.'

Leon opened his travelling bureau to begin the replies to
his mother and Kermit, but before he could dip his pen in the
inkwell Ishmael sounded the dinner gong. Leon groaned. He
had not fully recovered from his luncheon with Penrod. But
Ishmael's meals were not optional. They were obligatory.

The journey south to Lake Manyara was over brutally rough tracks for the first two hundred miles. The Vauxhall took cruel punishment and they were forced to stop and repair punctured tyres at least a dozen times. Manyoro and Loikot had become past masters at the art of locating and removing the thorns that had pierced them. In the sandy stretches of road the engine boiled over regularly and they had to wait for it to cool before they refilled the radiator.

The boundary between British and German East Africa was neither marked nor guarded. There were no signposts along the way, other than blazes on roadside trees and a few bleached animal skulls set on poles. Navigating chiefly by instinct and the heavens, they at last reached the tiny bush store run by a Hindu trader at Makuyuni river. Percy had left a pair of good horses with the store owner to await his arrival.

Leon parked the truck under a ficus tree at the back of the store and saddled up one of the horses. From there it was a ride of at least fifty miles to Percy's hunting camp, which was set on a promontory above the lake shore.

Leon and his Masai reached it an hour after dark on the following day. He found out that neither Percy nor his noble client had returned to camp. Percy's cook served Leon a dinner of grilled hippo heart and cassava porridge with pumpkin mash and thick Bisto gravy.

Afterwards Leon sat at the fire and watched the flamingoes flying across the moon in dark, wavering lines. A bush fire was burning on the far shore of the lake. It looked like a fiery snake crawling through the dark hills, and he could smell the smoke. It was past ten o'clock when he heard the horses coming out of the night and went to the perimeter of the camp to meet them.

As Percy dismounted stiffly and painfully from the saddle, he recognized Leon waiting in the shadows. His shoulders straightened and his face creased in a smile of welcome. 'Well met indeed!' he called. 'Your timing's immaculate, Leon. Come to the fire and I'll introduce you to his lordship. I might even be minded to pour you a dram of Talisker.'

Eastmont was a tall, gangling figure, with huge hands and feet and a head the size of a watermelon. His long, thin limbs were ill-matched to his bulky torso. Percy stood at a little more than six feet and his Masai tracker was an inch taller, yet Eastmont towered over them, and Leon realized that he must be six foot three. When he shook hands, his fist engulfed Leon's fingers as though they were a child's. In the flickering firelight Eastmont's features were gaunt and bony, his expression dark and morose. He said little but instead left the talking to Percy. Once the glasses were charged he sat staring into the fire while Percy described the day's hunting,

'Well, his lordship wanted a truly monumental buffalo and, by golly, we found one this morning. He was an old solitary and I swear by all that's holy he's fifty-five if he's an inch.'

'Percy, that's incredible! But I believe you,' Leon assured him. 'Show me the head. Are your people bringing it in tonight, or will the skinners come in with it tomorrow?'

There was an awkward silence, and Percy glanced across the fire at his client. Eastmont seemed not to have heard. He continued staring into the flames.

'Well,' said Percy, and paused again. Then he went on with a rush of words: 'There's a small problem. The buff's head is attached to his body, and the body is still very much alive.'

Leon felt a chill at the back of his neck, but he asked carefully, 'Wounded?'

Percy nodded reluctantly, then admitted, 'Yes, but pretty hard hit, I think.'

'How hard, Percy? In the boiler room or the guts? How much blood?'

'Back leg,' said Percy, then hurried on: 'Broke the gaskin bone, I do believe. He should be stiff and crippled by tomorrow morning.'

'Blood, Percy? How much?'

'Some.'

'Arterial or venous?'

'Hard to tell.'

'Percy, it's not hard to tell arterial from venous. You taught me how, so you should know. One is bright red, the other dark. Why did you find it hard to tell the difference?'

'There wasn't very much of it.'

'How far did you track him?'

'Until it got dark.'

'How far, Percy, not how long.'

'A couple of miles.'

'Shit!' said Leon, as though he truly meant it.

'The polite version of that word is "*merde*".' Percy tried for a touch of humour.

'I'll settle for good old Anglo-Saxon.' Leon did not smile.

They were silent for a few long minutes. Then Leon looked across at Eastmont. 'What calibre were you using, my lord?'

'Three seven five.' Eastmont did not look up as he spoke.

Shit again! Leon thought, but did not say. Goddamned pea-shooter! 'How thick is the cover he's in, Percy?'

'It's thick,' Percy admitted. 'We'll follow him up tomorrow at first light. He'll be stiff and sore. Shouldn't take too long to catch up with him.'

'I have a better plan. The two of you stay here and have a quiet day in camp. Rest your leg, Percy. I'll follow him up and finish the business,' Leon suggested.

His lordship let out a bellow like a bull sealion in mating season. 'You will do no such thing, you impudent whipper-snapper. It's my buffalo and I will finish him off.'

'With all due respect, my lord, too many guns could turn a potentially dangerous situation into a fatal one. Let me go. This is what you pay us so much money to do.' Leon smiled in an unconvincing attempt at diplomacy.

'I paid so much money for you to do as you're bloody well told, my lad.' Leon's mouth hardened. He looked at Percy, who shook his head.

'Leon, it'll be all right,' he said. 'We'll probably find him down tomorrow.'

Leon rose to his feet. 'As you wish. I'll be ready to ride at first light. Good night, my lord.' Eastmont did not reply and Leon turned back to Percy. He looked old and sick in the firelight. 'Good night, Percy,' he said gently. 'Don't worry. I have a good feeling about this. We'll find him down, I know it.'

L eon stood at the edge of the cliff with Manyoro and Loikot. The sun was not yet up, and a low bank of mist hung over the water. The dawn was windless and the lake was a polished pewter grey. Skeins of luminous pink flamingoes flew in long, wavering lines low along it, the unruffled grey waters reflecting their perfect mirror images. It was very beautiful.

'Bwana Samawati thinks his back leg is broken,' Leon said, still watching the flamingoes. 'Perhaps it will slow him down a little.' Loikot spat a small glob of mucus on to the black lava sand, and Manyoro picked his nose, then examined the crusty product on the end of his forefinger with attention. Neither replied to the fatuous statement. A broken leg would not slow down an angry buffalo bull.

Leon went on, 'Bwana Mjiguu wants to lead. He says it's his buffalo. He will shoot it.' The Masai had named Eastmont 'Mr Big Feet' and greeted this latest snippet of information with as much joy as they would news of the passing of a dear friend.

'Perhaps he will shoot it in the other leg. That will slow it down,' Manyoro suggested, and Loikot doubled over in paroxysms of mirth. Leon could not control himself. He had to join in, and the laughter eased their feelings a little.

Behind them Percy came out of his tent and Leon left the Masai to greet him. His complexion was as grey as the lake waters and his limp more pronounced.

'Morning, Percy. Did you have a good night?'

'Bloody leg kept me awake.'

'There's coffee in the mess tent,' Leon said, and they walked towards it. 'I saw Uncle Penrod in Nairobi. He asked me to tell you something.'

'Go ahead.'

'Eastmont was cashiered from the army in South Africa. Cowardice in the face of the enemy.' Percy stopped and stared at him. 'Back home he was found not guilty of drowning his extremely rich wife. Lack of evidence.'

Percy thought about that for a moment, then said, 'Do you know something? That doesn't surprise me one little bit. I had him right up against the buff yesterday. Twenty yards. Not an inch more. He shot it in the back leg because he was overcome with terror.'

'Are you going to let him lead today?'

'You heard him last night. We don't have much option, do we?'

'Do you want me to back him?'

'You think I can't cut it any more?' Percy looked bereft.

Leon was stricken with remorse. 'Hell, no! You're still a stick of dynamite.'

'Thanks. I needed to hear that. But Eastmont is still my client. I'll back him, but I'll be grateful to have you behind me.' At that moment Eastmont came out of his tent and shambled towards them. His gait was ungainly, like that of a performing bear on a chain. 'Good morning, my lord,' Percy greeted him brightly. 'Eager to pick up your buff?'

T hey rode for an hour before they reached the spot where Percy had abandoned the blood spoor the previous evening. It was a bad place. The thorn bush was dense and grew low to the ground. There were narrow aisles through it that had been trodden by rhino, elephant and buffalo herds.

Percy's tracker, who had been with him for thirty years, was named Ko'twa. He pointed out the stale spoor, which had been almost obliterated by the passing of other large animals during the night, and Manyoro and Loikot took it away at a jog trot.

The three hunters followed on horseback. Even though the bush was thick the ground was soft and sandy so they covered the first two miles quickly. Then the character of the soil changed, becoming hard gravel that resisted the prints of the buffalo's hoofs. There was little blood and it had dried black so it was almost impossible to pick out the specks in the mulch of dead leaves and dried twigs under the bushes. The horsemen stayed well back to let the three trackers perform their small miracles of detection without interference. Within another hour the sun was well up and baking hot. There was no breeze and the air was stifling. Even the birds and insects were quiescent. The silence was brooding and ominous, and the thorn grew thicker, until it was almost solid. The trackers squeezed through the narrow openings and aisles between the fanged, clawing branches. Even from horseback the view ahead was severely curtailed.

At last Leon checked his mount and whispered to Percy, 'We're making too much noise. The buffalo will hear us coming from a mile off. We don't want to push him and get him moving. That'll loosen up his wound. We must leave the horses.' They unsaddled and hobbled them, but gave them nosebags to keep them contented.

While they took a last drink from the water-bottles, Percy gave Eastmont a final briefing: 'When the buff comes, and I mean when he comes, not if he comes, he will come with his nose held high in the air. He will probably be quartering across your front. You might think he's moving slowly and that he's not actually coming for you. Don't delude yourself. He's coming very fast, and he's coming to get you. He'll look so big that you might be confused about where to place your shot. You might be tempted to shoot into the middle of him. Don't do it. There's only one place to shoot if you're going to stop him. You have to brain him. Remember, his nose is held high. Go for the end. It'll be wet and shiny and give you a good aiming mark. Keep shooting at his nose until he goes down. If he doesn't go down and just keeps coming, throw yourself to the left. I'll be at your right elbow, and you must give me a clear shot. Left! Throw yourself left. Have you got that?'

'I'm not a child, Phillips,' said his lordship, stiffly. 'Don't speak to me like one.'

No, you're not a child, Leon thought bitterly. You're the gallant gentleman who left his platoon to be shot to bits by the jolly old Boer. I think we might have some fun with you today, my lord.

'I beg your pardon,' Percy replied. 'Are you ready to move out?' They fell into battle formation. Eastmont was on the point, with Percy close to his right elbow, and Leon brought up the rear. All their rifles were loaded and locked on safety. Leon had two spare .470 cartridges held between the fingers of his left hand ready for a quick reload. They followed the trackers, who knew exactly what to do without being told. This was all in a day's work for them. As soon as the buffalo broke cover, their duty was to clear the front and leave Eastmont open ground in which to take on the animal. They went forward slowly and silently, communicating with each other by sign language.

The sun rose towards its zenith. The air was as hot as the breath of hell. The back of Eastmont's shirt was running with sweat. Leon saw drops sliding down the nape of his neck from his hairline. He could hear him breathing in the silence, short, wheezing gasps like an asthmatic's. They had covered no more than two hundred slow paces in the last hour, and tension seemed to crackle in the air around them, like static electricity.

Suddenly there was a sound from directly ahead, like two dry twigs tapped together. The trackers froze. Loikot was standing on one leg, the other stretched out to take the next step.

'What was that?' Eastmont asked. In the silence his voice sounded like a foghorn.

Percy seized his shoulder and squeezed hard to silence him. Then he leaned forward until his lips were almost touching Eastmont's ear. 'Buff heard us coming. He stood up from his couch. His horn touched a branch. He's close. Keep very quiet.'

Nobody else spoke, and nobody moved. Loikot was still on one leg. They were all listening, standing still as waxwork dummies. It lasted for an eternity and an aeon. Then Loikot lowered his foot to the ground, and Manyoro turned his head to look back. He made a graceful and eloquent gesture with his right hand to Leon. 'The buffalo has moved forward,' said the hand. 'We can follow.'

They went on cautiously but heard nothing and saw nothing. Now the tension was like the twanging of steel wires stretched to breaking point. Leon's thumb was on the safety catch of the Holland, and the butt of the rifle was clamped under his right armpit. He could mount, aim and fire instantaneously. He heard it then, soft as rain in the grass, faint as a sleeping babe's breath. He glanced left, and the buffalo was coming.

It had doubled back and waited in ambuscade, hidden in an impenetrable thicket of grey thorn. It had let the trackers pass and now it came out, black as charcoal and big as a granite mountain. The sweep of the great curved horns was polished and gleaming, wider than the full stretch of a tall man's arms. The points were dagger sharp, and the boss between them was gnarled like the shell of a gigantic walnut, and massive as a monolith of obsidian.

'Percy! On your left! He's coming!' Leon yelled with all the power of his lungs. He stepped out to give himself a clear field of fire, but as he lifted the rifle into his shoulder, the buffalo galloped behind an intervening clump of thorn scrub. He couldn't get a bead on him.

'Your bird, Percy! Get him!' Leon yelled again, and from the corner of his eye he saw Percy turn left and shuffle to get into position. But his crippled leg dragged and slowed him down. He braced himself and leaned into his rifle, levelling it at the charging bull. Leon knew that Percy would brain him from that range. Percy was an old hand. He wouldn't muck it up, not now, not ever.

But they had forgotten about Lord Eastmont. As Percy tightened his forefinger on the trigger, Eastmont's nerve snapped. He dropped his rifle, spun around and ran for safety. His eyes were wild and his face was ash-white with panic as he lumbered back down the path. He seemed not even to see Percy as he crashed into him with all his weight. Percy went down and the rifle flew from his grip as he hit the ground on his shoulders and the back of his head. Eastmont did not even check his run, but bore straight down on Leon. The path was too narrow for Leon to avoid him. He reversed his rifle and used the butt in an effort to fend off Eastmont's rush.

It was futile. Eastmont was an enormous man and he was mad with terror. Nothing could stop him. Leon hit him in the centre of the chest with the rifle butt. The walnut stock snapped cleanly at the pistol grip, but Eastmont did not even flinch. He came into Leon like an avalanche. Leon was flung aside by the collision. Eastmont kept going. Leon landed on his right shoulder on the side of the path. He had the stock of the broken rifle in his left hand and pushed himself up with the right. Desperately he looked along the path to where Percy had gone down.

Percy was struggling to his knees. He had lost his rifle and was dazed by the blow to the back of his head. Behind him Leon saw the buffalo burst out of the thorn scrub into the narrow pathway. Its little eyes were bloodshot and they fixed on Percy. It lowered its massive head and swerved towards him. Its off back leg was trailing and swinging limply on the shattered bone, but it came on the other three, swift and dark as a summer tornado.

Leon lifted the shattered rifle. The butt-stock was gone but he was going to fire single-handed. He knew that the recoil might break his wrist. 'Percy, get down!' he screamed. 'Fall flat! Give me a chance.' But Percy stood up to his full height, blocking his shot. He was shaking his head with confusion, staggering drunkenly and looking around vaguely. Leon tried to shout again but his throat seized with horror and he could not utter a sound. He watched the buffalo roll its head to one side, winding up for the hook, as it covered the last few yards to reach Percy. Its neck was as thick as a tree-trunk and bulging with muscle. It used all that pent-up power to swing the massive half-moon of horns.

The point of a horn caught Percy in the small of the back at the level of his kidneys. The buffalo tossed its head high and he was impaled. With disbelief Leon saw that the point of the long curved horn had emerged from Percy's stomach. The buffalo shook its head in an effort to dislodge the limp body. Percy was whipped around and his arms and legs flailed slackly, but the horn still transfixed his belly. Leon could hear his skin and flesh parting with a sound like tearing silk. Percy dangled over the buffalo's head and blindfolded it. Leon raced forward, slipping the safety catch off the broken rifle. Before he could reach them, the buffalo lowered its head and wiped Percy off against the ground. As soon as it was free it smashed its great boss into him and, standing over him, began to grind him into the earth. Leon heard Percy's ribs snapping like dry twigs. He could not fire into the bull's skull, for the bullet would have gone straight through and into Percy's pinned body.

He dropped to one knee beside the buffalo's shoulder and pressed the double muzzles of the Holland into the massive neck at the juncture of spine and body. He had expected the recoil of the rifle to snap his wrists, but such was his furious abandon that he barely felt it and thought that the cartridge had misfired. But the bull reeled away from the shot and dropped into a sitting position on its haunches, its forelegs braced in front of it. Its head was lowered, and at last Leon could reach the brain. He jumped up and ran forward again, careful to stay outside the sweep of those lethal horns. He thrust the muzzle of the unfired barrel into the back of the skull behind the horny boss and fired the second barrel. The bullet burst the beast's brain asunder in its casket of bone. It flopped forward, then rolled on to its side. Its good rear leg kicked convulsively, and it let out a long, mournful death bellow, then lay still.

Leon dropped the shattered stock of his rifle and wheeled back to where Percy lay. He fell to his knees beside him. Percy was on his back with his arms thrown wide as a crucifix. His eyes were closed. The wound in his stomach was hideous. The violent movements of the bull had enlarged it so that the torn and tangled intestines bulged through the opening, the contents of the ripped intestines pouring from the wound. From the murky colour of the blood he saw that Percy was bleeding from his kidneys.

'Percy!' Leon called. He was reluctant to touch him, fearful of inflicting further pain and damage. 'Percy?'

His partner opened his eyes and, with an effort, focused on Leon's face. He smiled regretfully, sadly. 'Well, I didn't get away the second time. The first was just my old leg, but now they've done for me, good and truly.'

'Don't talk such rot.' Leon's voice was harsh, but his vision was blurring. He felt moisture on his cheeks and hoped it was only sweat. 'As soon as I've patched you up, I'll get you back to camp. You're going to be all right.' He stripped off his shirt and bundled it into a ball. 'This might be a little uncomfortable, but we have to plug the leak you've got there.' He stuffed the shirt into the hole in Percy's abdomen. It went in easily, for the wound was wide and deep.

'I can't feel a thing,' Percy told him. 'This is going to be a lot easier than I ever imagined it would be.'

'Do shut up, old man.' Leon could not look into his eyes where the shadows were gathering. 'Now. I'm going to pick you up and carry you back to your horse.'

'No,' Percy whispered. 'Let it happen here. I'm ready for it, if you'll help me over.'

'Anything,' Leon told him. 'Anything you want, Percy. You know that.'

'Then give me your hand.' Percy groped for him, and Leon gripped his hand firmly. Percy closed his eyes. 'I never had a son,' he said softly. 'I wanted one, but I never had one.'

'I didn't know that,' Leon said.

Percy opened his eyes. 'I guess I'll just have to settle for you instead.' The old twinkle was in his eyes.

Leon tried to reply but his throat was choked. He coughed and turned his head away. It took him a moment to find his voice. 'I'm not good enough for that job, Percy.'

'No one ever wept for me before.' There was wonderment in Percy's voice.

'Shit!' said Leon.

'*Merde*,' Percy corrected him.

'*Merde*,' Leon echoed.

'Now, listen.' There was sudden urgency in Percy's tone. 'I knew this was going to happen. I had a dream, a premonition. I left something for you in the old tin cabin trunk under my bed at Tandala.'

'I love you, Percy, you tough old bastard.'

'Nobody ever said that either.' The twinkle in the blue eyes began to fade. 'Get ready. It's going to happen now. Get ready to squeeze my hand to help me across.' He closed his eyes tightly for a long minute, then opened them very wide. 'Squeeze, my son. Squeeze hard!' Leon squeezed and was startled by the power with which the old man squeezed back.

'Oh, God, forgive me my sins. Oh, sweet, loving Father! Here I come.' Percy took one last gulp of air. His body stiffened, and then his hand in Leon's went slack.

Leon sat beside him for a long while. He was unaware that the trackers had come back and were squatting close behind him. When Leon reached out and gently closed Percy's staring eyes, Ko'twa jumped up and raced back along the path brandishing his *assegai*.

Carefully Leon arranged Percy's limbs and lifted him in his arms as if he was a sleeping child. He started back towards where they had tethered the horses, Percy's head resting on his shoulder. He had not gone fifty paces before he heard wild shouts.

'Bwana, come quickly! Ko'twa is killing Mjiguu!' Leon recognized Manyoro's voice in the uproar. Still carrying Percy, he broke into a run. As he came around the next bend in the narrow pathway he was presented with a scene of wild confusion.

Eastmont was curled in a foetal position in the middle of the path. His knees were drawn up to his chest and his huge hands covered his head defensively. Ko'twa danced over him with his stabbing *assegai* raised. He was screaming at the prostrate body. 'Pig and son of pigs! You have killed Samawati! You thing that is no man! You left him to die. He was a man among men and you killed him, you worthless creature. Now I am going to kill you.' He tried to thrust the bright *assegai* head into Eastmont's back but Manyoro and Loikot were hanging on to his spear arm to prevent the thrust going home.

'Ko'twa!' Leon's voice cracked like a rifle shot, and reached the tracker even in his excess of grief. He looked at Leon, but his eyes were sightless with rage and sorrow.

'Ko'twa, your *bwana* needs you. Come, take him home.' He offered him the lifeless body. Ko'twa stared at him. Slowly he came back from the far regions of his mind, and the red stains of rage faded from his eyes. He dropped his *assegai*, and shrugged off the restraining hands of the two Masai. He came to Leon, face bathed in tears, and Leon laid Percy in his arms. 'Bear him gently, Ko'twa.' He nodded wordlessly and carried Percy away, back to where the horses waited.

Leon went to where Eastmont lay and spurned him with the toe of his boot. 'Get up. It's all over. You're safe. On your feet.' Eastmont was sobbing softly. 'Get up, damn you, you craven bastard!' Leon repeated.

Eastmont uncurled his enormous frame and looked at him with incomprehension. 'What happened?' he asked uncertainly.

'You bolted, my lord.'

'It wasn't my fault.'

'That must be a great consolation to Percy Phillips and the troopers you left to die at Slang Nek. Or, for that matter, the wife you drowned in Ullswater.'

Eastmont did not seem to understand the accusations. 'I didn't want it to happen,' he whimpered. 'I wanted to prove myself. But I couldn't help it happening again. Please try to understand, won't you?'

'No, my lord, I won't. However, I have a piece of advice for you. Don't speak to me again. Ever. I won't be able to stop myself if I hear any more of your whining. I'll wring that great grotesque head off your monstrously deformed carcass.' Leon turned away and summoned Manyoro. 'Take this man back to camp.' He left them and went back to where the buffalo carcass lay. He found the pieces of his rifle in the bushes beside the path where he had thrown them. When he reached the horses Ko'twa was waiting for him. He was still holding Percy.

'Brother, please let me take Samawati from you for he was my father.' Leon took the body from his grieving tracker and carried Percy to his horse.

W hen Leon reached the lakeside camp he found that Max Rosenthal had arrived from Tandala in the other vehicle. Leon told him to make the arrangements for Eastmont's luggage to be packed and loaded. When Eastmont, guided by Manyoro, arrived at the camp, he was hangdog and sullen.

'I'm sending you back to Nairobi,' Leon told him coldly. 'Max will put you on the train to Mombasa, and book you a berth on the next sailing for Europe. I'll send the buffalo head and your other trophies to you as soon as they have been cured. You will be happy and proud to know that your buffalo is well over fifty inches. I owe you some money as a refund for this curtailed safari. I will let you have a banker's order as soon as I have calculated the amount. Now get into the motor, and stay out of my sight. I have to bury the man you killed.'

T hey dug Percy's grave deep, under an ancient baobab tree on the headland above the lake. They wrapped him in his bedroll and laid him in the bottom of the hole. Then they covered him with a layer of the largest stones they could carry, before they filled it in. Leon stood beside the mound of earth while Manyoro led the others in the lion dance.

Leon stayed on after all the others had gone back to the camp. He sat on a dead branch that had fallen from the baobab and gazed out across the lake. Now, with the sun on the water, it was as blue as Percy's eyes had been. He made his last farewell in silence. If Percy was lingering near, he would know what Leon was thinking without having to be told.

Looking out across the lake, Leon was satisfied with the beautiful place he had chosen for Percy to spend eternity.

He thought that when his own time came he would not mind being buried in such a spot. When at last he left the grave and went back to the camp he found that Max had left for Nairobi with Lord Eastmont.

Well, at least I'm still drinking his whisky, Leon thought grimly. Those words had been Percy's summation of a safari that had gone horribly wrong.

Leon travelled the rough track to Arusha, the local administrative centre of the government of German East Africa. He went before the district Amtsrichter, and swore an affidavit as to the circumstances of Percy's demise. The judge issued a death certificate.

Some days later when he reached Tandala Camp, Max and Hennie du Rand were anxiously awaiting his return to find out what fate was in store for them now that Percy was gone. Leon told them he would speak to them as soon as he knew what was the position of the company.

After he had drunk a pot of tea to wash the dust out of his throat, he shaved, bathed and dressed in clothes freshly ironed by Ishmael. Then he faced the fact that he was deliberately marking time, reluctant to go to Percy's bungalow. Percy had been a private man and Leon would feel guilty of sacrilege if he ferreted around in his personal possessions. However, he steeled himself at last with the thought that this was what Percy had charged him to do.

He went up the hill to the little thatched bungalow that had been Percy's home for the last forty years. Yet he was still reluctant to enter and sat for a while on the stoep, remembering some of the banter that the two of them had enjoyed while seated in the comfortable teak chairs with their elephant-skin cushions and the whisky-glass coasters carved into the armrests. At last he stood up again and went to the front door. It swung open to his touch. In all those years Percy had never bothered to lock it.

Leon went into the cool, dim interior. The walls of the front room were lined with bookcases, the shelves packed with hundreds of books. Percy's library was a treasury of Africana. Instinctively Leon crossed to the central shelf and took down a copy of *Monsoon Clouds Over Africa* by Percy 'Samawati' Phillips. It was his autobiography. Leon had read it more than once. Now he flicked through the pages, enjoying some of the illustrations. Then he replaced it on the shelf and went into Percy's bedroom. He had never been in this room before and looked around diffidently. A crucifix hung on one wall. Leo smiled. 'Percy, you crafty old dog, I always thought you were an unrepentant atheist, but you were a secret Catholic all along.'

There was one other decoration on the monastically austere walls. An ancient, hand-coloured daguerreotype of a couple, sitting stiffly in what were obviously their best Sunday clothes, faced the bed. The woman held a small child of indeterminate sex on her lap. Despite his sideburns, the man was a dead ringer for Percy. The couple were unmistakably his parents, and Leon wondered if the child was Percy himself or one of his siblings.

He sat on the edge of the bed. The mattress was as hard as concrete and the blankets were threadbare. He reached under the bed and dragged out a battered steel cabin trunk. As it came it encountered resistance. He went down on one knee to see what had snagged it.

'My oath!' he muttered. 'I wondered what you'd done with that.' It required considerably more effort to drag the heavy item into plain view. Then he was gazing at a great ivory tusk, the pair of the one he had pawned to Mr Goolam Vilabjhi Esquire. 'I thought you'd sold it, Percy, but all along you had it squirrelled away.'

He resumed his seat on the edge of the bed and possessively placed both feet on the tusk, then threw back the lid of the trunk. The interior was neatly packed with all of Percy's treasures and valuables, from his passport to his accounts and his cheque book, from small jewellery boxes of cufflinks and dress studs to old steamline tickets and faded photographs. There were also several neat wads of documents tied with ribbon. Leon smiled again when he saw that one comprised all the clippings of the newspaper reports of the great safari, which had so prominently featured himself. On top of this hoard a folded document, sealed with red wax, was inscribed in block capitals: 'TO BE OPENED BY LEON COURTNEY ONLY IN THE EVENT OF MY DEATH'.

Leon weighed it in his hand, then reached for the hunting knife in its sheath on his belt. Carefully he prised open the wax seal and unfolded a single sheet of heavy manila paper. It was headed 'Last Will and Testament'. Leon glanced at the bottom of the page. It was signed by Percy, and his two witnesses were Brigadier General Penrod Ballantyne and Hugh, the 3rd Baron Delamere.

Impeccable, Leon thought. Percy couldn't have found more credible witnesses than those two. He started again at the top of the page and read the entire handwritten document carefully. The gist was clear and simple. Percy had left his entire estate, with nothing excluded, to his partner and dear friend Leon Ryder Courtney.

It took Leon some time to come to terms with the magnitude of Percy's last gift to him. He had to read the document three more times in order to assimilate it. He still had not the slightest idea of Percy's total wealth, but his firearms and safari equipment must have been worth at least five hundred pounds, to say nothing of the huge ivory tusk that Leon was using as a footstool. But the intrinsic value of the estate was of no concern to Leon: it was the gift itself, the earnest of Percy's affection and esteem, that was the real treasure.

He was in no hurry to examine the remaining contents of the trunk, and sat for a while, considering the will. At last he carried the trunk out to the stoep where the light was better and settled into the easy chair that had been Percy's favourite. 'Keeping it warm for you, old man,' he muttered apologetically, and began to unpack.

Percy had been meticulous in keeping his records in order.

Leon opened his cash book and blinked with astonishment when he saw the balances of the deposits held by the Nairobi branch of Barclays Bank, Dominion, Colonial and Overseas to the credit of Percy Phillips Esq. They totalled a little more than five thousand pounds sterling. Percy had made him a wealthy man.

But that was not all. He found title deeds to land and properties not only in Nairobi and Mombasa but in the city of Bristol, the place of Percy's birth, in England. Leon had no means of estimating what they might be worth.

The value was more readily apparent of the bundle of Consols, the 5 per cent perpetual bearer bonds issued by the government of Great Britain, the safest and most reliable investment in existence. Their face value was twelve and a half thousand pounds. The interest on that alone was more than six hundred per annum. It was a princely income. 'Percy, I had no idea! Where the hell did you get it all from?'

When it grew dark Leon went into the front room and lit the lamps. He worked on until after midnight, sorting documents and reading accounts. When his eyelids drooped he went through to the austere little bedroom and stretched out under the mosquito net on Percy's bed. The hard mattress welcomed his weary body. It felt good. After all his wanderings he had found a place that felt like home.

He woke to the dawn chorus of a thrush under the window. When he went down the hill he found Max Rosenthal and Hennie du Rand waiting anxiously in the mess tent. Ishmael had breakfast ready, but neither had touched it. Leon took his seat at the head of the table.

'You can relax, and stop sitting on the edge of your chairs. Help yourselves to the eggs and bacon before they get cold and Ishmael throws a tantrum,' he told them. 'C and P Safaris is still in business. Nothing changes. You still have your jobs. Just carry on exactly as you were before.'

As soon as he had finished breakfast he went out to the Vauxhall. After Manyoro had cranked the engine to life, he and Loikot scrambled into the back and Leon headed for town. His first stop was at the little thatched building behind Government House that served as the Deeds Office. The clerk notarized Percy's death certificate and his will, and Leon signed the entries in the huge leatherbound ledger.

'As the executor of Mr Phillips's estate, you have thirty days to file a statement of the assets of the estate,' the clerk told him. 'Then you must pay the duty before the remaining assets can be released to the named heirs.'

Leon was startled. 'What do you mean? Are you trying to tell me there's a charge for dying?'

'That's right, Mr Courtney. Death duties. Two and one half per cent.'

'That's blatant robbery and extortion,' Leon exclaimed. 'What if I refuse to pay?'

'We will seize the assets and probably lock you up to boot.'

Leon was still fuming at the injustice when he drove through the front gates of the KAR barracks. He parked the truck in front of the headquarters building and went up the steps, acknowledging the salutes of the sentries as he passed. The new adjutant was sitting in the duty room. To Leon's surprise, this was none other than Bobby Sampson. He now wore a captain's pips on his epaulettes. 'It seems that everybody around here is being promoted, even the lowest forms of animal life,' Leon remarked from the doorway.

Bobby stared at him blankly for a moment, then bounded up from his desk and rushed to pump Leon's hand joyously. 'Leon, my old fruit! A thing of beauty is a joy for ever! I don't know what to say, what? What?'

'You've just said it all, Bobby.'

'Tell me,' Bobby insisted, 'what have you been up to since last we met?'

They talked animatedly for a while, then Leon said, 'Bobby, I'd like to see the general.'

'I have no doubt that the Brig will be delighted to oblige,

what? Wait here and I'll have a quick word with him.' Minutes later he returned and ushered Leon through into the CO's office.

Penrod stood up and reached across his desk to shake Leon's hand, then indicated the chair facing him. 'This comes as a bit of a surprise, Leon. Didn't expect you back in Nairobi for another month or so. What happened?'

'Percy's dead, sir.' Leon's voice caught as he made the bald statement.

Penrod stared at him speechlessly. Then he left his desk and went to the window to stand gazing out across the parade-ground, his hands clasped behind his back. They were silent for a while, until eventually Penrod came back to his seat. 'Tell me what happened,' he ordered.

Leon did so, and when he had finished, Penrod said, 'Percy knew it was coming. He asked me to witness his will before he left town. Did you know he had made one?'

'Yes, Uncle. He told me where to find it. I've already lodged it with the registrar.'

Penrod stood up and placed his cap on his head. 'It's a bit early, sun isn't over the yardarm, but we're duty-bound to give Percy a decent wake. Come on.'

Apart from the barman, the mess was empty. Penrod ordered the drinks and they sat together in the quiet corner traditionally reserved for the commanding officer and his guests. For a while their conversation revolved around Percy and the manner of his dying. Finally Penrod asked, 'What will you do now?'

'Percy left everything to me, sir; so I'm going to keep the company running, if for no other reason than to honour his memory.'

'I'm pleased about that, for all the reasons of which you're well aware,' Penrod said, in hearty approval. 'However, I suppose you'll change its name.'

'I've already done so, Uncle. I registered the new name at the Deeds Office this morning.'

'Courtney Safaris?'

'No, sir. Phillips and Courtney. P and C Safaris.'

'You haven't dropped his name. Instead you've given it the priority over your own that it never had before!'

'The old name was decided on the spin of a coin. Percy really wanted it as it is now. This is just my way of trying to repay a little of all he did for me.'

'Well done, my boy. Now, I have some good news for you. P and C Safaris is off to a flying start. The Princess Isabella Madeleine Hoherberg von Preussen von und zu Hohenzollern has given her endorsement to your company. It seems that Graf Otto von Meerbach, a family friend of hers, spoke to her on her return to Germany and she recommended you without reservation. Von Meerbach has accepted the quotation from Percy that I sent him and has already paid the requested deposit into your bank account. He's confirmed that he'll be coming out to British East Africa with his whole entourage at the beginning of next year for a six-month safari.'

Leon grimaced and swirled the ice in his glass. 'Somehow it doesn't seem to matter very much, now that Percy has gone.'

'Cheer up, my boy. Von Meerbach is bringing out a couple of prototypes of his flying machines. Apparently he wants to test them under tropical conditions. Ostensibly he's developing them as mail-carriers, but on this safari he plans to use them to spot game from the air. Anyway, that's what he's saying but, given his connections with the German Army, I doubt that this is the whole truth. I believe he'll be using them to scout the back country along our border with German East Africa, with an eye to any future military offensives against us. Be that as it may, you might get the opportunity to fulfil your dream of sailing among the clouds while picking up some useful snippets of intelligence for me. Now, if you finish your drink we can return to my office. I'll give you a copy of the confirmation von Meerbach sent. It's the longest cablegram I've ever laid eyes upon, twenty-three pages in all, setting out his requirements for the safari. It must have cost him a ruddy fortune to send.'

Leon was waiting on the beach of Kilindini lagoon when the German tramp steamer SS *Silbervogel* anchored in the roadstead. He went out to her in the first lighter. When he went up the companion ladder five passengers were waiting to meet him on the afterdeck, the engineer and his mechanics from the Meerbach Motor Works, part of the team that Graf Otto von Meerbach had sent out as his vanguard.

The man in charge introduced himself as Gustav Kilmer. He was a muscular, capable-looking fellow in his early fifties, with a heavy jaw and close-cropped iron-grey hair. His hands were stained with embedded grease, and his fingernails were ragged from working with heavy tools. He invited Leon to take a glass of pilsener with him in the passenger saloon before they disembarked.

When they were seated with tankards in hand, Gustav went over the inventory of the cargo that was stowed in the *Silbervogel*'s holds, which comprised fifty-six huge crates weighing twenty-eight tons in total. There were also two thousand gallons of special fuel for the rotary aircraft engines in fifty-gallon drums, and another ton of lubrication oil and grease. In addition, three Meerbach motor vehicles were strapped under green tarpaulin covers on the afterdeck. Gustav explained that two were heavy transport trucks and the third was an open hunting car that had been designed jointly by himself and Graf Otto, and built in the Weiskirchen factory. It was the only one of its kind in existence.

It took the lighters three days to ferry this vast cargo ashore. Max Rosenthal and Hennie du Rand were waiting at the head of a gang of two hundred black porters to transfer the drums and crates from the lighters to the goods trucks that were standing in the Kilindini railway siding.

When the three motor vehicles were brought ashore and unwrapped from their heavy tarpaulin covers, Gustav checked them for damage they might have suffered during the voyage, Leon watching his every move with fascination. The trucks were big and robust, far in advance of anything he had ever seen. One had been fitted with a thousand-gallon tank to carry fuel for the motors and aeroplanes, and in a separate compartment between the fuel tank and the driver's seat there was a compact toolroom and workshop. Gustav assured Leon that, from the workshop, he could maintain all three vehicles and the aircraft anywhere in the field.

Leon was impressed by all of this, but it was the open hunting car that filled him with wonder. He had never seen such a beautiful piece of machinery. From the upholstered leather seats, fitted cocktail bar and gun racks to the enormous six-cylinder 100-horsepower engine under the long gleaming bonnet, it was a symphony of engineering genius.

By now Gustav had taken to Leon's boyish charisma, and was further flattered by his interest in and unstinted praise of his creations. He invited Leon to be his passenger on the long drive up-country to Nairobi.

When at last the main cargo had been loaded on to the railway wagons, Leon ordered Hennie and Max aboard to shepherd it to Nairobi. As the train pulled out of the siding and puffed away into the littoral hills, Gustav and his mechanics mounted the three Meerbach vehicles and started the engines. With Leon in the passenger seat of the hunting car, Gustav led the trucks out on to the road. The drive was much too short for Leon, every mile a delight. He sat in the leather seat, which was more comfortable than the easy chairs on the stoep of the Muthaiga Country Club, and was cosseted by the swaying Meerbach patented suspension. He watched the speedometer with amazement as Gustav pushed the great machine to almost seventy miles an hour on one particularly smooth and straight stretch of road.

'Not too long ago there was much debate as to whether or not the human body could survive speeds of this magnitude,' Gustav told him comfortably.

'It takes my breath away,' Leon confessed.

'Would you like to drive for a while?' Gustav asked magnanimously.

'I'd kill for half the chance,' Leon admitted. Gustav chortled jovially, and pulled to the side of the track to relinquish the steering-wheel.

They beat the goods train to Nairobi by almost five hours and were on the platform to welcome it when it chugged in, its steam whistle shrieking. The driver shunted the trucks on to a spur rail to be unloaded the following morning. Leon had hired a contractor who operated a powerful steam traction engine to haul the cargo to its final destination.

In accordance with one of the numerous instructions that had been cabled from Meerbach headquarters in Weiskirchen, Leon had already built a large open-sided hangar with a tarpaulin roof to serve as a workshop and storage area. He had sited this on the open plot of land he had inherited from Percy. It adjoined the polo ground, which he planned to use as a landing strip for the aircraft, which were still in their crates awaiting assembly.

These were busy days for Leon. One of Graf Otto von Meerbach's cables gave detailed instructions for the provision of creature comforts for himself and his female companion. At each hunting location, Leon was to prepare adjoining quarters to accommodate the couple; he had been issued with detailed specifications for these commodious and luxurious suites. Furniture for them was packed in one of the crates, and included beds, wardrobes and linen. He had also received instructions as to how the dining arrangements should be conducted. Graf Otto had sent full sets of crockery and silver, with a pair of enormous solid silver candelabra, each weighing twenty pounds, that were sculpted with hunting scenes of stag and wild boar. The beautiful bone-china dinner service and the crystal glassware were embellished in gold leaf with the Meerbach coat of arms: a mailed fist brandishing a sword and the motto 'Durabo!' on a banner below it. '"I shall survive!"' Leon translated the Latin. The fine white linen napery was embroidered with the same motif.

There were two hundred and twenty cases of the choicest champagnes, wines and liqueurs, and fifty crates of canned and bottled delicacies: sauces and condiments, rare spices like saffron, *foie gras* from Lyon, Westphalian ham, smoked oysters, Danish pickled herring, Portuguese sardines in olive oil, scallops in brine and Russian beluga caviar. Max Rosenthal was enraptured when he laid eyes for the first time on this epicurean hoard.

Apart from all of this there were six large cabin trunks labelled 'Fräulein Eva von Wellberg. NOT TO BE OPENED BEFORE ARRIVAL OF THE OWNER.' However, one of the largest had burst open and from it spilled a collection of magnificent feminine clothing and footwear suitable for every possible occasion. When Leon was summoned by Max to deal with the catastrophe of the damaged luggage, he gazed in wonder. The exquisite underwear, each separate article wrapped in tissue paper, caught his particular attention. He picked up a feathery wisp of silk and an enchanting, erotic fragrance wafted up from it. Prurient images bestirred themselves in his imagination. He repressed them sternly, and replaced the garment on the pile as he gave orders to Max to repack the trunk, then repair and reseal the damaged lid.

Over the weeks that followed, Leon delegated to Max and Hennie most of the petty details, while he spent every hour he could afford in the hangar at the polo field, watching Gustav and his team assemble the two aircraft. Gustav worked with precision and thoroughness. Each of the crates was marked with its contents so they were unpacked in the correct sequence. Slowly, day after day, the jigsaw puzzle of assorted engine parts, rigging wire and struts, wing and fuselage started to take on the recognizable shape of aircraft. When at last Gustav had completed the assembly, Leon was amazed by their size. Their fuselages were sixty-five feet long, and the wing spans a prodigious 110 feet. The framework was covered with canvas that had been treated with a cellulose derivative to give it the strength and tautness of steel. The aircraft were painted in marvellously flamboyant patterns and colours. The first was a dazzling chessboard of brilliant scarlet and black squares and the name painted on its nose was *Der Schmetterling*

– the *Butterfly*. The second was decorated with black and golden stripes. Graf Otto had christened it *Die Hummel* – the *Bumble Bee*.

Once the bodywork had been assembled, the aircraft were ready to receive their engines. There were four 250-horse-power seven-cylinder fourteen-valve rotary Meerbach engines for each. After Gustav had bolted them in turn on to test beds made of teak railway sleepers, he started them. Their roar could be heard miles away in the Muthaiga Country Club, and soon every layabout in Nairobi had arrived to swarm around the hangar, like flies around a dead dog. They seriously impeded the work, and Leon had Hennie erect a barbed-wire fence around the property to keep the gaping throng at a distance.

Once Gustav had tuned the engines, he declared he was ready to fit them to the wings of the two aircraft. One by one they were hoisted by block and tackle on gantries built over the wings. Then he and his mechanics manoeuvred them into position and fixed them into their mountings, two engines on each bank of wings.

Three weeks after the commencement of the work, the assembly of the machines was completed. Gustav told Leon, 'Now it is necessary to test them.'

'Are you going to fly them?' Leon had difficulty containing his excitement, but he was immediately disappointed when Gustav shook his head vehemently.

'*Nein!* I am not a crazy man. Only Graf Otto flies these contraptions.' He saw Leon's expression and tried to console him a little. 'I am only going to ground-taxi them, but you shall ride with me.'

Early the following morning Leon mounted the boarding ladder to the commodious cockpit of the *Butterfly*. Gustav, in a long black leather coat and matching leather helmet with a pair of goggles pushed up on to his forehead, followed him and seated himself on the pilot's bench at the rear of the cockpit. First, he showed Leon how to strap himself in. From there Leon watched Gustav's every move as he waggled the elevators and ailerons with the joystick, then did the same with the rudder bars. When he was satisfied that the controls were free he gave the signal to his assistants on the ground below, and they began the complicated starting routine. Finally all four engines were running smoothly, and Gustav gave the thumbs-up sign to his assistants, who dragged away the wheel chocks.

With Gustav playing the throttles as though they were the stops of a cathedral organ, the *Butterfly* rolled majestically out of the hangar and into the brilliant African sunshine. A cheer went up from the several hundred spectators who lined the barbed-wire boundary fence. Gustav's men ran beside the wing-tips to help steer the machine as, bumping and rocking, the *Butterfly* made four ponderous circuits of the polo ground.

Gustav saw Leon's yearning and, once again, took pity on him. 'Come, take the controls!' he shouted, above the din of the engines. 'Let's see if you can drive her.'

Joyfully Leon took his place on the pilot's bench and Gustav nodded his approval as Leon swiftly gained the feel of joystick and rudder bars, refining his touch on the quadruple throttle levers. '*Ja*, my engines can feel that you respect and cherish them. You will soon learn to get the very best out of them.'

At last they returned to the hangar, and when Leon had climbed back down the ladder to the ground, he reached up on tiptoe to pat the *Butterfly*'s scarlet and black chequered nose. 'One day I'm going to fly you, my big beauty,' he whispered to the towering machine. 'Damn me if I don't!'

Gustav came down behind him, and Leon took the opportunity to question him on something that had puzzled him for a while. He pointed out the racks of hooks and braces under the wings on each side of the fuselage. 'What are these for, Gustav?'

'They are for the bombs,' Gustav replied guilelessly.

Leon blinked but kept his manner only mildly curious. 'Of course,' he said. 'How many can she carry?'

'Many!' Gustav answered proudly. 'She is very powerful.

Let me give you the English numbers, which maybe you will understand better. She can lift two thousand pounds of bombs, plus a crew of five and her full tanks of fuel. She can fly at a hundred and ten miles per hour at an altitude of nine thousand feet for a distance of five hundred miles and after that return to her base.'

'She's amazing!'

Gustav stroked the gaudy fuselage, like a father caressing his firstborn. 'There is no other machine in the world to match her,' he boasted.

By noon the following day Penrod Ballantyne had cabled the precise performance figures of the Meerbach Mark III Experimental to the War Office in London.

Leon's next task was to select four landing strips in the wilderness, one at each of the widely separated locations where he intended to hunt with his client. Graf Otto had cabled him detailed instructions, setting out their required dimensions and their alignment to the prevailing winds. Once he had found suitable locations, Leon shot the levels with a theodolite and pegged out the runways. Meanwhile Hennie du Rand recruited hundreds of men from the surrounding villages and put them to work felling trees and smoothing the ground. In some places he had to dynamite termite mounds, in others to fill in numerous antbear holes and dongas. When each strip was completed he marked the periphery of the runways with lines of burned lime so that they were highly visible from the air. Then he raised one of the windsocks that Gustav had given him. It filled with the breeze and flew proudly at the top of its raw wood mast.

While Hennie built the airfields, Max Rosenthal was responsible for the construction of the elaborate camps that Graf Otto had specified. Leon had to drive both men hard to have everything in readiness for the imminent arrival of their guests. In the end they succeeded, but with only a few days to

spare before the ocean liner carrying Graf Otto von Meerbach
was due to anchor in Kilindini roads.

Leon bribed his way on board the pilot boat when it went
out through the mouth of Kilindini lagoon to meet the
German passenger liner SS *Admiral* from Bremerhaven
as she hove up over the horizon. The sea was calm, so it was
an easy transfer from the pilot boat to the liner. As he ran up
the companion ladder he was challenged by the ship's fourth
officer. When he mentioned his client's name, the man's
manner changed quickly and he led Leon up to the bridge.

From Kermit's description, Leon recognized Graf Otto von
Meerbach at first glance. He was standing in the wing of the
bridge smoking a Cohiba cigar and chatting to the captain,
whose attitude towards him was obsequious. Graf Otto was
the only passenger allowed on the bridge during the compli-
cated manoeuvre of anchoring the massive liner. Leon studied
him for a few minutes, then went up to him to introduce
himself.

Graf Otto wore an elegant cream tropical suit. He was as
big and hard as an oak tree, as Kermit had said. He gave the
impression of being all muscle, but carried himself with the
poise and overbearing self-assurance of a man of limitless
wealth and power. He was not handsome in any conventional
sense; instead his features were hard and uncompromising. His
mouth was wide, but a puckered white duelling scar ran from
one corner to just under his right ear so that it seemed frozen
in a lopsided sneer. His pale green eyes had an alert, intelli-
gent sparkle. He carried a white Panama hat in his left hand,
but for the moment his head was bare. His skull was well
shaped and proportioned, and his thick, short-cropped hair
bright ginger.

This is one tough, formidable bastard! Leon made a snap
judgement before he approached him. 'Do I have the honour

of addressing Graf Otto von Meerbach?' Leon gave him a minimal bow.

'*Jawohl*, you do indeed. May I ask who you are?' The Count's voice was stentorian, his tone dictatorial.

'I am Leon Courtney, sir, your hunter. Welcome to British East Africa.'

Graf Otto smiled with patronizing geniality, and extended his right hand. Leon saw that it was powerful and that the back was covered with golden freckles and curling ginger hair. He wore a gold ring set with a large white diamond on his third finger. Leon steeled himself for the handshake. He knew it would be crushing.

'I have been looking forward to meeting you, Courtney, ever since I spoke to both Mr Kermit Roosevelt and the Princess Isabella von und zu Hohenzollern.' Leon found he could match the power of that big freckled hand, but required all his strength to do so. 'Both have a high opinion of you. I hope you will be able to show me some good sport, *ja*?' Graf Otto spoke excellent English.

'Indeed, sir. I have every expectation of doing so. I have obtained hunting permits in your name for a full bag of species. But you must inform me which quarry interests you most. Lions? Elephant?' At last Graf Otto released his hand and the blood rushed back so painfully that it took all Leon's determination to prevent himself massaging it. He caught a glint of respect in the pale green eyes. He knew that the other's hand was also numbed, although he gave not the least indication that he was in pain.

'Your German is good, but this I was told,' Graf Otto replied, in the same language. 'To answer your question, I am interested in hunting both of those species, but especially lions. My father was ambassador to Cairo at the time of Kitchener's war with the Mahdi. This gave him the opportunity to hunt in Abyssinia and the Sudan. I have many of his lionskins at my hunting lodge in the Black Forest, but they are old now and some have been eaten by moths and worms. I have heard that the blacks here hunt the lions with a spear. Is that true?'

'It is, sir. For the Masai and the Samburu it is a test of the young warrior's courage and manhood.'

'I should like to witness this manner of hunting.'

'I shall arrange for you to do so.'

'Good, but I also wish to obtain several pairs of large elephant tusks. Tell me, Courtney, in your opinion, which is the most dangerous wild animal in Africa? Is it the lion or the elephant?'

'Graf Otto, the old Africa hands say that the most dangerous animal is the one that kills you.'

'*Ja*, that I understand. It is a typical English joke.' He chuckled. 'But what do you say, Courtney? Which is it?'

Leon had a vivid image of the curved black horn protruding from Percy Phillips's belly, and stopped smiling. 'The buffalo,' he replied seriously. 'The wounded buffalo in thick cover is the one that gets my vote.'

'I can see from your expression that you are speaking from the heart. No more English jokes, *nein*?' Graf Otto said. 'So, we hunt elephant and lions but most of all we hunt buffaloes.'

'You understand, sir, that although I will do my best to help you procure trophies, these are wild beasts and much will depend on luck?'

'I have always been a lucky man,' Graf Otto replied. It was a statement of fact, not a boast.

'That is abundantly obvious to even the most simple mind, sir.'

'And it is just as obvious that you do not have a simple mind, Mr Courtney.'

Like two heavyweight boxers at the opening of the first round, they watched each other's eyes as they smiled and feinted, keeping up their guard as they felt each other out, making quick assessments and subtly shifting their stance to meet every nuance in the charged current that flowed between them.

Then, unexpectedly, Leon became aware of a subtle perfume on the warm, tropical air. It was light and fragrant, the same enchanted scent that had captivated him once before as he held in his hand the silken garment from the ruptured cabin trunk. Then he saw Graf Otto's eyes flick to look over his shoulder. Leon turned his head to follow his gaze.

She was there. Ever since he had read Kermit's letter he had anticipated this meeting, but was still unprepared for the moment. He felt a flutter in his chest, like the wings of a trapped bird trying to escape from the cage of his ribs. His breath came short.

Her loveliness surpassed Kermit's meagre description a hundredfold. Kermit had been correct in one detail only: her eyes. They were an intense blue, a shade darker than violet and softer than dove grey, slanting up at the outer corners. They were wide-spaced and fringed with long, dense lashes that meshed when she closed them. Her forehead was broad and deep, and the line of her jaw finely sculpted. Her lips were full and parted slightly when she smiled to reveal a glint of small, very white teeth. Her hair was a lustrous sable. She wore it scraped back from her face but, beneath the brim of the fashionable little hat cocked at a jaunty angle over one eye, soft tendrils had escaped the retaining pins and curled out over her little pink ears. She was tall, almost reaching Leon's shoulder, but her waist was tiny.

The puffed sleeves of her piped velvet jacket left her arms bare from the elbows. They were shapely and lightly muscled, the limbs of an equestrienne. Her hands were elegantly formed, her fingers long and tapered, the nails pearly; the hands of an artist. From under her long, full skirts peeped the pointed toes of a pair of snakeskin riding boots. He imagined that the feet within the expensive leather must be as shapely as the hands.

'Eva, may I present to you Herr Courtney? He is the hunter who is to take care of us during our little African adventure. Herr Courtney, may I present Fräulein von Wellberg,' Otto said.

'Enchanted, Fräulein,' Leon responded. She smiled and

proffered her right hand, palm down. When he took it he found it was warm and firm. He bowed and lifted it until her fingers were an inch from his lips, then released it and stepped back a pace. She held his eyes for only a moment longer. Looking into their depths he saw that her regard was enigmatic and layered with innuendo. He had the sensation of gazing into a pool whose secret depths could never be fully fathomed.

When she turned away to speak to Graf Otto, he felt a pang of some emotion totally alien to any he had ever experienced before. It was a strange mixture of elation and regret, of attainment and numbing bereavement. In a blink of time it seemed he had discovered something of infinite value that, in almost the same instant, had been snatched away. When Graf Otto placed one large freckled hand on Eva's tiny waist and drew her closer to him, and she smiled up into his face, Leon hated him with a bitter relish that tasted like burned gunpowder in the back of his throat.

The transfer ashore was soon accomplished, for Graf Otto and his lovely consort had little luggage with them, fewer than a dozen large cabin trunks with some containers of Graf Otto's rifles, shotguns and ammunition. Everything else had been sent out in the first shipment aboard the SS *Silbervogel*. While this luggage was quickly loaded into the big Meerbach truck that stood above the beach ready to receive it, Graf Otto greeted his employees from Weiskirchen, who had lined up to welcome him. His manner towards them was that of a father to his young children: he greeted them by name and teased each in turn with little personal references. They wriggled like puppies, grinned and mumbled with gratification at his condescension. Leon saw that they worshipped Graf Otto as though he was God.

Then he turned to Leon. 'You may introduce your assistants,' he said, and Leon called Hennie and Max forward.

Graf Otto treated them in the same easy, condescending manner, and Leon watched them fall almost immediately under his spell. He had a way with men, but Leon knew that if anyone ever crossed or disappointed him he would turn on them vindictively and mercilessly

'*Sehr gut, meine Kinder*. Very well, children. Now we can go to Nairobi,' Graf Otto proclaimed. With the Meerbach mechanics, Hennie, Max and Ishmael climbed into the back of the waiting truck, Gustav took the wheel, and the huge vehicle roared away along the road to Nairobi.

'Courtney, you will ride with me in the hunting car,' Graf Otto told Leon. 'Fräulein von Wellberg will sit beside me, and you will take the back seat to show me the road and to point out to us the sights along the way.' He made a fuss of settling her in the front passenger seat, with a mohair rug to cover her lap, a pair of goggles to protect her eyes from the wind, kid gloves to keep the sun off her flawless hands and a silk scarf knotted under her pretty chin to prevent her hat being blown away. Finally he checked the three rifles in the gun rack behind his seat, then climbed behind the steering-wheel, adjusted his goggles, revved the engine and accelerated away in pursuit of the truck. He drove very fast but with effortless skill. More than once Leon saw Eva's grip on the door handle beside her tighten as he accelerated through a tight bend, corrected an alarming skid as the wheels hit a patch of floury dust, or bounced through a series of corrugations, but her expression remained serene.

Once the road had climbed away from the coast they entered the game fields and soon they were speeding past herds of gazelle and larger antelope. Eva was distracted by them from the rapidity of their progress: she laughed and clapped with delight at the multitudes and their alarm antics as the car roared past.

'Otto!' she cried. 'What are those pretty little animals, the ones that dance and prance in that delightful manner?'

'Courtney, answer the Fräulein's question,' Graf Otto shouted, above the rush of the wind.

'Those are Thomson's gazelle, Fräulein. You will see many thousands more in the days ahead. They are the most common species in this country. The peculiar gait you have noticed is known as stotting. It is a display of alarm that warns all other gazelle in sight that danger threatens.'

'Stop the car, please, Otto. I would like to sketch them.'

'As you wish, my pretty one.' He shrugged indulgently and pulled over. Eva balanced her sketchbook on her lap. Her charcoal flew over the page and, leaning forward unobtrusively, Leon saw a perfect impression of a stotting animal, its back arched and all four legs held stiffly, appear magically on the paper before his eyes. Eva von Wellberg was a gifted artist. He recalled the easel, the boxes of pastels and oil paints that had been shipped in on the SS *Silbervogel* ahead of her arrival. He had given them little thought at the time, but now their importance was clear.

From then onwards the journey was interrupted repeatedly at Eva's request as she picked out subjects she wished to draw: a roosting eagle on the top branches of an acacia tree, or a female cheetah sauntering long-legged across the sun-seared savannah with her three young cubs following her in Indian file. Although he humoured her, it was soon obvious that Graf Otto was becoming bored with these checks and delays. At the next stop he dismounted and took down a rifle from the gun rack. Standing beside the car he killed five gazelle with as many shots as they bounded across the road in front of the car. It was an incredible display of marksmanship. Although Leon despised such wanton slaughter he kept a civil tone as he asked, 'What do you wish to do with the dead animals, sir?'

'Leave them,' said Graf Otto, offhandedly, as he replaced the rifle in the rack.

'Do you not wish to examine them, sir? One has a fine set of horns.'

'*Nein*. You say there will be many more. Leave them to feed the vultures. I was merely checking the sights of my rifle. Let us go on.'

Eva's cheek was pale as they drove on, Leon noticed, and her lips were pursed. He took this as evidence of her disapproval, and his opinion of her was enhanced.

Graf Otto's attention was on the road ahead, and Eva had not looked directly at Leon since their first meeting on the ship's bridge. She had not spoken to him either: all her queries and remarks were relayed to him through Graf Otto. He wondered at this. Perhaps she was naturally extremely modest, or he did not like her to talk to other men. Then he recalled that she had been friendly with Gustav, and had chatted easily to Max and Hennie when they were introduced to her at Kilindini. Why was she so remote from and aloof with him? From the rear seat he was able surreptitiously to study her features. Once or twice Eva shifted uneasily in her seat, or tucked a tendril of hair under her scarf with a self-conscious gesture, and the cheek that was turned towards him flushed delicately as though she was fully aware of his interest.

A little after midday they came around another bend in the dusty road and found Gustav standing on the verge, waiting for them. He flagged down the car, and when Graf Otto braked to a halt, he ran to the driver's side. 'I beg your pardon, sir, but your luncheon has been prepared, if you should wish to partake.' He pointed to where the big truck was parked in a grove of fever trees two hundred yards off the road.

'Good. I'm ravenous,' Graf Otto replied. 'Jump up on the running-board, Gustav, and I'll give you a lift.' With Gustav clinging to the side of the car they bumped across the rough ground towards where the truck was parked.

Ishmael had spread a sun awning between four trees and in its shade he had set up a trestle table and camp chairs. The table was covered with a snowy linen cloth, silver cutlery and china. As they climbed stiffly out of the car and stretched their limbs Ishmael, in his red fez and long white *kanza*, came to each in turn with a basin of warm water, a bar of lavender-perfumed soap, and a clean hand towel over his arm.

As soon as they had washed, Max showed them to the

table. Platters of carved ham and cheese were laid out, with baskets of black bread, crocks of butter and an enormous silver dish filled with Russian beluga caviar. He drew the cork from the first of the platoon of wine bottles that were standing to attention on the side table and poured the crisp yellow Gewürztraminer into long-stemmed glasses.

Eva picked delicately at the food. She drank a few mouthfuls of wine, and ate a single biscuit spread with a tablespoon of caviar, but Graf Otto fell to like a trencherman. When the meal was over he had polished off two bottles of Gewürztraminer on his own account, and had left the caviar dish, the platters of ham and the cheese in sorry disarray. He showed no ill-effects from the wine when he took his place in the driver's seat once more and they drove on towards Nairobi, but his speed increased substantially, his laughter was unrestrained and his sense of humour less decorous.

When they came upon a party of black women walking in single file along the edge of the road with bundles of cut thatching grass balanced on their heads, Graf Otto slowed to a walking pace to study the girls' naked breasts openly. Then, as he pulled away, he laid a hand on Eva's lap in a possessive and familiar manner and said, 'Some like chocolate – but I prefer vanilla.' She grasped his wrist and replaced his hand on the steering-wheel. 'The road is dangerous, Otto,' she remarked evenly, and Leon seethed with outrage at the humiliation he had inflicted on her so casually. He wanted to intervene to protect her in some way but he sensed that Graf Otto in wine would be unpredictable and dangerous. For Eva's sake, he restrained himself.

But then his anger turned on her. Why did she allow herself to be the butt of such behaviour? She was not a whore. Then, with a shock, he realized that that was precisely what she was. She was a high-class courtesan. She was Graf Otto's plaything, and had placed her body at his disposal in return for a few tawdry ornaments, fripperies and, most probably, a harlot's wages. He tried to despise her. He wanted to hate her, but another thought shocked him, like a blow from a mailed fist between the eyes: if she was a whore then so was he. He thought of the princess, and the others to whom he had sold himself and his services.

We all have to survive the best we can, he thought, trying to justify himself and her. If Eva is a whore then we are all whores. But he knew that none of this was relevant. It was far too late to hate or despise her because he had already fallen hopelessly in love with her.

They drove into Tandala Camp as the sun was setting, and Graf Otto disappeared with Eva into the luxurious quarters that stood ready to receive them. Ishmael and three of his kitchen staff carried their dinner into their private dining room. The couple did not reappear until after breakfast the following morning.

'*Guten Tag*, Courtney. See to it that these letters are delivered at once.' Graf Otto handed him a bundle of envelopes sealed with red wax wafers and embossed with the double-headed eagles of the German Foreign Office in Berlin. They were addressed to the governor of the colony, and to all the other notables in Nairobi, including Lord Delamere and the officer commanding His Britannic Majesty's forces in British East Africa, Brigadier General Penrod Ballantyne. 'They are my letters of introduction from the Kaiserliche government,' he explained, 'and must be delivered today, without fail, *ja*?'

'Of course, sir. I'll see that this is done immediately.' Leon sent for Max Rosenthal and, in Graf Otto's presence, charged him with delivering the letters. 'Take one of the motors, Max. Don't come back until every one has been handed over.'

As Max drove away, Eva came from the private quarters to join them. She was dressed in riding kit and looked fresh and rested, her hair shining in the sunlight, her skin glowing with the sweet young blood under it.

Graf Otto scrutinized her approvingly, then turned back to

Leon. 'And now, Courtney, we will go to the airfield. I will fly my machines.' During the night the hunting car had been washed and polished. All three of them got into it, and Graf Otto drove through the town to the polo ground.

When they arrived Gustav already had the *Butterfly* and the *Bumble Bee* drawn up on the edge of the field. Graf Otto walked around each aircraft, inspecting them carefully, while he engaged in earnest discussion with Gustav. Eventually he climbed up on to the wings to check the tension of the rigging wires and the struts. He opened the engine cowlings and examined the fuel lines and throttle cables. He unscrewed the filler caps of the fuel tanks and used a dipstick to ascertain the levels.

It was the middle of the morning before he expressed his complete satisfaction with the two aircraft, then went to the boarding ladder and climbed into the cockpit of the *Bumble Bee*. He buckled the chinstrap of his flying helmet then beckoned Gustav. The two men had a muttered conversation, Graf Otto pointing to the hunting car. Then Gustav started the engines. When they had warmed up and were running sweetly, Graf Otto taxied down to the far end of the polo field and swung the huge machine around until its nose was pointing into the breeze.

The sound of the engines had summoned the entire population of Nairobi and, once again, they were lining the field in excited anticipation. The four engines burst into a lion-throated roar and the *Bumble Bee* started to roll back towards where Eva and Leon stood in front of the hangar. Leon was a few paces behind her, in a position of attendance rather than equality. Swiftly the *Bumble Bee* gathered speed. She lifted her tail wheel from the ground and Leon held his breath as he watched the massive undercarriage bounce lightly over the turf, then break free of gravity and rise into the air. With a mere twenty feet to spare, the machine bellowed over their heads. The crowd ducked instinctively – everyone except Eva.

As Leon straightened he saw that she had been watching him covertly. A faintly mocking smile lifted the corners of her mouth. 'Goodness me!' she taunted him lightly. 'Is this the intrepid hunter and fearless slayer of wild animals?'

It was only the second time since their meeting that she had looked him full in the face, and the first that she had addressed him directly. He was startled by how her demeanour changed when Graf Otto was not present. 'Fräulein, I hope this is the only time that I fall short of your expectations.' He gave her a small bow.

She turned away, deliberately terminating the brief contact, and shaded her eyes to watch the *Bumble Bee* circle the field. It was a light rebuff, but Leon savoured the memory of her smile, no matter that it had been mocking rather than friendly. He followed her gaze and saw that the *Bumble Bee* was already dropping towards the field for a landing.

Graf Otto touched down and taxied back to the hangar. He cut the engines and clambered down. The watching crowd cheered him wildly and he acknowledged them with a wave of his gloved hand. Gustav rushed to meet him, and the two men walked across to the *Butterfly* deep in conversation. Graf Otto left him at the foot of the ladder, climbed up into the cockpit and started the engines. He taxied her to the end of the polo field, turned her and came thundering back towards them. Once again Leon marvelled at the miracle of flight as the *Butterfly* left the ground and swept low over his head. This time he stood stock-still, and when he glanced at Eva she was watching him again. She inclined her head and her violet eyes sparkled with wicked fun. Her voice was drowned by the hubbub of the spectators, but he could read her lips as they formed a single word: 'Bravo!' The mockery was softened by another small, secret smile. Then she turned away to watch the aircraft circle the field twice before it lined up into the wind for the landing. It touched down and taxied to where they stood in front of the hangar.

Leon expected Graf Otto to cut the engines and disembark, but instead he leaned over the side of the cockpit and scrutinized the faces in the crowd below. He picked out Eva and signalled to her to come to him. She moved quickly to do his bidding, Gustav and two of his men running ahead of her with the boarding ladder. Halfway to the *Butterfly* the slipstream from the propellers caught her and flogged her skirts around her legs. Her broad-brimmed hat was whisked off her head, and her long dark hair tumbled around her face. She laughed and continued to run. Her hat was carried to where Leon stood and he caught it as it rolled past him.

Eva reached the bottom of the ladder and climbed lightly up the rungs. Clearly she had done it many times before. Leon watched her disappear over the rim of the cockpit. Then Graf Otto's helmeted head turned towards him and he beckoned. Taken by surprise, Leon touched his own chest in an interrogatory gesture. 'Who? Me?' Graf Otto nodded emphatically and beckoned again, this time more imperiously.

Leon ran through the slipstream, his heart pounding with excitement, and scrambled up the ladder. As he dropped into the cockpit he handed the hat to Eva. She barely turned her head in his direction as she took it from him. The playful exchanges of a few minutes earlier might never have taken place. From somewhere she had found herself a leather flying helmet, which she strapped under her chin. Then she covered her eyes with the smoked lenses of the goggles.

'Pull up the ladder!' Graf Otto shouted, and reinforced the command with a hand signal. Leon leaned over the side, lifted it and hooked it into the retaining brackets on the fuselage.

'Good. Sit here!' Graf Otto indicated the seat beside him. Leon sat in it and fastened the safety strap across his lap. Graf Otto cupped his hands into a trumpet and bellowed into his ear, 'You will navigate for me, *ja*?'

'Where are we going?' Leon shouted back.

'To the closest of your hunting camps.'

'That's more than a hundred miles away,' Leon protested.

'A short hop. *Ja!* We will go there.' He opened the throttles and taxied back to the far side of the field, paused to check the dials on his dashboard, then slowly pushed the four throttle levers forward to their full extent. The thunder of the Meerbach engines was deafening. The *Butterfly* bounded forward, bumping and thumping over every irregularity in the ground, her wings rocking and swaying as she gained speed swiftly. Leon clung to the rim of the cockpit, peering ahead. Tears started from his eyes as the wind ripped at them, but his heart was singing almost as loudly as the engines. Then, suddenly, all the rocking and bumping stopped with dramatic suddenness. Leon looked over the side and saw the earth dropping away below him. 'We're flying!' he shouted into the wind. 'We're really flying!' He saw the town below him but it took him moments to recognize it. Everything looked so different from that angle. He had to take his bearings from the snake of the railway line before he could pick out other landmarks: the pink walls of the Muthaiga Country Club; the shining corrugated-iron roof of Delamere's new hotel; the whitewashed bulk of Government House and the governor's residence.

'Which way?' Graf Otto had to shake his arm to get his attention.

'Follow the railway line.' Leon pointed westwards. With both hands he was trying to shield his eyes from the hundred-mile-an-hour wind that tore at his face. Graf Otto prodded his ribs with a bony finger and pointed at a small cubby-hole in the side of the cockpit. Leon opened it and found another leather flying helmet at the back. He pulled it over his head and buckled the strap under his chin, then adjusted the goggles over his eyes. Now he could see, and the side flaps of the helmet protected his eardrums from the roar of the rushing wind.

While he had been engrossed with fitting his helmet Eva had risen from her seat and moved to the front of the cockpit where she was standing, holding the handrail that ran around the rim. She resembled a figurehead on the bows of a man-o'-war, as she balanced gracefully against the motion of the *Butterfly*.

At that moment the aircraft plummeted sickeningly and unexpectedly. Leon grabbed at the nearest handhold in panic. He knew, without a shadow of doubt, that they were about to fall out of the sky and die a swift but violent death in a pile of wreckage on the earth far below. But the *Butterfly* was unperturbed: she waggled her wings in a dignified gesture of contempt at the forces of gravity and flew on serenely into the west.

Eva was still standing in the nose, and only then did Leon notice the safety-belt buckled around her waist and the karabiner snap-link at the other end of the lanyard hooked into a steel eye bolt in the floorboards between her feet. It had prevented her being hurled over the side when the *Butterfly* had dropped.

Graf Otto was still handling the controls with gentle touches of his big, freckled hands. He grinned at Leon around the unlit Cohiba cigar clamped in the corner of his mouth. 'Thermal!' he shouted above the wind. 'It is nothing.'

Leon was mortified by his own panicky display. He had read enough about the theory of flight to know that air acted in the same way as water, with all its unpredictable currents and eddies.

'Go forward.' Graf Otto gestured. 'Go forward to where you can see ahead to guide me.' Leon edged gingerly to the front of the cockpit. Without a glance in his direction Eva moved aside to make room for him and he took up his position beside her and fastened his safety belt to the ring bolt. They braced themselves with both hands on the rail. They were so very close that he fancied, despite the wind, that he could smell a trace of her special perfume. Facing forward, he glanced at her from the corner of his eye. The slipstream flattened the blouse and long skirt against her body and limbs so that every curve and contour was accentuated. For the first time he was able to make out the shape of her legs, long and slender, and then he looked to the twin mounds of her bosom under the velveteen jacket. He saw at once that her breasts were larger than they had seemed, rounder and fuller than Verity O'Hearne's had been. He forced himself to tear his eyes away and look ahead.

Already they were approaching the rim of the Great Rift

Valley. He picked out the glint of the steel tracks where the railway began its descent of the escarpment to the volcanic steppe of the valley floor. He looked back at Graf Otto and gave him a hand signal to turn ninety degrees southwards. The German nodded and the *Butterfly* dropped one wing and went into a lazy left-hand turn. Centrifugal force pushed Eva lightly against him, and for a long, exquisite moment Leon felt the outside of her warm thigh press against his. She seemed oblivious to this for she made no move to pull away. Then Graf Otto lifted the port wing and the *Butterfly* came back on to an even keel again. The contact was broken.

The Great Rift Valley opened before them. From this altitude it was a vista that belonged not to petty mankind but to God and his angels. Now Leon could truly appreciate the immensity of the land: the seared and rocky hills, the lion-coloured plains blotched with dark expanses of forest, and the blue palisades of hills and mountains stretching away into infinite distances.

Suddenly the deck canted under their feet as Graf Otto lowered the *Butterfly*'s nose and she dropped into the airy void. The cliffs of the escarpment rushed under them, so close that it seemed her wheels must bounce off the rocks. The valley floor loomed up to meet them. Leon saw Eva's fists tighten into balls on the handrail. He could see that the tension in her body was arching her back. To pay her back for her earlier sauciness he released his own grip on the rail, and placed his hands on his hips, leaning easily into the dive as the aircraft dropped. This time she could not ignore him, and shot him a quick glance as he balanced against the disparate forces that dragged at his body. Then she looked ahead, but lifted one hand from the rail and turned it palm upwards in a gesture of resignation.

Graf Otto pulled the *Butterfly*'s nose up out of her dive down the valley wall. Leon's knees buckled under the force of gravity and Eva was pushed against him once more. She swayed away as the *Butterfly* came back again on to an even keel. They barrelled along the escarpment with the wall flashing past on the port side, so close that it seemed the wing-tip might touch it at any moment.

Suddenly Leon saw what appeared to be a swarm of large black scarab beetles crawling along a mile or so ahead. It was only when the *Butterfly* raced down on them that he saw it was a large herd of buffalo charging away in panic from their approach. He made another hand signal to Graf Otto, and the *Butterfly* banked steeply towards the fleeing herd. Once again Eva was pressed against him, but this time she gave him a deliberate bump with her hip. With a surge like electricity through his loins, he understood she was letting him know that she was just as aware of these physical contacts as he was.

They flashed over the heaving backs of the buffalo, so close that Leon could see each pellet of dried mud sticking to their hair, and clearly discern the parallel pattern of scars across the shoulders of the leading bull, left by the raking claws of a marauding lion.

They flew on until Eva waved excitedly and pointed out on her side of the fuselage. Graf Otto banked in the direction she was pointing. Then the *Butterfly* was straight and lined up on five huge elephant bulls, wading through the dense thorny undergrowth a short distance ahead. Although she no longer had the excuse of gravity, Eva gave him another cheeky little bump with her hip. It was a titillating but dangerous game they were playing, right under Graf Otto von Meerbach's nose. Leon laughed into the wind and, without moving her head, Eva peeped at him through lowered lashes and smiled secretly.

They bore down on the running elephant. Leon saw that they were all old bulls and at least two carried tusks of more than a hundred pounds a side. Another had only a single, the other broken off at the lip, but the remaining one was colossal and dwarfed those of his companions. Otto dropped lower, then lower still, until it looked as though he meant to fly straight into the herd. The elephant seemed to realize that they could not outrun the *Butterfly*: they turned back and bunched up, shoulder to shoulder, forming a solid phalanx to confront this threat from the skies. Trumpeting so loudly that Leon could hear them above the engine, they charged head-long to meet the aircraft. As she skimmed over them they reared up, flaring their ears, and stretched out their serpentine trunks as though to snatch her out of the air.

Graf Otto climbed several hundred feet above the ground and flew on southwards. New and unexpected vistas opened before them. They flew over hidden valleys, secret re-entrants and salients in the walls of the Rift, some of which were not reflected on any survey map Leon had ever studied. Two or three valleys were fed by streams and pastured with green grass on which herds of large mammals, from giraffe to rhinoceros, had congregated. Leon tried to memorize the exact location of each one so that he could return to explore them, but they were flying so fast he found it difficult to keep track of their progress.

They climbed higher still until they could make out the vast massif of Kilimanjaro looming on the southern horizon a hundred miles or more ahead. The mountain was blue with distance, its crest wreathed in silver cloud through which the sun threw golden blades of light. Then Graf Otto waggled the wings to attract Leon's attention and pointed out a closer mountain, only twenty or thirty miles off. The table top was unmistakable, and was probably what had attracted his notice.

'Lonsonyo Mountain!' Leon cried, but his voice was lost in the roar of wind and engines. 'Go there!' He made vehement hand signals, and Graf Otto opened the throttles wide. The *Butterfly* rose upwards, but the table of Lonsonyo stood almost ten thousand feet above sea level, near the aircraft ceiling. At first she climbed rapidly, but as the altitude increased her speed bled off. She became so sluggish that they cleared the top of the cliffs by no more than fifty feet.

Before them, Lusima's cattle were spread out as they grazed on the sweet grasses of the high table land. Beyond them Leon picked out the pattern of the huts and cattle pens that formed the *manyatta*, and signalled to Otto to turn towards the village. Goats, chickens and naked herd-boys scattered at their approach. It was easy to single out Lusima's hut from the others, for it was the largest and grandest, closest to the spreading branches of her council tree. There was no sign of Lusima until they were almost directly overhead. Then, suddenly, she appeared, ducking out of the low doorway of her hut and staring up at him. She was naked except for her tiny red loincloth, and the colourful bangles and necklaces around her ankles, wrists and neck. She gazed up at the *Butterfly* with an expression of comical bewilderment.

'Lusima!' Leon yelled, and ripped off his helmet and goggles. 'Lusima Mama! It is me! M'bogo, your son!' He waved frantically and suddenly she recognized him. He was so close that he saw her face light up and she waved with both hands, but then they were past and dropping down the far side of the mountain.

Once again Graf Otto waggled the wings and, with hand signals, asked Leon to point out the course he should take to reach the hunting camp. They had left it on the far side of Lonsonyo Mountain, so Leon directed him into a right-hand circuit of the sheer cliffs below the table land. He had never seen this side of the mountain before. Up until now, he had always approached and ascended from the southern side.

The rock was as sheer and impregnable as the outer wall of some monumental medieval fortress and lichen had painted on it a patchwork of many colours. Then, unexpectedly, the *Butterfly* came level with a break in the wall, a vertical chimney of rock, splitting the cliff from the summit right down to the scree slope at the foot of the mountain. Over the lip of the cliff at the top of the chimney spilled a bright cascade of water, a stream that drained the rain-sodden table land above and fell in undulating lacy curtains down the moss-blackened stone. As they passed, the wind blew eddies of fine spray into their faces. It dewed their goggles, and was cold as snowflakes on their cheeks.

The waterfall fell several hundred feet into the pool at the base of the cliff. The sun's rays did not reach into that dark and mysterious gorge: it was filled with shadow that turned the pool black as an inkwell. It was so perfectly circular that it might have been built by ancient Roman or Egyptian architects. They were only able to gaze on this grand sight for a few short seconds before the *Butterfly* had sped past it; the rock flue seemed to close behind them with the finality of a massive cathedral door, shutting from view all trace of the waterfall.

When they flew out of the shadow of the mountain, the sun was already turning red as it passed through the haze of dust and smoke that hung low to the horizon. Leon gazed out over the purple plain, searching for his first glimpse of the hunting camp. At last, far ahead, he picked out the silver sausage of the windsock that marked the airstrip floating at the peak of its mast. He signed to Graf Otto to turn towards it, and soon they could make out the cluster of canvas and newly thatched roofs of what Leon had named Percy's Camp. Just behind it stood a small kopje, no more than a few hundred feet high but visible for many miles.

Graf Otto circled the camp to check the wind direction and the orientation of the landing strip. As they banked around on the far side of his camp, Leon looked down the wing on to a dense, seemingly impenetrable wilderness of hookthorn bushes. It stretched for many miles, and in its midst he spotted another cluster of those dark shapes. By their bulk he knew at once that they were buffalo bulls, three old bachelors. One thing was certain, and that was that those old recluses would be cantankerous and highly dangerous. When they raised their heads and stared malevolently up at the aircraft, Leon evaluated them quickly, then muttered to himself, 'Not a decent head among them. They're all wearing *yarmulkas*.' It was an irreverent reference to the Jewish prayer cap, used by the old hunters to describe a pair of buffalo horns so old and worn away that the points had gone, leaving only a skullcap of horn.

As Graf Otto touched down and let the *Butterfly* run out to the far end of the strip, they saw a cloud of dust tearing down the rutted track from the camp. A truck clattered into view with Hennie du Rand at the wheel, Manyoro and Loikot perched standing in the back.

'So sorry, boss!' Hennie greeted Leon, when he came down the ladder from the cockpit. 'We were not expecting you to arrive for another few weeks at least. You've taken us by surprise.' He was visibly flustered.

'I'm as surprised to be here as you are to see me. The Graf works to his own timetable. Is there food and liquor in camp?'

'*Ja!*' Hennie nodded. 'Max brought plenty from Tandala.'

'Is there hot water in the shower? Are the beds made up, and is there paper in the thunderbox?'

'There will be before you can ask again,' Hennie promised.

'Then we shall be all right. The Graf's family motto is "*Durabo*", I shall survive. We'll put it to the test this evening,' Leon said, and turned to Graf Otto as he came down the ladder.

'I'm pleased to be able to tell you that all is in readiness for you, sir,' he lied blithely, and led the couple to their quarters.

Somehow Hennie and his chef had performed a miracle of improvisation. They had put together a passable meal from the crates of provisions Max had brought from Tandala, and Leon waited for his guests in the mess tent. When Eva entered, he gaped at the vision she presented. It was the first time he had seen a beautiful woman in culottes, a most daring and avant-garde fashion that had not yet reached the colonies. Although they were cut full in the legs and seat, he could visualize what must lie beneath the fine material. He tore his eyes off her just before Graf Otto came in behind her.

Hennie had cooled a few cases of Meerbach Eisbock lager in the canvas wet-bags. This was a beer that had won innumerable gold medals at the annual Munich Oktober Bierfests. It was the product of a large Bavarian brewery that made up a small part of the Meerbach manufacturing empire. His own best customer, the Graf drank nearly half a gallon of it to whet his appetite before dinner was served.

When he took his seat at the head of the table, he changed his tipple from lager to Burgundy, a notable Romanée Conti 1896, which he had personally selected from his cellars at Weiskirchen. It went perfectly with the hors d'oeuvre of gerenuk liver pâté and the entrée of wild duck breasts on slices of fried *foie gras*. Graf Otto rounded off the meal with a few glasses of a fifty-year-old port and a Montecristo cigar from Havana.

He drew on the cigar and sighed with pleasure as he leaned back in his chair and eased his belt by a few notches. 'Courtney, you saw those buffalo we flew over while we were coming in to land, *ja?*'

'I did, sir.'

'They were in thick cover, *nein?*'

'They were, very thick. But not one is worth the price of a cartridge.'

'Ah, so, would they not be dangerous, then?'

'They would be very dangerous. Even more so if they were wounded,' Leon conceded, 'but—'

Graf Otto cut him off. 'But is a word I do not like very much, Courtney.' His mood had altered instantly and dramatically. 'Usually it is a signal that somebody is about to make an excuse to disobey me.' He scowled and the duelling scar across his cheek changed from glassy white to rose pink.

Leon had not yet learned that this was a danger sign. He went on regardless:

'I was just going to say that—'

'I have no great interest in what you were going to say, Courtney. I would rather you listened to what *I* have to say.'

Leon flushed at the rebuke, but then he saw Eva, who was sitting out of Graf Otto's direct line of sight, purse her lips and shake her head almost imperceptibly. He drew a deep breath and, with an effort, took heed of her warning. 'You wish to hunt those bulls, sir?'

'Ah, Courtney, you are not such a *Dummkopf* as you often appear to be!' He laughed as he switched back into geniality. 'Yes, indeed, I wish to shoot those bulls. I will give you an opportunity to show me how dangerous they truly are, *ja*?'

'I did not bring my rifle from Tandala.'

'You do not need it. I am the one who will do the shooting.'

'You wish me to accompany you unarmed?'

'Is the sauce too rich for your stomach, Courtney? If so, you may remain in bed tomorrow or under it. Wherever you feel warmest and safest.'

'When you hunt, I shall be at your side.'

'I am pleased that we understand each other. It makes everything simpler, does it not?' He drew on his cigar until the tip glowed brightly, then blew a perfect smoke-ring that rolled across the table towards Leon's face. Leon poked a finger through its centre and broke it before it reached him.

Eva intervened smoothly to quench the rising flames of their tempers. 'Otto, what was that beautiful flat-topped mountain you flew us over this afternoon?'

'Tell us about it, Courtney,' he commanded.

'It is called Lonsonyo Mountain, a sacred site to the Masai, and the home of one of their most powerful spiritual leaders. She is a seer who is able to divine the future with amazing accuracy.' Leon did not look in Eva's direction as he replied.

'Oh, Otto!' she exclaimed. 'That must have been the woman we saw coming out of the largest hut. What is her name, this prophetess?'

'You are amused by all this magical mumbo-jumbo, silly one?' Graf Otto asked indulgently.

'You know I love to have my fortune told.' She smiled prettily and the last of his anger evaporated. 'Don't you remember the Gypsy woman in Prague? She told me my heart truly belonged to a strong loving man, who would cherish me always. That was you, of course!'

'Of course. Who else could it have been?'

'Otto, what is her name, this diviner?'

He turned from her and raised a ginger eyebrow at Leon.

'Her name is Lusima, sir.' Leon had learned how to play this game of elliptical questions and answers.

'How well do you know her?' Graf Otto demanded.

Leon laughed lightly. 'She has adopted me as her son so we are well enough acquainted.'

'Ha, ha! If she has adopted you, it seems she is not a woman of good judgement. However . . .' Graf Otto spread his hands in surrender as he gazed at Eva '. . . I see that I will have no peace until I agree to this whimsy of yours. Very well, I will take you to visit this old woman of the mountain to have your fortune told.'

'Thank you so much, Otto.' Eva stroked the back of his hand. Leon felt an acidic flood of jealousy burn the lining of his stomach. 'Now you see that the Prague Gypsy was right. You are so kind to me. When will you take me there? After you have hunted these buffalo of yours, perhaps?'

'We shall see,' Graf Otto hedged, and changed the subject. 'Courtney, I will be ready at daybreak. It is no more than a few kilometres to where we last saw that herd. I wish to arrive before the sun is up.'

The hushed world was waiting for the sun and the chill of the night was still in the air when Graf Otto parked the hunting car at the edge of the thicket of thorn scrub beyond the airstrip. One of his men had driven it to the camp overnight. Manyoro and Loikot were squatting before a smoky little fire of dry twigs, warming their hands. They kicked earth over the flames and stood up as Leon jumped out and came to them. 'What do you have to tell me?'

'After the moon went down we heard them drink at the waterhole near the camp. When we found the spoor this morning, we tracked them from the waterhole to here. They are close by in the thorn. Only a short while ago we heard them moving about in there,' Manyoro reported, and went on, 'They are truly very old and very ugly. Is Kichwa Muzuru sure that he wishes to shoot one?' They had named Graf Otto 'Fire Head' for the colour of his hair and also for his apparent lack of fear, which the Masai admired greatly.

'Yes, he is certain. I could not make him change his mind,' Leon told him.

Manyoro shrugged with resignation. Then he asked, 'What *bunduki* will you carry, M'bogo? Your big one we left at Tandala.'

'I will not have a *bunduki* today. But no matter. Kichwa Muzuru shoots like a wizard.'

Manyoro looked at him askance. 'And if someone knocks over the beer pot, M'bogo, what then?'

'Then, Manyoro, I will poke the buffalo in the eye with this.' Leon hefted a heavy stick he had picked up from beside the track.

'That is not a weapon. It is not even a good louse-scratcher. Here.' Manyoro reversed one of his two stabbing spears, and handed it butt first to Leon. 'A real weapon for you to carry.'

It was a lovely blade, three foot long and sharpened along both edges. Leon tested it on his forearm. It shaved the hairs as cleanly and effortlessly as his straight razor would have done. 'Thank you, my brother, but I hope I shall not need to use it. Take the spoor again, Manyoro, but be ready to run if Kichwa Muzuru kicks over the beer pot!'

Leon left them and went back to the hunting car where Graf Otto was taking his rifle out of its leather slip case. Leon felt a little easier when he saw that it was a large-calibre double-barrelled weapon, probably a continental 10.75mm. It had more than enough knock-down power to deal effectively with a buffalo.

'So, Courtney, are you ready for a little sport?' Graf Otto asked, as Leon came up to him. He had an unlit cigar between his lips and a loden hunting hat pushed to the back of his head. He was loading steel-jacketed cartridges into the open magazine of the rifle.

'I hope you're not planning on having too much fun, sir, but, yes, I'm ready.'

'I see that you are.' He grinned at the spear in Leon's hand. 'Are you hunting rabbits or buffalo with that?'

'If you stick it into the right place it will do the job.'

'I make you a little promise, Courtney. If you kill a buffalo with that I will teach you to fly an aeroplane.'

'I'm overwhelmed by your magnanimity, sir.' Leon bowed slightly. 'Will you please ask Fräulein von Wellberg to remain in the car until we return? These animals are unpredictable, and once the first shot is fired, anything might happen.'

He removed the cigar from his mouth to address Eva. 'Will you be a good girl today, *mein Schatz*, and do as our young friend asks?'

'Aren't I always a good girl, Otto?' she asked, but something in her eyes negated the sugary response.

He replaced the cigar in his mouth and handed her his silver Vesta case. She flipped open the lid and shook out a red-tipped match, struck it against the sole of her boot, and when it flared, she held it at arm's length to burn off the sulphur smoke, then applied the flame to the tip of the cigar. Graf Otto was watching Leon's eyes as he puffed at the Cohiba. Leon knew that this little demonstration of domination and subservience was probably for his benefit. The other man was not unobservant: he must be able to sense the emotional thunder in the air and was marking his thrall over Eva. Leon kept his expression neutral.

Then Eva intervened again softly: 'Please be careful, Otto. I would not know what to do without you.'

Leon wondered if she was protecting him from the Graf's jealous anger. If that was her motive, it worked well.

Graf Otto chuckled. 'Worry for the buffalo, not for me.' He shouldered the rifle and, without another word, followed the Masai into the thorn thicket. Leon fell in behind him, and they went forward quietly.

Once the three bulls were in heavy cover they had spread out to feed and their tracks meandered back and forth. It would have been only too easy while following one to run straight into another of the trio, so they moved slowly, checking the way ahead after every few paces. They had taken no more than a hundred when they heard the crackle of breaking twigs, followed by a soft snort nearby. Manyoro held up a hand, the signal to stand still and be quiet. There was silence for a full minute, which seemed much longer, then the rustle of vegetation. Something large was pushing its way through the thorn, coming directly towards them. Leon touched Graf Otto's arm, and he slipped the rifle from his shoulder and held it at high port across his chest.

Suddenly the wall of thorn bush parted directly ahead and the head and shoulders of a buffalo pushed through the opening. It was a scarred and battered old creature, one horn broken off to a jagged stump, the other almost worn away by constant sharpening against tree-trunks and termite mounds. The neck was scrawny and bald in patches. The nearest eye was white and glassy, completely blinded by fly-borne ophthalmia. At first it did not see them. For a while it stood and chewed at a clump of grass, loose straws and strings of saliva hanging from the corners of its mouth. It shook its head to drive away the little black flies that crawled around the lids of the blind eye, swarming to drink the yellow pus that dribbled down the buffalo's cheek.

Poor old blighter, Leon thought. A bullet in the head will be a real kindness. He touched Graf Otto's shoulder. 'Do it,' he whispered, and braced himself for the shot. But nothing could have prepared him for what followed.

Otto threw back his head and let out a wild shout: 'Come, then! Show us how dangerous you can be.' He fired a shot over the buffalo's head. The bull recoiled violently and spun to face them. It stared at them through its one good eye, then let out a loud snort of consternation and wheeled away. Bursting into a full gallop, it fled straight back into the thorn

palisade. At the moment before it disappeared Graf Otto fired
again.

Leon saw dust fly from the top of the buffalo's haunch, a
hand's breadth to the left of the knotty vertebrae of the spine
that showed through the scarred grey hide. He stared after the
fleeing bull with dismay. 'You wounded him deliberately!' he
accused, in a tone of utter disbelief.

'*Jawohl!* Of course. You said they needed to be wounded if
we wanted some sport. Well, now it is wounded, and I am
going to tickle up the other two as well!' Before Leon could
recover from the shock, Graf Otto let out another savage
war-cry and took off in pursuit of the stricken animal. The
two Masai were as stunned as Leon, and the three stood in a
bewildered group, staring after the German.

'He is mad!' Loikot said, in awed tones.

'Yes,' said Leon, grimly. 'He is. Listen to him.'

There was uproar in the scrub just ahead: the drumming of
many hoofs and the breaking of branches, snorts of anger and
alarm, the detonation of rifle shots and the *whump!*, *whump!*
of heavy bullets striking flesh and bone. Leon realized that
Graf Otto was shooting at all three bulls, not to kill but to
wound. He swung around to the Masai. 'There is nothing
more you can do here. Kichwa Muzuru has smashed the beer
pot into a hundred pieces. Go back to the car,' he ordered.
'Take care of the memsahib.'

'M'bogo, that is a great stupidity. We go forward together
or not at all.'

There was another shot, and this one was followed by the
death bellow of one bull. At least one was down, Leon
thought, but there were two more to go. There was neither
time nor latitude for argument. 'Come on, then,' Leon
snapped. They ran forward, and came upon Graf Otto standing at the edge of a small opening in the thorn. At his feet
lay the carcass of a dead bull. Its back legs were still kicking
convulsively in its death throes. The beast must have charged
at him as he stepped into the clearing. He had dropped it
with a bullet through the brain.

'You were wrong, Courtney. They are not so dangerous,' he remarked coolly, as he slid another round of ammunition into the breech of the rifle.

'How many others have you wounded?' Leon barked.

'Both of them, of course. Don't worry. You may still have a chance to learn to fly an aeroplane.'

'You have proved your courage beyond any doubt, sir. Now, give me your rifle and let me finish the job.'

'I never send a boy to do a man's work, Courtney. Besides, you have your good spear. For what reason do you need a rifle?'

'You are going to get somebody killed.'

'*Ja*, perhaps. But I don't think it'll be me.' He strode forward towards the wall of thorn bush on the far side of the clearing. 'One of them went in there. I am going to pull him out by his tail.'

It was futile to try to stop him. Leon held his breath as Graf Otto reached the far end of the clearing.

The wounded buffalo was waiting for him behind the first fringe of vegetation. It let him come in close, then charged at him from a mere five yards. The thorn exploded before its rush. Graf Otto had the rifle to his shoulder in an instant, and the muzzles were almost touching the bull's wet black nostrils when he fired. It was another perfect brain shot. The buffalo's front legs collapsed under it. However, the momentum of its charge carried it forward and it slid into its tormentor's legs like a black avalanche. He was sent spinning backwards, the rifle thrown from his hands, and hit the ground flat on his back. Leon heard the breath forced in a rush from his lungs. He sat up painfully, wheezing, as Leon ran forward to help him.

Leon was in the centre of the clearing when Manyoro shouted an urgent warning behind him. 'On your left side, M'bogo. The other one is coming!'

He swerved to the left and saw the third wounded buffalo almost upon him, so close that it was already lowering its head to hook at him with its horns. He saw the bull's suppurating blind eye – this was the first animal Graf Otto had fired at. Leon wheeled to face it and gathered himself, standing on the balls of his feet, his body in perfect balance, judging his moment. As the bull closed with him he swayed into the beast's blind side, and it lost sight of him, hooking wildly at where he had been the second before. If the horn had not been broken and foreshortened it would probably have ripped Leon's belly open, and even though he pirouetted clear, the ragged tip snagged his shirt, but then it tore free. Leon arched his back and the bull's massive body brushed against him, splashing the legs of his trousers with blood as it thundered past.

'Hey, Toro!' Graf Otto shouted encouragement. He was struggling to his feet, his voice hoarse with laughter despite the agony of his empty lungs. 'Hey, Torero!' He was still laughing wheezily as he stooped to pick up his rifle.

'Shoot it!' Leon yelled, as the bull skidded to a halt, its front legs braced.

'*Nein!*' Graf Otto shouted back. 'I want to watch you use your little spear.' He was holding the rifle with the muzzles pointed at the ground. 'You want to learn to fly? Then you must use the spear.'

His first bullet had broken the bull's back leg at the hip, so it was slow to recover from its abortive charge. But then it swung around awkwardly and again focused its single eye on Leon. It plunged forward, coming at him in a full gallop. Leon had learned from the bull's first pass: he held the spear in the classic Masai grip, the long blade aligned with his forearm like a fencing foil, and let the bull come in close, waiting until the very last instant before he swung his body out of the line of the charge and into the buffalo's blind spot again. As the great black body brushed against his legs he leaned in over the shoulder and placed the point of the spear in the hollow between the shoulder-blades. He did not try to stab with it. Instead he let the impetus of the bull's own charge carry it on to the blade. He was astonished at how easily the razor-sharp steel slid in. He hardly felt the jolt as the entire three feet vanished into the heaving black body. He released his grip on the haft and let the bull carry away the spear, plunging and swinging its head from side to side, fighting the biting agony of the blade. Leon saw that these violent movements were working the steel around in its chest, slashing the heart and lung tissue.

Once again the bull bucked to a halt on the far side of the clearing. It was still swinging its head, trying to find him. He stood motionless. At last the bull spotted him and turned towards him, but its movements were slow and uncertain. It staggered, but kept coming. Before it reached him it opened its mouth and let out a long, low bellow. A thick gout of blood from its lacerated lungs burst through its jaws and it fell on to its knees. Then it rolled slowly on to its side.

'Olé!' Graf Otto shouted, but this time his tone was without mockery, and when Leon looked at him, he saw new respect in the man's eyes.

Manyoro went slowly to where the buffalo lay. He stooped and, with both hands, took hold of the *assegai* haft that protruded from between its shoulder-blades. He straightened up, leaned back and drew the bloody steel out of the wound. Then he saluted Leon with the spear. 'I praise you. I am proud to be your brother.'

When they returned to camp Graf Otto turned breakfast into a celebration of his own prowess. He sat at the head of the table wolfing ham and eggs, and swigging the coffee he had laced generously with cognac while he regaled Eva with a highly coloured description of the hunt. He gave a passing mention to Leon at the end of the long account. 'When there was only one old blind animal still on its feet, I let Courtney have it. Of course, I had wounded it so badly that it was not a real challenge, but I will say this for him, he managed to kill it in quite workmanlike fashion.'

At that moment his attention was taken by sudden activity outside the tent. Hennie du Rand was with the skinners, who were getting into the back of a truck. They were armed with axes and butcher's knives. 'What are those people doing, Courtney?'

'They are going to bring in your dead buffaloes.'

'What for? The heads are worthless, as you have already told me, and surely the meat will be so old and tough that it will be inedible.'

'When it is smoked and dried the porters and other labourers will eat it with relish. In this country any meat is much prized.'

Graf Otto wiped his mouth on his napkin and stood up. 'I will go with them to watch.'

This was another of his typically idiosyncratic decisions, but still it took Leon by surprise. 'Of course I will come with you.'

'No need for that, Courtney. You can stay here and see to the refuelling of the *Butterfly* for the flight back to Nairobi. I will take Fräulein von Wellberg with me. She will be bored sitting in camp.'

I would do my best to entertain her if you gave me half a chance, Leon thought, but kept the sentiment to himself. 'As you wish, Graf,' he acquiesced.

Hennie was overawed to have such illustrious company travelling with him in the truck, even for the short ride to where the carcasses lay. As he climbed into the driver's seat, Graf Otto put him more at ease by offering him a cigar. After the first few puffs Hennie had relaxed to the point at which he was able to answer the man's questions coherently, rather than in an embarrassed mumble.

'So, du Rand, they tell me you are South African, *ja*?'

'No, sir. I am a Boer.'

'Is that different?'

'*Ja*, it is very different. South Africans have British blood. My blood is pure. I am one of a chosen *Volk*.'

'To me it sounds as though you do not like the British very much.'

'I like some of them. I like my boss, Leon Courtney. He is a good *Sout Piel*.'

'*Sout Piel*? What is that?'

Hennie glanced unhappily at Eva. 'It is man's talk, sir. Not fit for the ears of young ladies.'

'Do not worry. Fräulein von Wellberg speaks no English. Tell me what it is.'

'It means "salty penis", sir.'

Graf Otto began to grin, anticipating a good joke. 'Salty prick? Explain this to me.'

'They have one foot in London and the other in Cape Town, with their cocks dangling in the Atlantic,' Hennie said.

Graf Otto let out a hearty guffaw. '*Sout Piel! Ja*. I like it! It is a good joke.' His chuckles died away, and then he picked up the conversation from where it had been diverted. 'So, you do not like the British? You fought against them in the war, did you?'

Hennie thought about the question carefully, while he nursed the vehicle over a particularly rough stretch of the track. 'The war is finished,' he said at last, his tone flat and non-committal.

'*Ja*, it is finished, but it was a bad war. The British burned your farms and killed your cattle.'

Hennie did not reply, but his eyes shaded. 'They put your women and children in the camps. Many died there.'

'*Ja*. It is true,' Hennie whispered. 'Many died.'

'Now the land is ruined and there is no food for the children, and your *Volk* are slaves to Britain, *nein*? That is why you left, to escape the memories.'

Hennie's eyes were filled with tears. He wiped them away with a calloused thumb.

'Which commando did you ride with?'

Hennie looked directly at him for the first time. 'I did not say I rode with any commando.'

'Let me guess,' Graf Otto suggested. 'Perhaps you rode with Smuts.'

Hennie shook his head with an expression of bitter distaste. 'Jannie Smuts is a traitor to his people. He and Louis Botha have gone over to the khaki. They are selling our birthright to the British.'

'Ah!' Graf Otto exclaimed, with the air of a man who already knew the answer to his question. 'You hate Smuts and Botha. I know then who you rode with. It must have been Koos de la Rey.' He did not wait for an answer. 'Tell me, du Rand, what manner of man was General Jacobus Herculaas de la Rey? I have heard tell that he was a great soldier, better than Louis Botha and Jannie Smuts put together. Is that true?'

'He was no ordinary man.' Hennie stared at the track ahead. 'To us he was a god.'

'If there were ever to be another war, would you follow de la Rey again, Hennie?'

'I would follow him through the gates of hell.'

'The others of your commando, would they follow him also?'

'They would. We all would.'

'Would you like to meet de la Rey again? Would you like to shake his hand one more time?'

'That is not possible,' Hennie mumbled.

'With me everything is possible. I can make anything happen. Say nothing to anybody else. Not even to your *Sout Piel* boss, whom you like. This is between you and me alone. One day soon I will take you with me to see General de la Rey.'

Eva was crammed in beside him. She was obviously uncomfortable and swiftly becoming bored with the conversation in a language she did not understand. Graf Otto knew that her only languages were German and French.

1

Leon refuelled the *Butterfly* from one of the fifty-gallon drums that had been brought from Nairobi by Gustav in the big Meerbach truck. While he was doing this he sent Manyoro and Loikot to the top of the hill above the camp to join in with the Masai grapevine and gather any news that might be of interest. Once or twice he looked up from refuelling to listen to the shrill distant voices, calling to each other from hilltop to hilltop. The *chungaji* used a type of verbal shorthand, and he could make out a few isolated words but he could not follow the whole sense of their exchanges.

Not long after he had topped up the last of the *Butterfly*'s four fuel tanks and was washing his hands in the basin in front of his tent, the two Masai came down from the hill. They began to report to him the few items of interest they had gathered.

It was said that on the next full moon, as was customary at this time of the year, Lusima would preside over a conference of the Masai tribal elders on Lonsonyo Mountain. She would sacrifice a white cow to the ancestors. The welfare of the tribe depended on the observance of these rituals.

It was said also that there had been a raid by a war-party of Nandi. They had run off thirty-three head of prime Masai cattle, but the avenging *morani* had caught up with them on the banks of the Tishimi river. They had recovered all the missing cattle and thrown the corpses of the rustlers into the river. The crocodiles had disposed of this evidence. At the moment the district commissioner was holding an inquiry at Narosura, but it seemed that the entire area was suffering from an attack of amnesia. Nobody knew anything about stolen cattle or missing Nandi warriors.

It was further said that four lions had come down into the Rift Valley from the direction of Keekorok, all young males. They had been given a drubbing by the big dominant male and driven out of the pride into which they had been born: he would not tolerate any competition when it came to breeding with his females. Two nights previously the youngsters had killed six heifers from the *manyatta* directly to the west of Lonsonyo Mountain. The call had gone out to the *morani* to gather at this village, which was named Sonjo. They were going to deal out to these four cattle-killing lions a summary lesson in manners.

Leon was pleased with this news. Graf Otto had expressed a keen desire to watch a ceremonial hunt, and this was a most fortuitous coincidence. He despatched Manyoro to the Sonjo *manyatta*, which was hosting the lion hunters, with a gift of a hundred shillings for the local chieftain, and a request that he allow the *wazungu* to be spectators at the hunt.

By the time Graf Otto returned with Hennie in the Vauxhall from butchering the buffalo carcasses, Leon had the horses saddled and the pack mules loaded with sufficient supplies for the side expedition to Sonjo. As his client disembarked Leon hurriedly told him the good news.

Graf Otto was excited. 'Quickly, Eva! We must change into riding clothes and go at once. I do not want to miss the show.'

They pushed the horses along at a canter, covering almost twenty miles before it became too dark to see the ground ahead. Then they dismounted and unsaddled. They ate a cold dinner and slept rough. The next morning they were away again before it was fully light.

Some time before noon the next day, as they neared the village of Sonjo, they heard drums and singing. Manyoro had come from the village to await their arrival and was squatting beside the track. He stood up and came to meet the horses. 'All is arranged, M'bogo. The chief of the *manyatta* has agreed to delay the hunt until you arrive. But you must hurry. The *morani* are becoming restless. They are eager to blood their spears and win honour. The chief cannot keep them on the leash much longer.'

The *morani* were gathered in the centre of the cattle pen, an élite band who had been selected by the elders, the bravest and best. They were young men, fifty strong, dressed in red leather kilts decorated with ivory beads and cowrie shells. Their naked torsos gleamed with a coating of fat and red ochre. Their hair was dressed in an elaborate style of coiled plaits. They were lean and long-limbed, hard and elegantly muscled, their features handsome and hawkish, eyes bright and rapacious, showing their eagerness for the hunt to begin.

They had formed up in a single rank, shoulder to shoulder. At their head was a senior *morani*, an experienced warrior who wore five lion tails in his kilt, one for every Nandi he had killed in single combat. His war-bonnet was the headskin of a black-maned lion, further proof of his prowess. Single-handed, he had taken the lion with the *assegai*. He had a signal whistle made from the horn of a reed buck hanging on a thong around his neck.

Several hundred older men, with women and children, lined the outer stockade to watch the dance. The women clapped and ululated. As the three whites rode into the *manyatta* the drums took on an ever more savage and frenetic rhythm. The drummers pounded on the hollow logs, working the warriors into a fighting frenzy until they broke into the lion dance, singing and bounding high in the air on stiff legs, grunting like lions as they came back to earth.

Then the leader blew a shrill command on his whistle and the troop began to sally forth from the cattle pen, retaining their single file. Evenly spaced, they formed a long, sinuous serpent, which wound away down the grassy slope, the sunlight reflecting in bright sparks off the steel of their *assegais*. They carried on their shoulders their long rawhide shields, each painted with a single large eye of black and ochre, the pupil glaring white.

'Why do they have eyes on their shields, Otto?' Eva asked.

'Answer the question, Courtney.'

'The *morani* say they will provoke the lions into charging. Come, we must not be left behind. When it happens, it will happen very fast.' The riders followed the long, winding file of warriors.

'How do they know where to find the quarry?' Graf Otto asked.

'They have scouts watching over the lions,' Leon answered. 'But the lions will not have gone far. They have killed six cattle, and they will not leave until they have finished all that meat.'

Manyoro was running at Leon's stirrup. He said something and Leon stooped in the saddle to listen to him. When he straightened up he told Graf Otto, 'Manyoro says the dead cattle are lying in a shallow basin over the next rise.' He pointed ahead. 'If we circle out to the right, and take up position on the high ground, we will have a grandstand view.' He led them off the track and they cantered in a wide circle to get ahead of the file of *morani*, reaching the lookout point as the head of the long line of warriors breasted the ridge and started down into the basin.

Manyoro had given them good advice. When they reined in on the crest, they had a fine view over the grassy dale. The rotting carcasses of the cattle lay in full view, bellies ballooned with gas. Some had been partially devoured, but others seemed untouched.

Now the single file of warriors changed formation. As they reached a predetermined spot, each *morani* turned in the opposite direction to the man in front of him. Like a chorus line of well-choreographed dancers, the single file split into two. The twin lines opened to form a noose that would encircle the grassy hollow. Then, at a sharp blast on the whistle, the heads of the files of warriors began to converge. Swiftly the manoeuvre was completed. A wall of shields and spears ringed the basin.

'I cannot see the lions,' Eva said. 'Are you sure they have not escaped?'

But before either man could answer her, a lion stood up in full view. He had been lying flat against the earth, his coat blending perfectly with the sun-scorched brown grass. Although he was young, he was big and rangy. His mane was short and sparse, a mere fuzz of red hair. He snarled at the *morani*, his lips peeling back from his long, bright fangs.

They returned his greeting: 'We see you, evil one! We see you, killer of our cattle.'

The sound of fifty voices alarmed the other lions. They rose from their hiding places in the short grass, crouched low and glared, with eyes of topaz yellow, at the ring of shields. Their tails twitched nervously, they snarled and growled with fear and anger. They were young and this was beyond their experience.

The buckhorn whistle shrilled again and the *morani* began to chant the chorus of the Lion Song. Then, still singing, they moved forward in unison, shuffling and stamping. Slowly they closed in on the four lions as a python tightens its coils on its prey. One lion made a short mock-charge at the wall, and the *morani* shook their shields and called to him, 'Come! Come! We are ready to welcome you!'

The lion broke off his charge, coming up short on stiff front legs. He glared at the men, then spun around and ran back to join his siblings. They circled and milled uneasily, growling, and erected their manes in a threatening display, making short rushes at the wall of shields, then breaking off and turning back.

'The one with the ginger mane will be the first to charge home.' Graf Otto made his judgement and, as he spoke, the largest of the four lions launched himself in a swift, determined charge, straight at the shields. The senior *morani*, with the black-mane headdress, blew a blast on his buckhorn whistle. Then, with his spear, he pointed out a man in the file who was directly in the line of the charge. He shouted the man's name: 'Katchikoi!'

The warrior who had been chosen sprang high in the air to acknowledge the honour, then broke out of the line and raced to meet the charging lion with long, bounding strides. His comrades egged him on with a savage, rising ululation. The lion saw him coming, and swerved towards him, grunting with each stride, a tawny streak snaking low against the ground, his black-tufted tail slashing against his flanks. His glittering yellow eyes were fastened on Katchikoi.

As they came together the *morani* altered the angle of his charge, turning into the lion, forcing him to come in from the right, into his spear arm. Then he dropped on one knee behind his shield. The point of his *assegai* was aimed at the centre of the lion's chest, and the beast ran straight on to the steel. The long silver blade disappeared with magical suddenness, full length into the tawny body. Katchikoi released his grip on the haft, leaving the blade buried in the lion's chest. He raised the rawhide shield and the lion crashed headlong into it. He did not try to resist the weight and momentum of the great cat's leap, instead he rolled over backwards and curled himself into a ball holding the shield interposed. Despite the *assegai*, which transfixed him, the lion's strength and rage were undiminished. He tore at the shield with both front paws, the yellow claws raking deep gouges in it. He was growling hideously and trying to bite into the shield, but the leather had dried iron-hard and his fangs could not find a grip.

The hunt master blew a short blast on his buckhorn and four of Katchikoi's comrades left the ring of warriors and raced forward, then separated, two on each side. The lion was concentrating all his effort on Katchikoi so he did not see them coming until they had him surrounded. Their *assegais* rose and fell as, repeatedly, they drove the long blades deep into the lion's vital organs. The beast gave a mighty groan that carried clearly to the horsemen on the rise, then collapsed and rolled off the shield. He stretched out and lay still.

Katchikoi sprang to his feet, seized the handle of his *assegai*, placed one foot on the lion's chest and drew the blade clear. Brandishing the bloody steel, he led his four companions back to their places in the ring of warriors. They were greeted with shouts of acclamation that seemed to ring against the sky, and a salute of raised spears. Then the ring of *morani* moved forward again, tightening inexorably around the remaining three lions. As the ring contracted the warriors compacted into a solid wall, the outer edges of their shields overlapping.

In the centre the three lions rushed back and forth, seeking escape. They charged, then broke off and turned back with tails between their legs. At last one screwed its courage to the fatal point and charged home. The *morani* who met him drove the blade of his *assegai* fully home, but as he went over backwards with the lion on top, its claws hooked around the edge of the shield and ripped it aside, exposing the man's head and his naked torso. While its claws tore the man's chest open, the mortally wounded lion opened its jaws to their full extent and engulfed the man's head. It bit down until the long fangs interlocked, crushing the human skull like a walnut in a nutcracker. The dead man's comrades speared the lion in a fury of vengeance.

In quick succession the last two lions charged into the front rank of warriors, which broke over them, like an ocean wave upon a rock. They died under the spears, crackling with snarls, lashing out with hooked claws and desperate futility, as the razor steel stabbed deeply into them.

His circumcision brothers lifted the torn body of the dead *morani* out of the grass, and laid him on his shield. Then, to the full extent of their raised arms, they lifted him high in the air and bore him home singing his praise song. As they passed the watchers on the hilltop, Graf Otto lifted a clenched fist in a salute to the corpse. The *morani* acknowledged it with raised *assegais* and a wild shout.

'There was a man who died a man's death.' Graf Otto spoke with solemn intensity, a tone Leon had not heard him use before, and lapsed into silence. All three were deeply moved by the sublime tragedy. Then Graf Otto spoke again. 'What I have witnessed here today makes all the ethics of the hunt that I have believed in seem ignoble. How can I count myself a true hunter until I have stood to meet such a magnificent beast with only a spear in my hand?' He swivelled in the saddle and glared at Leon. 'This is not a request, Courtney, it is an order. Get me a lion, a full-grown black-maned lion. I will take him on foot. No guns. Just the beast and me.'

T hey camped that night at the *manyatta* of Sonjo and lay awake listening to the drums beating a dirge for the *morani* killed in the lion hunt, the keening of the women and the singing of the men.

In the darkness before dawn, they rode out again. When the sunrise broke over the escarpment of the Rift Valley it swamped the eastern sky with a blazing grandeur of gold and crimson, dazzling their eyes and warming their bodies so that they shrugged off their overcoats and rode on in shirtsleeves. Somehow this sunrise was a fitting epilogue to the lion hunt. It excited their senses and lightened their mood so that they saw beauty in all around them and wondered at the small things that before might have gone unremarked: the azure jewel of a kingfisher's breast as it darted across the track ahead, the grace of an eagle soaring high against the gold-drenched sky on outstretched pinions, a gazelle lamb kneeling on its front legs under its dam's belly and greedily bumping her udders with its snout, her milk running down its chin. The ewe watching them pass, unafraid, huge soft eyes glistening.

The mood was upon Eva also. She pointed with her riding crop and called out gaily, 'Oh, Otto! See that small creature snuffling around in the grass like an old man who has lost his reading glasses? What is it?'

Although she was addressing Graf Otto, Leon had the feeling that she was sharing the moment with him alone and answered, 'It is a honey badger, Fräulein. Although he appears gentle, he is one of the most ferocious creatures in Africa. He is without fear. He is immensely powerful. His pelt is so tough that it resists bee stings and the claws and fangs of much larger animals. Even the lion gives him a wide berth. Interfere with him at your peril.'

Eva gave him a flash of her violet eyes, then turned to Graf Otto with a purr of sweet laughter. 'In all of that he resembles you. In future I shall think of you as my honey badger.'

Which of them was she speaking to? Leon wondered. With this woman a man could never be sure of anything. There was always so much about her that was either enigmatic or ambiguous.

Before he could decide, she had spurred forward and, standing in the stirrups, pointed towards the southern horizon. 'Look at that mountain over there!' The distant shape of the flat-topped summit was dramatically highlighted by the rising sun. 'Surely it must be the mountain we flew over, the mountain on which the Masai prophetess lives.'

'Yes, Fräulein. That is Lonsonyo Mountain,' Leon confirmed.

'Oh, Otto, it is so close!' she cried.

He chuckled. 'For you it is close because that is where you want to go. For me it is a day's hard ride away.'

'You promised to take me there!' Her voice was dulled by disappointment.

'Indeed I did,' he agreed. 'But I did not promise when.'

'Then promise me now. When?' she demanded. 'When, darling Otto?'

'Not now. We must return to Nairobi at once. This delay was an indulgence. I have important business to see to. This African safari was not all for pleasure.'

'Of course not.' She grimaced. 'With you it is always business.'

'How else could I afford to have you as my friend?' Graf Otto asked, with heavy humour, and Leon turned away so as not to reveal his quick anger at the unkind remark. But Eva seemed to neither hear nor care, and Graf Otto went on, 'Perhaps I shall buy property here. It seems that there is room for investment in a new land with such resources to exploit.'

'And when your business is done, will you take me to Lonsonyo Mountain?' Eva persisted.

'You do not give up easily.' Graf Otto shook his head in mock-despair. 'Very well. I will make a bargain with you. After I have killed my lion with the *assegai* I will take you to see this witch.'

Once again Eva's mood altered subtly. Her eyes were masked, her expression closed and cool. Just when Leon had felt he might glimpse something beyond the veil, she had become once more remote and unfathomable.

They rested the horses at noon, off-saddling in a grove of stately pod mahogany trees beside a small reed-enclosed pool in an unnamed stream. After an hour they saddled up to ride on, but standing beside her mare Eva exclaimed irritably, 'The safety clasp on my right stirrup is locked. If I were to fall I would be dragged.'

'See to it, Courtney,' Graf Otto ordered, 'and make sure it does not happen again.'

Leon threw his reins to Loikot and went quickly to Eva's side. She moved a little to allow him to reach the stirrup leather, but she was close beside him as Leon stooped to examine the steel. Both of them were hidden from Graf Otto's view by the body of the horse. Leon found she was right: the safety clasp was locked. It had been open when they had left Sonjo *manyatta* that morning – he had checked it himself. Then Eva touched his hand, and his heart tripped. She must have opened the clasp herself as an excuse to have him alone for a moment. He glanced sideways at her. She was so close that he could feel her breath on his cheek. She wore no perfume, but she smelled as warm and sweet as a milk-fed kitten. For an instant he looked into the violet depths of her eyes and saw beyond the veil to the woman behind the lovely mask.

'I must go to the mountain. There is something there for me.' Her whisper was so soft he might have imagined it. 'He will never take me. You must.' There was the slightest check in her voice, and then she said, 'Please, Badger.' The heartfelt plea and the new pet name with which she had dubbed him made him catch his breath.

'What is the matter, Courtney?' Graf Otto called. Always alert, he had sensed something.

'I am angry that the clasp was locked. It might have been dangerous for Fräulein von Wellberg.' Leon drew out his knife and used the blade to prise open the clasp. 'It will be all right now,' he assured Eva. They were still screened by the mare, so he dared to stroke the back of the hand that lay on the saddle. She did not pull it away.

'Mount up! We must ride on,' Graf Otto ordered. 'We have wasted enough time here. I wish to fly back to Nairobi today. We must reach the airstrip while there is still sufficient daylight for the flight.' They rode hard, but the sun was lying red and bleeding on the horizon, like a dying *morani* on his shield, when at last they scrambled up the ladder into the cockpit of the *Butterfly*. Inexperienced as he was, even Leon knew that Graf Otto had cut the take-off beyond the limits of safety. At this season of the year twilight would be short-lived: it would be dark in less than an hour.

When they crossed the wall of the Rift Valley they were flying just high enough to catch the last rays of the sun, but the earth below was already shrouded in impenetrable purple shadow. Suddenly the sun was gone, snuffed out like a candle, and there was no afterglow.

They flew on in darkness, until Leon picked out the tiny cluster of lights far ahead that marked the town, insignificant as fireflies in the dark immensity of the land. It was completely dark when at last they were over the polo ground. Graf Otto repeatedly revved, then throttled back on the engines as he circled. Suddenly the headlights of the two Meerbach trucks lit up below them, at opposite ends of the landing field, shining down the grassy runway. Gustav Kilmer had heard the *Butterfly*'s engines and hurried to the rescue of his beloved master.

Guided by the lights Graf Otto put the *Butterfly* down on the turf as gently as a broody hen settling on a clutch of eggs.

Leon believed that the flying visit to Percy's Camp down in the Rift Valley and the wild buffalo hunt in the thorn signalled the commencement of the safari in earnest. He thought that the Graf was at last ready to head out into the blue. His assumption was incorrect.

The second morning after their return from Percy's Camp and the nocturnal landing at the polo ground, Graf Otto sat at the head of the breakfast table at Tandala Camp with a dozen envelopes stacked in front of him. Every one was a response to the official letters from the German Foreign Office in Berlin that Max Rosenthal had distributed to all the dignitaries of British East Africa.

Graf Otto translated excerpts from each missive to Eva, who was sitting opposite him nibbling daintily on slices of fruit. It seemed that all of Nairobi society was agog to have in their midst a man like Graf Otto von Meerbach. Like any other frontier town, Nairobi needed little excuse for a party, and he was the best excuse they had been presented with since the opening of the Muthaiga Country Club three years previously. Every letter contained an invitation.

The governor of the colony was hosting a special dinner at Government House in his honour. Lord Delamere was holding a formal ball at his new Norfolk Hotel to welcome him and Fräulein von Wellberg to the territory. The committee of the Muthaiga Country Club had voted Graf Otto an honorary member and, not to be outdone by Delamere, were also throwing a ball to initiate him into club membership. The officer commanding His Britannic Majesty's armed forces in East Africa, Brigadier General Penrod Ballantyne's invitation was to a banquet at the regimental mess. Lord Charlie Warboys had invited the couple to a four-day pig-sticking party on his fifty-thousand-acre estate on the edge of the Rift Valley. The Nairobi Polo Club had voted Graf Otto full membership, and asked him to play on their first team in a challenge match against the King's African Rifles on the first Saturday of the coming month.

Graf Otto was delighted by the furore he had stirred up. Listening to him discuss each invitation with Eva, Leon realized that their departure from Nairobi had receded to some time in the remote future. Graf Otto accepted every one of the invitations, and in return issued his own to spectacular dinners, banquets and balls that he would host at the Norfolk, the Muthaiga or out at Tandala Camp. Leon now understood why he had sent out such enormous supplies of food and drink on the SS *Silbervogel*.

However, the Graf's masterstroke of hospitality, which warmed every heart in the colony and earned him the instant reputation of being a cracking good fellow, was his open day. He issued a public invitation to a picnic on the polo ground. At this gathering, selected guests such as the governor, Delamere, Warboys and Brigadier General Ballantyne would be given a flight over the town in one of his aeroplanes. Then Eva exerted her influence, and persuaded him to extend the invitation to every boy and girl between the ages of six and twelve: they were all to be given a flight.

The entire colony went into raptures. The ladies were determined to turn the open day into an African equivalent of Ascot. From a simple picnic it snowballed into an almost royal occasion. Lord Warboys donated three prime young oxen to be roasted on spits over beds of coals. Every member of the Women's Institute got busy with her oven, turning out cakes and pies. Lord Delamere took over the supply of beer: he sent an urgent-rate cable to the brewery at Mombasa and received an assurance that a large quantity would be on its way within days. Word of the invitation went out into the hinterland and settler families on the remote farms loaded their wagons in preparation for the trek to Nairobi.

There were only four dressmakers in town and their services were immediately booked out. The open-air barbers on Main Street were busy clipping beards and trimming hair. The boys' school and the girls' convent declared a holiday, and rumour flew through the classrooms that every child who made a flight would be presented by Graf Otto with a commemoration gift in the form of a perfect scale model of the *Butterfly*.

Leon was sucked into all this feverish activity. Graf Otto decided he needed a second pilot to deal with the hordes of eager children who would be queuing for a flight. He would pilot the senior guests, but he was not enthusiastic about filling his cockpit with their offspring. As he remarked to Eva in Leon's hearing he preferred children in their sweet spirit rather than in their clamorous, noisome flesh.

'Courtney, I promised I would teach you to fly.'

Leon was taken by surprise. This was the first time Graf Otto had mentioned the flight instruction since the buffalo hunt, and he had thought the promise conveniently forgotten. 'So we go to the airfield immediately. Courtney, today you learn to fly!'

L eon sat beside Graf Otto in the cockpit of the *Bumble Bee* and listened intently as he described the functions and operation of each dial and instrument, the taps and switches, the levers and controls. Despite their complexity, Leon already had a working knowledge of the flight-deck layout, acquired on the 'monkey see, monkey do' principle. When Graf Otto listened as Leon repeated everything he had just learned, he chuckled and nodded. '*Ja!* You have been watching me when I fly. You are quick, Courtney. That is good!'

Leon had not expected he would make a good instructor, and was pleasantly surprised by the Graf's attention to detail and his patience. They began on engine start-up and shut-down, then moved on quickly to ground taxiing: cross wind, down wind and into the wind. Leon started to feel the controls and the big machine's response to them, like the reins and stirrups of a horse. Nevertheless he was surprised when Graf Otto tossed him a leather flying helmet. 'Put it on.' They had taxied to the far end of the polo ground, and he shouted above the engine roar, 'Nose to wind!' Leon put on full starboard rudder and gunned the two port engines. Already he had assimilated the use of opposing thrust to manoeuvre the machine. The *Bumble Bee* came around handily and put her nose into the wind.

'You want to fly? So fly!' Graf Otto shouted into his ear.

Leon gave him a horrified, disbelieving look. It was too soon. He wasn't ready yet. He needed a little more time.

'*Gott im Himmel!*' Graf Otto bellowed. 'Why are you waiting? Fly her!'

Leon took a long, slow breath and reached for the bank of throttles. He opened them gradually, listening for the beat of the separate engines to synchronize. Like an old lady running for a bus, the *Bumble Bee* broke into a trot, then a canter and finally a sprint. Leon felt the joystick come alive in his hands. He felt the lightness of impending flight in his fingertips, in his feet on the rudder bars and in his spirit. It was a feeling of absolute power and control. His heart began to sing in the rush of the wind. The nose veered off line and he met it with a touch of rudder and brought it back. He felt the *Bumble Bee* bounce lightly under him. She wants to fly, he thought. We both want to fly!

Beside him Graf Otto made a small gesture, and Leon understood what it meant. The joystick was trembling in his fingers, and he pressed it gently forward. Behind him the massive tailplane lifted clear of the grassy surface, and the *Bumble Bee* reacted gratefully to the decrease in drag. He felt her quicken in his hands, and as Graf Otto made the next signal he was already easing the joystick back. Once, twice, the wheels bounced and then she was flying. He lifted the nose and settled it on the horizon ahead, in the attitude of climb. They went up and up. He shot a glance over the side of the cockpit and saw the earth falling away below. He was flying. His hands were the only ones on the stick, his feet alone were on the rudder bars. He was really flying. He soared on upwards joyfully.

Beside him Graf Otto nodded approvingly, then gave him

the signal to level out of the climb, to bank left and bank right. Stick and rudder together, Leon put the *Bumble Bee* over, and she responded docilely.

Graf Otto nodded again and raised his voice so that Leon could catch the words: 'Some are born with the wind in our hair and the starlight in our eyes. I think you may be one of us, Courtney.'

Under his instructions Leon circled wide, then lined up on the runway. He had not yet learned how to slow the machine and at the same time lose height. He should have held the nose up and let her bleed off speed, sinking under her own weight. Instead he pushed the nose down and dived towards the field, coming in much too fast. The *Bumble Bee* was still flying when she hit the ground with a crash and ballooned up off the grassy strip. He was forced to open the throttles wide and go around again. Beside him Graf Otto laughed. 'You still have much to learn, Courtney. Try again.'

On the next approach he did better. With her vast wing area the *Bumble Bee* had a low stall speed. He came in over the fence of the polo ground at thirty feet above the ground, with forty knots of air speed indicated. He held her nose up, and let her sink to the earth. She touched down with a jolt that clashed his teeth but did not bounce, and Graf Otto laughed again. 'Good! Much better! Go around again.'

Leon was getting the feel of it quickly. Each of the next three landings was an improvement on the preceding effort, and the fourth was a perfect three-point touch-down, the main undercarriage and tail wheel kissing the ground in unison.

'Excellent!' Graf Otto shouted. 'Taxi to the hangar!'

Leon felt heady with success. His first day of instruction had been a triumph and he knew he could look forward to continued improvement over the days ahead.

When he swung the *Bumble Bee* around in front of the hangar he reached for the fuel cock to shut off the engines, but Graf Otto forestalled him. 'No! I am getting out, but you are not.'

'I don't understand.' Leon was puzzled. 'What do you want me to do?'

'I promised to teach you how to fly, and I have done so. Now go and fly, Courtney, or go and kill yourself. It is all the same to me.' Graf Otto von Meerbach scrambled over the side of the cockpit and disappeared, leaving Leon, after the grand total of three hours' tuition, facing his first solo flight.

It took a deliberate effort of mind and body to force himself to reach forward and grip the throttle handle. His mind was in a spin. He had forgotten everything he had just learned. He began his take-off run with the wind behind his tail. The *Bumble Bee* ran and ran, building up air speed so gradually that he was only able to wrench her into the air seconds before she hit the boundary fence. He cleared it with three feet to spare, but at least he was flying. He glanced over his shoulder and saw Graf Otto standing in front of the hangar with his fists on his hips, his head thrown back and his whole body convulsed with laughter.

'Wonderful sense of humour you have, von Meerbach. Deliberately wounding a couple of buffalo and sending up a complete novice to kill himself. Anything for a laugh!' But his anger was ephemeral and forgotten almost immediately. He was flying solo. The earth and the sky belonged to him alone.

The sky was bright and clear except for a single silver cloud that seemed not much larger than his hand. He put the *Bumble Bee* into a climb and banked towards it. It seemed almost solid as the earth and he flew close over the top. Then he turned and came back, and this time he touched the top of the silver billows with his wheels as though he was landing upon them. 'Playing with clouds,' he exulted. 'Is this how the angels and the gods pass their time?' He dropped down through the cloud bank and was blinded for a few seconds in the silver mists, then burst out through them into the sunlight, laughing with the joy of it. Down and down he plummeted and the great brown land rushed up to meet him. He levelled out, his wheels skimming the treetops. The wide expanse of the Athi plains opened ahead and he dropped even lower. Thirty feet above the earth and at a hundred miles an hour he charged across the treeless wilderness. The game herds scattered in pandemonium under his wheels. He was so low that he had to lift his port wing-tip to avoid collision with the outstretched neck of a galloping bull giraffe.

He climbed again and turned towards the line of the Ngong Hills. From two miles out he picked out the thatched roofs of Tandala Camp. He flew over it so low that he could recognize the faces of the camp staff who stared up at him in amazement. There were Manyoro and Loikot. He leaned over the side of the cockpit and waved, and they danced and cavorted, waving back in wild exuberance.

He looked for a white face among them, not just any white face but that special one, and felt a throb of disappointment that she was not there. He turned back towards the airstrip, and was skimming the tops of the Ngong Hills when he saw the horse. It was on the skyline directly ahead, the grey mare she always favoured. Then he saw her standing at its head. She wore a bright yellow blouse and a wide-brimmed straw hat. She looked up at the approaching aircraft but showed no animation.

Of course, she doesn't know it's me. She thinks it's Graf Otto. Leon smiled to himself and dropped towards her. He pushed back his goggles and leaned over the side of the cockpit. He was so close to her that he saw the moment she recognized him. She threw back her head and he saw the flash of her teeth as she laughed. She snatched off her hat and waved it as he thundered over her, so close that the mare pranced and tossed her head with alarm. He fancied he could even make out the colour of Eva's eyes.

As he climbed away he twisted in the seat to look back at her. She was still waving. He wanted her in the cockpit beside him. He wanted to be able to reach out and touch her. Then he remembered the signal pad in the locker beside him. Graf Otto had used a page of it to illustrate a point of instruction. A pencil was attached to it on a length of twine. He held the pad between his knees and scribbled quickly, keeping his other hand on the controls. 'Fly away with me to Lonsonyo Mountain. Badger.' He ripped the page out and folded it into a tiny square. In the locker where he had found the pad there was a ball of scarlet message ribbons, each six feet long. He pulled one out. One end was weighted with a lead slug the size of a musket ball and at the other there was a small, buttoned pocket. He slipped the folded page into it and closed it, then turned the *Bumble Bee* back.

She was still on the hilltop, but now she was mounted on the grey. She saw the *Bumble Bee* coming back and rose in the stirrups. He made a hasty calculation of height and speed, then dropped the signal ribbon over the side of the cockpit. It unrolled in the slipstream and fluttered down.

Eva turned the mare and galloped after the falling scrap of scarlet. When he turned the machine in a tight circle back towards her, he saw her swing down from the saddle as she found the ribbon. She opened the pocket, and pulled out his note, read it and waved both hands above her head, nodding vigorously. Her teeth flashed as she laughed.

Graf Otto von Meerbach's open day at the airfield gradually grew in status until it seemed to overshadow almost any other event in the history of the colony, including the arrival of the first train from the coast or even the visit of Theodore Roosevelt, former President of the United States of America.

As one of the wags at the long bar of the Muthaiga Country Club remarked, Colonel Teddy had not been dishing out free rides in an aeroplane.

By sunrise of the great day a small city of tents surrounded the polo ground. Most housed the settler families who had come in from the surrounding countryside, but the others were refreshment booths from which Lord Delamere dispensed free beer and lemonade, and the Women's Institute handed out chocolate cakes and apple pies.

The chef from the Norfolk Hotel was supervising the roasting of the oxen on spits over live coals. The KAR band was tuning its instruments in readiness for the arrival of the governor. Gangs of small boys and pariah dogs roamed the field looking for titbits and mischief. The refreshment booths were doing a roaring trade, and the betting was three to one that the shipment of beer would be insufficient to last the day. Gustav Kilmer's mechanics were busy fine-tuning the aircraft engines and topping up the fuel tanks. Lines of excited children were queuing for the promised flights, squealing with excitement every time one of the engines bellowed.

By this time Leon had flown a total of twelve hours in the *Bumble Bee* and Graf Otto assured anxious parents that their offspring would be quite safe with such an experienced pilot at the controls. Eva assumed responsibility for controlling the hordes of children. She press-ganged their mothers and the members of the Polo Club committee to act as her marshals. Some had a little German or French, and they all seemed to understand each other well enough. Every time Leon glimpsed her during the morning she had a small child on her hip and half a dozen others hanging on to her arms or skirts.

This was a different woman from Graf Otto's beautiful enigmatic consort. Her maternal instincts had been aroused, her face was radiant and her eyes shone. Her laughter was quick and unrestrained, as she passed little ones up into the cockpit of the *Bumble Bee*, where Leon and Hennie du Rand strapped them on to the benches. When the cockpit was filled almost to overflowing with tiny humanity Leon started the engines and the children squeaked in delicious terror. From the sidelines the KAR band struck up a rousing military march. Then the *Bumble Bee* taxied out on to the field, following Graf Otto in the *Butterfly* with his more dignified and illustrious passengers. The two aircraft took off in formation and circled the town twice, then returned to the field for landing. Eva was at the *Bumble Bee*'s ladder, helping the children back to the ground. Hennie and Max Rosenthal handed out the model aircraft, and the next band of little passengers was lifted aboard.

Leon was fascinated by this new manifestation of Eva. She had raised the shutters to allow her inner warmth and her womanly capacity for kindness and affection to shine out. The children saw this in her and were drawn to her like ants to a sugar bowl. It seemed to Leon that Eva had become a child herself, totally happy and natural. As the day wore on and the lines of children seemed never to grow shorter, most of her assistants were flagging in the heat, but Eva was indefatigable. Leon watched as she knelt in the dust, sweat-damp strands of her hair coming down over her eyes so that she had to purse her lips and blow them aside while she cleaned up a small girl who had been airsick. Her boots were dusty and her skirts bore the marks of grubby fingers, but her face shone with perspiration and happiness.

Leon glanced around. Graf Otto had taken off in the *Butterfly* for his next circuit, carrying with him Brigadier General Penrod Ballantyne and the manager of Barclays Bank. Gustav Kilmer was by the hangar, his back turned to them as he removed the bung from another drum of fuel. For the moment they were not under surveillance.

'Eva!' he called.

She returned the child to her mother and came to the side of the aircraft where she pretended to fuss with those who were waiting. She spoke to Leon without looking at him. 'You like to live dangerously, Badger. You know we should not talk in public.'

'I must seize every chance to have you alone.'

'What did you want to tell me?' Her expression had softened, but she looked away quickly.

'You're very good with the babies,' he told her. 'I didn't expect that of such a grand lady as you.'

Again she looked at him, smiling, her eyes bright and candid, concealing nothing. 'If you think I'm a grand lady, you don't know me very well.'

'I think you know how I feel for you.'

'Yes, Badger. I know. You're not good at keeping secrets.' She laughed.

'Is there no way we can ever be alone together? There is so much I want to say to you.'

'Gustav is watching us. We have already spoken too long. I must go.'

By mid-afternoon the waiting lines of children were almost exhausted, and so was Leon. He had lost count of the number of take-offs and landings he had executed. Not all had been perfect but he had done no obvious damage to the *Bumble Bee*, and he had received no complaints from his small customers. Now he eyed the queue wearily. There were five children remaining so this would be his last flight of the day.

Then something caught his attention. Somebody was waving at him from beyond the boundary fence. It took him a moment to recognize the face, and might have taken longer, were it not for the line of small girls in bright saris who stood behind him.

'My solemn oath!' Leon perked up immediately. 'It's Mr Goolam Vilabjhi Esquire and his cherubs.' Then he saw that the smallest cherub was weeping and the others looked as though their hearts were about to break. He stood up in the cockpit and beckoned them to him. They started for the gate into the field in a compact family group, but one of the committee members of the Polo Club, who was acting as a marshal, was guarding it to keep out undesirable elements. He was a large, beefy man, with a beer-barrel belly and a very red, sunburned face. Leon knew him as a recent settler who had come out from the Old Country to take up his four-thousand-acre grant. Clearly he had availed himself unstintingly of Lord Delamere's free beer. He intercepted Mr Vilabjhi with shaking head. The dismay on the faces of the children was pathetic.

Leon jumped down from the cockpit and started for the gate, but he was too late: Eva had beaten him to it. She flew at the marshal like a Jack Russell terrier at a rat, and he retreated hastily before her onslaught. She grabbed two of the Vilabjhi girls by their hands and Leon ran to gather up the rest. He spoke to her over their heads: 'When will we have a chance to be alone?'

'Be patient, Badger. Please. No more now. Gustav is watching us again.' She pushed the last child up the ladder into the cockpit and went to where Mr Vilabjhi was watching anxiously from the gate. When Leon brought the *Bumble Bee* back into the field after the flight she was still standing at the gate in earnest conversation with him.

Every man in the colony is fascinated by her and I am right at the back of the queue. Leon was surprised by the strength of his own jealousy.

Ladies' Night at the KAR regimental mess was another towering success for all but Leon. He stood at the bar and watched Penrod waltzing with Eva. His uncle was a striking figure in his dress uniform and danced gracefully. Eva was light and lovely in his arms, her shining dark hair swept up and her shoulders bare. Her dress was in a subtle shade of violet that enhanced her eyes and emphasized the satin skin of her *décolleté*. Her bosom was full and shapely. Her arms were long and sleek. Her skin glowed and her cheeks were slightly flushed as she laughed at one of Penrod's sallies. As they whirled past, Leon picked up snatches of their conversation. They were talking French, and Penrod was at his most charming and urbane.

The old bastard! Leon thought bitterly. He's old enough to be her grandfather, but I wouldn't put anything past him. Then he saw the sparkle of Eva's eyes and the flash of her perfect white teeth as she smiled up at him. She's no better than he is. Can't she resist the temptation to sparkle at every man who passes through her life?

The evening dragged on interminably. The jokes of his brother officers creaked with age, the speeches were dull, the music loud and tuneless and even the whisky tasted sour. The night was hot and the air in the hall suffocating. He felt caged in. The wallflower with whom he was doing his duty suffered from halitosis and he returned her to her large, hopeful mother, then escaped thankfully into the night.

The air was sweet, the sky clear, and the stars were wondrous. Scorpio stood on his head with his sting raised, ready to strike. Leon thrust his hands into his pockets and sauntered glumly around the parade-ground. As he completed the circuit and came back towards the mess, he saw a small group of men on the veranda. They were smoking cigars, and Leon heard a familiar braying voice holding forth from the centre of the group. It was answered almost immediately by another that jarred on his nerves as painfully as the first. Froggy Snell and his grovelling boot-licker Eddy Roberts, he thought irritably. Just when I was starting to feel better, the last two people in the world I wanted to meet.

Fortunately there was a rear entrance to the dance hall so he made his way quietly along the side wall of the building, which was covered with a dense trumpeter vine.

As he turned the corner a Vesta flared in the darkness close by and he saw a couple standing among the concealing curtain of the vine's leaves and flowers. The woman had her back to him. She had struck the Vesta and was holding it for the man, who stooped over the flame to light his cigar. He straightened up, puffing out streamers of smoke. The Vesta was still burning and by its light Leon saw that the man was Penrod. Neither he nor the woman was aware of his presence.

'Thank you, my dear,' Penrod said, in English. Then he spotted Leon and his expression changed to one of mild alarm. 'It's Leon!' he exclaimed.

An odd remark, Leon thought. It sounded like a warning rather than a friendly greeting. The woman whirled around to face him, still holding the burning Vesta. She let it drop and put her foot upon it to snuff out the flame, but he had seen the expression on her face. She and Penrod were behaving like a pair of conspirators.

'Monsieur Courtney, you made me jump. I didn't hear you coming.'

She spoke in French – but why, only seconds before, had Penrod been speaking to her in English? 'Forgive me. I'm intruding.'

'Not at all.' Penrod denied it. 'The air in the hall is oppressive. Those little punkah fans are worse than useless. Fräulein von Wellberg was affected, and needed a breath of fresh air. And I, on the other hand, needed a smoke.' He switched to French when he addressed Eva: 'I was telling my nephew that you were a little indisposed by the heat and the stale air.'

'I am feeling perfectly well now,' she replied, in the same language, and though Leon could not see her face she sounded utterly composed once more.

'We were discussing the band and their musical repertoire,' Penrod said. 'Fräulein von Wellberg feels that their rendition of Strauss resembles a tribal war-dance, and she prefers the way they deal with the polka.'

Uncle, it seems to me that you are protesting too much, Leon thought, with a touch of bitterness. Something very strange is going on here. For a little longer he joined in their inconsequential conversation, then bowed to Eva. 'Please excuse me, Fräulein, but I am not as strong as you two are. I shall go home to get some sleep. Will you and the Graf be returning to Tandala Camp after the ball, or will you stay at the Norfolk Hotel?'

'I understand that Gustav will drive us back to the camp in the hunting car,' Eva replied.

'Very well. I have instructed my staff to have everything ready for your return. If there is anything you need you have only to let them know. I imagine that tomorrow you and Graf Otto may wish to sleep late. Breakfast will be served when you order it.' He nodded at Penrod. 'Even though duty calls loud and clear, sir, I find that the flesh is weakening fast. One or two more duty dances and then I will be lost in a cloud of dust as I head for my bed.'

'I shall give you an avuncular mention in despatches, my boy. You have held high the honour of the regiment. The manner in which you trotted the light fantastic with Charlie Warboys's fat daughter was a joy to watch. You have been weighed in the balance and not found wanting.'

'Jolly kind of you to say so, Uncle.' He left them, but when he reached the door of the hall he glanced back. They were two dark figures and he could not see their faces, but there was something in the way they leaned towards each other, an alertness in the way they held their heads, that convinced him they were no longer discussing the band's rendition of the polka, but something of much deeper import.

Just what are the two of you up to? Who are you really, Eva von Wellberg? The closer I get to you, the more elusive you become. The more I learn about you, the less I know.

L eon was awakened by the sound of the Meerbach hunting car coming down the track from the town and the Graf singing the beer-hall drinking song 'I Lost My Heart In Heidelberg' at the full pitch of his lungs. He sat up in bed, struck a Vesta and checked the time on Percy's silver hunter, which lay on the bedside table. It was six minutes to four in the morning. He heard the car come to a halt in the camp, and the slamming of its doors, Graf Otto's voice shouting goodnight to Gustav, and Eva's laughter. Leon felt a stab of jealousy and muttered to himself, 'By the sound of it you've taken a skinful, Graf. You should be more careful about drinking with Delamere. I hope you have a brutal hangover in the morning. You deserve it, you bastard.'

He was to be disappointed. Graf Otto appeared in the mess tent a little after eight, looking cheerful and rested. The whites of his eyes were as clear and bright as a baby's. He shouted to Ishmael to bring coffee, and when it arrived he poured a dram of cognac into the steaming mug. 'Drinking makes me extremely thirsty. That mad Englishman Delamere ran out of people to toast so towards the end of the evening we were hailing his favourite horse and his hunting dog. He is mad, that one. He should be locked up for his own good and the good of everyone else.'

'As I recall, it wasn't Lord Delamere who stood on his head in the middle of the dance floor and drank a glass of cognac while inverted.'

'No, that was me,' Graf Otto admitted. 'But I was challenged by Delamere. I had no choice in the matter. Did you know that he was bitten by a lion when he was younger? That is why he limps.'

'Everybody in the colony knows the story.'

'He was trying to kill it with a knife.' Graf Otto shook his head sadly. 'Madman! He really should be locked away.'

'Tell me, Graf Otto, is it not just as crazy to try to kill one with an *assegai*?'

'*Nein!* Not at all! A knife is stupid, but a spear is extremely logical.' Graf Otto drained his coffee and slammed his mug on the table. 'I am grateful to you for reminding me, Courtney. I have had enough of these schoolboy larks, as mad Delamere terms them. I have drunk toasts to all the world and danced with every fat British matron in the colony. I have flown their puking brats in my beautiful machines. In short, I have observed all the niceties and fulfilled my social obligations to the governor and the citizens of this colony. Now I want to go out into the wilderness and do some real hunting.'

'I am delighted to hear you say so, sir. Like you, I have had enough of Nairobi for a while.'

'Good! You may leave at once. Summon those two tall heathens of yours and take *Die Hummel* to the hunting grounds. Spread the word to the tribes the length and breadth of the Rift Valley that I am searching for the biggest lion that ever came out of Masailand. I will pay a reward of twenty cattle to the chief whose people find it for me. Go now, and do not return until you have good news to bring me. Remember, Courtney, he must be big and his mane must be as black as the hell hound.'

'At once, Graf, but may I finish this cup of coffee before I leave?'

344

'Another good English joke. *Ja*, it is funny. Now I will crack a good German joke. Find my lion or I will kick your arse until you limp a damned sight worse than Delamere. Now that is really a funny joke, no?'

When Eva entered the mess tent an hour later Graf Otto was alone at the long table, a sheaf of documents stacked in front of him. He was poring over one that bore the black eagle crest of the German Ministry of War and making entries in his notebook. He laid it aside and looked up at her as she stood in the entrance to the tent with the morning light behind her. She wore sandals, and a light summer dress in a lovely floral pattern that made her as winsome as a schoolgirl. Her hair was freshly washed, and brushed out in a cascade of sable wavelets down her back. Her lips were unpainted. She came to stand behind him and draped an arm over his shoulder. He took her hand, opened her fingers and kissed the palm. 'How can you be so beautiful?' he asked. 'Do you not feel guilty that you make every other woman around you seem drab and ugly in comparison?'

'Don't you feel guilty that you lie so readily and convincingly?' She kissed him full on the mouth, then giggled and broke away as he reached for her breasts. 'You must feed me first, darling Otto.'

Ishmael had been poised for her arrival. He wore his best scarlet fez with a black tassel, and his *kanza* had been carefully laundered, then ironed crisp as a fresh fall of snow. His teeth flashed brightly when he smiled. 'Good morning, Memsahib. May your day be filled with the perfume of roses and flavoured with sweet fruits such as these.' He spoke in French as he placed a platter of sliced mangos, banana and papaya before her.

'*Merci beaucoup*, Ishmael. Where did you learn to speak such good French?'

'I worked for many years for the consul in Mombasa,

Memsahib.' Ishmael beamed. She had cast her spell over all the staff of Tandala Camp.

'Away with you, you smirking infidel,' Graf Otto intervened. 'My coffee is cold. Get me a fresh pot.' As soon as Ishmael had gone, his manner changed and he became serious and businesslike. 'Well, I've got rid of Courtney. I sent him out into the hunting grounds to find the lion we have spoken of so often. He will be well out of the way for as long as it takes to see to the real business. Despite his guileless manner and his engaging personality I do not trust him. He is much too astute for my taste. Last evening he was wearing army uniform. That was the first inkling I had that he is on the British Army reserve list. Also, I learned from Delamere that Brigadier General Ballantyne is his uncle. His connections with the British military are strong. In future we must be more circumspect with him.'

'Of course, Otto.' She took the chair beside him and turned her attention to the platter of fruit.

'There was a cable from Berlin yesterday. They have arranged my meeting with von Lettow for the seventeenth,' he continued. 'It's a long flight to Arusha, but I cannot afford to be gone long. There are too many people watching us. Pack some of your pretty things, Eva. I want to be proud of you.'

'Do you really need me with you, Otto? It will be all men's talk and so dull. I would rather stay here and do some painting.' She speared a slice of ripe mango.

Her attitude of mild disinterest in his affairs of business and state was a pose she had perfected over her long association with him. It yielded far greater fruits than if she had tried to wheedle information from him. Once again her patience had paid off handsomely. For the first time since they had left Weiskirchen he had mentioned von Lettow Vorbeck. She knew that this was the real purpose of their African expedition. This was what lay at the heart of all the make-believe and play-acting.

'Yes, indeed, *Liebling*. You know that I always need you with me.'

'Who else will be there other than von Lettow? Will there be any other women?'

'I doubt it. Von Lettow is a bachelor. It is possible that Governor Schnee may be there, but he and von Lettow do not get on together, or so I believe. It will not be a social occasion. The most important person at the meeting will be the South African Boer, Koos de la Rey. He is the pivot on which it all hinges.'

'Maybe I'm just a silly girl, as you often say I am, but isn't this a very convoluted way of meeting? Would it not have been easier for this Boer general simply to have come to Berlin – or couldn't we have sailed to Cape Town in the comfort of an ocean-going liner like the *Admiral*?'

'In South Africa de la Rey is a marked man. He was one of the Boer leaders who fought so hard and bitterly against the British. Since the armistice he has made no secret of his anti-British feelings. Any contact between him and our government would set off alarm bells in London. The meeting has to be outside his own country. Ten days ago, in great secrecy, he was picked up off the South African coast by one of our submarines and brought to Dar es Salaam. After our meeting he will return by the same route.'

'Meanwhile, you are on a big-game safari in an adjoining country. There is nothing to lead anybody to suspect that the two of you ever made contact. I see now that it is a rather neat conspiracy.'

'I am glad you approve.' He smiled sarcastically.

'The whole business must be very important for you to have spent so much time on it when you might have been hunting.'

'It is.' He nodded seriously. 'Believe me, it is.'

Instinct warned her that she had gone far enough for the moment. She sighed and murmured, 'Very important, and deadly boring. If I come with you, will you buy me a nice present when we get back to Germany?' She pouted at him and fluttered her long dark lashes, using her eyes artfully. This was more in line with the character she had built up to please him. It was the type of shallow response he had come to expect of her. During the time they had been together she had worked out precisely how to handle every situation that arose between them, and how best to fulfil all his expectations. She understood precisely what he needed from her. He did not want her to be a companion, or someone who gave him intellectual stimulation – there were many others who could do that. He wanted her as an ornament, an uncomplicated and compliant beauty, someone who could first arouse, then skilfully satisfy his animal passions. He wanted her as a pleasurable possession, who excited the envy and admiration of other men and women; a decoration that enhanced his own position and social standing. As soon as she became tiresome he would discard her as readily as he would throw away a pair of shoes that pinched his toes. She was fully aware that hundreds of other beautiful women would be delighted to take her place. It was a measure of her skills as a courtesan that he had kept her so long at his side.

'It will be the prettiest present we can find in all of Berlin,' he agreed easily.

'Shall I take the Fortuny frock you bought for me in Paris? What do you think General von Lettow Vorbeck will think of it?'

'One look at you in that dress and his thoughts would probably have him locked behind bars in any decent society.' Graf Otto chuckled, then raised his voice to a shout: 'Ishmael!'

'Send for Bwana Hennie!' Graf Otto ordered, as soon as Ishmael appeared. 'Tell him to come at once.'

Within minutes Hennie du Rand appeared in the fly of the tent. The frown on his brown, weather-beaten face was anxious, and he held his stained slouch hat across his chest, twisting it between grease-stained fingers.

'Come in, Hennie. Don't just stand there.' Graf Otto greeted him with a friendly smile, then looked at Eva. 'You must forgive us, *Liebling*. You know that Hennie has no German so we will be speaking English.'

'Please, Graf Otto, do not worry about me. I have my book of birds and my binoculars. I shall be quite happy.' She stooped to kiss him as she passed his chair, then went to sit just outside the tent where she had a good view of the birdbath and feeding table Leon had set up for her entertainment. Noisy flocks of songbirds gathered around it: fire finches, waxbills, weavers and wild canaries.

Although they were within earshot she ignored the conversation of the two men in the mess tent as she concentrated on capturing in her sketchpad the forms and colours of the tiny jewel-like creatures.

Almost at once Graf Otto forgot her and gave Hennie his full attention. 'How well do you know Arusha and the country around it, Hennie?'

'I worked for a timber company there for two years. They were logging on the lower slopes of Mount Meru. I came to know the area well.'

'There is a military fort on the Usa river, *ja*?'

'*Ja*. It is a local landmark. People thereabouts call it the Icing Sugar Castle. It is painted brilliant white, and there are turrets and battlements along the top of the walls. It looks like something from a child's picture book.'

'We are going to fly there. Do you think you can find it from the air?'

'I have never flown in an aeroplane, but I am sure that a blind man could pick out that building from fifty miles away.'

'Good. Be ready to leave tomorrow morning at first light.'

'I can scarcely believe I will be flying in one of your machines, sir.' He grinned. 'I can help with the maintenance and refuelling.'

'Don't worry about that. Gustav takes care of those details. That's not why you are coming. I need you to introduce me to an old friend of yours.'

349

The sun was still below the horizon when the *Butterfly* took off from the polo ground. It was cold in the rush of pre-dawn air, and everyone in the cockpit was bundled up in greatcoats. Graf Otto headed due south at three thousand feet above the ground, and not long after they crossed the escarpment of the Rift Valley the sun shot above the horizon with startling rapidity and lit the great mountain bastion of Kilimanjaro, which, even though it was more than a hundred miles away, still dominated the southern horizon.

Eva was alone in the rear seat of the cockpit, out of view of Graf Otto, who sat forward at the controls. She was huddled down behind the windscreen in her heavy loden coat. Her hair was covered with her helmet; her eyes with the smoked lenses of her goggles. Gustav and Hennie were in the front of the cockpit, absorbed in the view ahead. None of them looked back at her. Usually every eye was on her, and it was strange to be unobserved. For once she did not have to act. For once she was able to slip her emotions off the short leash on which she kept them and allow them to run free.

Gazing over the starboard side of the cockpit, she had a sweeping vista of the great brown land, the length and breadth of the wide Rift Valley. The immense spaces enhanced her loneliness. They made her feel tiny and insignificant. A sense of total isolation from any meaningful human contact overwhelmed her. She contemplated the depths of her despair and wept. It was the first time she had shed tears since the cold November day six long years ago when she had stood at the graveside and watched her father's coffin lowered into the earth. She had been alone ever since. It was too long.

Masked by the helmet, she wept silently and secretly. This sudden weakness terrified her. In all the years she had been forced to live the life of illusion and disillusion, to play the game of shadows and mirrors, she had never been assailed by such feelings as these. She had always been strong. She had always known her duty and been steadfast in her resolve. But now something had changed, and she did not understand what it was.

Then she felt the aircraft bank steeply under her and saw a mountain appear high above. She had retreated so deeply into herself that she thought it was a trick of her mind. The mountain was so ethereal that it floated on a silver cloud. She knew it could not be real. Was it a beacon of hope in the midst of her desolation? Was it her haven in the sky where she could hide from the wolf packs that pursued her? Thoughts as insubstantial and fanciful as this dream mountain flitted through her mind.

Then, with a start, she realized it was not the stuff of dreams. It was Lonsonyo. The clouds on which it seemed to float were a solid bank of silver mist at its base. Even as she watched, it began to dissipate in the warmth of the rising sun and the massif of Lonsonyo was revealed.

She felt the despair slough off her soul like an old skin and strength flow back into her. She understood the changes that had overwhelmed her so suddenly and completely. Until now she had believed that strength alone held her on her charted course, but now she knew it was resignation. There had been no other road open to her. But that had changed. It was not despair that had overwhelmed her so suddenly but hope. A hope so strong it transcended all else.

'The hope that springs from love,' she whispered to herself. She had never been able to love a man before. She had never been able to trust a man before. She had never before let a man into her secret, well-guarded places. That was why the feeling had been so alien. That was why she had not known it immediately. Now she had found a man who had made her dare to hope. Until this moment she had resisted him, for she knew him as little as he knew her. But now her resistance had crumbled. She had let him in. Despite herself she had surrendered to him. For the first time in her life she had given someone her trust and her unconditional love.

She felt this new hope stemming her tears and steeling her resolve. Badger, oh, Badger! I know that the road we must travel together will be long and hard. So many snares and pitfalls stand in our way. But I know with equal certainty that together we can win through to the summit of our mountain.

G raf Otto flew on through the airy canyons of the sky, with the eternal snowfields and the gleaming glaciers of Mount Kilimanjaro towering high above them and casting their shadow over them. The *Butterfly* was tossed about wantonly by the winds that swirled around the mountain's three extinct volcanic peaks. Then she broke free of Kilimanjaro's influence and sailed out into the sunlight. But there was another mountain range directly ahead of them and Meru was so different from the great massif they had left behind. Eva fancied that if Kilimanjaro was the male, Meru was the female. She was lower and gentler in aspect, covered with dense green forests rather than harsh rock and ice.

Hennie du Rand gestured to Graf Otto, indicating the new course. He banked sharply along the lower slopes of Meru and flew on past the town of Arusha that huddled at the foot of the mountain. Then Hennie pointed ahead and they all saw the white gleam of the crenellated walls of Fort Usa sitting above the river. As they flew closer they could make out the flag upon the central turret, which billowed in the light breeze, the twin-headed black imperial eagle of Germany on a ground of red, yellow and black.

Graf Otto flew low past the white walls, and the uniformed figures on the battlements looked up at them. A staff motorcar drove out through the main gates and headed towards the open ground along the bank of the Usa river, dragging a pall of dust behind it. The Graf nodded with gratification: the vehicle was one of the latest models from his own factory. There were two men in its back seat.

As Graf Otto had requested, a strip of ground had been cleared parallel to the river bank in preparation for their arrival. The earth was as raw as a ploughed field, and uprooted trees were piled haphazardly along the edge. At the far end a windsock floated from the top of a tall mast. The layout of the landing ground was exactly as he had stipulated it should be in his cables to Colonel von Lettow Vorbeck. Lightly he touched down and let the *Butterfly* run to where the staff car was parked. A uniformed German officer stood beside the open front door of the vehicle with one booted foot on the running-board.

As soon as Graf Otto had clambered down the boarding ladder the officer came forward to greet him. He was a tall, spare but broad-shouldered figure in a field grey tunic and a felt-covered tropical helmet. He wore red and gold staff officer's tabs on his collar, and the Iron Cross, first class, at his throat. His clipped moustache was flecked with grey, and his regard was direct and piercing.

'Count Otto von Meerbach?' he asked, as he saluted smartly. 'I am Colonel Paul von Lettow Vorbeck.' His voice was brisk and precise, given to command.

'Indeed, Colonel. After all our correspondence, I am delighted to meet you.' Graf Otto shook his hand and examined his features keenly. Before leaving Berlin he had made a special visit to Army Headquarters on Unter den Linden, where he had been given access to von Lettow Vorbeck's service record. It was an impressive document. There was probably no other officer of equivalent rank who had seen as much active duty as he had. In China he had taken part in the campaign to put down the Boxers. In German South-west Africa he had fought under von Trotha during his ruthless genocide of the Hereros. Sixty thousand men, women and children had been exterminated, more than half of the entire tribe. After that von Lettow Vorbeck had gone on to command the Schutztruppe in the Cameroons, before being given the same task here in German East Africa.

'Colonel, may I present Fräulein von Wellberg?'

'Enchanted, Fräulein.' Von Lettow Vorbeck saluted again, then clicked his heels and bowed as he held open the door to the staff car for Eva to take her seat in the back. They left

Gustav and Hennie to secure the *Butterfly* and drove up towards the fort.

Graf Otto came directly to the main business. He knew the colonel would expect and appreciate a forthright approach. 'Has our visitor from the south arrived safely, Colonel?'

'He is waiting for you in the fort.'

'What do you make of him? Does he live up to his reputation?'

'Difficult to say. He speaks no German or English, only his native Afrikaans. You will have some difficulty communicating with him, I fear.'

'I have made allowance for that. One of the men I brought with me is an Afrikaner. In fact, he fought under de la Rey against the British in South Africa. He also speaks fluent English, as I know you do, Colonel. We shall have no trouble in communicating.'

'Excellent! That will certainly make matters easier.' Von Lettow Vorbeck nodded as they drove through the gates into the interior courtyard. 'After your journey, you and Fräulein von Wellberg will want to bathe and rest for a while. Captain Reitz will conduct you to the quarters that have been prepared for you. At four o'clock, that is in two hours' time, Reitz will return and bring you to the meeting with de la Rey.'

As von Lettow Vorbeck had promised, Reitz knocked on the door of the guest suite at precisely four o'clock.

Graf Otto checked his watch. 'He is punctual. Are you ready, Eva?' Punctuality was something he expected of everybody around him, including her. He looked her over, from the top of her shining head to her small neat feet. She had taken care with her appearance and knew how lovely she was.

'Yes, Otto. I am ready.'

'That is the Fortuny dress. It suits you admirably.' He called Captain Reitz, who entered and saluted respectfully. Behind him, Hennie du Rand stood in the open doorway. He wore a fresh shirt, had shaved and slicked down his hair with pomade.

'You look very smart, Hennie,' Eva told him. He had

sufficient rudimentary German to understand her and blushed
with pleasure under his tan.

'If you are ready, will you please follow me, sir?' Reitz
invited Graf Otto, and they followed him along the stone-
flagged passageway to the circular staircase that led up to the
battlements. There, on the terrace, Colonel von Lettow Vorbeck waited for them under a canvas awning. He was sitting
at a heavy teak table on which was set out a selection of
drinks and refreshments.

At the far end of the battlements stood another tall figure
in a black frock coat. His back was turned to them and his
hands were clasped behind it. He was staring out across the
river at the bulk of Mount Meru, which hovered in the distant
mist.

Von Lettow Vorbeck stood to welcome them, and once he
had enquired politely as to the comfort of their quarters, he
eyed Hennie with interest.

'This is du Rand, the man I told you about.' Graf Otto
introduced them. 'He rode commando with de la Rey.' At
the mention of his name, the black-clad figure standing at the
far end of the battlements turned towards them. He was in
his sixties, and his silver-shot hair had receded to leave his
forehead high and domed; the skin was white and smooth
where it had been protected by his hat from the sun. His
remaining locks hung to his shoulders, speckling the dark
cloth of his coat with flakes of dandruff. His beard was dense,
profuse and untamed. His nose was large, the line of his
mouth grim and unyielding. His deep-set eyes were as piercing
and fanatical as those of a Biblical prophet. Indeed, he carried
a small Bible in his right hand, which he stuffed into the
pocket of his frock coat as he strode towards Graf Otto.

'This is General Jacobus Herculaas de la Rey,' von Lettow
Vorbeck introduced him, but before he reached them Hennie
ran forward to intercept him and went down on one knee in
front of him.

'General Koos! I beg you to give me your blessing.'

De la Rey stopped and looked down at him. 'Don't kneel

for me. I am not a priest, and I am no longer a general. I am a farmer. Get up, man!' Then he peered more closely at Hennie. 'I know your face, but I have forgotten your name.'

'Du Rand, General. Hennie du Rand.' Hennie beamed with pleasure to be remembered. 'I was with you at Nooitgedacht and Ysterspruit.' Those were two of the notable victories the Boers had won during the war. At Ysterspruit de la Rey's flying commando had captured such huge quantities of British stores that the little Boer Army had been rejuvenated, given the will and means to fight on for another year.

'Ja, I remember you. You were the one who guided us to the river crossing after the fight at Langlaagte when the khaki had us surrounded. You saved the commando that night. What are you doing here, man?'

'I came to shake your hand, General.'

'That will be my pleasure!' de la Rey replied, as he seized Hennie's hand in a powerful grip. It was plain to see why his men held him in such awe and reverence. 'Why did you leave the Orange Free State Republic, Hennie?'

'Because it was no longer a republic and it was no longer free. They have made it part of a foreign land that they call the British Empire,' Hennie replied.

'It will be a republic again. Then will you come back with me? I need good fighting men like you.'

Before Hennie could reply Graf Otto stepped forward. 'Please tell the general that I am deeply honoured to meet such a brave soldier and patriot.' Hennie fell quickly and readily into the role of translator, first making the introductions, and then taking his place at de la Rey's side under the sun awning.

At first both von Lettow Vorbeck and the general were stiff and awkward with Eva at the conference table, and Graf Otto apologized to them: 'I hope you do not mind Fräulein von Wellberg being present at our deliberations. I vouch for her. Nothing that is said here today will go with her when she leaves. The Fräulein is an artist of repute. With your permission, gentlemen, and as a memento of such a historic conclave I have asked her, while we talk, to make portraits of you.' Von Lettow and de la Rey nodded. Eva thanked them with a smile, then laid her sketchpad and pencil on the table and began to work.

Graf Otto turned back to de la Rey. 'You have Hennie du Rand to translate for you, General. Colonel von Lettow Vorbeck and I are fully conversant with English so that is the language we will use. I hope that is agreeable to you?' When Hennie translated this, de la Rey inclined his head, and Graf Otto continued, 'First I want to present a letter of introduction and authority from the minister of Foreign Affairs in Berlin.' He handed it across the table.

Hennie read it aloud while de la Rey listened carefully, then said, 'I would not have come on such a terrible journey under the sea if I had not known who you are, Graf Otto. Germany was a staunch ally and a good friend of my people during the war with the British. That I will never forget. I look upon you as a friend and an ally still.'

'Thank you, General. You do me and my country great honour.'

'I am a simple man, Graf. I like straight and honest talk. Tell me why you have invited me here.'

'Despite the great courage and determination with which they fought, the Afrikaner people have suffered terrible defeat and humiliation.' De la Rey said nothing but his eyes were dark and tragic. Graf Otto was silent with him for a moment, then went on, 'The British are a warlike and rapacious nation. They have seized and dominated most of the world, and still their appetite for conquest is unassuaged. Although we Germans are a peaceable people, we are also proud and prepared to defend ourselves against aggression.'

De la Rey listened to the translation. 'We have much in common,' he agreed. 'We were willing to make a stand against tyranny. It cost us dearly, but I and many like me do not regret it.'

'The time is coming on apace when you may be forced to make the decision again. Fight with honour or capitulate with shame and disgrace. Germany will face the same dreadful choice.'

'It seems that the fates of our two peoples are linked. But Britain is a terrible enemy. Her navy is the most powerful in all the oceans. If Germany were forced to oppose it what would be your battle plan? Would the Kaiser send an army to defend your colonies in Africa?' de la Rey asked.

'There are differing opinions on that. The prevailing view in Germany is that our colonies must be defended in the North Sea, not on their own ground.'

'Do you subscribe to that view, Graf? Would you abandon your African colonies, and your old allies?'

'Before I answer that question, let us review the facts. Germany has two colonies in sub-Saharan Africa south of the equator, one on the south-west coast, the other here on the east coast. Both are thousands of miles from Germany, and widely separated from each other. At present the forces defending them are tiny. In German South-west Africa there are approximately three thousand regular Schutztruppe, and seven thousand settlers, most of whom are on the army reserve list or have received military training. Here, in German East Africa, the numbers are comparable.' Graf Otto looked at von Lettow Vorbeck. 'Am I correct, Colonel?'

'Yes, they are very similar. I have two hundred and sixty white officers and two and a half thousand *askari* under my command. In addition there is a police gendarmerie of forty-five white officers and a few more than two thousand police *askaris*, who will help to defend the colony if it comes to war.'

'It is a pitifully small force with which to defend such a vast territory,' the Graf pointed out. 'With the British Royal Navy in command of the oceans around the continent, the chance of reinforcing and supplying these two tiny armies would be negligible.'

'It is a daunting prospect,' von Lettow Vorbeck agreed. 'We would be forced to adopt the same guerrilla tactics that you Boers employed so successfully in South Africa against them.'

'All that would change most dramatically if South Africa entered the war on the side of Germany,' Graf Otto said softly. Both he and von Lettow Vorbeck looked hard at de la Rey.

'None of this is completely new to me. I also have given much thought to these matters, and consulted many of my old companions in arms.' De la Rey stroked his beard thoughtfully. 'However, Smuts and Botha have gone over heart and soul to the British. They have a grip on the reins of power. A firm but not unshakeable grip. A large part of the South African population is of British descent and their hearts and loyalties lie with Britain.'

'What is the state of the South African Army?' Graf Otto asked. 'What are the numbers and who is in command?'

'Without exception, all the senior officers are Afrikaner and fought against the British,' de la Rey replied. 'That includes Smuts and Botha, who have gone over to them. However, there are many who have not followed their lead.'

'The war ended almost twelve years ago,' von Lettow Vorbeck pointed out. 'Much has changed since then. All four of the old South African republics have been amalgamated into the Union of South Africa. The Boers have twice the power and influence they had before. Will they be satisfied with this, or will they risk it all by siding with Germany? Are the Boers not tired of war? They are now part of the British Empire. Would Smuts and Botha succeed in turning their old comrades away from Germany?' Von Lettow and Graf Otto waited for the old Boer to respond.

'You may be right,' he said at last. 'Perhaps time has healed some of the wounds of the Afrikaner *Volk*, but the scars are still there. However, I run ahead of myself. Let us consider the existing army of South Africa, the Union Defence Force, as it is now known. It is formidable, perhaps sixty thousand strong and well equipped. It is quite capable of controlling all of southern Africa from Nairobi and Windhoek down to the Cape of Good Hope. Whichever government commands it will have control of the sea routes and the harbours around the continent. It will have under its control the monumental resources of the Witwatersrand gold fields, the Kimberley diamond mines and the new steel and armament works in the Transvaal. If South Africa threw in its lot with Germany, Britain would come under enormous strain. She would have to divert a large army from Europe to try to recapture the country, and the Royal Navy would be stretched to its limit to defend and supply it. South Africa might well be the pivot on which the outcome of such a war would turn.'

'If you decided to ride against the British again, which way would your old comrades go? We know Botha and Smuts would support Britain, but what of the other old commando leaders? Which way would de Wet, Maritz, Kemp, Beyers and the others go? Would they be with you or with Botha?'

'I know these men,' de la Rey said softly. 'I have fought with them and seen into their hearts. It was a long time ago, but they have not forgotten the terrible things that the British did to them, their women and children, and to the land we love. In my heart I know they would ride out on commando with me against the enemy, and for me the enemy is still Britain.'

'That is what I hoped to hear you say, General. I have been given total authority by the Kaiser and by my government to promise you whatever you require in the way of supplies, arms and money.'

'We will need all of those things,' de la Rey agreed, 'especially in the beginning, before we have been able to wrest control from Botha and before we have seized the army arsenals and the vaults of the Reserve Bank in Pretoria where the money is.'

'Tell me what you will need, General. I will get it for you from Berlin.'

'We will not need food or uniforms. We are the farmers who grow the crops so we will feed ourselves. We will fight, as we did before, in our workaday clothes. We will not need small arms. Every man of us still has his Mauser.'

'What will you need, then?' Graf Otto persisted.

'For a start, I will need one hundred and fifty heavy machine-guns and twenty trench mortars, with the ammunition and bombs for them. Say, one million rounds of ammunition and five hundred mortar bombs. Then we will need medical supplies . . .' Graf Otto made shorthand notes on his pad, as de la Rey enumerated his requirements.

'Heavy cannon?' von Lettow Vorbeck suggested.

'No. Our first attacks will rely on speed and surprise. If they succeed we will capture the government arsenals and the heavy artillery will fall into our hands.'

'What else do you need?'

'Money,' de la Rey replied simply.

'How much?'

'Two million pounds in gold sovereigns.'

For a minute they were all silenced by the enormity of the request. Then Graf Otto said, 'That is a great deal of money.'

'That is the price of the richest land in the southern hemisphere. It is the price of an army of sixty thousand trained and battle-hardened men. It is the price of victory over the British. Do you really believe it to be too high, Graf?'

'No!' Graf Otto shook his head emphatically. 'When you put it like that, it's a fair price. You shall have the full two million. I will see to it.'

'All of this, all the money and arms, will be to no avail until it is delivered to our bases in South Africa.'

'Tell me how we should get it to you.'

'You could not smuggle it in through one of the main harbours, not through Cape Town or Durban. Customs surveillance is too strict. However, South Africa has a common border with your colony in the south-west. They are joined by a good railway line. The management and employees of South African Railways are almost exclusively Afrikaners. We can rely on them to sympathize with our cause. An alternative route might be from here in German East Africa across Lake Tanganyika by boat to the copperbelt in Rhodesia and from there south, once again by the railway line.'

Von Lettow Vorbeck looked grave. 'It would take weeks or

even months to get the supplies to you by those routes. At every turn there would be danger of the shipment's discovery and interception by the enemy. It would be too risky.' Both men looked to Graf Otto for an alternative plan.

'How could you deliver the goods to us?' de la Rey demanded. They all waited expectantly for his reply.

Eva went on sketching imperturbably. Obviously she had not followed a single word of the discussion, but Graf Otto glanced at her, then at Hennie, and frowned slightly. For a little longer he remained silent, drumming his fingers on the table, thinking deeply. Then he seemed to reach a decision. 'It can be done. It will be done. I give you my word, General. I will deliver everything that you need to wherever you need it. But from now on our watchword must be secrecy. I shall inform only you and Colonel von Lettow much nearer the time of the method of delivery that we will employ. At this stage I must ask you to trust me.'

De la Rey stared at him with those smouldering fanatical eyes, and Graf Otto returned his gaze calmly. At last de la Rey picked up the sheet of paper with the eagle letterhead that still lay on the table in front of him. 'This is the guarantee of your Kaiser and your government. It is not sufficient incentive to persuade me to lead my *Volk* into the holocaust once again.'

Graf Otto and von Lettow Vorbeck continued staring at him wordlessly. The whole design seemed on the point of collapse.

Then de la Rey went on, 'You have given me another guarantee, Graf. You have given me your word. I know you are a man who has moved great mountains. Your accomplishments are the stuff of legend. I know you are a man who does not even admit the possibility of failure.' He paused again, perhaps to gather his thoughts. 'I am a humble man, but in one respect alone I am proud. I am proud of my ability to judge horses and men. You have given me your word, and now I give you mine. On the day that the scourge of war sweeps across Africa once again, I will be ready for you with an army of sixty thousand fighting men at my back. Give me your hand, Graf. From this day on I am your ally to the death.'

From dawn to dusk over the past four days Leon Courtney had flown the *Bumble Bee* at treetop height over the wide savannah. Manyoro and Loikot were perched in the front of the cockpit, vigilant as cruising vultures, watching and searching. They had found many lions, probably more than two hundred, females and cubs, young males and toothless old solitaries. But Kichwa Muzuru had told them, 'He must be big and his mane must be as black as the hell hound.' So far, they had found no animal that came close to that description.

On the fourth day Manyoro had wanted to give up the search in Masailand and fly up to the Northern Frontier District, to the wild land between Lake Turkana and Marsabit. 'There we will find lions under every acacia tree. Lions big enough and fierce enough to make even Kichwa Muzuru happy.'

Loikot had strenuously opposed the move. He had told Leon of a pair of legendary lions that held a huge territory between Lake Natron and the west wall of the Rift Valley. 'I know those lions well. Many times I have seen them over the years that I herded my father's cattle. They are twins, brothers born from the same lioness on the same day. That was in the season of the locust plagues, eleven years ago, when I was just a child. Year after year I have watched them grow in size, strength and daring. By now they are in their prime. There is not another lion to compare with them in all the land. They have killed a hundred head of cattle, maybe more,' Loikot had said. 'They have killed eighteen of the *morani* who set out to hunt them down. No man has been able to stand against them for they are too fierce and cunning. Some of the *morani* believe they are ghost lions that can change themselves into gazelle or birds when they hear the hunters coming after them.'

Manyoro had scoffed, rolled his eyes and touched his temple with a forefinger to indicate the depth of Loikot's dementia. But Leon had backed him, so for the last few days they had scoured the wide brown grassland. They had seen huge herds of buffalo, and countless thousands of smaller plains game, but the lions were either very young or very old and not worthy of the spear.

That evening, as they sat around the campfire, Loikot tried to keep up their flagging enthusiasm. 'I tell you, M'bogo, these two are the paramount chieftains of all the lions in the valley. There are no others greater, fiercer or more cunning. These are the ones that Kichwa Muzuru has sent us to find.'

Manyoro hawked and spat in the fire, then watched the slug of his phlegm boil and bubble in the flames before he gave his opinion. 'For many days I have listened to this story of yours, Loikot. There is one part of it that I have come to believe, that these lions you speak of can change their shape to birds. That is what they must have done. They have become little sparrows and flown away. I think we should leave these bird-lions, and go up to Marsabit to find a real one.'

Affronted, Loikot folded his arms across his chest and stared at Manyoro loftily. 'I tell you, I have seen them with my own eyes. They are here. If we stay we will find them.' They looked at Leon for a decision.

While he drained the coffee in his mug and flicked the grounds into the fire, Leon considered the choice. They were already low on fuel for the *Bumble Bee* and had enough for only a day or two more. If they moved up to the north, they would need to transport more supplies by road. That would take many more days, and Graf Otto was not a patient man. 'One more day, Loikot.' He made the decision. 'Find those beasts of yours tomorrow or we leave them and go up to Marsabit.'

They took off before sunrise and resumed the search at the point where they had left off the previous evening. An hour later and twenty miles out from the airstrip at Percy's Camp, Leon picked out an enormous herd of buffalo streaming back across the savannah from the lake shore where they had drunk. There must have been more than a thousand animals. The big bulls were bunched up in the vanguard, with the cows, calves and younger beasts strung out over almost a mile of grassland behind them. He banked towards them. He knew that lion prides often followed such large herds to pick off the weaklings and stragglers.

Suddenly in the front of the cockpit Loikot was making agitated hand signals, and Leon leaned forward to see what had excited him. A pair of buffalo had become separated from the main herd, and were trailing a quarter of a mile or so behind it. They were crossing a glade of long golden grass, walking side by side. Only their backs were visible above the grass, and from this Leon judged that they were bulls, heavy and black in the body, but young, and he wondered why Loikot was making such a fuss about them.

Then, as he studied them, the pair emerged from the long grass into shorter, more open pasture, and Leon felt every nerve in his body snap tight. They were not buffalo but lions. Never before had he seen lions of that size or colour. The early-morning sun was behind them, highlighting their regal, stately progress. Their manes were deepest Stygian black and shaggy as haystacks, ruffling in the breeze as they stopped to stare up at the approaching aircraft.

Leon throttled back the engines and let the *Bumble Bee* drop until her landing wheels were skimming the ground. As he headed straight towards the lions, they swelled out their manes and swung their long black-tufted tails against their flanks in mounting agitation. One sank down and flattened himself in the short grass while the other spun around and broke into a weighty, swinging trot, heading for a patch of dense bush on the verge of the open ground. Leon passed low over the crouching animal and looked down into its implacable yellow stare. Then he was roaring down on the second. As it heard the aircraft approaching, it broke into a gallop, maned shoulders driving and belly swinging, filled with the meat of its kill. Once again it turned its great maned head to snarl up at Leon as he flashed over.

Leon put the aircraft into a gentle climb, and turned towards the landing strip below the camp. It would take twenty minutes' flying time, but he needed to land so that he could discuss a plan of action with the two Masai. Manyoro seemed to have forgotten his earlier opposition to continuing the search, and was stamping and laughing with as much wild abandon as Loikot.

'Those lions are good reason for such joy. Graf Otto von Meerbach, you had better sharpen your *assegai*. You're going to need it.' Leon laughed into the wind. He was sorely tempted to turn back for one more look at those magnificent animals. However, he knew it would be unwise to disturb them again. If they were as cunning and wary as Loikot had said, he might easily drive them from the grassy savannah into the forests of the escarpment where they would be much more difficult to come at.

Let them be, he decided. Let them settle down until I can get mad von Meerbach here to deal with them.

As Leon touched down and let the *Bumble Bee* roll out on the airstrip below Percy's Camp, the two Masai were still celebrating the find. When he cut the engines, Loikot shouted joyously, 'Did I tell you, Manyoro?' and answered himself immediately: 'Yes, I told you! But did you believe me, Manyoro? No, you did not! Of the two of us, who is the stupid and stubborn one? Is it me, Manyoro? No, it is not! Which of us is the great hunter and finder of lions? Is it you, Manyoro? No, it is Loikot!' He adopted a noble and heroic pose, while Manyoro covered his face with his hands in mock-chagrin.

'You are the greatest tracker in Africa and surpassingly beautiful, Loikot,' Leon interrupted, 'but now I have work for you. You must return to your lions and stay with them until I can bring Kichwa Muzuru for the hunt. You must follow them closely, but not so closely that you alarm them and scare them away.'

'I know those lions. They will not elude me,' Loikot vowed. 'I have them in my eye.'

'When I return and you hear the sound of the engines, you must light a smudge fire. The smoke will guide me to you.'

'I will have the lions in my eye, and the sound of your engines in my ear,' Loikot boasted.

Leon turned to Manyoro, 'Who is the chief of the area in which we found the lions today?'

'His name is Massana and his *manyatta* is at Tembu Kikuu, the Place of the Great Elephant.'

'You must go to him, Manyoro. Tell him there is a bounty of twenty cattle on each of his lions. But tell him that we will bring him a *mzungu* who will hunt them in the traditional way. Massana must bring together fifty of his *morani* for the hunt, but the killing will be done by Kichwa Muzuru alone.'

'I understand, M'bogo, but I do not think Massana will understand. A *mzungu* hunting a lion with the *assegai*? It has never been heard of before. Massana will think Kichwa Muzuru is mad.'

'Manyoro, you and I know that Kichwa Muzuru is indeed as crazy as the wildebeest with snot worms in his brain. But tell Massana not to worry too much about the condition of Kichwa Muzuru's head. Tell him to consider rather the twenty head of cattle. What do you think, Manyoro? Will Massana help us with the hunt?'

'For twenty head of cattle Massana would sell all his fifteen wives and their daughters, perhaps his own mother as well. Of course he will help us.'

'Is there a place close to his *manyatta* where I can land the aeroplane?' Leon asked.

Manyoro picked his nose thoughtfully before he replied. 'There is a dry salt pan close to the village. It is flat and without trees.'

'Show it to me,' Leon ordered. They took off again and Manyoro guided him towards it. It was a huge expanse, flat and glaring white, clearly visible from many miles out. As they drew closer a small herd of oryx galloped across it, and Leon saw with relief that their hoofs did not break through the white crust. Some such pans were death traps: often deep, sinking mud, soft as oatmeal porridge and sticky as glue, was concealed beneath the fragile crust. He put the *Bumble Bee* down gingerly, letting the wheels just touch the surface, prepared to lift her off again if he felt mud grab the undercarriage. When the surface supported her weight he let her settle. He taxied to the edge of the pan, and turned the plane. But he did not shut down the engines. 'How far is it to the *manyatta* from here?' he shouted at Manyoro above the din.

'It is close.' Manyoro pointed ahead. 'Some of the villagers are coming already.' A small group of women and children were running towards them through the trees.

'And how far to where we left the lions, O great hunter?' Leon demanded of Loikot. With his spear he pointed out a small segment of the sky, indicating two hours' passage of the sun. 'Good. So, here you are close to the *manyatta* and the lions. I will leave both of you. Watch for my return. When I come back I will have Kichwa Muzuru with me.'

Leon left the two Masai on the salt and took off again. He circled the pan once before heading back to Nairobi. The Masai waved at him and then he saw them separate: Loikot trotted away to pick up the tracks of the lions, and Manyoro went to meet the women from Massana's village.

As Leon made the initial approach to the Nairobi polo ground he looked out anxiously for the *Butterfly*. He was worried that Graf Otto might have taken off on another of his mysterious, unpredictable jaunts into the blue and would not reappear for many days, by which time Loikot might have lost contact with the quarry.

'Thank the Lord for that!' he exclaimed, as he made out the gaudy scarlet and black shape of the *Butterfly* parked in front of the hangar at the far end of the field. Gustav and his assistants were working on her engines. However, there was no sign of the hunting car, so instead of landing he circled out over Tandala Camp and found it parked outside Graf Otto's private quarters. Leon made another pass over the camp and the Graf emerged from his tent, shrugging on a shirt over his naked torso.

Leon felt a sharp pang of jealousy and resentment. Of course he has Eva in there with him, he thought. She has to earn her keep. The idea made him feel sick. Graf Otto gave him a perfunctory wave, then went to the hunting car. Leon turned the *Bumble Bee* back towards the polo ground, but the taste of anger and jealousy were strong and rank on the back of his tongue.

Pull yourself together, Courtney! You know that Eva von Wellberg isn't a vestal virgin. She's been under the same mosquito net as him every night since they arrived, he told himself, as he lined up for the landing. As he side-slipped the *Bumble Bee* in over the boundary fence, his heart bounded as he saw her sitting at her easel in the shade of the *Butterfly*'s chequered wing. Until that moment she had been hidden from him by the fuselage. It seemed ridiculous, but he was relieved to know that Graf Otto had been alone in the private quarters.

As he set the aircraft down and taxied towards the hangar, Eva jumped up from her easel and started impulsively towards him. Even at this distance he could see the eagerness in her smile. Then she seemed to realize that Gustav was watching, checked herself and came on at a more demure pace. She hung back as he placed the boarding ladder against the fuselage, and Leon swarmed down it. He glanced at her over the heads of the other men, and saw that she was flustered and nervous. He was accustomed to her always being poised and cool, but now she was like a gazelle with the scent of a hunting leopard in its nostrils. Her agitation affected him, but he was able to hide his feelings sufficiently to nod casually at her. 'Good day, Fräulein,' he said politely, then turned to

Gustav. 'The starboard number-two engine's running rough and blowing blue exhaust smoke.'

'I'll check it at once,' Gustav said, and shouted to his assistants.

When his head disappeared into the engine cowling, Leon and Eva were alone. 'Something has happened to you – something's changed,' he told her softly. 'You're different, Eva.'

'And you're perceptive. Everything's changed.'

'What is it? Has there been trouble with Graf Otto?'

'Not with him. This is between you and me.'

'Trouble?' he stared at her.

'Not trouble. The very opposite. I have made a decision.' Her voice was low and husky, but then she smiled.

Her smile was the most beautiful thing he had ever seen. 'I don't understand,' he said.

'Nor do I, Badger.'

Her use of that name was too much for him. He took a step towards her, and reached out a hand. She recoiled sharply. 'No, don't touch me. I can't trust myself not to do something stupid.' She indicated the dust thrown up by the hunting car as it drove towards them. 'Otto is coming. We must be careful.'

'I cannot go on like this much longer,' he warned her.

'Neither can I,' she replied. 'But for now we must keep away from each other. Otto is no fool. He will see that something has happened between us.' She turned away and went to where Gustav was balanced on a wing, peering into the engine housing.

As he drove the hunting car in through the gate of the boundary fence, Graf Otto called, 'So you are back, Courtney. You have been gone long enough. Where were you? Cape Town? Cairo?'

The brief exchange with Eva had left Leon in an ebullient and reckless mood. 'No, sir. I was looking for your bloody lion.'

Graf Otto saw Leon's elation and his own face lit up, his

370

duelling scar turning pink with anticipation. He jumped out and slammed the door behind him. 'Did you find it?'

'I wouldn't have come back if I hadn't.'

'Is he a big one?'

'He's the biggest lion I've ever seen, and the other is even bigger.'

'I don't understand. How many lions are there?'

'Two,' said Leon. 'Two enormous brutes.'

'When can we leave to go after them?'

'As soon as Gustav has checked the engine of the *Bumble Bee*.'

'I can't wait that long. The *Butterfly*'s tanks are full, all our gear is loaded and she is ready to go. We will leave now! At once!'

Graf Otto was at the controls of the *Butterfly* as they took off from the Percy's Camp airstrip, where they had stopped to refuel after the flight in from Nairobi. He headed south-west towards the *manyatta* of Massana. Eva sat beside him, Ishmael squatted on the deck with his precious kitchen bundle, while Leon, Gustav and Hennie were bunched at the front of the cockpit.

They had been flying for little more than twenty-five minutes when Leon spotted a feather of smoke on their port quarter, rising straight into the still, breathless heat of midday. 'Loikot!' Leon knew it was him, even before he made out the slim figure standing beside the smudge fire. Loikot flapped his *shuka* to ensure that they had seen him, then pointed with his spear towards the jagged outline of a small kopje not far ahead. He was indicating the whereabouts of the quarry.

Swiftly Leon assessed the changed situation. The gods of the chase had been kind to them. During his absence the lions must have headed in the direction of Massana's *manyatta*. They were now many miles closer to it than they had been when they had first spotted them. He looked at the distant escarpment of the Rift to orientate himself, then picked out the ghostly shape of the salt pan where he had left the two Masai only three days ago. It lay almost equidistant between the *manyatta* and the kopje where the lions were now lying up. Couldn't be better, he exulted, and moved back quickly to where he could talk to Graf Otto above the engines. 'Loikot signalled that the lions are lying up among the rocks on that hillock.'

'Where is the nearest place I can land?'

'Can you see that salt pan?' Leon pointed it out. 'If you put us down there, we'll be close to the quarry and to the village where the *morani* are assembling for the hunt.'

Massana's *manyatta* was larger than most others in the valley. A hundred or more large huts were laid out in a wide circle around the cattle pen. Graf Otto circled the settlement at low level. A dark mass of humanity had gathered in the central cattle pen. Although Leon could not pick out Manyoro in the press of *shuka*-clad figures, he had done his job, and prevailed on Massana to assemble his *morani* for the great hunt. Satisfied that all was in readiness for them, Leon asked Graf Otto to turn the *Butterfly* towards the salt pan. He landed and taxied to the treeline along its western edge before he shut down the engines.

'We will be camping here for a while,' Leon told him, 'so we can make ourselves comfortable before the *morani* arrive.' All the equipment for a fly camp was packed into the cargo hold of the *Butterfly*. It did not take Leon long to set it up. He sited the tents in the shade beneath the aircraft's wings. Ishmael built his kitchen and cooking fire at a safe distance from the aircraft and was soon serving coffee and ginger snaps.

Leon drained his mug, then looked up at the sky to judge the time. 'Loikot will be here any minute now,' he told Graf Otto, and had barely finished the sentence when Loikot trotted out from among the trees.

Leon left the shade and walked into the sunlight to greet him. He was desperately eager to hear Loikot's report, but he knew Loikot could not be hurried. The more portentous his tidings, the longer Loikot took to divulge them. First he took a little snuff, standing on one leg and leaning on his spear. Then they agreed that it had been three days since they had last seen each other, a long time, that the weather was hot for this season of the year, and that it would probably rain before sunset, which would be good for the grazing.

'So, Loikot, mighty hunter and intrepid tracker, what of your lions? Do you still have them in your eye?'

Loikot shook his head lugubriously.

'You have lost them?' Leon asked angrily. 'You have let them escape?'

'No! It is true that the smaller lion has disappeared but I still have the larger one in my eye. I saw him no more than two hours ago. He is alone, still lying up from the heat on top of the hillock I pointed out to you earlier.'

'We should not bewail the disappearance of the other,' Leon consoled him. 'One lion on his own will be easier to work with. Two together might be one too many.'

'Where is Manyoro?' Loikot asked.

'After we left you we flew over the *manyatta* of Massana. The *morani* hunters were gathered there, but they must already be on their way to join us. The *manyatta* is not far off. They will be here soon.'

'I will go back to keep watch on my lion,' Loikot volunteered. 'When it is dark, he might move a great distance. I will return early tomorrow morning.'

It was still two hours from sunset when they heard singing and saw the people coming through the open forest towards where they were camped on the edge of the pan. Manyoro was leading them, and he was followed by the long file of armed *morani* decked out in full hunting regalia, carrying shields and *assegais*.

Behind them came hundreds of men, women and children. They had gathered from every *manyatta* for fifty miles around. Like a flock of gorgeous sunbirds, the unmarried girls fluttered behind the regiment of eligible *morani*. By the time the sun had set, this agglomeration of humanity was encamped around the *Butterfly*, and the night air was redolent with the aromas from the cooking fires. Excitement was running at fever pitch and the singing and happy laughter of young people went on throughout the night.

The next morning, before it was light, Loikot returned from his scouting expedition. He reported that, by the light of the moon, the lion had taken a young kudu cow and was still feeding on the carcass. 'He will not leave his kill,' Loikot said with conviction.

The hunters waited for the sun with mounting anticipation. They sat around the fires preening and dressing their hair, sharpening their *assegais* and tightening the sinews of their shields. When the first rays of the sun struck the cliffs of the escarpment, the master of the hunt blew a blast on his whistle to signal the start. They sprang up from their sleeping mats and formed up on the white salt plain in their ranks. They began to dance and sing, softly at first but with increasing abandon as the excitement built up.

The young girls formed a ring around them. They started to ululate, to stamp their feet and jerk their hips, to clap their hands and bob their heads. They joggled their breasts and oscillated their plump round buttocks for the men, egging them on. The *morani* began to sweat as they danced. Their eyes glazed over with a ferment of blood-lust and arousal.

Suddenly Graf Otto appeared from the tent that had been erected in the shadow of the *Butterfly*'s wide wings and marched on to the white pan. A roar went up from the *morani* ranks when they saw him. He was dressed in a red tribal *shuka*. The skirt was belted around his waist and the tail was thrown back over one shoulder. The skin of his upper torso and limbs was exposed, white as an egret's wing. The hair on his chest and forearms was as bright as copper wire. His shoulders were wide, his chest was broad and his limbs were hard and muscled, but his belly was full, beginning to bulge and soften with age and good living.

The young girls shrieked with laughter, and clung to each other in raptures of mirth. They had never imagined a *mzungu* to dress in tribal costume. They flocked to him and gathered around him, still giggling. They touched his milky skin, and stroked his red-gold body hair in wonder. Then Graf Otto began to dance. The girls backed away, and soon they were no longer giggling. They clapped the rhythm for him and urged him on with shrill, excited cries.

Graf Otto danced with extraordinary grace for such a big man. He leaped high, spun, stamped and stabbed at the air with the *assegai* in his right hand. He flourished the rawhide shield that he carried on his left shoulder. The prettiest and more daring of the girls took it in turns to come forward and dance face to face with him. They shot out their long, crane-like necks and rattled the collars of beadwork that festooned them. Their breasts were polished with fat and red ochre, and with each stiff-legged jump they bounced tantalizingly. The air was thick with the dust raised by their flying bare feet, musky with the smell of their sweat, and charged with the prospect of blood, death and carnality.

Leon leaned against the fuselage of the *Butterfly* and seemed to give his full attention to this display of primeval abandon. However, almost within arm's length of where he stood Eva was perched on the leading edge of the *Butterfly's* wing, legs dangling. From this angle he was able to study her face without seeming to do so. Eva showed no emotion at the display other than mild amusement. Once again, Leon wondered at her ability to hide her true feelings so completely.

Graf Otto was her man, and ostensibly she was his woman, yet he was participating in a blatantly sexual ritual with dozens of nubile, half-naked and frenzied young females. If she felt demeaned and insulted by his boorish behaviour, she did not show it, but Leon seethed on her behalf.

Almost as though she could feel his eyes on her, she looked down at him from her perch on the wing. Her expression was calm and her eyes were secretive, betraying nothing. Then, as their gazes locked, she allowed him to see into the secret, well-guarded places of her soul. Such manifest love for him shone forth from her violet eyes that he caught his breath.

All at once he was aware of the depth of the change that had overtaken them. No matter what had gone before, they were now committed to each other. Nothing and nobody else counted. Looking into each other's eyes they exchanged vows that were silent but irrevocable.

The moment was shattered by the blast of a whistle and a great shout from the *morani*. The hunters formed up in a column. Loikot took his place in the front rank to guide them to where the quarry was lying up. Still singing the Lion Song, the *morani* followed him, winding through the trees, with the gleaming white body of Graf Otto in their midst. The spectators trooped after them. Gustav and Hennie were swallowed up in the crowd and borne away with it.

Leon and Eva were left alone. He went to where she sat on the wing. 'If we are to be in at the death, we must hurry.'

'Help me down,' she replied. She lifted her arms and leaned towards him. He reached up, placed his hands around her narrow waist, and when he set her on her feet she pressed against him for a brief moment. He smelled her particular perfume and felt the warmth of her belly against his. She read his eyes, and felt the stiffening of his loins through their clothing. 'I know, Badger. I know so well how you feel. I feel it too. But we must be patient a little longer. Soon! Soon, I promise.'

'Oh, God!' He groaned. 'I wish ... Otto ... the lion. If only ...'

Her eyes quickened with real fear. 'No, don't say it!' She placed a finger on his lips. 'Don't wish for that to happen. It would bring us the worst possible luck.' She dropped her hand from his face, and he saw that Manyoro had come silently and was standing at his shoulder. He had the Holland rifle in one hand and the ammunition bandolier in the other.

'Thank you, my brother,' Leon said, as he took them.

'Graf Otto said there were to be no guns on this hunt,' Eva reminded him.

'Can you imagine what might happen if he wounds that lion and it gets in among all those people?' Leon asked grimly.

'It's one thing for him to have a pact with the devil, but quite another if he intends to include a dozen women and children in the bargain.' He opened the breech of the rifle, and while he loaded it with two fat brass cartridges, he asked, 'Can you run in that skirt and those boots?'

'Yes.'

'Then let's see you do it.' He took her arm and they raced after the column of *morani*, which was drawing away rapidly from the rabble of spectators.

Leon was surprised by how well Eva kept up. She lifted her long gabardine skirts to the tops of her knee-high boots and ran with the grace and lightness of a newly roused doe. He took her arm to steady her over the rougher footing, and boosted her up the steep bank of a ravine. They passed the stragglers and caught up with the main body of hunters, and were not far behind the leading warriors when the hunt master blew his whistle again. The *morani* evolved smoothly into their twin-horned battle formation.

'They have caught up with the lion.' Leon was breathing heavily with exertion.

'How do you know? Can you see it?' she panted.

'Not from here, but they can. Judging from the way they're moving, it must be lying up in that dense scrub at the foot of the kopje.' He pointed ahead at a jumble of rocks and silver-leaf scrub.

'Where is Otto?' She gasped to catch her breath and leaned against him for a moment to rest. Her forehead was damp and shining with perspiration, and he delighted in her warm, womanly odour.

'He's right in the thick of it. Where else would we expect him to be?' Leon pointed, and she saw his pale form standing out clearly in the first rank of dark warriors that was closing like a mailed fist around the rocky prominence of the hillock.

'Can you see the lion yet?' Her tone was agonized.

'No. We'll have to get closer.' He took her arm and they began to run again. The first line of *morani* was no more than a hundred and fifty paces ahead of them when Leon stopped abruptly. 'Oh, sweet God! There he is! There is the lion.' He pointed.

'Where? I can't see it.'

'There, on the high ground.' He put an arm around her shoulders and turned her to face it. 'That huge black thing on top of the highest rock. That's him. Listen! The *morani* are challenging him.'

'I can't see . . .' But then the lion raised and fluffed out his mane, and she gasped. 'I was looking right at it. I never realized it would be so big. I thought it was a gigantic boulder.'

The lion swung his massive head from side to side, surveying the host of enemies that surrounded him. He snarled and bared his teeth. Even at that distance Leon and Eva could clearly see the ivory flash of his fangs and hear the furious crackling growls. Then he lowered his head and flattened his ears against his skull as he picked out the moon-pale flash of Otto von Meerbach's body in the centre of the ranks. He had been driven off his kill and he was angry. He needed no further provocation than the sight of that alien body. He growled again, then launched his charge, bounding down the side of the kopje straight at Graf Otto.

A challenging shout went up from the *morani* ranks and they drummed on their shields, goading the lion. As he reached level ground at the foot of the slope he flattened out with the speed and power of his rush, snaking low to the earth, the dust spurting up from under the massive paws, grunting with every stride.

Without a moment's hesitation Graf Otto lifted his shield and held it high as he charged forward to meet the great beast. Leon and Eva came up short and, with a sense of inevitability, watched it happen. Eva was clinging to Leon's hand and he felt her fingernails sink into his flesh, drawing blood. 'It's going to kill him!' she whispered, but at the last possible instant Graf Otto moved with the timing and co-ordination of a consummate athlete. He dropped to one knee and covered himself with the rawhide war-shield. At the same time he brought up the *assegai* in his right hand and presented the point to the charging lion. The beast took it in the centre of his chest, and it went in full length, so deep that Graf Otto's right hand, which held the haft, was buried in the coarse black fleece of the mane, and the lion's heart was spitted cleanly by the razor steel. His jaws gaped wide as he roared, and from his throat shot a fountain of bright blood that sprayed over Otto von Meerbach's head and shoulders. The lion reeled back with the spear still buried in his heart, staggered in a circle and collapsed into the grass, all four legs kicking in the air. It was a perfect kill.

Graf Otto threw aside the shield and bounded to his feet, bellowing triumphantly, whirling in a dervish dance, his face contorted under the glistening coating of the lion's blood. A dozen *morani* rushed forward to stab the blades of their *assegais* into the corpse. The Graf confronted them, bellowing possessively, keeping them away from his kill. He ripped his own spear from the lion's chest and shook it at the warriors as they crowded forward, driving them back, shouting in their faces, beating his chest with his fists in a berserker rage, threatening them with his raised spear. They yelled back furiously at him, drumming on their shields with their own blades. They were demanding to share the glory, their entitlement to wash their spears in the blood of the lion. Graf Otto lunged at one, and the *morani* was only just quick enough to deflect the thrust with his shield. Graf Otto screamed with rage and hurled the *assegai* at him, like a javelin. The warrior raised his shield but the blade cut through the rawhide targe and slashed open the blood vessels in his wrist. His companions roared with fury.

'Dear God! The madness is on him,' Eva panted. 'Someone will be killed, either himself or the Masai. I must stop him.' She started forward.

'No, Eva. They're all mad with blood rage. You cannot stop them. You will only be hurt.' He seized her arm.

She tugged against his grip. 'I've been able to quiet him before. He will listen to me . . .' Again she tried to pull away, but now he grabbed her shoulders with his left arm, and hefted the rifle in his right hand. Strong as she was, and no matter how she struggled, she was helpless in his grip.

'It's too late, Eva,' he hissed into her ear and, holding the heavy rifle as though it were a pistol, he pointed with the barrel over the heads of Graf Otto and the wounded *morani*. 'Look up there, on top of the kopje.'

She looked as he directed, and saw the second lion, the missing twin. He was standing on the crest of the hillock, a huge creature, bigger even than the one Graf Otto had killed, but his mane was fully erect with rage so he seemed to double in size. He hunched his back, opened his jaws wide and held them close to the ground as he roared, a full-throated earth-splitting blast. The hubbub of the watchers, the tumult of Graf Otto and the embattled warriors died away into a deathly silence. Every head was turned to the summit of the kopje and the beast that stood there.

The two lions had separated three days previously when the elder had been lured away by an irresistible perfume on the cool pre-dawn breeze. It was the odour of a mature lioness in full oestrus. He had left his younger twin and hurried to answer the wind-borne invitation.

He found the lioness an hour after sunrise, but another lion was already mating with her, a younger, stronger and more determined suitor. The two had fought, roaring, slashing and ripping at each other with fangs and bared claws. The older lion had been injured, driven off with a deep gash across the ribs and a bite in the shoulder that had cut down to the bone. He had come back to join his twin, limping with pain and aching with humiliation. The two lions had been reunited a little after moonrise and the wounded one had fed on the carcass of the kudu killed by his twin, then retreated to a rocky overhang in the side of the hill where he had lain up to rest and lick his wounds.

He had been too sore and stiff to take any part in the attack by the *morani* hunters, but the angry roaring and the death throes of his twin had brought him out of his hiding place. Now he looked down on the killing ground where the corpse of his sibling lay. He did not know the human feelings of grief, sorrow or loss, but he knew rage, a terrible consuming rage against the world and especially against the puny creatures in front of him. The figure of Graf Otto was closest, and the pale colour of his body acted as a focal point for the lion's anger. He sprang forward and charged down the slope.

A dreadful wail went up from the women, who scattered like a flock of chickens before the stoop of a peregrine. The *morani* were taken completely off-guard: one minute they had been brawling with Graf Otto and then the lion had appeared, as if by virtue of his magical powers.

By the time they had rallied to face this new threat the beast had covered most of the ground to reach Graf Otto. Leon thrust Eva behind him and shouted at her, 'Stay here. Don't come any closer!' Then he raced forward in an attempt to protect his client. He and the *morani* were far too late.

At the last instant Graf Otto threw up his arms in a futile effort to protect himself, but the lion smashed into him with all its speed and massive weight. He was bowled over backwards with the beast on top of him. It enfolded him in the crushing embrace of its forelegs, and drove its claws like butcher's meat-hooks deep into the flesh of his back. At the same time its back legs raked the front of his lower body and thighs, cutting deep gouges into his flesh and slicing open his belly. Now it was crouched on top of him and went for his face and throat, but Graf Otto thrust his forearm into the gaping jaws in an effort to keep it away. The lion bit down, and as Leon ran up he heard the bones splinter. The lion bit again, this time crushing Graf Otto's right shoulder. Like a kitten worrying a ball of wool, its back legs were busy, ripping long yellow claws through Graf Otto's thighs and belly.

Leon slipped the safety catch off the rifle and rammed the muzzles into the lion's ear. At the same instant he pulled both triggers. The bullets tore through the skull and blew out through the opposite ear, taking most of the brains with them. The lion flopped on to its side and rolled off Graf Otto.

Leon stood over the man, ears singing from the blast of the rifle, and stared in horrified disbelief at the damage the animal had inflicted in just a few seconds. For the moment he could not bring himself to touch Graf Otto: he was awash with blood, and more spurted from the hideous wounds in his arm and shoulder. It poured, too, from the deep gouges in the front of his thighs and from the slashes in his belly.

'Is he still alive?' Eva had ignored his instruction to stay back. 'Is he alive or dead?'

'A little of each, I think,' Leon told her grimly, but her voice had snapped him out of the inertia of horror that had gripped him. He handed the rifle to Manyoro as he ran up, then dropped to his knees beside his client's body, drew his hunting knife from its sheath and started to cut away the blood-soaked *shuka*.

'Sweet God, it's torn him to shreds. You'll have to help me. Do you know anything about first aid?' he asked Eva.

'Yes,' she said, as she knelt beside him. 'I've had training.' Her tone was calm and businesslike. 'First we must stop the bleeding.'

Leon stripped away the last of Graf Otto's tattered *shuka* and cut it into strips as bandages. Between them they placed tourniquets on the shattered arm and the torn thighs. Then they strapped pressure pads to the other deep punctures left by the lion's fangs.

Leon watched Eva's hands as she worked quickly and neatly. She showed no repugnance although she was bloodied to the elbows. 'You know what you're doing. Where did you learn?'

'I could ask you the same question,' she retorted.

'I was taught the basics in the army,' he replied.

'The same with me.'

He stared at her in astonishment. 'The German Army?'

'One day I may tell you my life story, but for the moment we must get on with the job.' She wiped her bloody hands on her skirt while she appraised what they had done, then shook her head. 'He may survive the injuries, he's tougher than most, but infection and mortification will probably kill him,' she said.

'You're right. The fangs and claws of a lion are more deadly than poison arrows. They're caked with rotten flesh and dried blood, a seething hothouse of germs. Dr Joseph Lister's little friends. We must get him to Nairobi right away, so that Doc Thompson can stew him in a hot iodine bath.'

'We can't move him until we've done something about the tears in his belly. If we try to lift him now, his bowels will fall out. Can you stitch him?' she asked.

'I wouldn't know where to begin,' Leon said. 'That's a job for a surgeon. We'll just strap him up and hope for the best.' They bound up his stomach with lengths of *shuka*. Leon was watching Eva, waiting for her to express some emotion. She did not seem to be grieving. Did she have any feelings for him at all? She seemed to be working with professional detachment and avoided his eyes so he could not be certain.

At last they were able to lift Graf Otto on to a war-shield. Six of the *morani* took up the burden and carried him at a run in the direction of the salt pan where the *Butterfly* stood waiting.

Under Manyoro's supervision they lifted the makeshift litter into the cockpit and Leon lashed it to the ring bolts in the deck. Then he looked up at Eva. Pale and dishevelled, she was squatting opposite him, her skirts filthy with blood and dust.

'I don't think he'll make it, Eva. He's lost too much blood. But perhaps Doc Thompson can pull off one of his miracles, if we get him to Nairobi in time.'

'I'm not coming with you,' Eva said softly.

He stared at her in amazement. It was not only the words themselves, but also the language in which she had spoken them. 'You speak English. That's a Geordie accent,' he said. Its lyrical cadence was sweet to his ears.

'Yes.' She smiled sadly. 'I am from Northumberland.'

'I don't understand.'

She pushed the hair back from her eyes and shook her

head. 'No, Badger, you cannot understand. Oh, God! There's so much you don't know about me, and which I can't tell you . . . yet.'

'Tell me one thing. What do you truly feel for Otto von Meerbach? Do you love him, Eva?'

Her eyes widened, then darkened with horror. 'Love him?' She gave a short, bitter laugh. 'No, I don't love him. I hate him with all my heart and to the depths of my soul.'

'Then why are you here with him? Why do you behave towards him as you do?'

'You're a soldier, Badger, as I am. You know about duty and patriotism.' She drew a long, deep breath. 'But I've had enough. I cannot go on. I'm not going with you to Nairobi. If I do I'll never be able to escape.'

'Who are you trying to escape from?'

'Those who own my soul.'

'Where will you go?'

'I don't know. Some secret place where they cannot find me.' She reached out to him and took his hand. 'I was relying on you, Leon. I hoped you could find a place where I might hide. Somewhere to which we could escape together.'

'What about him?' He indicated the blood-smeared body lying on the deck between them. 'We cannot leave him to die, as he surely will if we don't do something soon.'

'No,' she agreed. 'Despite my feelings towards him, we cannot do that. Find me a place to hide. Leave me there. Come back for me as soon as you can. That is my only chance of winning my freedom.'

'Freedom? Aren't you free now?'

'No. I am the captive of circumstances. You don't believe that I chose to be what I have become, what they have made me, do you?'

'What are you? What have you become?'

'I have become a whore and an impostor, a liar and a cheat. I am caught in the jaws of a monster. Once I was like you, good, honest and innocent. I want to be like that again.

I want to be like you. Will you have me? Shop-soiled and dirty as I am, will you take me?'

'Oh, God, Eva, there's nothing I want more. I've loved you from the first moment I laid eyes on you.'

'Then no more questions now. I beg you. Hide me here in the wilderness. Take Otto to Nairobi. If anybody there asks about me, and I mean anybody at all, don't tell them where I am. Tell them simply that I've disappeared. Leave Otto at the hospital. If he survives they will send him back to Germany. But as soon as you can, you must return to me. I will explain everything to you then. Will you do it? The Lord knows there's no reason why you should, but will you trust me?'

'You know I will,' he said softly, then he shouted, 'Manyoro! Loikot!' They were waiting close at hand. The orders he had for them were short and to the point. It took him less than a minute to issue them. He turned back to Eva. 'Go with them,' he told her. 'Do as they tell you. You can trust them.'

'I know I can. But where will they take me?'

'To Lonsonyo Mountain. To Lusima,' he answered, and watched all the worry disappear from her violet eyes.

'To our mountain?' she said. 'Oh, Leon, from the first moment I saw it I knew Lonsonyo had a special significance for us.'

While they were speaking Manyoro had found the carpet bag in which Eva carried her personal things. He dragged it out of the stowage hatch at the rear of the cockpit and tossed it down to Loikot, who was standing below the fuselage, then vaulted over the side. For the moment Leon and Eva were alone together. They gazed at each other wordlessly. He reached out to touch her, and she came into his arms with a swift, lissom grace. They clung to each other, as though they were trying to meld their bodies into a single entity. Her lips quivered against his cheek as she whispered, 'Kiss me, my darling. I have waited so long. Kiss me now.'

Their lips came together, as lightly at first as two butterflies touching in flight, then stronger, deeper, so that he could taste her essence and savour the warmth of her tongue and the pink, fragrant recesses of her mouth. That first kiss seemed to last an instant yet all of eternity. Then with an effort, they broke apart and stared at each other in awe.

'I knew I loved you, but not until this moment did I realize how much,' he said softly.

'I know, for I feel it also,' she replied. 'Until this moment, I never knew what it would be like to trust and love somebody completely.'

'You must go,' he told her. 'If you stay another minute I cannot trust myself to let you go.'

She tore her eyes from his and looked out across the pan to where the *morani* and the villagers were streaming back towards them. Some were carrying the carcasses of the two lions slung on poles, their heads hanging.

'Gustav and Hennie are coming,' she said. 'They must not see me leave or know where I have gone.' She kissed him again swiftly, then broke away. 'I shall wait for you to come back to me, and every second that we are apart will be agony and an eternity.' Then, with a rustle and flurry of skirts, she sprang out of the cockpit. With Manyoro and Loikot on each side of her she ran for the trees, screened from Gustav and Hennie by the fuselage of the aircraft. When they reached the treeline Eva paused to look back. She waved, then vanished into the forest. He was surprised by the desolation that came over him now that she was gone, and he made a conscious effort to shake off the mood and brace himself to meet Gustav, who was scrambling into the cockpit.

He fell on his knees beside Graf Otto's body. 'Oh, my God, my good God!' he cried. 'He is killed!' Unaffected tears streamed down his weathered cheeks. 'Please, God, spare him! He was more than my own father to me.' Apparently Gustav had forgotten the existence of Eva von Wellberg.

'He's not dead,' Leon told him brusquely, 'but he soon will be if you don't get the engines started so I can take him to a doctor.' Gustav and Hennie sprang to work, and within a few minutes all four engines were rumbling and popping blue smoke scented with castor oil as they warmed up. Leon swung the *Butterfly*'s nose to the wind, and waited for the engines to settle down to a steady beat, then shouted at Gustav and Hennie, 'Hold him steady!'

They crouched beside the makeshift stretcher on which Graf Otto lay and took a firm grasp. Leon pushed the throttles forward to the stops. The aircraft roared and rolled forward. As he lifted her over the trees he looked over the side, searching for Eva. He saw her then. She and the Masai had covered the ground, and they were already a quarter of a mile beyond the perimeter of the pan. She was running a little behind the other two. She stopped and looked up, swept off her hat and waved. Her hair tumbled down her shoulders and she was laughing, and he knew that her laughter was for his encouragement. He felt his heart squeezed by her courage and fortitude, but he dared not return her wave for it might draw Gustav's attention to the little figure far below. The *Butterfly* roared on, climbing towards the rampart of the Rift Valley wall.

It was late afternoon and the sun was setting when Leon set the *Butterfly* down on the Nairobi polo ground. It was deserted, for nobody was expecting them. He taxied to the hangar where the hunting car was parked, shut down the engines and, between them, they manhandled the stretcher over the side of the cockpit and lowered Graf Otto to the ground.

Leon examined him briefly. He could detect no breathing, and Graf's skin was deathly pale, damp and cold to the touch. He showed no signs of life. Leon felt a guilty jolt of relief that his wish for the man's death had been so swiftly realized. But then he touched Graf Otto's neck under the ear and felt the carotid artery throbbing feebly and irregularly. Then he placed his ear to the man's lips and heard the faint hiss of air, in and out of his lungs.

Any normal human being would have been dead long ago,

but this bastard is as tough as the skin on an elephant's backside, he thought bitterly. 'Bring the hunting car,' he told Gustav. They placed the litter across the back seat, where Gustav and Hennie held it securely while he drove carefully to the hospital, avoiding the ruts and bumps in the track.

The hospital was a small building of mud-brick and thatch, across the road from the new Anglican church. It comprised a clinic, a rudimentary operating theatre and two small, empty wards. The entire building was deserted and Leon hurried to the cottage at the rear.

He found Doc Thompson and his wife sitting down to their dinner, but they left it on the table and rushed with Leon to the hospital. Mrs Thompson was the only trained nursing sister in the entire colony and took over immediately. Under her supervision Gustav and Hennie carried Graf Otto into the clinic and lifted him off the stretcher on to the examination table. While the doctor cut away the makeshift bandages, they dragged in a galvanized iron bath and filled it with hot water into which Mrs Thompson emptied a quart bottle of concentrated potassium of iodine. Then they lifted Graf Otto's broken body off the table and lowered him into the steaming brew.

The pain was so excruciating that he was jerked out of the dark fog of coma, shrieking and struggling as he tried to drag himself out of the caustic antiseptic. They held him down mercilessly so that the iodine could soak into the deep, terrible wounds. Despite his antipathy towards the man, Leon found the spectacle of his agony harrowing. He backed to the door and slipped quietly out of the clinic into the sweet evening air.

By the time he reached the polo ground the sun had set. Paulus and Ludwig, two of the Meerbach mechanics, had got there before him: they had heard the *Butterfly*'s earlier landing and had come to find out what was happening. Leon gave them a brief account of the Graf's mauling, then said, 'I must get back. I don't know what has happened to Fräulein von Wellberg. She is there alone. She may be in danger. The

Butterfly's fuel tanks are almost empty. What about the *Bumble Bee?*'

'We filled her up after you brought her in,' Ludwig told him.

'Help me to get the engines started.' Leon went to the aircraft, and the mechanics ran after him.

'You cannot fly in darkness!' Ludwig protested.

'The moon is only two nights from full and will rise within the next hour. Then it will be as bright as day.'

'What if it clouds over?'

'Not at this time of year,' Leon told him. 'Now, stop arguing. Give me a hand to get her started.' He climbed into the cockpit and began the routine, but halfway through he stopped and tilted his head to listen to the galloping hoof-beats coming up the track from the town. 'Damn it to hell,' he muttered. 'I was hoping to sneak away without attracting any unwelcome attention. Who's this?' He crouched below the cockpit coaming and watched the dark shape of horse and rider materialize out of the night. Then he sighed as he recognized the tall, portly figure in the saddle, even though he could not yet make out the face. 'Uncle Penrod!' he called.

The rider reined in. 'Leon? Is that you?'

'None other, sir.' Leon tried to keep the tone of resignation from his voice.

'What's happening?' Penrod asked. 'I was having dinner with Hugh Delamere out at the Muthaiga Country Club when we heard the aircraft arriving. Almost immediately there were all sorts of rumours flying around the bar. Somebody had seen von Meerbach brought in on a stretcher. They were saying he'd been in an accident, bitten by a lion, and that Fräulein von Wellberg was dead or missing. I went up to the hospital but I was told that Doc was operating and wouldn't talk to me. Then I realized that as there are only two people in the colony who can fly an aeroplane, and von Meerbach was apparently in no condition to do so, it had to have been you who had flown in. I came to look for you.'

Leon laughed ruefully. It was not easy to beat Brigadier General Ballantyne to the punch. 'Uncle, you're a bloody genius.'

'So everybody keeps telling me. Now, my boy, I want a full report. What in the name of all that's holy are you up to? What has really happened to von Meerbach, and where is the lovely Fräulein?'

'Some of the rumours you heard are correct, sir. I brought von Meerbach in from the field. He was badly mauled by a lion, as you heard. I left him with Doc. I don't think he'll pull through. He's badly hurt.'

'How could you let it happen, Leon?' Penrod's tone betrayed his outrage. 'By Gad, all my hard work gone to pot.'

'He insisted on taking on the lion in the Masai fashion with the *assegai*. It had him down before I had a chance to prevent it.'

'The man's a bloody fool,' Penrod snapped, 'and you're not much better. You should never have let him get himself into such a position. You knew how important it was, how much we were hoping to learn from him. Damn it! You should have stopped him. You should have looked after him as though he was a baby.'

'A big bad baby with a mind of his own, sir. Not easy to look after.' Leon's tone was sharp with anger.

Penrod changed tack smoothly. 'Where is von Wellberg? I hope you haven't fed her to the lions too.'

The taunt riled Leon, as Penrod had intended it to. The truthful reply leaped angrily to his lips but, with an effort, he stopped it there. Eva's warning echoed in his ears: *If anybody there asks about me, and I mean anybody at all, don't tell them where I am. Tell them simply that I've disappeared.*

Anybody at all. Had she meant to include Penrod in that warning? His mind raced. He recalled the incident at the regimental dinner when he had come across them in the garden. His suspicions at that time must have been well founded. Eva would never have dropped her guard like that unless there was some special understanding between them. Then he recalled how Eva had adumbrated her connections to the military. Penrod was the commander of the armed forces in the colony. It was all starting to take on a shadowy shape in his mind.

I am caught in the jaws of a monster, she had said. Was Penrod the monster? If so, then Leon had been on the point of betraying her. He took a deep breath and said firmly, 'She disappeared, sir.'

'What in hell do you mean, "disappeared"?' Penrod barked.

His swift, sharp reaction confirmed Leon's suspicions. Penrod was at the centre of the murky mystery.

You are a soldier, Badger, as I am. You know about duty and patriotism.

Yes, he was a soldier, and here he was, lying to his superior officer. Once before he had been found guilty of disobeying a superior officer and dereliction of duty. Now he was committing the same capital offences, but this time he was doing it deliberately and wilfully. Like Eva, he was caught in the jaws of the monster.

'Come on, boy, spit it out. What do you mean she disappeared? People don't just disappear.'

'At the time of the lion attack I was trying to protect von Meerbach. He was the one in real jeopardy, not . . .' he had almost said 'Eva' but corrected himself '. . . not the lady. I told her to stay well back, and I ran forward among the Masai. I lost sight of her in the confusion. Then, when the lion got von Meerbach down and ripped him up, I had only one thing on my mind, and that was to patch him up and get him to Doc Thompson. I didn't think about Fräulein von Wellberg again until I was airborne, and by then it was too late to turn back for her. I trusted Manyoro and Loikot to find her and take care of her. I believe they will have taken her to safety. But right now I'm going to risk a night flight into the valley to make sure she's all right.'

Penrod pushed his horse close alongside the fuselage and glared up at Leon, who was certain that his guilt must be stamped clearly on his features. He blessed the darkness that hid his face from Penrod's harsh scrutiny.

'Listen to me, Leon Courtney! If any harm comes to her you will answer to me. Now, here are my orders. Mark them well. You will go back to where you left Eva von Wellberg in the bush and bring her out. You will conduct her to me – directly to me and nobody else. Do I make myself clear?'

'Abundantly, sir.'

'If you let me down, I will teach you the meaning of the words "pain" and "suffering". What Freddie Snell did to you will seem like a pat on the head in comparison. You have been warned.'

'Indeed I have, sir. Now, if you will kindly move away from the wash of the propellers, I'll be on my way to obey your orders.'

Ludwig drove the big von Meerbach truck to the far end of the polo ground and parked it so that its headlights lit the landing strip. As Leon roared down the field on the take-off run, he saw Penrod, silhouetted by the headlights, hunched on his mount. He could almost feel the heat of his uncle's anger.

As soon as he had cleared the tops of the bluegum trees at the end of the field he turned on to a heading for Percy's Camp. As he gained altitude the moon seemed to rush eagerly over the black horizon to light him on his way. From fifteen miles out, the hill above the camp was gilded by moonlight, guiding him in on the last leg of the journey. To attract Max Rosenthal's attention he circled the camp three times, revving the engines, then throttling back. On the last circuit he saw headlights switched on below him, then watched the truck grind its way over the rough track to the airstrip. Max understood what was required of him and lined up the vehicle to orientate Leon for the landing.

As soon as Leon had parked the *Bumble Bee* he threw his pack over the side, then grabbed the Holland rifle and bandolier which he had taken from the *Butterfly*. He scrambled down and hurried towards the truck.

'Max, I want four of our best horses and one of the grooms to go with me. We'll each ride a horse, and take the spares on lead reins.'

'*Jawohl*, boss. Where are you going? When do you want to leave?'

'Don't worry about where I'm going, and I want to leave at once.'

'*Himmel!* It's eleven o'clock at night. Can't it wait until morning?'

'I'm in a hurry, Max.'

'*Ja*, so it seems.'

Leon hurried to his tent and threw a few essential items into his light pack, then went down to the picket lines. There, the horses were already waiting, but instead of four animals, as he had ordered, there were five. Leon's frown cleared, replaced by a grin as he recognized the figure mounted on the black mule. 'May the Prophet shower blessings on you!' he greeted him.

Ishmael's teeth flashed white in the moonlight. 'Effendi, I knew that you would starve without me.'

They rode hard for the rest of that night, changing horses twice. In the dawn the shadowy blue bulk of Lonsonyo Mountain lay low on the distant horizon ahead. By noon it filled half of the eastern sky, but this aspect was unfamiliar to Leon. He had never before approached the mountain from this direction. Now it was presenting its more rugged northerly slope, the one he and Eva had flown over with Graf Otto at the controls of the *Butterfly*.

By this time they had been riding for almost thirteen hours since leaving Percy's Camp and he had pushed the horses hard. Despite his impatience to be reunited with Eva he knew he could not demand more of the animals or the men. He had to rest the men and let the horses graze and drink. They unsaddled beside a small waterhole and hobbled the animals, then turned them loose to graze.

While they were busy Ishmael brewed coffee, then cut slices of cold venison and pickled onions on to a hunk of unleavened bread. When he had eaten Leon slept until nightfall. Then they saddled up and rode on into the darkness. In the cool night the horses went with a will and at dawn the mountain towered above them. Leon stared up at its cliffs in awe: the high walls were decked with brilliantly coloured lichens. He picked out the silvery gleam of falling water in one of the gorges that rent the massive ramparts. Although from this low angle the circular dark pool was hidden, he realized that this must be the waterfall he and Eva had looked down upon from the air.

Leon knew from Loikot that there was a pathway beside the waterfall that scaled the cliffs to the summit, and this was the route by which they had intended to take Eva to Lusima. But he was still too far off to pick out the track even with the help of binoculars. Instead he concentrated on estimating the distances and direction from which the others would come, hoping he might intercept them before they began their ascent. It was more likely, though, that they were already on the path ahead of him.

Either way he knew Eva was close at hand, and his spirits soared. Ishmael and the groom were unable to keep pace with him as he urged his mount forward. Within another hour he reined in sharply, swung down from the saddle and squatted beside one of the numerous game trails that criss-crossed the savannah. Three sets of human footprints were freshly impressed in the fine dust. Manyoro had been in the lead – Leon would have recognized that limp anywhere: the slight drag of the toe was unmistakable. Loikot had followed, with his long, lithe paces, Eva behind them.

'Oh, my darling!' Leon murmured, as he touched one of her neat, narrow prints. 'Even your little feet are beautiful.'

The tracks were headed directly towards the mountain, and he remounted and followed them at a canter. The path climbed the first pitch of the slope, becoming steeper with each pace. The cliff reared up until it seemed to fill the sky and the clouds sailing above gave Leon the uncomfortable delusion that the mountain was collapsing on top of him.

Soon the path was so steep that he was forced to dismount and lead his horse. At intervals he picked up the tracks Eva's boots had left, which encouraged him to keep on upwards at his best speed. The severity of the slope made it impossible to see more than a short way ahead, but he strode on, the rest of his party struggling after him but losing ground rapidly. He reached a step in the mountainside, and as he topped it he stared in wonder.

Before him lay the circular pool. It was much larger than it had seemed from the aeroplane, but its size was dwarfed by the magnitude of the cliff above it and the thunderous white deluge of the waterfall. So copious was the flood that it sent eddies of cool air swirling around the rock cauldron.

Then he heard a voice, faint and almost drowned by the din of cascading waters. It was hers, and his heart surged with excitement. Eagerly he scanned the cliffs on both sides of the pool, for the echoes were deceptive and he was uncertain of the direction from which she was calling. 'Eva!' he shouted at the cliffs, and the diminishing echoes mocked him.

'Leon! Darling!' This time the direction was more obvious. He turned to the left side of the pool and threw back his head. He saw a flash of movement high above and realized she was standing on a ledge that angled up the cliff face. But as he watched she started back down towards him, running with the speed and agility of a rock hyrax over the treacherous footing.

'Eva!' he yelled. 'I'm coming, my darling!' He dropped his horse's reins and scrambled up the mountainside to meet her. Now he could see the two Masai on the path above her. Even at this distance he could read the astonishment on their faces as they watched this extraordinary display. He and Eva reached the beginning of the ledge at almost the same time, but he was below the lip and she was on top of it, six feet above his head.

'Catch me, Badger!' she called and, trusting in his strength, flung herself over the edge. As she dropped he caught her, but her weight and momentum brought him to his knees. He knelt over her, hugging her protectively to his chest as they laughed.

'I love you, you crazy girl!'

'Never let me go again!' she said, as their lips came together.

'Never!' he promised, speaking into her sweet mouth.

Much later when they drew apart to breathe, they saw that Manyoro and Loikot had followed Eva back down the path, and were squatting on the ledge just above them, watching their performance with grins of delight.

'Go and make nuisances of yourselves somewhere else!' Leon ordered them. 'You're not welcome here. Take my horse and go down the mountain until you meet Ishmael. Tell him to make camp at the foot. Wait for us. We'll sleep there tonight.'

'Ndio, Bwana,' Manyoro answered.

'And stop giggling like that.'

'Ndio, Bwana!'

Manyoro's voice was muffled with mirth as he scrambled down, but Loikot remained on the ledge above him. Suddenly he squeaked at Manyoro, in a falsetto imitation of Eva's voice, 'Cashy mia, Bazzer!' and threw himself from the ledge as Eva had done. He crashed into Manyoro with such force that he bowled him over. The two rolled down the slope locked in each other's embrace, howling and hooting with laughter. 'Cashy mia!' they screamed. 'Cashy mia, Bazzer.'

Neither Leon nor Eva could contain themselves and burst out laughing again. Eventually Leon found his voice: 'Go, you idiots!' he ordered them. 'Get out of my sight. I don't want to see either of you again for a long, long time!'

They staggered down the mountain, still racked with paroxysms of laughter, hugging themselves and each other with glee.

'Cashy mia, Bazzer!' Manyoro howled.

'Luff you, clazy gel!' Loikot slapped his cheeks and shook his head. 'Luff you!' he repeated, and jumped three feet into the air.

'That was, without doubt, the funniest incident ever to be recorded in the history of Masailand. You and I will go down in tribal mythology,' Leon told Eva, as the two men disappeared down the path. He picked her up in his arms and she locked hers around his neck. He carried her to a flat ledge beside the pool and sat with her in his lap. 'You don't know how I've longed to hold you like this,' he whispered.

'All my life,' she replied. 'That's how long I've waited for this to happen.'

He stroked her face, tracing the arches of her eyebrows with his fingertips, then burrowed his fingers into the tresses of her hair, filling his hands with the thick, glossy locks, gloating on every facet of her beauty, like a miser fondling his hoard of gold coins. She seemed so fragile and delicate that he was afraid he might hurt her, startle or alarm her. Her loveliness awed him. She was nothing like the other women he had known. She made him feel inadequate, unworthy.

She understood his dilemma. His timidity reawakened in her feelings of tenderness such as she had not experienced for a very long time. But she wanted him desperately and could not wait. She knew she must take the lead.

He felt her unbuttoning his shirt and one of her hands slipped through the opening and began to caress the muscles of his chest. He shivered with delight. 'You're so hard, so strong,' she murmured.

'And you're so soft and tender,' he countered.

She leaned back a little way so that she could look into his eyes. 'I'm not breakable, my Badger. I'm flesh and blood as you are. I want what you want.' She took the lobe of his ear between her teeth and nibbled it softly. He felt goosebumps rise on the nape of his neck. When she thrust her tongue deep into his ear he shuddered deliciously.

'I have sensitive places, just like you do.' She took his hand and placed it on her breast. 'If you touch me here and here, like this and that, you will see for yourself.'

He felt the hooks and eyes of her blouse under his fingers and slipped open the top one. He did it diffidently, expecting a rebuke, but she drew back her shoulders so that her breasts swelled out to meet his exploring fingers.

'There's a clever boy! You found one of my places without any help from me.'

Her words, and the tone in which she uttered them, roused in him a feverish impatience. He threw aside all restraint and caution, plucked open her blouse and reached inside. Her breasts were hot and silky, and he felt the tips harden and pucker. Her breathing was coming faster as she whispered, 'They are yours, my darling. All I have is yours.'

She drew back just enough and moved so that her breasts brushed lightly against his face. She shrugged off her blouse and silken slip, and was naked to the waist. Again she let her breasts swing against his face, and he took one of her nipples into his mouth. She gasped and lay back in the circle of his arms, then took a double handful of the hair at the back of his head and used it to direct his mouth to the other.

'Forgive me, my darling, but I cannot wait any longer,' she cried, her tone almost desperate as she wriggled off his lap and knelt in front of him, her naked breasts heavy and full, just brushing his face as she tugged at his belt. When she had opened the buckle and unbuttoned his fly, he lifted himself just enough to enable her to push his breeches down to his knees. She hoisted her long skirt to her lower ribs – she wore nothing under it – and her waist was fluted, like the neck of a Grecian vase, curving into the swell of her hips. The skin of her belly was nacreous and unblemished. Her thighs were strong but shapely and between them nestled her womanly bush, dark and curling luxuriantly in its marvellous profusion. She raised one of her knees over him, mounting him as she would a horse, and as her thighs parted he glimpsed, through the dark curtain of hair, the gape of her sex. It was pouting and damp with the lubricious juices of her arousal. Then, with a single adroit thrust of her hips, she engulfed him to the hilt, and they cried out together as though in pain.

For both, it happened so swiftly and intensely that they were left unable to speak, barely able to move, clinging together like the survivors of some devastating earthquake or typhoon. It took them some time to drift back from the far frontiers of their minds and bodies to which they had been transported.

Eva spoke first: 'I never imagined it could be like that.' She laid her head on his chest to listen to his heart. He stroked her hair and she closed her eyes. They slept, and came awake to the barking of a troop of baboons high on the cliff face, their challenge reverberating through the gorge. She sat up slowly and pushed the hair back from her face. It was still wet with sweat and her cheeks were flushed. 'How long were we asleep?' She blinked.

'Is it important?' he asked.

'It's very important. I don't want to waste a single moment of the time we have together in sleeping.'

'We have the rest of our lives.'

'I pray God that is so. But this world is so cruel.' She looked forlorn and bereft. 'Please don't ever leave me.'

'Never,' he said fiercely, and when she smiled the violet lights glowed in her eyes.

'You're right, Badger. We're going to be happy for ever. I refuse to be sad on this wonderful day. The world can never catch us.' She sprang to her feet and pirouetted on the ledge. 'This day will last for ever,' she sang, and as she danced she shed her clothing, scattering it over the rock.

'What are you doing, you shameless hussy?' He laughed with delight as she danced for him, naked in the sunlight. Her body was very lovely, young and perfectly proportioned, her movements lithe and graceful.

'I'm going to take you for a swim in our magical pool,' she cried. 'Throw off those dusty old clothes, sir, and come with me.' She stopped dancing and watched with her full attention as he hopped on one foot to pull off his boots.

'All of your things bounce and joggle when you do that,' she observed.

'So do yours.'

'Mine aren't as pretty and useful as yours.'

'Oh, yes, they jolly well are.' He flung aside his breeches and started after her. 'Let me show you just how useful yours really are.' She squealed with mock-alarm, ran to the end of the ledge and paused there for just long enough to make certain he was still pursuing her. Then she clasped her hands above her head and dived into the pool. She struck the water like an arrow, her limbs perfectly aligned with her body so that there was almost no splash as she slipped beneath the surface. She went deep, her image wavering beneath the ripples, then shot up again so swiftly that her white body burst out to the level of her belly button before she fell back with her hair slicked over her shoulders, like the pelt of an otter.

'It's cold! My bet is that you're too much of a sissy to chance it,' she shouted.

'You lose your bet, and here I come for my payment.'

'You must catch me first.' She laughed and set off for the far side of the pool, kicking up a froth behind her.

He dived in and ploughed after her with long, powerful, overhead strokes. He caught her before she was halfway across, and seized her from behind. 'Pay up!' he demanded, and turned her to face him.

She placed both arms around his neck and her lips on his. Kissing, they sank deep below the surface only to come up again, spluttering, choking and laughing. She had her long legs locked around his waist and her arms around his neck. She lifted herself out of the water and used her weight to force his head under, then twisted out of his grip and darted away. She only looked back when she reached the far side of the pool. The waterfall thundered down in two separate streams, leaving an area of quiet water between them. In the centre of this haven a single rock thrust its top above the surface, black and smooth, polished by the waters. She pulled herself up on to it and sat with her legs dangling below the surface. With both hands she thrust her wet hair back from her eyes as she looked around for Leon. At first she was laughing, but then, as she saw no sign of him, she became anxious. 'Badger! Leon! Where are you?' she cried.

He had followed her across the pool, but as she approached the black rock he had taken a deep breath and duck-dived, swinging his legs high in the air so that their weight forced his body under. Once he was below the surface he swam on downwards. He had imagined that the pool was probably bottomless, for he had seen no overflow at the surface. The huge volume of water pouring over the falls must have another means of escape. But as he swam down he found he had been mistaken. The bottom appeared below him and, even at this depth, the water was so clear that he could see it was covered with a jumble of rocks that must have fallen from the cliffs.

By now his eardrums were aching with the pressure and he stopped to clear them, holding his nose and blowing air through the Eustachian tubes. His ears squealed and popped, the pain subsided and he swam on down. He reached the bottom and found that among the rocks was scattered a bizarre collection of Masai artefacts: ancient *assegais* and axes, mounds of pottery shards, necklaces and bracelets made from trade beads, small carvings of hardwood and ivory, primitive jewellery and other artefacts so old and rotten that they were unidentifiable, all offerings made by the Masai over the ages to their tribal gods.

By now he had expended most of his oxygen so he took one last look around, and the mystery of the overflow was solved. The wall below the waterfall was pierced by a number of almost horizontal adits that had probably been blown out in antiquity by boiling lava and gas from the volcano under the mountain. It was these dark and sinister passages that drained away the overflow from the pool and kept it at a constant level. By now his lungs were heaving for air and he swam for the surface. As the light strengthened he saw above him a pair of long, shapely feminine legs dabbling below the surface. He swam up under them, seized the ankles and jerked their owner into the pool on top of him. They came to the surface again, clinging together and gasping for air.

Eva recovered her voice before he did. 'You heartless

swine! I thought you were drowned or swallowed by a crocodile. How can you play such a cruel trick on me?'

They swam back to where they had left their clothes.

'We don't want you to catch your death of cold,' Leon told
her, and made her stand naked on the ledge while he dried
her with his shirt.

She held her hands above her head and revolved slowly to
allow him to reach the difficult places. 'What big eyes you
have, sir. You're doing a great deal more looking than drying.
So is your one-eyed friend down there. I should make both of
you wear a blindfold,' she said, as she came around to face
him.

'And who is the heartless one now?' he asked.

'Not me!' she cried. 'Let me prove to both of you what a
kind heart I have.' She reached out and grasped his friend
firmly but tenderly. In the first divine madness of their passion
they were insatiable.

I t was almost dark when, hand in hand, they went down
the pathway. As soon as they topped the fold of ground
that concealed the pool they saw the campfire burning not
far below. When they reached it they found that a log had
been placed in front of the flames as a bench for them. When
they had settled themselves on it, Ishmael appeared, bearing
two mugs of strong black coffee, with evaporated milk.

Eva sniffed the air. 'What is that delicious aroma, Ishmael?'

He showed no surprise that, for the first time, she was
speaking English rather than German or French. 'It is green-
pigeon casserole, Memsahib.'

'Ishmael's celestial version thereof,' Leon added. 'It should
only be eaten with bared head on bended knee.'

'I'm so starving that I'm prepared to go down on both
knees. It must be the swimming, or something else, that is so
good for the appetite,' she said.

He laughed. '*Viva!* That little something else.'

Immediately they had eaten, they were overwhelmed by a wonderful weariness. Manyoro and Loikot had built a small thatched shelter for them, well away from their own huts, and Ishmael had cut a mattress of fresh grass and covered it with blankets. Over it he had hung Leon's mosquito net. They shed their clothes and Leon blew out the candle stub before they crept under the net.

'It's so safe and intimate and cosy in here,' she whispered, and he lay behind her and enfolded her in his embrace. She pushed her round warm buttocks into his belly so that their bodies fitted together like a pair of spoons. The reflection of the campfire played shadow games on the netting over their heads, and the piping duet of two scops owlets in the branches of the tree above them was both plaintive and lulling.

'I have never been so pleasantly exhausted in my entire life,' she murmured.

'Too exhausted?'

'That's not what I meant, you silly man.'

She woke in the dawn to find Leon sitting cross-legged over her. 'You've been watching me!' she accused him.

'Guilty as charged,' he admitted. 'I thought you were never going to wake up. Come on!'

'It's midnight, Badger!' she protested.

'Do you see that big shiny thing peeking at you through the chinks in the thatching? It's called the sun.'

'Where do you want to go at this ridiculous hour?'

'For a swim in your magical pool.'

'Well, why didn't you say so?' she asked, and threw back the blanket.

The waters were cool and slippery as silk over their bodies. Afterwards they sat naked in the early sunlight to dry off. When the warmth had soaked into them and charged their blood, they made love yet again. Afterwards she said solemnly, 'I thought nothing could be better than yesterday, but today is.'

'I want to give you something that will always remind you of how happy we were on this day.' Leon stood up and dived from the ledge.

She watched him growing smaller and less distinct as he swam down, until finally he had faded into the depths. He was down for so long that she grew anxious until, with a lift of relief, she saw him coming up. He broke through the surface and, with a shake of his head, flicked his wet hair out of his eyes. He swam to the bank below her and clambered up on to the ledge. Then he held up a necklace of ivory beads strung on a leather thong.

'It's beautiful!' She clapped her hands.

'Two thousand years ago, when she passed this way, the Queen of Sheba offered it to the gods of the pool. Now I give it to you.' He looped the necklace around her throat and tied it at the nape of her neck.

She looked at the beads as they lay between her breasts, and stroked them as though they were living things. 'Did the Queen of Sheba really pass this way?' she asked.

'Almost certainly not.' He laughed at her. 'But it makes a good story.'

'They're so lovely, so smooth and delicate.' She turned one between her fingers. 'Oh, I wish I had a mirror.'

He led her to the end of the ledge and stood beside her with his arm around her waist. 'Look down,' he told her. Silently and seriously they regarded their naked images in the mirror-like surface of the water. At last Leon asked softly, 'Who is that girl in the water? Her name isn't Eva von Wellberg, is it?' He watched her expression crumble and her eyes mist with incipient tears. 'I'm so sorry. I promised not to make you sad.'

'No!' She shook her head. 'You did the right thing. We've had our little dream together, but now it's time to face reality.' She turned away from the reflections in the pool and looked up at him. 'You're right, Leon. I'm not Eva von Wellberg – von Wellberg was my mother's maiden name. My name is Eva Barry.' She took his hand. 'Come and sit with me and I'll tell you all you want to know about Eva Barry.' She led him back to the ledge and they sat cross-legged, facing each other.

'I must warn you that it's a mundane and grubby little tale, not much for me to be proud of, and very little in it for your comfort, but I shall try to make it as painless as possible for both of us.' She drew a deep breath, then went on: 'Twenty-two years ago I was born in a little village in Northumberland. My father was an Englishman, but my mother was German. I learned the language at her knee. By the time I was twelve my German was almost as good as my English. That was the year my mother died of a terrible new disease, which the doctors called infantile paralysis or poliomyelitis. The sickness paralysed her lungs and she suffocated. Within days of her death my father was struck by the same disease and his legs withered away. He spent the rest of his life in a wheelchair.'

At first she spoke deliberately but then the words spilled out of her in short, breathless rushes. Once she began to weep. He took her in his arms and hugged her. She pressed her face to his chest, and her tears were hot on his skin.

He stroked her hair. 'I didn't mean to cause you distress. You don't have to tell me. Hush now. It's all right, Eva, my darling.'

'I do have to tell you, Badger. I have to tell you everything, but please hold me tight while I do it.'

He picked her up and carried her to a place in the shade away from the waterfall so that it would not drown her voice. He sat with her in his lap as though she was a hurting little girl. 'If you must, then tell me,' he invited her.

'Daddy's name was Peter, but I called him Curly because he had not a hair on his head.' She smiled through the tears. 'He was the most beautiful man in the world, despite his bad legs and his bald head. I loved him so very much, and wouldn't allow anybody else to look after him. I did everything for him. I was a clever child and he wanted me to go to the university in Edinburgh to develop my natural gifts, but I wouldn't leave him. Despite his ruined body he had an extraordinary mind. He was an engineering genius. Sitting in his wheelchair, he dreamed up revolutionary mechanical principles. He formed a small company and hired two mechanics to help him build the models of his designs. But he hardly had enough money to feed us after he had paid his workmen's wages and for the materials. Without money, the patents were worthless. With money, they might have been converted into something of real value.'

She broke off and sniffed back her tears, then wiped her wet nose on his chest. It was such a childlike gesture that he was deeply touched. He kissed the top of her head, and she cuddled against him. 'You don't have to go on,' he said.

'Yes, I do. If I am ever to mean anything to you, you have a right to know all these things. I don't want ever to hide anything from you.' She took a deep breath. 'One day a man came with great secrecy to Curly's workshop. He said he was a lawyer, and that he represented a client who was enormously rich, a financier, who owned factories that built steam engines and rolling stock, motor-cars and aeroplanes. The client had seen Curly's registered designs in the patents office in London. He had recognized their potential value. He proposed an equal partnership. Curly would provide his intellectual properties and this man the finances. Curly signed an agreement with him. The financier was German so the contract was in German. Although his wife had been German, Curly understood no more than a few simple words of the contract. He was a gentle, gullible genius, not a businessman. I was a child of fifteen, and Curly never mentioned the contract to me before he signed it. He should have done so because I would have been able to read it to him. I handled all our expenses, and I had become good with money. Perhaps he realized that if I had known of the contract I would certainly have tried to dissuade him, and Curly hated arguments. He always chose the easier option, and in this case it was simply not to tell me about it.' She broke off and sighed, then visibly braced herself to continue.

'The name of Curly's new partner was Graf Otto von Meerbach. Only he wasn't a partner, he was the owner of the company. In a very short time Curly learned that by signing the contract he had sold the company and all the patents it owned to Meerbach Motor Works for a pitifully small sum. One of Curly's patents led directly to the creation of the Meerbach rotary engine, another to a revolutionary differential system for Meerbach heavy vehicles. Curly tried to find a lawyer to help him regain what rightfully belonged to him, but the Meerbach contract was iron-clad and no lawyer would touch the case.

'The money from the sale of the company did not last us long. Although I scrimped and saved, Curly's medical expenses ate it up. Doctors and medicines . . . I never knew they cost so much. Then there was the rent, gas and warm clothes for Curly. The circulation in his legs was bad and he felt the cold terribly but coal was so expensive. In winter he was always ill. For a few months he had a job in the mill, but he was off sick from work so often that they dismissed him. He could get no other work. Bills, bills and more bills.

'Two days after my sixteenth birthday Curly had one of his attacks. I ran to fetch the doctor. We already owed him more than twenty pounds but Dr Symmonds never refused to come when Curly needed him. When he and I got back to the room in which we lived, we found that Curly had killed himself with his old shotgun. Many times before I had tried to sell that gun to buy food, but he would never part with it. Only as I stood beside his headless corpse did I realize why he had been so stubborn about keeping it. That marvellous brain of his was splattered all over the wall behind his wheelchair. Later, when the undertaker had taken him away, I had to mop up the stain.'

Her body was racked by silent sobs, and he could find no words to console her. He pressed his lips to the top of her head and held her until the storm abated. 'That's enough, Eva. This is taking too much out of you.'

'No, Badger. It's cathartic. I've kept it bottled up inside me for years. Now I have somebody I can tell it to. Already I can feel the benefit of letting the poison pour out at last.' She pulled back and saw the pain in his eyes. 'Oh, I'm sorry. I'm being selfish. I didn't realize what this was doing to you. I'll stop now.'

'No. If it helps you, let it all out. Go on. It's hard for both of us, but this is one way I can get to know and understand you.'

'You've become my rock.'

'Tell me the rest.'

'There's not much more to tell. I was alone and the funeral took all the money I had left. I didn't have enough to pay the rent. I didn't know which way to turn. I took a job in the mill for two shillings a day. Curly had a friend with whom he had played chess and he and his wife took me in. I paid them what I could and helped his wife with their children.

'One day a stranger came to visit me. She was very elegant and beautiful. She said she was a childhood friend of my mother's but that they had lost track of each other. She had only heard my tragic story recently and had determined to find me and look after me for the sake of my mother's memory. She was so kind and friendly that I went with her unquestioningly.

'Her name was Mrs Ryan and she had a splendid house in London. She gave me my own room and new clothes. I had a tutor and a dancing teacher. A woman came twice a week to instruct me in etiquette. I had a riding instructor, and my own horse, a darling little filly called Hyperion. The strangest thing was how assiduously Mrs Ryan made me practise my German. She was quite ruthless. I had a succession of German teachers and worked with them for two hours a day, six days a week. I read aloud all the German newspapers and discussed them with my tutors. I read aloud histories of the German nation from the time of the Holy Roman Empire to the present. I did the same with the works of Sebastian Brandt, Johann von Goethe and Nietzsche. Within the first year of this intensive study I could have passed readily as an educated native-born German speaker.

'Mrs Ryan was like a mother to me. She knew so much about me and my family. She told me things about them that I hadn't known. She knew how Curly had been tricked out of his company, and told me about Otto von Meerbach. We spoke of him often. She said he had murdered Curly just as surely as if it had been his finger on the trigger of the shotgun. Although I had never laid eyes on him, I began to hate him with a burning passion, and Mrs Ryan subtly fuelled the flames of my loathing. She had an important job in the government. Not until much later did I have any idea what it might be, but we spoke often about how privileged we were to be the subjects of such a noble monarch, and citizens of the most powerful and far-reaching empire the world had ever seen. We should welcome any opportunity to serve King and empire. We should train ourselves to meet any call that might be made on us. We should be ready to make any sacrifice that duty and patriotism demanded.

'I took her words deep into my heart and worked even harder than she demanded. I was never given the opportunity to meet any men except the servants, my tutors and teachers, so I had never known how beautiful I was, or that most men would find me irresistible.' She broke off and shook her head ruefully. 'Oh dear. Please forgive me, Badger. That sounds terribly immodest.'

'No. It's the simple truth. You're beautiful beyond the telling of it. Please go on, Eva.'

'Beauty and ugliness are random occurrences. The difference is that beauty fades and becomes another form of ugliness. I place no value on mine, but others did. It was one of the three reasons why they chose me. The second was my intelligence.'

'What was the third?'

'I had suffered a terrible wrong, and I was eager for retribution.'

'I find this fascinating in a dreadfully sinister way. My skin is beginning to creep.'

'For my nineteenth birthday the dressmaker made me a magnificent ballgown. Mrs Ryan stood beside me as I tried it on for the first time. Together we looked at my reflection in the full-length mirror. She said, "You're very beautiful, Eva. You've become everything we hoped you might be." There was something sad and regretful in the way she said it. I thought little of it at the time because, of course, I had no idea what they were planning. Then she smiled and the sadness vanished. "Tomorrow night I'm holding a birthday party for you," she told me.' Eva laughed. 'It was a very strange birthday party. Mrs Ryan and I went in a cab to a house in Whitehall, one of those magnificent government buildings. Four men were waiting for us. I had imagined that there would be dozens of young people, but there were just these four old men – the youngest was at least forty. Three were dressed in gorgeous military uniform. They must have been very senior officers for they wore glittering decorations, stars and medals. The fourth was thin and severe-looking. Mrs Ryan introduced him as Mr Brown. He was the only civilian in the group. He wore a black frock coat and a high collar.

'We sat down to dinner at a round table in the centre of a large room, with massive chandeliers suspended from the ceiling. The panelled walls were hung with huge canvases of battle scenes – I remember one was a painting of Nelson dying on the deck of the Victory at Trafalgar, and another was of Wellington and his officers at Quatre Bras, watching the charge of Napoleon's hussars. A band was playing in the gallery and, one after another, the officers danced with me. While they did so, they questioned me as though I were in the dock.

'I cannot remember what we ate because I was so nervous that I lost all appetite. A servant poured champagne into my glass, but Mrs Ryan had warned me and I didn't touch it. At the end of the meal all four men conferred in low tones that I couldn't follow, then seemed to come to some agreement, for they nodded and looked extremely pleased with themselves. The evening ended with a speech from Mr Brown about duty and sacrifice. That was the end of my birthday party.

'Two days later I met Mr Brown again, this time in less salubrious circumstances. We were in a musty office, filled with files of old papers in another part of Whitehall. He was kind and avuncular. He told me I was privileged to have been selected for a task of the utmost delicacy, which was vital to the interests and security of our beloved Britain. The storm-clouds of war were gathering over the continent, he said, and soon the nation would be engulfed in flames. I couldn't understand what this had to do with me – and all his rhetoric had a stultifying effect upon me until he mentioned the name of Otto von Meerbach. My attention was immediately riveted. He suggested that I was in a position to perform a memorable service for King and Empire, and at the same time find retribution for the terrible wrongs my father and I had suffered at the hands of Graf Otto. All I had to do was induce him to tell me information that would be vital to Britain's military interests.'

She laughed again but this time with genuine amusement. 'Can you imagine, Badger? I was such a naïve and innocent little ninny that I hadn't the faintest idea how I was supposed to make him tell me his secrets. I asked Mr Brown outright, and he looked mysterious and exchanged a glance with Mrs Ryan. "If you agree to do as we ask you will be taught," he said.

'As I recall, my exact words to him were "Of course I will. I just want to know how."' She broke off, sat upright and looked solemnly into Leon's face with the violet eyes he adored. 'Nearly a year after I made that contract with the devil they deemed I was perfect in the role they had chosen for me. I learned everything there was to know about Graf Otto except, of course, the secrets I was to wheedle out of him. By then I knew that he was estranged from his wife of ten years, but as both he and she were good Catholics they were unable to divorce. There would be no question of my being coerced into marrying him once he had fallen under my fatal spell.' She laughed without humour at this piece of hyperbole. 'Mr Brown and Mrs Ryan placed me in the way of Graf Otto von Meerbach. It was arranged through one of the military attachés at the British Embassy in Berlin that I should be invited to his hunting lodge at Weiskirchen. I had been taught my duty and I did it,' she said flatly but, like a drop of dew on the petal of a violet, a single tear clung to her bottom eyelashes. 'I was a virgin when I met Otto von Meerbach, and in mind and spirit I still was, until yesterday. My darling Badger, I don't want to go into any more detail, and even if I did you would not want to hear it.'

They were silent for a while, then Eva could contain herself no longer. 'Now that you know about me, do you despise me?'

Her voice was muted and her expression stricken. He reached out to her with both hands and cupped her face, gazing into her eyes so that she could see the truth of what he was about to tell her. 'Nothing you have done, or ever will do, could make me despise you. You have let me into your soul and I have found only goodness and beauty there. You must remember also that when you look at me you are not looking at a saint. It was you who told me we are both soldiers. I have killed men in the name of duty and, like you, I have done many other things that I'm ashamed of. None of that matters. All that matters is that we are together now and we love each other.' With his thumb he gently wiped away the tear.

At last she smiled. 'You're right. We love each other and we have each other. That is all that matters.'

T he funeral procession stretched the full length of Unter
den Linden. As the head of it reached the Brandenburg
Gate the tail was out of sight at the far end of the
boulevard. It was a wet, grey day, and the mourners lined both
sides of the road, ten persons deep, under the drizzle. They
were silent, except for the women's weeping. A single drum-
mer tapped out the Death March. A full squadron of cavalry
led the procession: the hoofs of their horses clattered on the
paving, and the pale light reflected dully from the blades of
the drawn sabres. Eva stood in the front rank of mourners.
She wore full-length black leather gloves, and a hat with
black ostrich feathers on the crown. A black veil covered her
eyes and the top half of her face.

Kaiser Wilhelm II rode his black charger ahead of the gun
carriage that bore the coffin. He wore a shining spiked helmet
with a golden chain chinstrap, and his black cloak was flared
back from his shoulders over the rump of his mount. His
expression was fiercely tragic. A team of magnificent black
horses drew the gun carriage. The coffin upon it was enormous
and made of transparent crystal so that Otto von Meerbach's
corpse was clearly visible to the mourners. He was dressed in
the costume of a Roman emperor with a crown of laurel leaves
on his head. In each of his great hairy fists he held an *assegai*,
the blades crossed over his chest. Incongruously a Cuban cigar
was clamped between his teeth.

Eva was filled with a consuming joy and a profound sense
of relief. Otto was dead. The nightmare was over and she was
free to go to Leon. Lying in his crystal coffin Otto opened one
eye, looked directly at her and blew a perfect smoke-ring. She
began to laugh, she could not stop, and the bell-like peals
rang out across Unter den Linden.

Kaiser Wilhelm turned in his saddle and glared at her.
Then he urged his horse forward and leaned over her to
reprimand her. 'Wake up, Eva!' he told her sternly. 'Wake up.
You're dreaming!'

'Otto is dead!' she answered him. 'It will be all right now. Now they will have to let me go. I will be free. It's over.'

'Wake up, my darling,' said the Kaiser, and leaned out from the saddle to take her by the shoulder and shake her briskly. The fact that he was the Emperor of Germany and that she had been presented to him at court on more than one occasion was no excuse for such familiar behaviour. She was quite offended. How dare he call her 'darling'?

'I am Leon's darling, not yours!' she told him primly, and sat up. Leon had lit the candle, so it was light enough in the hut on Lonsonyo Mountain for her to make out his face close to hers and see his anxious expression. 'Otto is dead,' she told him.

'You were dreaming, Eva.'

'I saw him, darling Badger. He really is dead.' She paused to consider this statement. 'Even if my dream was a fantasy, even if he is out there somewhere, living and breathing, for me he is dead. He no longer means anything to me. I don't even hate him any longer. Now that I've found love with you, there is no place in my life for barren emotions like hatred and revenge.'

She reached out for him, and he took her within the circle of his arms and held her tightly. 'Together we will transform all this ugliness into something bright and beautiful,' he promised.

'I want you to take me to Lusima Mama,' she whispered. 'The very first time you spoke of her I felt as though I already knew her. I have a strange feeling that I am spiritually connected to her. Somehow I know that she holds the key to our happiness.'

'We will go to her today, as soon as it is light enough to take the pathway to the summit.'

Manyoro and Loikot warned Leon that the last section was too steep and narrow for the horses so he sent Ishmael and the groom back down to the base of the mountain with orders to circle to the southern side and bring the horses up along the easier, more familiar route.

Once they had disappeared, Leon, Eva and the two Masai started up the track beside the waterfall. The way became more difficult with every step they climbed. At some places they were forced to traverse the face of the mountain on ledges along which only one could pass at a time, and always the exposure to height became more severe. For the most part the waterfall was hidden by rock, but twice as they edged around a buttress they were presented with a spectacle that bated their breath. The torrent seemed to swirl around them in silvery sheets, confounding their senses. The rocky walls and the shelf under their feet were wet and slippery with a coating of slimy algae. Their upward progress became more and more laborious.

The sun was reaching its noon when they came out on the plateau of the summit. Manyoro and Loikot sought shade under one of the trees and threw themselves down to rest and take a little snuff. Leon led Eva by the hand to the brink of the precipice. There they sat together with their feet dangling over the void. Leon picked up a pebble the size of his fist that had cracked from the ledge on which they sat and dropped it over the edge. They watched with fascination as it fell three hundred feet without touching the rock wall. The tiny splash it made as it struck the surface of the pool was barely apparent in the tumultuous waters. Neither spoke, for words seemed superfluous in the midst of such splendour. At last Manyoro called them and, reluctantly, they stood up and backed away from the void.

'How far to Lusima Mama's *manyatta*?' Leon asked.

'Not far,' replied Loikot. 'We will be there before sunset.'

'A mere stroll of twenty miles or so.' Leon smiled. 'Let's

go.' The two Masai picked out the overgrown pathway unerringly and set an easy pace. For once there was no hurry and the three men could enjoy their surroundings, which seemed so remote from the floor of the Rift Valley. It was Eva's first visit to the mountain, so the scenery and vegetation fascinated her. She delighted in the flowering orchids that hung in festoons from the high branches of the rainforest trees, and laughed at the antics of the Colobus monkeys that scolded them as they passed. Once they stopped to listen as a herd of heavy animals crashed away through the undergrowth, alarmed by their presence.

'Buffalo,' Leon answered her silent question. 'There are some enormous brutes up here in the mist.'

At one point they descended into a steep gorge and climbed up the far side to reach an open tableland as flat as a polo ground and devoid of trees. At one end the cliff fell away abruptly for hundreds of feet. A pair of large, reddish antelopes stood against the forest at the opposite end of the clearing. Creamy stripes were emblazoned across their shoulders and their ears were large and trumpet-shaped. Their horns were massive black spirals with sharp white tips. 'How beautiful they are!' Eva exclaimed, and at the sound of her voice they slipped into the forest, without disturbing a leaf of the dense shrubbery. 'What were they?'

'Bongo,' Leon told her. 'The rarest and shyest of all our animals.'

'I hadn't known how beautiful everything is in this country of yours.'

'When did you make the discovery?' He laughed at her enthusiasm.

'At about the same time that I realized I was in love with you.' She laughed back. 'I don't ever want to leave this land. Can we live here for ever, Badger?'

'What a splendid idea,' he said, but she could see he was distracted.

'What is it?' she asked.

'This!' With a sweep of one arm he indicated the clearing

in front of them. Then he strode down the length of it, counting his paces and examining the ground underfoot. She noticed that at no point was the undergrowth higher than his knee. Suddenly she felt hot and tired. She found a tree stump and sank down on it thankfully, mopping her face with her bandanna. On the far side of the clearing Leon and the two Masai were in deep conversation, and it was obvious to her that they were discussing this unusual extent of open ground. After a while Leon came back to her. 'What did you find? Gold or diamonds?' she teased him.

'Loikot says that in the time of his grandfather the Mkuba Mkuba, the great god of the Masai, was displeased so he threw down a bolt of lightning to warn the tribe of his anger. No trees or large plants have grown here since that day.'

'And you believe that?' Eva challenged him.

'Of course not,' Leon replied, 'but Loikot does and that's what counts.'

'Why are you so fascinated by this bare ground?'

'Because this is a natural landing strip, Eva. If I side-slipped her between those tall trees at the end of the clearing I could put the *Bumble Bee* down here as sweetly as spreading a spoonful of honey on a slice of buttered toast.'

'Why on earth would you want to do that, my darling man?'

'That's the only thing I don't like about flying,' he answered. 'Every time you take off you have to think about where you're going to land. I've got into the habit of making a note of every possible landing strip I come across in the bush. I might never need it, but if I ever did I imagine I'd need it pretty damn badly.'

'But on top of this mountain? Aren't you carrying your search a little too far? I'll give you a kiss if you give me one good reason why you might ever want to put her down here.'

'A kiss? Now you have my interest.' He lifted his hat and scratched his head thoughtfully. 'Eureka! Got it!' he exclaimed. 'I might want to bring you up here for a champagne picnic on our honeymoon.'

'Come and get your kiss, clever boy!'

As they left the clearing it started to rain, but the drops were as warm as blood and they didn't bother to take shelter. An hour later, with dramatic suddenness, the rain stopped and the sun burst out again. At the same time they heard distant drums.

'Such a stirring sound.' Eva cocked her head to listen. 'It's the very pulse of Africa. But why are the drums beating in the middle of the day?'

Leon spoke quickly to Manyoro, and then he told her, 'They are welcoming us.'

'But how could anyone know we're coming?'

'Lusima knows.'

'Another of your little jokes?' she demanded.

'Not this time. She always knows when we're coming, sometimes before we know it ourselves.'

The drums urged them forward and they quickened their pace. The sun was low and smoky red when they emerged from the forest and smelled woodsmoke and cattle pens. Then they heard voices and the lowing of the herds, and at last they saw the rounded roofs of the *manyatta* and a crowd of figures in red *shukas* coming towards them, singing the songs of welcome.

They were swept up by the crowd and carried along with the laughing, singing throng to the village. As they approached the large central hut the others hung back and left Leon and Eva standing alone before the hut.

'Is this where she lives?' Eva asked, in an awed whisper.

'Yes.' He took her arm possessively. 'She will make her entrance after keeping us in suspense for a while. Lusima enjoys a little drama and theatrics.'

As he spoke she appeared before them through the doorway of the great hut, and Eva started with surprise. 'She's so young and beautiful. I thought she'd be an ugly old witch.'

'I see you, Mama,' Leon greeted her.

'I see you also, M'bogo, my son,' Lusima replied, but she was staring, with those mesmerizing dark eyes, at Eva. Then she glided towards her with regal grace. Eva stood her ground as Lusima stopped in front of her. 'Your eyes are the colour of a flower,' she said. 'I shall call you Maua, which means "flower".' Then she looked at Leon. 'Yes, M'bogo.' She nodded. 'This is the one of whom you and I spoke. You have found her. This is your woman. Now, tell her what I have said.'

Eva's expression lit with joy as she listened to the translation. 'Please, Badger, tell her I've come to ask for her blessing.'

He did so.

'You shall have it,' Lusima promised her. 'But, child, I see that you have no mother. She was carried away by a terrible disease.'

The smile faded from Eva's face. 'She knew about my mother?' she whispered to Leon. 'Now I believe all that you have told me about her.'

Lusima reached out with both hands and cupped Eva's face between smooth pink palms. 'M'bogo is my son, and you shall be my daughter. I shall take the place of your mother who has gone to be with her ancestors. Now I give you a mother's blessing. May you find the happiness that for so long has eluded you.'

'You are my mother, Lusima Mama. May I give you a daughter's kiss?' Eva asked.

Lusima's smile was a thing of such loveliness that it seemed to light the gloom. 'Although it is not the custom of our tribe, I know that this is the *mzungu* way of showing respect and affection. Yes, my daughter, you may kiss me, and I shall kiss you back.' Almost shyly Eva went into her embrace. 'You smell like a flower,' Lusima said.

'And you smell like the good earth after rain,' Eva replied, after a pause to hear Leon's translation.

'Your soul is full of poetry,' Lusima said, 'but you are hurt and tired to the depths of it. You must rest in the hut we have built for you. Perhaps, here on Lonsonyo Mountain, your wounds will be healed and you will be made strong again.'

The hut to which Lusima's handmaidens led them was

newly built. It smelled of the smoke of the herbs that had been burned to purify it, and of the fresh cow dung with which the floors were plastered. There were bowls of stewed chicken, roasted vegetables and cassava meal waiting for them, and after they had eaten, the maidens led them to the bed of animal skins with carved wooden headrests set side by side. 'You will be the first to sleep here. Let our joy at your coming be your joy also,' they told them as they withdrew and left them alone.

In the morning the girls came to fetch Eva and take her to the pool in the stream that was reserved for the women. When she had bathed they braided her hair with flowers. Then they brought her a fresh unworn red *shuka* to replace her own torn and dusty clothing. Giggling and caressing her as though she was a pretty child, they showed her how to fold and arrange the *shuka* like a Roman toga. Then, barefooted, they took her to the great council tree under which Lusima was waiting. Leon was already there, and the three shared a breakfast of sour milk and sorghum porridge.

After they had eaten they talked together for the rest of the morning. Eva and Lusima sat side by side watching each other's faces and eyes, every now and then holding hands. They were in such complete accord that Leon's translations were mostly superfluous, for they seemed to understand each other implicitly on a level above that of speech.

'You have been alone for a long time,' Lusima said at one stage.

'Yes, I have been alone for too long,' Eva agreed, then glanced at Leon and reached out to touch his hand. 'But no longer.'

'Loneliness erodes the soul as water wears away rocks.' Lusima nodded.

'Will I ever be alone again, Mama?'

'You wish to know what the future holds, Maua?' she asked.

Eva nodded. 'Your son M'bogo says that you can see what lies ahead for all of us.'

'He is a man, and men try to make all things simple. The future is not simple. Look up!' Eva raised her head obediently and gazed at the sky. 'What do you see, my flower?'

'I see clouds.'

'What shape and colour are they?'

'They are many shapes and shades, changing even as I watch them.'

'Thus it is with the future. It takes many shapes and it changes as the winds of our lives blow.'

'So you cannot foretell what will become of M'bogo and me?' Eva's disappointment was so childlike that Lusima laughed.

'That is not what I said. Sometimes the dark curtains open and I am given a glimpse of what lies ahead, but I cannot see all of it.'

'Look into my future, please, Mama. Tell me if you find a glimpse of happiness there,' Eva asked eagerly.

'We have been together only a short time. As yet, I know little about you. When I have looked deeper into your soul, perhaps I will be able to scry your future better.'

'Oh, Mama! That would make me so happy.'

'Do you think so? Perhaps I will come to love you so well that I will not want to tell you what I see.'

'I don't understand.'

'The future is not always kind. If I see things that would make you sad and unhappy would you want to hear them?'

'All I want is that you tell me M'bogo and I will be together for ever.'

'If I said that will not be, what would you do?'

'I would die,' Eva said.

'I do not want you to die. You are too lovely and good. So if I see in the future that the two of you will be parted, shall I lie to you to keep you from dying?'

'You make it very difficult, Mama.'

'Life is difficult. Nothing is certain. We must take the days allotted to us and make of them what we can.' She studied Eva's face, saw the pain and took pity on her. 'This much I can tell you. As long as you are together, you and M'bogo will know true happiness, for your hearts are linked like these two plants.' She laid her hand on an ancient vine that twisted around the trunk of the council tree like a python. 'See how the vine has become part of the tree. See how the one supports the other. You cannot separate them. That is the way it is with the two of you.'

'If you see dangers that lie ahead for us, will you not warn us? I beg you, Mama.'

Lusima shrugged. 'Perhaps, if I think it will be to your advantage to know. But now the sun has reached its noon. We have talked the morning away. Go now, my children. Take what remains of the day and be happy together. We will talk again tomorrow.'

So the days passed, and under Lusima's gentle counsel and guidance, Eva's fears and uncertainties gradually faded and she entered a realm of happiness and contentment so complete that she had never suspected its existence.

'I knew we had to come here, but I never knew why until now. These days spent on Lonsonyo Mountain are more precious than diamonds. No matter what happens they will be with us for ever,' she told Leon.

Five days after their arrival at the village Ishmael brought the horses up the southern pathway from the plain below. It had taken him that long to circle the base of the mountain. He was appalled to find Eva barefoot and wearing a *shuka*. 'A great and beautiful lady like you should not be dressed like one of these infidel savages,' he reprimanded her sternly in French.

'This *shuka* is so comfortable and, besides, my old clothes have fallen into rags,' she told him.

He looked distraught. 'At least, I will be able to feed you civilized food, not this swill that the Masai eat.'

The days flew by in such a dreamlike blur that they lost track of time. Like two children, they wandered hand in hand through the enchanted forests of Lonsonyo Mountain. With each small delight they came across – a tiny sunbird of brilliant plumage or a monstrous horned beetle whose armoured carapace clicked as it marched – the worries of the outside world receded further from their minds. When first Leon had met her she had hidden her true nature behind a mask of solemnity. She had seldom smiled and almost never laughed. But now that they were alone and safe on the mountain she doffed the mask and allowed her real self to shine through. For Leon the laughter and smiles enhanced her beauty a hundredfold. They spent every moment they could together. Even the briefest separation was painful to them both. Eva's first waking thought each morning was, Otto is dead and nobody knows where we are hiding. We are safe and nobody can come between us.

Even when Ishmael's carefully hoarded store of coffee was exhausted, they laughed when he told them the tragic news. 'It is no fault of yours, O Beloved of the Prophet. It is a sin that shall not be written against your name in the golden book,' Leon comforted him, but Ishmael went away muttering dolefully.

The people of the village watched them fondly, smiling when they passed, bringing Eva small presents, sticks of sugarcane, bouquets of wild orchid blooms, fans of pretty feathers or bead bracelets they had woven. Lusima revelled in their love almost as much as they did. She spent hours with them each day, sharing her wisdom and understanding of life.

The 'little rains' began and they lay in each other's arms at night, listening to the drumming on the roof of their hut, whispering and laughing, warm and safe in their love. Then the rains ceased and Leon realized that almost two months had passed since they had climbed the pathway beside the waterfall to the summit. When he pointed this out to her she smiled comfortably. 'Why do you bother to tell me, Badger? Time means nothing, just as long as we are together. What are we going to do today?'

'Loikot knows where there is an eagles' breeding site in the cliffs on the far side of the mountain not far from Sheba's Falls. Generation after generation of the great birds have nested there since as far back as men can remember. At this season there will be chicks in the nest. Would you like to visit it and see the young ones?'

'Oh, yes, please, Badger!' She clapped her hands, as excited as a child at the promise of a birthday party. 'Then on our way back we can go to the falls and swim once again in those enchanted waters.'

'That will make it a long trek. We'll be away for several days.'

'We have all the time in the world.'

It took them three days of easy travel to cross the mountain at its widest point, for the gorges were deep and rugged, the forest was dense and there were delightful distractions at every turn of the path. But at last they sat on the brink of the precipice and watched a pair of eagles sailing in elegant flight far below them, circling their eyrie calling to each other and their young ones in the nest, bringing in the carcasses of their prey to feed them, hyrax and hares, monkeys and game birds dangling from their talons.

However, the eyrie was hidden by the overhang of the rocky buttress on which they sat. Eva was disappointed. 'I wanted to see the chicks. Surely Loikot knows of a vantage-point from which we can see down into the nest. Won't you ask him, Badger?' She sat impatiently listening to the long discussion in Maa of which she understood not a single word.

At last Leon turned back to her with a shake of the head. 'He says there is a way down the cliff, but it is hard and dangerous.'

'Ask him to show it to us. He brought us all this way with a promise that we would see the chicks, and I'm going to hold him to his word.' Loikot led them along the edge of the cliff to a crack in the rock. He laid aside his *assegai* and crept into it. The opening was just wide enough to admit Leon's larger frame. He propped the Holland rifle against a tree-trunk and wriggled down into the opening. Eva tucked up the skirts of her *shuka* between her long legs and followed him.

In semi-darkness they descended an almost vertical natural shaft lit by only a feeble reflection of light from the surface, just enough for them to make out the hand and footholds. Then, gradually, light began to filter up from below, and at last they crawled through a narrow gap on to an open ledge. The shaft had brought them out below the overhang of the buttress. However, there was still no sight of the eyrie, but the eagles had seen them appear on the ledge above their nest and screeched with anger and alarm, flying in closer to glare at them with fierce yellow eyes.

The ledge was narrow and precarious, so they edged along it with their backs to the cliff wall until, suddenly, it widened. Loikot stretched out flat on the rock and peered over the edge, then grinned at Eva, beckoning her to join him. She crawled cautiously to his side and looked down. 'There they are!' she exclaimed with delight. 'Oh, Badger, come and see them.'

He lay beside her and placed one arm around her shoulders. The nest was no more than thirty feet directly below, a massive platform of dried sticks wedged into a cleft in the rock. The top was dish-shaped and lined with green leaves and reeds. In the centre of the indentation two eaglets crouched on wobbly legs, so young they could barely hold their heads upright. Their huge beaks were out of proportion to their fluffy grey bodies, and they had not yet shed the hooks on the tips with which they had battered their way through the tough shell of the egg as they hatched.

'They're so adorably ugly. Look at those big milky eyes.' Eva laughed, then ducked with alarm as the air around their heads was disrupted and filled with the sound of great wings. Shrieking with outrage, first the female and then the male eagle dived in at them, talons extended, ready to defend their nest and the young birds in it.

'Keep your head down,' Leon warned, 'or those talons will take it off for you. Keep still. Don't move.' They pressed themselves to the rocky floor of the ledge. Gradually the fury and deadly intent of the eagles abated, as they realized there was no direct threat to their brood. At last the female returned to the nest and settled upon it, furling her wings and standing over her chicks protectively before tucking them away beneath her breast. On the ledge above them Leon and Eva lay patiently making no movement, and the birds relaxed further, until at last they ignored the human presence and resumed their natural behaviour.

It was a fascinating experience to be allowed so close to such magnificent wild creatures and observe them caring for and feeding their young. Leon and Eva spent the rest of the day on the ledge. When at last daylight was fading and it was time to go, they left reluctantly. In the rudimentary overnight shelter that Loikot and Manyoro had built for them they lay under a single blanket.

'I will never forget this day,' Eva whispered.

'Every day we spend together is unforgettable.'

'You will never take me away from Africa, will you?'

'This is our home,' he agreed.

'When I watched those funny little eaglets I had the strangest sensation.'

'It's a common female affliction, known as becoming broody,' he teased her.

'We will have babies of our own, won't we, Badger?'

'Do you mean right this moment?'

'Well, I don't know about that,' she conceded, 'but perhaps we could start practising. What do you think?'

'I think you're a ruddy genius, woman. Let's waste no more time in idle chatter.'

T heir return to Lusima's village was a happy home-
        coming. The herd-boys spied them from afar and
        shouted the news to the villagers, who trooped out to
welcome them with singing and laughter. Lusima was waiting
for them under the council tree. She embraced Eva and made
her sit on her right-hand side. Leon took the stool on her
other side and helped with translation when their intuitive
understanding faltered. Suddenly he broke off in the middle
of a sentence and raised his head to sniff the air. 'What on
earth is that wonderful aroma?' he demanded, of no one in
particular.

'Coffee!' cried Eva. 'Wonderful, glorious coffee!' Ishmael
came towards them with a pair of mugs in one hand and a
steaming coffee pot in the other. His grin was triumphant.
'You are a worker of miracles!' Eva greeted him in French.
'That is the only thing I needed to make my life perfect.'

'I have also brought you many of your beautiful clothes
and shoes so that you no longer have to wear the garments
of the infidel.' He indicated her *shuka* with a grimace of the
deepest disapproval and disgust.

'Ishmael!' Leon's voice was sharp with alarm. 'While we
were away, did you go down to Percy's Camp to fetch the
coffee and the memsahib's clothes?'

'*Ndio*, Bwana.' Ishmael grinned with pride. 'I rode hard on
my mule and I was there and back in only four days.'

'Did anybody see you? Who else was at the camp?'

'Only Bwana Hennie.'

'Did you tell him where we are?' Leon demanded.

'Yes, he asked me,' Ishmael answered. Then his face fell as
he saw Leon's expression. 'Did I do wrong, Effendi?'

Leon turned away as he struggled to suppress his anger and
the dread that had engulfed him. When he turned back his
face was blank. 'You did what you thought was right, Ishmael.
The coffee is excellent, as good as any you've ever brewed.'
But Ishmael knew him too well to be taken in by his words.

427

It was not clear to him how he had erred, but he was stricken with guilt as he backed away to his kitchen hut.

Eva was watching Leon. Her face was pale and her hands were clenched in her lap. 'Something dreadful has happened, hasn't it?' Her voice was soft and calm but her eyes were dark with worry.

'We cannot stay here any longer,' Leon told her grimly, and turned to look into the west where the sun was already on the horizon. 'We should leave at once, but it's already too late. I don't want to chance the track down the mountain in the dark. We'll go at first light tomorrow.'

'What is it, Badger?' Eva reached across to take his hand.

'While we were at the eagle's nest, Ishmael went down to Percy's Camp to fetch supplies. Hennie du Rand was there. Ishmael told him where we are. Hennie has no idea of the delicate circumstances that have overtaken you and me. We cannot chance it, Eva. If Graf Otto is alive he will come after you.'

'He is dead, my darling.'

'So you dreamed, but we cannot be sure. Then there are your masters in Whitehall. If they find out where you are, they will not let you go. We must run.'

'Where to?'

'If we can get to one of the aircraft, we can fly across the German border to Dar es Salaam, and from there take a ship to South Africa or Australia. Once we get there we can change our names and disappear.'

'We don't have any money,' she pointed out.

'Percy left me enough. Will you come with me?'

'Of course,' she replied, without hesitation. 'From now on, wherever you go, I go also.'

Leon smiled at her and said simply, 'My heart, my dear heart.' Then he turned back to Lusima. 'Mama, we have to leave.'

'Yes,' she agreed at once. 'This I have foreseen, but I could not tell it to you.'

Somehow Eva understood what Lusima had said. 'Have

you been given a glimpse beyond the curtain, Mama?' she demanded eagerly.

Lusima nodded, so she went on, 'Will you tell us what you have seen?'

'It is not much, and little of it is what you want to hear, my flower.'

'I will hear it nonetheless. You may have something to tell us that will be our salvation.'

Lusima sighed. 'As you wish, but I have warned you.' She clapped her hands and her girls came running to kneel before her. Lusima gave them their orders and they scampered away to her hut. By the time they returned, carrying the paraphernalia Lusima used for divination, the sun had set and the brief twilight was fading into night. The girls laid her tools close to Lusima's hand, then built up the small fire. She opened one of the small leather bags and scooped from it a handful of dried herbs. Muttering an incantation, she threw it into the fire, and it burned up in a puff of acrid smoke. One of the girls brought a clay pot and placed it on the fire in front of her. It was filled to the brim with a liquid that reflected the flames like a mirror.

'Come and sit beside me.' She motioned to Eva and Leon. They formed a circle with her around the pot. Lusima dipped a horn cup into the liquid and offered it to each in turn. They swallowed a mouthful of the bitter brew, and Lusima drank what was left.

'Look into the mirror,' she ordered, and they stared into the pot. Their own images wavered on the surface, but neither saw anything beyond that. The liquid began to bubble and boil as Lusima chanted softly, and her eyes glazed as she stared into the rising clouds of steam. When at last she spoke her voice was harsh and strained: 'There are two enemies, a man and a woman. They seek to sever the chain of love that binds you to each other.'

Eva gave a small cry of pain, but then was silent.

'I see that the woman has a silver flag on her head.'

'Mrs Ryan in London,' Eva whispered, when Leon translated this for her. 'She has a streak of silver in the front of her hair.'

'The man has only one hand.'

They looked across the pot at each other, but Leon shook his head. 'I don't know who that might be. Tell us, Mama, will these two enemies succeed in their designs?'

Lusima moaned as though in pain. 'I can see no further. The sky is filled with smoke and flame. The whole world is burning. It is obscure, but I see a great silver fish above the flames that brings hope of love and fortune.'

'What fish is this, Mama?' Leon asked.

'Please explain your vision to us,' Eva pleaded, but Lusima's eyes had cleared and focused again.

'There is no more,' she said regretfully. 'I warned you that little of it is what you wanted to hear, my flower.' She reached forward and overturned the clay pot, spilling its contents on to the fire, extinguishing it in a cloud of hissing steam. 'Go to your rest now. This may be your last night on Lonsonyo Mountain for a long, long while.'

Before they went to their hut Leon issued instructions to the two Masai and Ishmael to have the horses saddled and make all preparations for departure at dawn on the morrow.

The night was quiet and still but they slept only fitfully. When they started awake they reached out for each other instinctively, seized by a formless sense of dread. When the birds in the surrounding forest began their symphonic chorus of greeting to the dawn, and first light showed through the chinks in the walls, they made love with a desperate abandon they had never known before; a passion storm that, when it passed its climax, left them trembling in each other's arms, their naked bodies drenched with sweat, their hearts racing wildly. At last they drew apart and Leon whispered, 'Time to go, my beloved. Get dressed.'

He rose and threw on his clothes before he went to the door and pulled it open. He stooped through the opening and stood upright. The forest around him was black. The morning star was still aloft, and pricked the dark velvet sky. The light was leaden and dull. Eva came through the doorway behind him and he placed his arm around her. He was about to speak when he saw the men. For a moment he thought they must be his own, for they were leading horses.

They had been waiting in the darkness at the edge of the forest, but now they came towards them, and as they drew closer, Leon saw that there were seven. Five *askaris* and two officers. They all wore slouch hats and khaki campaign uniform. The *askaris* carried rifles slung over their shoulders, the officers only sidearms. The senior man stopped in front of them, but he ignored Leon and saluted Eva.

'How did you find us, Uncle Penrod? Did you have somebody watching Percy's Camp who followed Ishmael here?'

Penrod nodded. 'Of course.' He turned back to Eva. 'Good morning, Eva, my dear. I have a message for you from Mrs Ryan and Mr Brown in London.'

Eva recoiled. 'No!' she said. 'Otto is dead and it's all over.'

'Graf Otto von Meerbach is not dead. I grant you, it was a close call. The doctor had to amputate his left arm, which was rotten with gas gangrene, and sew the rest of him together. The Graf was completely *non compos mentis* for a long time – in fact, until very recently. But he is as hard as granite and as tough as elephant hide. He is still very weak but he is asking for you, and I had to make up a cock-and-bull story to explain your absence. I think he truly loves you, and I have come to take you back to him so that you can finish the job you were sent to do.'

Leon stepped between them. 'She is not going back. We love each other and we are going to marry as soon as we can get back to civilization.'

'Lieutenant Courtney, may I remind you that I am your commanding officer and the correct form of address is either "sir" or "General"? Now, step aside at once.'

'I can't do that, sir. I can't let you take her back.' Leon hunched his shoulders stubbornly.

'Captain!' Penrod snapped, over his shoulder, and the younger officer stepped forward smartly.

'Sir?' he said. Leon recognized his voice, but in his distress it was a moment before he grasped that it was Eddy Roberts, Froggy Snell's toady.

'Arrest this man.' Penrod's expression was grim. 'If he resists, shoot him in the kneecap.'

'Sir! Yes, sir!' Eddy sang out jubilantly. He drew his Webley revolver from its holster and Leon started towards him. Eddy stepped back, cocked the hammer and raised the weapon, but before he could level it Eva jumped between them and spread her arms. Now the pistol was aimed at her breast.

'Hold your fire, man!' Penrod shouted. 'For God's sake, don't harm the woman.' Eddy lowered the weapon uncertainly.

Immediately Eva switched her attention from Eddy to Penrod. 'What do you want of me, General?' She was very pale but her voice was cold and calm.

'Just a few minutes of your time, my dear.' Penrod took her arm to lead her away, but Leon intervened again.

'Don't go with him, Eva. He'll talk you around.'

She glanced back at him, and he saw that her eyes were veiled and the spark had been extinguished. His guts shrank: she had gone back to that place where nobody could follow her, not even the man who loved her. 'Eva!' he pleaded. 'Stay with me, my darling.'

She gave no indication that she had heard him, and allowed Penrod to walk her away. He led her to the edge of the cliff so that Leon could not hear a single word of their conversation. Penrod towered over her, head and shoulders. He was twice her bulk. Eva looked like a child beside him as she gazed up solemnly into his face and listened to what he was saying. He placed both hands on her shoulders and shook her gently, his expression grave. Leon could barely restrain himself. He wanted to protect and defend her. He wanted to wrap her in his arms and cherish her for ever.

'Yes, Courtney, do it!' Eddy Roberts said, in a gloating tone. 'Just give me the excuse. You got away with it last time, but that won't happen again.' The hammer was cocked, his finger was on the trigger and the weapon was aimed at Leon's right leg. 'Do it, you bastard! Give me the excuse to blow your bloody leg off.'

Leon knew he meant it. He clenched his hands until his fingernails dug into his palms, and ground his teeth. Eva was still staring up into Penrod's face as he talked. Occasionally she nodded expressionlessly and Penrod kept talking, in his most charming and convincing manner. At last Eva's shoulders slumped in capitulation and she nodded. Penrod placed an arm around her shoulders in an avuncular, concerned manner, then led her back to where Leon stood under the menace of Eddy's pistol. She did not look at him. Her expression was dead.

'Captain Roberts!' Penrod said. He would not look at Leon either.

'Sir?'

'Use your handcuffs to restrain the prisoner.'

Eddy unhooked the bright steel chains from his webbing belt and snapped the bracelets on to Leon's wrists.

'Keep him here! Don't harm him, unless he deserves it,' Penrod ordered. 'Don't allow him off this mountain until you receive orders from me. Then take him to Nairobi under guard. Don't let him speak to anyone there. Bring him directly to me.'

'Yes, sir!'

'Come along, my dear.' He turned back to Eva. 'We have a long ride ahead of us.' They walked to the horses, and Leon called after them, his voice cracked with despair, 'You can't go, Eva. You can't leave me now. Please, my darling.'

She paused to look back at him with opaque, hopeless eyes. 'We were two silly children playing a game of make-believe. It's over now. I have to go. Goodbye, Leon.'

'Oh, God!' He groaned. 'Don't you love me?'

'No, Leon. The only thing I love is my duty.' And he was not to know that her heart was breaking as she walked away, the lie still scalding her lips.

As soon as Penrod and Eva had gone down the mountain, Eddy Roberts had his *askari* drag Leon back into the hut and sit him down with his legs on each side of the central pole that supported the roof. Then he unlocked the cuffs from his wrists and clamped them on to his ankles. 'I'm not taking any chances with you, Courtney. I know just what a slippery brute you are,' Eddy told him, with sadistic relish. He allowed Ishmael to visit Leon in the hut once a day to feed him, to carry away the night-soil bucket and then to wash his backside, as if he was an infant. But apart from that Leon was forced to sit there for twelve long, degrading days until Penrod Ballantyne's messenger came up the mountain track with a note written on yellow order paper. Then Eddy Roberts allowed him out of the hut and the *askari* lifted him on to his horse. His ankles were so swollen and raw where the manacles had galled him that he could barely walk. Nevertheless Eddy ordered his men to rope his ankles together under the horse's belly.

It was an unpleasant journey up the Rift Valley to the railway. Eddy made it more so by riding behind Leon's mount and prodding it into a trot over the rough ground. With his ankles bound, Leon was unable to pace with the gait of his mount and was bounced around savagely.

Penrod was furious when two *askari* almost carried his nephew into his office in the KAR headquarters building in Nairobi. He came out from behind his desk and helped him into a chair. 'I did not intend you to be treated in that fashion,' he said, which was as close to an apology as Leon had ever heard him come.

'That's perfectly all right, sir. I suppose I made it impossible for you to do anything else but have me hog-tied.'

'You were asking for it,' Penrod agreed. 'You're just bloody lucky that I didn't have you shot out of hand. The thought did cross my mind.'

'Where is Eva, Uncle?'

'She's probably somewhere in the Suez Canal by now, well on her way back to Berlin. I only sent for you when the liner steamed out of Mombasa.' His expression softened. 'You're well out of the whole sorry business, my lad. I think I did you a great service by bringing you to your senses and getting rid of her for you.'

'That's as may be, sir, but I cannot say that I'm overflowing with gratitude to you.'

'Not now, perhaps, but you will be later. She's a spy, did you know that? She's totally scheming and unscrupulous.'

'No, sir. She's a British agent. She's a beautiful young woman of great courage who has done more than her patriotic duty for you and Britain.'

'There's a name for women like her.'

'Sir, if you speak it aloud, I will not be responsible for my actions. This time you really will have to shoot me.'

'You're an idiot, Leon Courtney, a lovesick puppy, incapable of rational thought.' He reached for his uniform tunic, which was hooked over the back of his chair.

As he buttoned it on Leon saw three stars and crossed-swords insignia on the shoulders. 'If you've finished insulting me, sir, perhaps you might allow me to congratulate you on your meteoric rise to the lofty rank of major general.'

Leon had broken the tension and Penrod accepted the peace-offering. 'So, no hard feelings, then. We all did what we had to do. Thank you for your congratulations, Leon. Did you know that while you were honeymooning on Lonsonyo Mountain some Serbian madman assassinated the Archduke Franz Ferdinand of Austria-Hungary and the heavy-handed retaliation of that country against the Serbs has set off a chain reaction of violence? Half of Europe is already at war, and Kaiser Wilhelm is spoiling to get into it. It's all happening just as I predicted. Full-scale war within a few months.' He searched his pockets for his cigarette case and lit a Player's. 'I was with "Bloody Bull" Allenby in the Boer War, and now he's in charge of the Egyptian Army. They're ready to go into Mesopotamia, and he wants me to take command of his cavalry. I sail for Cairo next week. Your aunt will be pleased to have me home for a few days.'

'Please give her my love, sir. Who's taking over from you here in Nairobi?'

'Good news for you. Your old friend and admirer Froggy Snell has been promoted to colonel and given the job.' He saw Leon's face fall. 'Yes, I know what you're thinking. However, I can perform one last favour for you before I leave. Hugh Delamere is raising a volunteer unit of light horse unconnected with the KAR. I have transferred you from the reserves to act as liaison and intelligence officer to him. He's keen to have you fly reconnaissance for his unit. He knows about your rift with Snell and will protect you from him.'

'Very decent of him. But there's one small problem. I have no aeroplane for these reconnaissance flights.'

'The minute Kaiser Wilhelm declares war you'll have your aeroplane – in fact, you will have two. Hugh Delamere borrowed a seaplane pilot from the Royal Navy base at Mombasa and sent him to Percy's Camp to ferry the *Bumble Bee* up here. Both of von Meerbach's aircraft are safely parked in the hangar at the polo ground.'

'I'm not sure I understand. Didn't he take them with him when he sailed?'

'No, he left them with his mechanic, Gustav Kilmer, to take care of them. As soon as war breaks out they become the property of an enemy alien. We'll lock up Kilmer in a concentration camp and commandeer the planes.'

'That's good news indeed. I've become addicted to flying, and wasn't relishing the thought of having to give it up. As soon as you dismiss me, sir, I intend to go out to Tandala

Camp to check on what Max Rosenthal and Hennie du Rand have been up to in my absence. After that, I'll go down to the polo ground and make sure Gustav has the aircraft safely stowed.'

'Oh, you won't find du Rand at Tandala. He's gone to Germany with von Meerbach.'

'Good Lord.' Leon was genuinely surprised. 'How did that come about?'

'The Graf must have taken a shine to him. Anyway, he's gone. As I will have next Friday. I expect you to be at the station to give me a hearty send-off.'

'Wouldn't miss it for the world, General.'

'A bit of *double-entendre* there, I suspect.' Penrod stood up. 'You're dismissed.'

'One last question, if I may, sir?'

'Go ahead and ask it, but as I suspect I already know what your enquiry concerns, I don't promise to answer.'

'Do you have an arrangement in place for exchanging messages with Eva Barry while she's in Germany?'

'Ah! So that's the young lady's real name. I knew that von Wellberg was a *nom de guerre*. It seems you know a great deal more about her than I do. I apologize if that's another *double-entendre*.'

'None of that answers my question, General.'

'It doesn't, does it?' Penrod agreed. 'Shall we leave it at that?'

Leon rode out to Tandala Camp, and when he went into his tent he found Max Rosenthal packing his kitbag. 'Leaving us, Max?' Leon asked.

'The locals are starting a pogrom against us. I don't want to spend this war in a British concentration camp, like the ones Kitchener put up in South Africa, so I'm heading for the German border.'

'Wise man,' Leon told him. 'Things are going to change

around here. I'm going to the polo ground to talk to Gustav about the two aircraft. If you're there at first light tomorrow morning, I may be able to give you both a lift south to Arusha and safety.'

It was dusk when Leon rode down the main street of Nairobi, but the entire town was bustling. He had to weave his way through the throng of Scotch carts and wagons, all crammed with the families of settlers coming in from the remote farms. A rumour was flying about that von Lettow Vorbeck had massed his troops on the border ready to march on Nairobi, burning and plundering the farms along the way. Major General Ballantyne's men were erecting army tents on the KAR parade-ground to accommodate the refugees. The women and children were already settling in while their menfolk headed for the recruitment office in the Barclays Bank building where Lord Delamere was taking on men for his irregular regiment of light horse.

When Leon rode past the front of the bank the volunteers were standing in excited groups on the dusty street, discussing the prospect of war and how it would affect them in the colony. Their horses were saddled up, and they were dressed in hunting clothes. Most were armed with sporting rifles, ready to ride out to oppose von Lettow Vorbeck and his murderous *askari*. Leon knew that few of them had had any military training. He smiled pityingly. Silly beggars. They think it's going to be a guinea-fowl shoot. They haven't considered the possibility of the Germans shooting back.

At that moment a man ran out of the cablegram office across the street from the bank, waving a buff form over his head. 'Message from London! It's started!' he yelled. 'Kaiser Bill has declared war on Britain and the Empire! All aboard for glory, lads!'

There was a raucous chorus of cheers. Beer bottles were lifted high, and there were shouts of 'Rot the bastard!'

Bobby Sampson was among a group of men, most of whom Leon knew. Leon was about to dismount and join them when a thought occurred to him. How is Gustav going to react to this declaration of war? What orders did Graf Otto leave for him to cover this eventuality?

He whipped up his horse and pointed its nose in the direction of the polo ground.

It was dark when he reached it. He pulled his mount down to a walk as he approached the hangar. There had been rain earlier and the ground was soft. The turf muffled the sound of the horse's hoofs, and he saw light in the hangar through the tarpaulin wall. At first he thought that somebody was moving around inside with a lantern. Then he realized that the light was too ruddy, and that it was flickering.

Fire!

His premonition of trouble had been realized. He kicked his feet out of the stirrups and dropped to the ground. Silently he ran to the door and paused to assess the situation. The flame he had seen was a burning torch, which Gustav was holding aloft. By its light Leon saw that both aircraft were parked tail to tail on their usual stands at opposite ends of the hangar. Each had its own doorway, an arrangement that allowed them to be wheeled in or out without the other machine having to be moved.

Gustav had chopped up most of the heavy packing crates in which the planes had been shipped out from Germany and had piled the wood in a pyramid under the *Butterfly*'s fuselage. His back was turned and he was so preoccupied with his preparations to burn the planes that he was unaware of Leon's presence in the doorway behind him. He held the burning torch in his right hand, an open schnapps bottle in the left. He was in the middle of a drunken valediction to the two flying machines.

'This is the hardest thing I have ever been asked to do. You are the fruit of my mind. You are the creation of my hands. I dreamed up every line of your lovely bodies, and I built you with my own hands. I laboured on you through long days and longer nights. You are a monument to my skills and genius.' He broke off with a sob, took a long swig of schnapps and belched as he lowered the bottle. 'Now I must destroy you. Part of me will die with you. I wish I had the courage to throw myself on your pyre, for after you are gone my life will be ashes.' He hurled the torch towards the pile of wood, but the schnapps had affected his judgement and it arched up, leaving a trail of sparks. It struck the propeller of the near-side port engine and rebounded, falling to the floor of the hangar and rolling back to Gustav's feet. With an oath he stooped to pick it up.

Leon rushed at him. He crashed into Gustav from behind just as his fingers closed on the handle of the burning torch. He knocked the German off his feet and the schnapps bottle shattered as it struck the floor, but somehow Gustav managed to keep his grip on the torch.

With amazing agility for such a big man he rolled on to his knees and glared at Leon. 'I will kill you if you try to stop me!' He threw the torch again, and this time it lodged on the wood. Leon wondered if Gustav had soaked it with petrol, but although the flame was still burning it did not explode. He ran forward, trying to reach it before the fire took hold.

Gustav staggered to his feet and blocked his path. He was leaning over, his head held low and his arms spread to prevent Leon reaching the spluttering torch. Leon ran straight at him, but before Gustav could grab him he used the momentum of his run and kicked him in the crotch. The rowel of his spurs ripped into the soft flesh between Gustav's thighs. He screamed and reeled back, clutching his injured genitals with both hands.

Leon shouldered him aside and reached the wood. He grabbed the torch and hurled it towards the door. One of the planks of the packing crates was burning. He pulled it free, threw it to the ground and stamped on it to extinguish the flames.

Gustav leaped on to his back and wrapped a muscular arm around his neck in a deadly stranglehold. He had both legs locked around Leon's body, riding him like a horse. He tightened his grip, and Leon choked.

Through streaming eyes he saw one of the propeller blades

of the big Meerbach rotary engine hanging in front of him at head level. It was made of laminated wood, but the leading edge was clad with metal, like a knife blade. He pirouetted quickly, bringing Gustav in line with the blade, then ran backwards. It slashed into the back of the man's skull, cutting to the bone and stunning him. His grip loosened and Leon tore himself free. Gustav was staggering in a circle, blood spurting from the wound. Leon clenched his right fist and punched the side of his jaw. Gustav went down, sprawling on his back.

Gasping for breath, Leon looked around wildly. The torch was lying in the doorway where he had thrown it. It was still alight but there was nothing for the flames to catch. More dangerously, though, he had not managed to extinguish the plank before Gustav leaped upon him. Now the flames had rekindled and were burning up brightly. Leon picked it up and ran with it to the entrance. He hurled it outside, then turned his attention to the torch. As he bent to pick it up he heard a scuffling sound behind him and ducked to one side. He heard something hiss past his right ear. He whirled around.

Gustav had armed himself with an eight-pound sledgehammer from the workbench against the wall. Then he had charged at Leon and, both hands gripping the long handle, had swung it at Leon's head. If Leon had not ducked, it would have shattered his skull. The force of the swing had set Gustav off-balance, and before he could recover, Leon grabbed him in a bear-hug, trapping the hammer between their bodies. They spun around in a deadly waltz, shifting weight and balance, trying to trip or lift the other off the ground.

Leon was the taller by four inches, but Gustav matched him in weight and was solid muscle, tempered and hardened by a lifetime of physical work. The punishment Leon had dealt him would have incapacitated a lesser fighter, and Gustav's resilience was frightening. His strength seemed to increase as the adrenalin coursing through his body countered the agony of his injuries. He drove Leon back towards the doorway where the burning torch lay. Leon felt its heat on the back of his legs. Then Gustav swivelled and pushed his hip under his adversary. For a fleeting second Leon was off-balance and Gustav aimed a mighty kick at the torch. He sent it bouncing across the floor until it slammed into the base of the wooden pyramid. The hangar was filled with smoke and the smell of burning.

Like a leopard mad with rage, Leon found a hidden reservoir of strength. He shifted in Gustav's arms and hooked one of the man's heels with his toe, tripping him backwards. Gustav crashed to the ground with Leon's full weight on top of him. The air was forced out of his chest in a loud *whoosh*. Leon broke away, vaulted to his feet like a gymnast and ran to retrieve the torch from the wood. Two pieces were already alight but he had just enough time to drag them out of the pile and hurl them aside before Gustav was on him again. He was swinging the sledgehammer in great sweeps at Leon's face, forcing him to back away. The German was wheezing as he sucked air into his lungs. The back of his shirt was black with blood from the wound in his scalp and the front of his breeches from where Leon's spur had gouged him, but he was beyond pain. The hammer swung like a metronome, back and forth, and Leon was forced to give ground before the menace of its heavy steel head.

He came up short with his back against the corner of the hangar wall. The angle prevented him breaking out and he knew that Gustav had him trapped. With both hands Gustav lifted the hammer high, and paused with it aimed at Leon's head. Leon knew that when the blow came he could not avoid it. There was simply not enough space for him to dodge. He stared into Gustav's eyes, trying to read his intention, trying to control him with the force of his gaze, but schnapps and pain had turned the man into an animal. In his eyes there was no trace of recognition or mercy.

Then Gustav's expression changed subtly. The mad rage faded from his eyes, replaced by bewilderment. He opened his mouth, but before he could speak a thick gout of bright blood spewed over his lips. The hammer dropped and clattered to the hangar floor. He looked down at his body.

The blade of a Masai *assegai* stood out three hands' breadth from the centre of his chest. He shook his head as though in disbelief at what he was seeing. Then his legs buckled. Manyoro was standing close behind him, and as Gustav fell, he plucked out the blade from where he had driven it home. The German's heart must still have been beating, for a small fountain of blood spurted from the gaping wound and shrivelled as Gustav died.

Leon stared at Manyoro. His mind seethed with wild conjecture. The last time he had seen Manyoro was almost a week ago on Lonsonyo Mountain. How had he arrived so fortuitously? Then he saw that Loikot was with him and, before he could stop him, had plunged his own *assegai* into the inert body.

Leon was assailed by horror and dread. No matter the circumstances in which it had happened, they had killed a white man. There would be retribution in the form of the hangman's noose. The administration of the colony could not afford to condone such a heinous offence in a land where whites were outnumbered fifty to one by tribesmen. It would set too dangerous a precedent. His mind racing, Leon demanded of the two Masai, 'How did you get here?'

'When the soldier took you from Lonsonyo we followed you.'

'I owe my life to you. The Bula Matari would have killed me, but you know what will happen if the police catch you.'

'No matter,' Manyoro said, with dignity. 'They can do with me as they wish. You are my brother. I could not stand by and watch him kill you.'

'Does anybody else know you are in Nairobi?' Leon asked, and they shook their heads. 'Good. We must work quickly.'

Between them they wrapped Gustav's corpse in a tarpaulin from the storeroom with a fifty-pound crank shaft lashed to his feet. They trussed it securely with lengths of hemp rope, then carried it to the *Butterfly* and loaded it into the main bomb bay in the fuselage. Still working fast, they tidied the hangar, getting rid of any trace of the fight and the fire. They carried out the remains of the packing cases and stacked them on the woodpile behind the Polo Club. Then they spread fresh earth over the bloodstains, trampled it down and sprinkled engine oil over the spot to disguise the nature of the stains. If any questions were asked about Gustav's disappearance it would be assumed that he had gone on the run to escape arrest and incarceration in a concentration camp.

When Leon was satisfied that they had covered up as much of the incriminating evidence as they could, they wheeled the *Butterfly* out of the hangar and he climbed into the cockpit to begin his start-up procedures. The two Masai stood ready to swing the propellers. Then they stiffened and stared into the darkness from which came the sound of a horse at full gallop.

'Police?' Leon muttered. 'I have the corpse of a murdered man on board. This could mean trouble.'

He held his breath, then released it as Max Rosenthal rode out of the night and dismounted. He carried a large rucksack slung on his back as he hurried to the side of the *Butterfly*. 'You told me you'd help me,' he said, looking hunted and terrified. 'Up at the parade-ground they've just shot three Germans they accused of being spies. Mr Courtney, you know I'm no spy.'

'Don't worry, Max, I'll take you out,' Leon reassured him. 'Climb aboard!'

As soon as the engines started, the two Masai scrambled up to join Max in the cockpit and, with the waxing moon lighting the way, Leon took off and turned south, heading for the border with German East Africa. Three hours later the silver expanse of Lake Natron came up ahead, shining like a mirror in the moonlight. Leon let the *Butterfly* sink down until they were skimming its surface. He flew into the centre before he pulled the lever that opened the bomb bay, then leaned over the side of the cockpit and watched the tarpaulin-shrouded corpse plummet into the soda-rich water. It raised a splash of white foam. He circled back low over the surface to make certain that it had not floated, but the metal ballast had pulled it under and there was barely a ripple to be seen.

He turned back for the eastern shore. Lake Natron overlapped the boundary between the German and British territories. At this dry season of the year the beaches were exposed and as the water was rich in soda they were brilliant white, the soda hard-packed. Leon could land the *Butterfly* safely on one of them. The difficulty lay in deciding which to trust. He made a pass down a stretch of beach, which seemed firm and hard, came around again and touched down gently. The *Butterfly* settled and began to slow. Then, heart sinking, he felt her wheels break through the soda crust into the soft mud beneath. The plane stopped so abruptly that they were all thrown heavily against their safety straps.

Leon cut the engines and they climbed down on to the beach. A hasty inspection revealed no apparent damage to the landing gear or fuselage, but the wheels were bogged axle deep in the mire. Leon walked in a circle around the *Butterfly* to test the surface. They had been unfortunate to run into a small mudhole. Fifty feet ahead the ground was firm, but there was no hope of the four men being able to manhandle the heavy machine that far.

'Where are we, Manyoro?'

The two Masai discussed the question before they replied.

'We are in the land of the Bula Matari. It is half a day's walk back to the border.'

'Are there any Germans close by?'

Manyoro shook his head. 'The nearest post is at Longido.' He pointed south-east. 'It will take more than a day for the soldiers to get here.'

'Are there any villages close by where we can find men to help us?'

'*Ndio*, M'bogo. Less than an hour's walk along the shore from here there is a large village of fisherfolk.'

'Do they have trek oxen?'

Manyoro consulted Loikot and at last they both nodded.

'Yes. It is a large village and the chief is a rich man. He has many oxen.'

'Go to him, my brethren, as fast as you can run. Tell him if he brings a span of his oxen to pull us out of the mud I will make him even richer. He must bring ropes too.'

Leon and Max settled down in the cockpit to wait, but dense clouds of mosquitoes whined around their heads and kept them awake until dawn. At last they heard voices and the lowing of oxen from the direction in which Manyoro and Loikot had disappeared. Then a crowd of people and animals came towards them along the shore. Manyoro was in the vanguard, trotting far ahead.

Leon jumped down from the cockpit and hurried to meet him.

'I have brought two full spans of oxen.' Manyoro was grinning with his accomplishment as they came together.

'I praise you, Manyoro. You have done work of great value. Have they brought ropes?' Leon asked.

Manyoro's smile faded. 'Only short leather traces, which will not stretch across the mudhole to our *indege*,' he admitted. He tried to look downcast, but Leon had seen the twinkle in his eyes.

'A man of such wisdom as you must have thought of another plan?' Leon asked.

Manyoro gave his sunniest smile.

'What have you brought me, brother?'

'Fishing nets!' he cried, and dissolved into a gale of giggles.

'That is a very good joke,' Leon said, 'but now tell me the truth.'

'It *is* the truth.' Manyoro staggered weakly with an excess of mirth. 'You shall see, M'bogo, you shall see, and then you will praise me even more.'

The thirty-six oxen were driven down the lake shore by several hundred fisherfolk, with their women and children. On the back of each ox was strapped an enormous brown bundle of some amorphous material. Under Manyoro and Loikot's stern supervision, the bundles were unloaded and laid out on the beach. When they were unrolled they proved to be two-hundred-foot lengths of hand-woven netting. The mesh was little more than an inch across and the knots were neat and firm. Leon stretched a section over his shoulders and tried with all his strength to break it. The villagers danced and hooted when he turned red with his vain efforts.

'Look at his face!' they told each other. 'It is the colour of a turkey buzzard's wattles. Our nets are the finest and strongest in the land. Even the largest crocodiles cannot tear them.'

The nets were laid out, joined together, then carefully rolled into a long, bulky hawser two or three feet in diameter, thicker and heavier than the mooring ropes of an ocean liner. Gangs of villagers carried one end out to where the *Butterfly* stood, her wings canted at a forlorn, abandoned angle. Leon wound the end around the landing gear and secured it with the leather thongs that the villagers had brought with the nets. The teams of oxen were backed to the edge of the mud and inspanned to the far end of the hawser. Leon, Max and the two Masai took up positions at each of the *Butterfly*'s wing-tips to prevent her rocking dangerously and digging one into the mud. Then, with shouts of encouragement from the onlookers and the cracking of whips by the drivers, the oxen heaved. The hawser lifted from the mud and came up straight and hard. For a minute nothing further happened, but then, gradually, the landing wheels broke out of the mud and the *Butterfly* trundled on to dry ground.

When the hysteria of celebration and self-congratulation abated, Leon gave the village headman a generous gift, sufficient to purchase several more oxen. Then he bade Max farewell and watched him set off jauntily on foot for the German police post at Longido, his rucksack on his back. As soon as he had disappeared into the bush, Leon and the Masai started the *Butterfly*'s engines and climbed into the cockpit. When he was airborne, Leon turned north on to a heading for Nairobi.

T he following days were feverishly busy as Leon reported to Lord Delamere and took over his new job as his lordship's intelligence and liaison officer. Despite all this distraction, Eva was never far from his mind. Her image rose unexpectedly to haunt him at odd hours of his day.

When Penrod left for his new assignment in Egypt Leon was at the railway station to see him off. Their relationship had cooled noticeably since Eva had come between them. At the last moment, as they stood on the railway platform and the train conductor gave a blast on his whistle, Leon could contain himself no longer. Once again he asked his uncle if there was any way in which he could contact Eva now that Germany and Britain were at war and all regular channels of communication had been closed.

'You should forget about that young lady. I've pulled your irons out of the fire once already and I don't want to be forced to do it again. She can bring you nothing but trouble and heartbreak,' Penrod replied, and climbed up on to the balcony of his carriage. 'I shall give your love to your aunt. That will please her.'

It was almost a week later and Leon was leaving Lord Delamere's office in the Barclays Bank building. As he stepped out through the main doors into the road he felt a small soft hand press into his. Startled, he looked down – into the huge dark eyes of a Vilabjhi cherub. 'Latika! My sweet lollipop!' he greeted her.

'You remembered my name,' she exclaimed, with delight.

'Of course I did. We're friends, aren't we?'

Only then did she remember her errand. She placed a small folded square of paper in his hand. 'My daddy said I should give this to you.'

Leon unfolded it and read quickly: 'I must speak to you. Latika can bring you to my emporium as soon as you can come. Signed by Mr Goolam Vilabjhi Esq.'

Latika was tugging at his hand, and he allowed her to lead

him away to where his horse stood at the hitching rail down the street. He mounted, then reached down from the saddle to take the child under her armpits and lift her behind him. She clasped him around the waist, and they rode the length of the street with Latika squeaking and wriggling ecstatically.

When they entered Mr Vilabjhi's shop Leon saw that his own little shrine had been maintained assiduously, and now contained more memorabilia: pictures of him in flying gear, and newspaper articles about the open day at the polo ground.

Mr Vilabjhi rushed out of the back room to welcome him, and his wife brought in a tray of strong Arabic coffee and sweetmeats. She was followed by all of their daughters, but before they could entrench themselves their father drove them out, with fond cries of 'Be gone, you wicked and rowdy female personages!' He bolted the door behind them. Then he came back to Leon. 'I have a most pressing and urgent matter on which I plead for your wise counsel.'

Leon sipped the coffee and waited for him to proceed.

'Without any doubt you are aware that your uncle, the eminent sahib Major General Ballantyne, asked me to receive messages from the lovely memsahib von Wellberg on his behalf and forward these to the correct authority.' He looked at Leon quizzically.

Leon was about to deny any knowledge of this arrangement, but then he realized that would be a mistake so he nodded. 'Of course,' he agreed, and Mr Vilabjhi looked relieved.

'The reason that the general chose me is that I have a niece who lives with her husband in Altnau, a small town in Switzerland on the north shore of Lake Bodensee. Across the lake is the town of Weiskirchen in Bavaria. This is where the castle of the German count is situated, and also the main factory of the Meerbach Motor Works. It is also where Memsahib von Wellberg lives.' Mr Vilabjhi had phrased it delicately. 'My niece works in the Swiss cablegram company. Her husband has a small fishing-boat on the lake. The shore is not heavily guarded by the egregious Germans, so it is easy for them to

cross the water at night and pick up any message at Weiskirchen, then return home and telegraph it to me. I take it to
General Ballantyne. But now the esteemed general has gone.
Before he left he told me I should deliver any future messages
to the man who has taken over his job at KAR Headquarters.'

'Yes. Colonel Snell,' Leon said calmly, although his heart
raced at the prospect of messages coming directly from Eva.

'Ah, of course I am telling you nothing that is not already
well known to you. However, a terrible thing has happened.'
Mr Vilabjhi broke off and rolled his eyes tragically.

Leon's heart was chilled with dread. 'Something has happened to Memsahib von Wellberg?' he asked.

'No, not in the very least, not to the memsahib, but it has
happened to me. After the departure of the general I took
the first despatch from my niece to the office of Colonel
Snell. I learned in no ambivalent terms that the man is an
enemy of the general. Now that he has left for Egypt, Snell
will not pursue or foster any enterprise initiated by your
honourable avuncular relative. I think it is because the praise
and success arising from it would redound to the general's
credit, rather than to Snell himself. Also it seems he knows
that you and I are friends and he looks upon you as an
enemy. He knew that if he insulted me and questioned my
veracity, he would be getting at you. He drove me away with
harsh words.' Mr Vilabjhi paused. It was obvious that he had
been deeply hurt by his encounter with Snell. Then he went
on bitterly, 'He called me a "devil-worshipping wog", and
told me not to go back to him with my vaunting claptrap
about secret despatches.' Tears welled in his dark eyes. 'I am
at the end and far limit of my wits. I know not what to do
so I appeal to you.'

Leon rubbed his chin thoughtfully. His mind was racing.
He knew that if he wanted ever to lay eyes on Eva again he
needed Mr Vilabjhi as his ally. He chose his words carefully.
'You and I are loyal subjects of King George the Fifth, are we
not?'

'Indeed we are, Sahib.'

'If the beastly man Snell is a traitor, then you and I are not.'

'No! Never! We are true and resolute Englishmen.'

'In the name of our sovereign, we have to take over this enterprise from Snell and steer it to a victorious conclusion.' Leon had picked up Mr Vilabjhi's floral turn of phrase.

'I rejoice to hear such words of wisdom, Sahib! This is what I hoped you would say.'

'First, you and I must read the message that Snell has rejected. Have you kept it safe?'

Vilabjhi sprang up from his desk and went to the iron safe in the wall. He brought out a large cash book bound in red leather. Tucked under the rear cover was one of the distinctive Post Office envelopes. He handed it to Leon. The flap was sealed.

'You did not open it?'

'Of course not. That is not my business.'

'Well, it is now,' Leon told him, and split the envelope with his thumbnail. He drew out the folded buff sheet, his hands trembling with excitement as he unfolded and spread it on the desk. Then he sagged with dismay. It was covered with rows and columns of numbers, no letters.

'Damn it to hell! It's in code,' he lamented. 'Do you have the key?'

Mr Vilabjhi shook his head.

'But of course you know how to send a reply?'

'Of course. I arranged the link with the memsahib through my niece.'

1

Eva ran lightly down the magnificent marble staircase of the *Schloss*. Her riding boots made no sound on the carpeted treads. The panelled walls were hung with canvases depicting Otto's ancestors down the centuries and there were suits of armour at each landing. At first she had found the architectural style and heavy furnishings depressing, but now she no longer noticed them. As she reached the lowest landing she heard voices coming up the stairwell. She stopped to listen.

Otto was in conversation with at least two other men, and she recognized the voice of Alfred Lutz, the commodore of his fleet of dirigible airships, and that of Hans Ritter, the senior navigator, who seemed to be arguing with the Graf.

Otto's tone was loud and hectoring. Since his mauling by the lion his previously overbearing manner had become ever more authoritarian. Eva thought that Ritter should have known this by now and taken care not to provoke him. 'We will leave from Weiskirchen and overfly Bulgaria and Turkey, then go on to Mesopotamia where our forces are already occupying the northern part of the country. We will land there to top up our tanks with fuel, oil and water. From there we go on to Damascus, then across the Red Sea to the Nile valley, Khartoum and the Sudan.'

It sounded as though Otto was illustrating his lecture to Lutz and Ritter on the large-scale pull-down map on the far wall of the library.

He went on, 'From the Sudan we will cross the Great African Lakes and fly on down the Rift Valley to Arusha, where Schnee and von Lettow Vorbeck are holding stores of fuel and oil for us. From there, we go to Lake Nyasa and Rhodesia. We will observe strict radio silence until we are over the central Kalahari. Only then will we contact Koos de la Rey by radio to our relay station at Walvis Bay on the west coast of Africa.'

She felt a deep sense of accomplishment. This was the

most vital piece of information, which until now she had been unable to discover. Now she knew exactly how Otto intended to convey his cargo of arms and bullion to the South African rebels. Penrod had suggested that it would be sent by submarine to some uninhabited beach on the west coast of South Africa. No one had thought of a dirigible airship. But now she had the entire plan, even a precise description of the route Otto would take down the African continent. With this information she would have given Penrod Ballantyne everything he needed, except the date that the journey would begin.

She started as she heard the library doors opening and the voices were louder and clearer. Footsteps warned her that Otto and his aviators were coming out into the hall. She must not be found eavesdropping. She ran on down the last flight of stairs, making no attempt to cover the sound of her descent. The men were standing in a group in the centre of the hall. The airmen saluted her respectfully, and Otto's face lightened with pleasure.

'You are going out for a ride?' he asked.

'I told Chef I would go into Friedrichshafen and see if the old lady in the market has any black truffles for your dinner. I know how you love them. You don't mind if I leave you for a few hours, Otto? I might stop on my way back to sketch a view of the lake.'

'Not at all, my dear. Anyway, I am going to the factory with Lutz and Ritter to check the final assembly of the new airship. I might be gone for some time. I shall probably lunch with Commodore Lutz in the senior managers' mess. However, do not make any plans for next week.'

'Are you almost ready to fly the airship?' She clapped her hands in feigned excitement.

'Perhaps, perhaps not,' he teased, with heavy humour. 'But I would like you to be there when we walk her out from her hangar for her maiden flight. I think you will find it extremely exciting.' He lifted his left arm and clicked open the metal thumb and finger of the prosthesis that was fitted to the end of the stump. He placed a Cuban cigar in the jaws of the metal appendage and secured it in place with a lateral twist of his wrist. Then he lifted it, and placed the tip between his lips, and Lutz struck a Vesta and held it for him while he puffed out clouds of smoke.

Eva suppressed a shiver of unease. The artificial hand frightened her. It had been made for Otto by the engineers in his factory to his own design. It was an extraordinary creation with which he had already developed an alarming dexterity. Holding a bottle between the steel fingers he could pour wine for his dinner guests without spilling a drop, button the front of his coat, clean his teeth, deal a hand of cards or tie his shoelaces.

He had devised a number of other fittings to replace the metal finger and thumb, which included a selection of fighting knives, a grip for a polo stick and a rest to hold the forestock of a rifle steady while he aimed the weapon with his usual accuracy. However, most formidable of all was a spiked battle mace. With this terrible club replacing his hand, Otto was able to splinter a heavy oak beam to kindling. She had seen him put a horse with a broken leg out of its misery with a blow that had shattered its skull.

Otto kissed her, then led his guests down the front steps of the *Schloss*. They climbed into a glistening black Meerbach touring car, Otto dismissed the chauffeur, took the wheel in his steel fist and they roared off in the direction of the factory. Eva waved him out of sight. Then, with a sigh of relief, she ran down to the forecourt, where one of the grooms was holding her favourite mare. As soon as she was out of sight of the *Schloss* she kicked her heels into the mare's flanks and urged her into a headlong gallop down the bridlepath through the forest to the lake. These solitary rides were her only escape from the gloomy old castle and Otto.

Since she had known Leon it had become almost impossible for her to sustain her carefully rehearsed role as the Graf's dutiful and doting mistress, and to satisfy his endless physical demands. There were nights when, with his naked muscular body pounding into hers, his flesh latticed by vivid red scars inflicted by the lion's claws, his face swollen and inflamed with passion, sweat dripping from it on to her own, she had barely been able to prevent herself clawing with her fingernails at his passion-glazed eyes and throwing herself out of the great four-poster bed. She could not go on much longer before she made a mistake and he discovered that he had been gulled. When that happened his vengeance would be merciless. She was afraid, and longed to be safe in Leon's arms, shielded by his love. There was not a moment of her waking existence when she did not miss him.

'I love him but I know I'll never see him again,' she whispered, and the tears blew back across her cheeks with the speed of the mare's gallop. At last they burst out on her favourite view across Lake Bodensee to the snow-clad heights of the Swiss Alps on the far side. She stopped on the high ground, wiped away her tears and gazed out across the blue waters. There were many sails in sight, but she picked out a tiny fishing-boat, running before the wind under a reefed mainsail and jib. A man was slumped lazily over the tiller in the stern, and a dark girl in a brightly coloured dress sat cross-legged on the foredeck. With an inscrutable expression she gazed across the water at Eva. Though they knew each other well, they had never spoken, and this was the closest they had ever been to an actual meeting. Eva did not know her name. Their relationship had been arranged by Penrod Ballantyne and Mr Goolam Vilabjhi.

The girl turned her head and said something to the man in the stern. He put the tiller over and tacked the fishing-boat. As it came across the wind, the blue swallow-tailed pennant at the masthead unfurled and flapped open. It was the signal that there was a message for Eva. The boat came about on the starboard tack and settled on a course for the Swiss shore of the lake.

Eva was relieved. For the past weeks she had been expecting a response to her last signal to Penrod in Nairobi. His silence had made her feel even more vulnerable. Although she was still bitter that he had separated her and Leon, Penrod was the only ally she had in all her lonely world. She gathered the reins and trotted the mare along the shore in the direction of Friedrichshafen. The Meerbach estates stretched for many miles.

At one point ahead a copse came to the water's edge, the trees marking the juncture of the boundary wall with the lake. She reached the wall and dismounted to open the gate in it. The wall was a substantial construction of dry-packed stone blocks. Otto had boasted to her that it had been built originally by the Roman legionaries of Tiberius. She hitched the mare to the gate, climbed up on to the stone blocks and, her sketchpad open in her lap, gazed about as though she was admiring the scenery.

When she had satisfied herself that she was not observed, she reached down casually and lifted a mossy stone from its niche. In the recess beneath it lay the folded sheet of thin rice paper that the dark girl had placed there for her.

Eva put back the stone carefully before she unfolded the paper. She was alarmed to see that the script was in clear language, not coded. Her first thought was that a trap had been set for her. Swiftly she scanned the two lines of text, then gasped with astonishment. 'Uncle gone stop What code are you using query Badger.'

Joy surged through her. 'Badger!' she exclaimed. 'My darling Badger, you've found me.' Although he was half a world away she was no longer completely alone. The knowledge armed her and strengthened her wounded heart. She put the scrap of rice paper into her mouth, chewed it and swallowed. Then, struggling to control her soaring emotions, she began a sketch of the lake shore, with the spire of the Weiskirchen in the background. Finally, satisfied that Otto had not sent any of his men to spy on her, she tore a small strip from the foot of the pad and wrote in neat block capitals: 'MACMILLAN ENGLISH DICTIONARY JULY 1908 EDITION STOP FIRST NUMERAL GROUP IS PAGE STOP SECOND NUMERAL GROUP IS COLUMN STOP FINAL NUMERAL GROUP IS WORD FROM

THE TOP STOP.' She paused, searching for words to express her feelings adequately. Finally she wrote, 'YOU ARE IN MY HEART FOR EVER.' She did not add a signature. She folded the sheet and placed it carefully in the niche under the stone in the top of the wall. The girl from across the lake would come for it after dark. She would transmit it to Mr Goolam Vilabjhi, and by tomorrow evening Badger would be reading it in Nairobi. She sat for a while longer, bowed over the sketchpad, pretending to draw, but her spirits were bubbling like a freshly opened bottle of Dom Pérignon champagne.

'To get back to Africa and the man I love. This is all I desire. Please, dear God, have mercy on me,' she prayed aloud.

Leon spent the morning in conference with Hugh Delamere and his other officers. The little man had thrown himself wholeheartedly into the formation and training of his tiny force. Already he had raised more than two hundred troopers and had mounted and equipped them from his own pocket. Delamere was renowned throughout the colony for his energy and enthusiasm, but keeping pace with him was exhausting. It had taken Delamere less than two weeks to bully and cajole the regiment into a state of campaign readiness. Now he wanted an enemy to fight and had turned to Leon to find one.

'You're the only pilot we have, Courtney. Our border with the Hun is long and the bush is thick. I agree with you that the best way to keep an eye open for the movements of von Lettow and his *askaris* is from the air. You have the job. My guess is that he will try to reach Nairobi by forced marches up the Rift Valley from the main German base at Arusha. I want you to fly regular reconnaissance patrols from Percy's Camp. I also know you have a network of Masai *chungaji* keeping watch for elephant coming into your area. You should let your boys know that, for the time being, we are more interested in the Hun than in ivory.'

By noon Leon's notebook was half filled with his lordship's orders and instructions. Delamere dismissed his officers for lunch with orders to return promptly at fourteen hundred hours. His lordship enjoyed his food and his siesta, so two hours was plenty of time to get out to the club for a bite of lunch and back again before Delamere ordered him flogged. But when he strode out into the street Latika was waiting for him by the hitching rail in front of the bank. She was feeding his horse with sugar cubes, which both of them were enjoying.

'Hello, Lollipop. Did you come to see me or my horse?'

'My daddy sent me to give this to you.' She pulled a sealed buff envelope from her apron pocket and offered it to him. She watched his face as he opened it and read the cablegram. 'Is it a letter from someone who loves you?' she asked wistfully.

'How did you know that?'

'Do you love her back?'

'Yes, very much.'

'Don't forget I love you too,' she whispered, and he saw she was close to tears.

'Then you won't mind if I give you a ride home on horseback, will you?'

Latika sniffed back her tears and forgot her potential rival. Mounted up behind him, she chattered happily all the way to her father's shop.

Mr Goolam Vilabjhi Esquire came out on to the pavement to welcome them. 'Welcome! Welcome! Mrs Vilabjhi is serving her world-famous chicken curry and saffron rice for lunch. She will be cross and sad if you do not sample it with us.'

While Mrs Vilabjhi and her daughters put the finishing touches to the luncheon table, Leon went to stand in front of the bookshelf and ran his eye over the display of books. Then he grunted with satisfaction and took a copy of Macmillan's *English Dictionary* from the upper shelf. 'May I borrow this for a while?' he asked.

Mr Vilabjhi touched the side of his nose with a finger and

looked knowing. 'General Ballantyne kept a copy of that book on his desk. It was the first thing he reached for whenever I took him a cable from Switzerland. Maybe Memsahib von Wellberg has sent you the code.' Then he covered both ears with his hands and said, 'But do not tell me about it. I am like the monkey who hears no evil. We secret agents must always be discreet.'

The curry was exquisite but Leon, eager to compose his response to Eva, hardly tasted it. As soon as the girls were clearing away the empty dishes he sequestered himself in Mr Vilabhji's office and, within twenty minutes, had encoded a message to be sent to Eva. He began with a fervent protestation of his love, then explained Penrod's absence and went on, 'With my uncle transferred to Cairo I am left in the dark stop I need to have all intelligence that you have in your possession stop Eternal love stop Badger.'

Four days later he received Eva's reply. He sat in Mr Vilabjhi's office using the dictionary to decode it. She had briefly outlined the information she had gleaned during the flying visit with Otto and Hennie to German African territory to meet von Lettow Vorbeck and Koos de la Rey. She explained the plot to raise a rebellion in South Africa at the outbreak of war, and listed the materials and stores for which de la Rey had appealed and that Graf Otto had promised to deliver.

When he read the inventory Leon whistled softly. 'Five million German marks in gold coin! That's the equivalent of almost two million pounds sterling. Enough to buy the whole damned African continent, let alone just the tip.' He sat back in Mr Vilabjhi's chair and pondered the possibility of such an audacious scheme succeeding. He remembered the deeply rooted anger and bitterness that had infected Hennie du Rand and thought, there are a hundred thousand other Boers just like him, trained and battle-hardened soldiers. Given the means, they could seize the entire country within days. Damned right the plot could succeed. But is there any way we can prevent it?

Mr Goolam Vilabjhi appeared in the doorway. 'Another message has just arrived.' He came to the desk and laid the envelope in front of Leon.

Leon worked quickly with the dictionary, then leaned back in his chair. 'Airship! Not by ship but by bloody great airship, and my little darling has discovered the exact route they will fly. If only she could tell us when they plan to come.'

W hen the house party finished breakfast Graf Otto led them down the steps to the *Schloss*, where five elephantine black Meerbach touring limousines were drawn up. There were five high-ranking officers from the War Office in Berlin, all accompanied by their wives. The women were dressed as though they were off to the races, with parasols and feathered hats, the men in dress uniform, with swords hanging on their belts, their chests glittering with medals and diamond-studded orders. Etiquette was so strictly observed that it took time to get them into the waiting vehicles without violating military orders of precedence, but finally Eva found herself in the third car with an admiral of the fleet and his large, horsy wife as her companions.

It was a twenty-minute drive to the main Meerbach factory, and as he approached the main gate in the high barbed-wire fence that surrounded it Graf Otto, at the wheel of the leading limousine, sounded his horn. The gates swung open and the guards presented arms, then stood stiffly to attention as the convoy rolled through.

This was Eva's first visit to the citadel at the centre of the Meerbach engineering empire, which sprawled over an area of almost twelve square kilometres. The streets were paved with cobblestones, and in the square in front of the administrative headquarters a magnificent marble fountain shot water fifty feet into the air. The three sheds that housed the fleet of dirigibles stood at the furthest corner of the complex. She was

unprepared for their sheer size: they seemed as tall and commodious as Gothic cathedrals.

The weather was delightfully sunny and warm as the party
dismounted before the high, rolling doors of the central
building and made their way to the row of armchairs set out
for them under spreading umbrellas, which all bore the coat
of arms of the House of Meerbach. When they were seated,
three waiters in white jackets came down the row carrying
silver trays laden with crystal glasses of champagne. When
everyone had a glass in hand, Graf Otto mounted the dais
and gave a short but pithy speech of welcome. Then he went
on to set out his own vision of the role his dirigibles were
destined to play during the fateful years ahead.

'Their ability to stay aloft for long periods is their main
attribute. Non-stop flights across the Atlantic Ocean are now
easily within our grasp. One of my airships loaded with
passengers or even with a hundred-and-twenty-ton bombload
could take off from Germany and be over New York City in
less than three days. It could return without having to refuel.
The possibilities are staggering. Observers could hover over
the English Channel for weeks on end, keeping watch over
the enemy fleet and radioing its position to Berlin.' He was
too shrewd a salesman to bore his audience, half of whom
were women, with too many technical details. He kept his
canvas broad, his brushstrokes heavy and vividly colourful.
Eva knew that his speech would last seven minutes, which
he had calculated long ago was the maximum attention span
of the average listener. Surreptitiously she timed him with
her gold and diamond wristwatch. She was out by only forty
seconds.

'My friends and distinguished guests.' He turned to the
shed's gigantic doors and spread his arms like a conductor
calling his orchestra to attention. 'I give you the *Assegai*!'
Ponderously the doors trundled open and a magnificent sight
was revealed. His guests rose to their feet and burst into
spontaneous applause, heads thrown back to gaze up at the

110-foot-high monster that filled the shed from wall to wall, and from the floor to within two feet of the high ceiling. Painted across the nose in ten-foot-high scarlet letters was her name, *Assegai*. Graf Otto had chosen it to commemorate his African lion hunt. The airship had been carefully 'weighed off' so the lift of her hydrogen-filled gas chambers exactly balanced the 150,000 pounds dead weight of the hull. The watchers gasped with surprise as ten men lifted her off the landing bumper set along her keel, on which she rested when she was on earth. They were dwarfed by her size, as tiny as ants bearing the carcass of a huge jellyfish.

Slowly they carried her through the tall doors into the sunlight, which reflected off her outer skin in a dazzling blaze. Gradually her entire hull was revealed. Her handlers manoeuvred her to the sturdy mooring tower in the centre of the field and secured her to it by the nose. She lay there, her true size now apparent. She was more than twice the length of a football field, 795 linear feet from stem to stern. Her four massive Meerbach rotary engines were housed in boat-shaped gondolas that hung on steel arms beneath her keel. They could be reached from the main cabin along the central companionway, which ran along the length of the airship. Two were positioned under the bows and the other two at the stern, where they could assist in steering the ship in flight. There was a ladder down each suspension arm, by means of which the mechanic on duty could descend from the companionway to take his post beside the engine, either to carry out maintenance or to respond to telegraph signals from the bridge for changes in the power settings. The propellers were made of laminated wood and the leading edges of the six heavy blades were sheathed with copper.

The keel acted as a conduit along the hull for the passage of crew members or for fuel, lubrication oil, hydrogen and water to be piped to where it was needed. In flight the trim of the airship could be adjusted by pumping the liquid cargo forward or aft.

The control car was well forward under the nose. From

here, the airship was flown by the captain and navigator. The long passenger coach and cargo holds hung beneath the centre where their weight was evenly distributed.

After he had given them time to admire his creation, Graf Otto invited them to board her, and they assembled in the luxurious lounge. Glass observation windows ran the length of the outer walls of the long room. The guests were seated in leather-covered easy chairs, and the stewards served more champagne while they were divided into three separate groups. Then Graf Otto, Lutz and Ritter led them on a guided tour, pointing out the main features and answering questions. They returned to the main lounge for a lunch of oysters, caviar and smoked salmon, washed down with more champagne.

When they had finished eating, Graf Otto asked jovially, 'Which of you has flown before?'

Eva was the only one who held up her hand.

'Ah, so!' He laughed. 'Today we will change that.' He looked across at Lutz. 'Captain, please take our honoured guests on a little flight over the Bodensee.' They crowded to the observation windows, chattering and laughing like children, as Lutz started the engines. The *Assegai* seemed to come to life and quivered eagerly on her moorings. Then she rose gently aloft and her link to the mooring tower dropped away.

Lutz flew them as far as Friedrichshafen, then back down the centre of the lake. The water was a magical shade of azure, and the snows and glaciers of the Swiss Alps glowed in the sunlight. Then the airship returned to the Weiskirchen factory and hovered three thousand feet above the field. Quite unexpectedly, Graf Otto returned from the control car to the lounge, and his guests stared at him, perplexed: he had a large rucksack on his back held in place by an elaborate arrangement of harness straps.

'Ladies and gentlemen, you must have realized by now that the *Assegai* is an airship of surprises and wonders. I have one more to show you. The contraption on my back was dreamed up by Leonardo da Vinci more than four hundred years ago.

I have taken his idea and made it reality, by fitting it into a canvas pack.'

'What is it?' a woman asked. 'It looks very heavy and uncomfortable.'

'We call it a *Fallschirm*, but the French and the British know it as a parachute.'

'What does it do?'

'Exactly as the name implies. It breaks your fall.' He turned to two crew members and nodded. They slid aside the boarding doors. The guests standing nearest to them backed nervously away from the opening.

'Goodbye, dear friends! Think of me when I am gone.' Otto ran across the cabin and launched himself head first through the open door. The women shrieked and covered their mouths. Then there was a rush for the observation windows and they stared down in horror at Graf Otto's body, dwindling rapidly in size as it fell towards the earth. Then, abruptly, a long white pennant streamed from the bulky rucksack strapped to his back, snapped open and assumed the shape of a monstrous mushroom. Graf Otto's death plunge came to an abrupt halt and, miraculously, he was suspended in mid-air, in defiance of the laws of nature. The horror of the watchers was transformed to wonder, their chorus of despair to cheers and clapping. They watched as the gently sinking figure reached the ground and tumbled in an untidy heap, shrouded in the white sheet. Quickly Graf Otto struggled back to his feet and waved to them.

Lutz vented the valves on the airship's main hydrogen tanks and it sank down as softly as a feather from the breast of a high-flying goose. It settled on its bumpers along the keel and the ground crew rushed forward to secure the mooring line to the anchor mast.

When the main doors of the cabin were opened Graf Otto was standing at the threshold to welcome his guests back to earth. They crowded around him to shake his hand and heap their praises on him. Then once more they mounted the convoy of vehicles and drove back to the *Schloss*, their excited laughter and cries of congratulation on Graf Otto's extraordinary achievement echoing through the forest.

Dinner that evening was a formal occasion in the main dining room at a long walnut table, which could be extended to seat two hundred and fifty, as an orchestra played light airs in the high gallery. The walls were panelled with oak that had taken on the patina of age, and were hung with portraits of the von Meerbach ancestors, scenes of the hunt, and trophies, including racks of stag antlers and arrangements of wild boar tusks.

The men were in full dress uniform, with swords and decorations. The ladies were glorious in silks, satins and a dazzling array of jewels. Eva von Wellberg far outstripped the others in beauty and elegance, and Otto was unusually attentive to her. On many occasions he spoke to her down the length of the table, to include her in an anecdote or to solicit her opinion or confirmation on a topic under discussion.

When the band struck up a sequence of Strauss waltzes he monopolized her as his dance partner. For such a big man, Otto was remarkably light on his feet and possessed an animal presence such as that of a great African buffalo. In his arms Eva was as slim and graceful as a reed bending and swaying in a breeze off the lake. He was fully aware of what a striking pair they made, and thoroughly enjoyed the stir that followed them around the floor.

As the evening drew to a close, a trumpeter blew a flourish to draw the attention of the company. Then the band and the servants were sent out of the hall. The butler locked the windows, then doors behind him, after he, too, had withdrawn. Armed sentries stood outside the soundproof doors, but the select company were alone. Otto had not been able to resist this opportunity to celebrate his triumph. He wanted them to know the full extent of his achievements, and to revel in their adulation.

At last the senior officer present, Vice Admiral Ernst von Gallwitz, rose to his feet to make a speech of thanks to the host for his hospitality, dwelling at length on the technological marvels they had been shown at Weiskirchen. Then, choosing his moment skilfully, he said, 'The world and our enemies will soon be given a demonstration of the power and potential of Graf Otto's wondrous creation. As we are among friends, I can tell you that Kaiser Wilhelm the Second, our revered leader, has from the very beginning taken an intense interest in the development of this extraordinary machine. While we were changing for dinner, I was able to report to him by telephone and to inform him of what we have seen here today. I am delighted to tell you that he gave his unconditional sanction for Graf Otto to embark immediately on a daring plan that will stun the enemy with its genius.'

He turned to Graf Otto at the head of the table. 'Ladies and gentlemen, it is not gross overstatement to tell you that the man sitting among us quite literally holds the outcome of this war in his hands. He is about to set off on an epic journey, which if he accomplishes it successfully, will deliver an entire continent into our hands to the total confusion of our enemy.'

Graf Otto rose to his feet to acknowledge the applause. He glowed with pride, but his short speech of thanks to the admiral was modest and self-deprecating. They admired him all the more for it.

Much later, when they were upstairs in Otto's private wing of the *Schloss* readying themselves for bed, Eva heard him singing in his bathroom and, at intervals, letting fly a guffaw.

In tune with his mood she put on one of her most fetching satin nightdresses. She brushed her hair on to her shoulders, as she knew he liked it, and touched her lashes with mascara, skilfully giving her face a haunted and sorrowful aspect. As she worked she whispered to her image in the mirror, 'You have no inkling of the fact yet, dear Otto, but I know where you're going, and I'm going back to Africa with you ... to Africa and to Badger.'

When Otto strode into the bedroom he was wearing a dressing-gown she had never seen before. This was not surprising as the wardrobes in his dressing room were stuffed with such an accumulation of clothing that it required four full-time valets to keep it in order. He had never worn half of it. This dressing-gown was gold and imperial purple, its inner lining scarlet, with skirts that almost swept the ground. Despite its flamboyance he wore it with natural panache. He was still buoyed up by the success of the day, flushed with the honour and acclaim showered on him. With Otto this led inevitably to an elevated level of arousal, and she could see the bulge of his manhood thrusting out under his silk robe as he came towards her.

Eva was standing in the centre of the room, drooping tragically. For a few moments he did not seem to notice her distress, but as he held her in his arms and began to fondle her breasts he became aware of the coolness of her response and drew back to study her face. 'What is it that troubles you, my love?'

'You're going away again, and this time I know I will lose you for ever. Last time I so nearly lost you to the lion, and then I was taken by those savage Nandi tribesmen. Now something equally horrible is going to happen.' She let tears swamp her violet eyes. 'You can't leave me again,' she sobbed. 'Please! Please! Don't go.'

'I have to go.' He sounded bewildered, uncertain. 'You know I cannot stay. It is my duty and I have given my word.'

'Then you must take me with you. You cannot leave me behind.'

'Take you with me?' He seemed totally at a loss. He had never considered the idea.

'Yes! Oh, yes, please, Otto! There is no reason why I should not go with you.'

'You do not understand. It will be dangerous,' he said, 'very dangerous.'

'I have been in danger before with you at my side,' she pointed out. 'I will be safe if I am with you, Otto. I will be in much greater danger here. Soon the British may send their aeroplanes to bomb us.'

'What nonsense!' he scoffed. 'Only an airship can fly so far. The British do not have airships.' But he stood back from her to give himself space in which to gather his wits.

For once he was uncertain. In all these years he had never dared enquire too deeply into why she had stayed at his side for so long, apart from the material benefits she received from him. But surely by now even those must have palled. There must be some other more compelling incentive. He had never wanted to know those deeper reasons because they might devastate his manhood. Now he gazed deep into her eyes before he asked the question that had scorched his tongue for so long: 'You have never told me, and I have never dared ask, what do you truly feel for me, Eva, in your heart? Why are you still here?'

She had known that, in time, she would be faced with that question. She had prepared herself for the reply she must give, and had rehearsed it so often that it resonated with sincerity and conviction:

'I am here because I love you, and I want to be with you as long as you will have me.' For the first time ever, he looked vulnerable in a childlike way.

He sighed softly but deeply. 'Thank you, Eva. You will never know how much those words mean to me.'

'So you will take me with you?'

'Yes.' He nodded. 'There is no reason why we should ever be apart again as long as we both shall live. I would marry you if it were in my power to do so. You know that.'

'Yes, Otto. However, we have agreed not to speak of it again,' Eva reminded him.

Athala, his wife of almost twenty years and mother of his two sons, still refused to release him from his vows – God knows he had tried often enough to persuade her to do so. He smiled and straightened his shoulders. Visibly his usual ebullience and self-confidence flowed back into him. 'Then pack your bag. Take a pretty dress for the victory parade,' he said. 'We are going back to Africa.'

She rushed to him and stood on tiptoe to kiss his mouth. For once not even the taste of his cigar repelled her. 'To Africa? Oh, Otto, when shall we leave?'

'Soon, very soon. As you saw today, the airship is battle-ready, the crew is fully trained and aware of what is required of them. Now all depends on the moon phase and the forecasts for wind and weather. Ritter will be navigating day and night and he needs the light of the full moon. Full moon is on September the ninth, and our departure must be within three days either side of that date.'

F or most of that night Eva lay awake, listening to Otto's snores. Every once in a while he startled himself awake with their force and fury, but then he grunted and lapsed back into sleep. She was thankful for this last opportunity to consider what she had to do before they left on their journey. She must get one last message to Leon, confirming that Otto was bringing the Assegai to Africa, laden with arms and bullion for the Boer rebels, and that, almost certainly, he would fly down the Nile and through the Rift Valley on his way southwards. When she told him the date on which the Assegai would come, Leon's duty would be to prevent the airship getting through by any means, including, as a last resort, attacking it with lethal force. However, her immediate dilemma was whether or not she should warn him that she would be on board. If he knew she was, his concern for her safety might weaken his resolve. At the very least it would be deleterious to his performance of his duty. She decided not to tell him, and they would both have to take their chances when they met again in the high blue African skies.

The outbreak of the Great War had been signalled not by the stroke of a pen or a single fateful pronouncement. It had taken place like a train smash in which coach after coach had run without braking into a huge pile of wreckage. Driven by the impetus of their treaties of mutual aid, Austria had declared war on Serbia, Germany had declared war on Russia and France, and finally, on 4 August 1914, Britain had declared war on Germany. The fire and smoke that Lusima had foreseen had spread out to envelop the world.

Once more the population of the newly united South Africa was divided. Louis Botha was the former commander of the old Boer Army and his comrade in arms, General Jannie Smuts, had fought at his side against the combined forces of the British Empire. Most of the other Boer leaders hated the British and were strongly in favour of joining the conflict on the side of the Kaiser's Germany. It was only by the narrowest margin that Louis Botha carried Parliament with him and was able to send a cable to London informing the British Government that they were free to release all the imperial forces in southern Africa because he and his army would take over the defence of the southern half of the continent against Germany. Gratefully, London accepted his offer, then asked if Botha and his army could invade the neighbouring German South-west Africa and silence the radio stations at Lüderitzbucht and Swakopmund, which were sending a steady stream of vital information to Berlin, detailing all movements of the Royal Navy in the southern Atlantic. Botha agreed immediately, but in the meantime bloody revolt was brewing among his men.

Botha was only one of three former Boer leaders and heroes known as the Triumvirate. The other two were Christiaan de Wet and Herculaas 'Koos' de la Rey. De Wet had already declared for Germany, and all his men went with him. They were holed up in their fortified encampment on the edge of the Kalahari desert, and Botha had not yet sent a force to bring them in. Once he did, rebellion would break out in full force and the ravening beasts of civil war would burst raging from their cage.

Although de la Rey had not come out openly against Botha and Britain, nobody doubted that it was only a matter of time before he did so. They did not suspect that he was awaiting news from Germany on the flight of the *Assegai* from Weiskirchen to his succour. This news would be sent from Berlin through the powerful radio installation at Swakopmund in German South-west Africa, just over the border from South Africa.

In Weiskirchen the *Assegai* was taking on her final cargo. Graf Otto von Meerbach and Commodore Alfred Lutz struggled all night with the loading manifest. Much of the calculation was a matter of guesswork and instinct: no man alive had experienced flight in an airship over the Sahara desert during the summer months when air temperatures could range from fifty-five degrees centigrade at noon to zero at midnight.

The *Assegai*'s total gas volume was 2.5 million cubic feet of hydrogen, but daily she would be obliged to valve off large volumes of this to compensate for the weight of fuel she was burning. Otherwise she would become so light that she would go into an uncontrolled rush to upper space, where her crew would perish from cold and lack of oxygen. The main tanks were filled to the brim with 549,850 pounds of fuel, 4,680 pounds of oil and 25,000 pounds of water ballast. Her crew, of twenty-two men and one woman, and their severely restricted personal luggage weighed 3,885 pounds. Theoretically, this allowed a useful cargo of 35,800 pounds to be taken on board. But in the end Graf Otto decided to abandon 7,000 pounds of mortar bombs to make way for additional gold bullion. That would be the weight to swing the arms of the scale in their favour.

All the coin had been struck in eighteen-carat gold. There were almost equal amounts of authentic British sovereigns and

Deutsches Reich ten-mark coins. The money was packed first into small canvas bags, which were placed in sturdy ammunition cases, the lids securely screwed down. The final tally was 220 cases. Each case packed with coin weighed 110 troy pounds. This was the usual pack carried by an African porter on safari. Historically gold was always valued in American dollars and it had been fixed at twenty-one dollars per fine ounce for decades. Graf Otto was quick with figures: the value of his cargo in round terms would be nine million dollars, which, despite the current chaos in the exchange markets caused by the outbreak of war, was the equivalent of two million pounds sterling.

'That should be enough to keep the Boers smiling sweetly for a long time to come!' He personally supervised the baggage-handlers as they packed the chests in neat rows down the length of the main salon of the *Assegai* and lashed each one to the ring bolts in the deck. On top he laid the cases of live ammunition and the crates of Maxim machine-guns.

By the time the last had been secured, there was little space for the crew to move around the airship and attend to their duties. In an attempt to alleviate the problem, Graf Otto ordered that the bulkheads between the cabins be taken out and the bunks removed. The crew would be forced to sleep on the wooden deck. He had the chart and radio rooms knocked down, then moved forward to the control gondola under the bows. Three latrines were stripped out to make extra space; only one remained to provide for the needs of twenty-three people. There was to be no differentiation between the men and the woman, the senior officers and the Lascar cook. The laundry was dispensed with and the galley halved in size. A small electric stove would be enough to heat soup and coffee and turn out a pot of porridge each morning, but there would be no other hot food. The milk would be powdered; sausage, cold meat and hard biscuit would make up any shortfall. He would allow no alcohol on board. It would be a bare-bones ship, stripped of all but the necessities.

The last dinner before departure was a banquet held in the

Assegai's shed under the massive silver bulk of the airship. At the last moment one of the Meerbach limousines, driven by a uniformed chauffeur, brought Eva from the *Schloss*. She was wearing her flying gear, with boots, gloves and a goggled helmet. The chauffeur carried her valise, which was all the luggage she had.

Until she arrived the crew had not known she would be travelling with them. Her beauty and charm had made her a universal favourite, so they gave her a hearty welcome. Hennie du Rand had not seen her since the voyage back from Mombasa on the SS *Admiral*. Rough and graceless man of the soil that he was, he bowed and kissed her hand. His companions hooted with glee and he blushed like a schoolboy.

Eva was touched and felt a pang of guilt that she had deceived him with her pretence of not understanding what had taken place during his meeting with the Boer general.

When Graf Otto called her, she went to join him at the head of the dinner table. He introduced her as the expeddition's mascot. The company clapped and cheered. They were happy and excited, eager to set off on a journey that they knew would be considered an epic of airship travel.

The plates were piled high with Bavarian delicacies. Only the liquor was stinted: Graf Otto wanted clear heads and eyes on board when they took to the skies. The toasts were drunk in a light pilsener, in which the presence of alcohol was barely detectable.

At 2100 hours precisely Graf Otto came to his feet. 'Ah, so! My friends, it is time we were on our way to Africa.' There was another burst of cheering, then the crew hurried aboard and stood at their action stations. The ship was weighed off carefully, then walked out to her mooring mast. Standing in his makeshift radio room Graf Otto made final contact with Berlin Central. He received the Kaiser's personal good wishes and was told, 'God speed'. He turned off the transmitter and gave the launch orders to Commodore Lutz. The *Assegai* slipped her nose cable, rose gently into the golden summer twilight and turned on to a heading of 155 degrees.

Over the past weeks they had planned the flight in detail so there was little need to discuss it now. Lutz knew precisely what Graf Otto required of him and his crew. Showing no lights they ascended to their maximum safe cruising altitude of ten thousand feet as they floated over the Bodensee and ran on due south to cross the Mediterranean coastline a little after midnight a few miles west of Savona. They went on southwards, keeping the lights of the Italian coastal towns in sight on their port side.

They had a strong following wind as they crossed the island of Sicily, which carried them swiftly to their landfall on a nameless, bleak stretch of the Libyan desert somewhere west of Benghazi. As the sun rose Eva stood at the forward observation windows of the saloon and watched their gigantic shadow flitting across the ridges and dunes of the rugged brown terrain below. Africa! she exulted silently. Wait for me, my love. I am coming back to you.

The heat came up at them, sunlight reflected by the rock, and powerful eddies swirled around the ship, like the currents of some great ocean. She was lighter now that her four great Meerbach engines had burned off six thousand pounds of fuel and oil, but the sun heated the hydrogen in its chambers, increasing their lift. Inexorably the airship began to rise, and Lutz was forced to valve off 230,000 cubic feet of gas, but still she continued to climb until at fifteen thousand feet the crew felt the enervating effects of oxygen starvation. At the same time the temperature climbed dramatically and was soon registering 52 degrees centigrade in the control room. The engines had to be shut down in rotation to allow them to cool and for fresh oil to be pumped through the systems.

They were now flying light with six degrees of down angle on the controls. The airspeed bled away from 100 knots to fifty-five and the *Assegai* was failing to respond adequately to the helm. Then the forward port engine surged and cut out. With this sudden loss of power the airship stalled and dropped from thirteen thousand to six thousand feet before she responded to her helm again and came back on an even keel.

It had been an alarming plunge and part of the main cargo had broken loose.

Even Graf Otto was shaken by the *Assegai*'s erratic behaviour in the superheated air and agreed without argument to Lutz's suggestion that they should land and anchor the ship for the remainder of the day, to continue the journey in the evening. Lutz picked out an outcrop of black rock on the desert floor ahead that would afford an anchor point for the mooring cable and eased the ship downwards, valving off great quantities of hydrogen.

They were only fifty feet above the desert floor when a party of mounted men in flowing white burnous burst out from the rocks and galloped down a wadi towards them, brandishing curved short swords and firing up at the *Assegai* with long-barrelled jezails. A bullet smashed through the observation window beside Graf Otto and showered him with glass. He swore with annoyance and stepped across to the Maxim machine-gun mounted at the front of the gondola.

He levered a round into the breech, then swung the gun downwards on its mounting. He fired a short burst and the leading rank of charging Arabs disintegrated. Three horses went down, taking their riders with them. He traversed the gun right and fired again. Four more horses dropped, kicking, into the sand and the survivors scattered. Eva counted the casualties. Seven men were down, but two horses lunged back on to their feet and galloped after the rest.

'I don't think they'll be coming back,' he said casually. 'You can stand the watch down until eighteen hundred hours, Lutz. Then we'll start the engines again to fly on in the cool of the night.'

The last cablegram that Mr Goolam Vilabjhi had received from his niece in Altnau contained only a single number group. When Leon decoded it he found it was the date that Eva had promised to send him: that on which the *Assegai* would commence its flight from Weiskirchen. In her previous cables, she had given him the name that Graf Otto had chosen for his machine, with its design number. The *Assegai* was a Mark ZL71. She had already outlined the course he intended to follow on his flight to South Africa. From this Leon had calculated when the airship might arrive over the Great Rift. Now all he needed was a plan of action that offered even a remote chance of success in bringing the massive ship to earth, then capturing its crew and cargo. With Penrod gone and Frederick Snell able to block his efforts, Leon was on his own.

He had seen drawings of the type of airship he was up against. When Graf Otto had been evacuated from Nairobi to Germany after his mauling, he had left piles of books and magazines in his private quarters at Tandala Camp. They were mostly technical engineering publications and one contained a long, illustrated article on the construction and operation of a large dirigible. It had included numerous drawings of the various types, including the Mark ZL71. Now Leon retrieved it and studied it carefully.

Far from being of help or inspiration, he found the illustrations and descriptions thoroughly discouraging. The airship was so enormous and so well protected, it flew so fast and high, that there seemed no possible way to prevent it getting through. He tried to imagine a comparison for the little *Butterfly* and this behemoth of the skies: a field mouse alongside a black-maned lion, perhaps, or a termite beside a pangolin?

He cast his mind back to the prophecy that Lusima had made for them when first he had taken Eva to Lonsonyo Mountain to meet her. She had conjured up the image of a great silver fish obscured by smoke and flame. When he looked at the illustration, in Graf Otto's book, of the airship with its mighty fish-tailed rudder and generally piscine shape, he had no doubt that this was what she had foreseen. He wondered if there was any more she could tell him, but that was unlikely: Lusima never enlarged on an original prediction. She gave you the kernel, and it was up to you to make of it what you could.

Leon was isolated and abandoned. He had lost Eva and he knew that there was only a remote chance that he would see her again. It was as though a vital part of his body had been cut away. Penrod was gone too. He never thought he would miss his uncle, but he felt the loss intensely. He needed help and advice, and there was only one person left in his life who might provide it.

He called for Manyoro, Loikot and Ishmael. 'We're going to Lonsonyo Mountain,' he told them.

Within half an hour they were airborne and winging down the Rift Valley, headed for Percy's Camp. When they landed he found it in disarray. Both Hennie du Rand and Max Rosenthal had been gone for some time and Leon had been so distracted by Eva that he had taken no interest in the day-to-day operation of the camp. He had left it to his untrained and unsupervised staff.

He was not seriously concerned by this state of affairs. The future was uncertain, and it was highly unlikely that there would be any hunting guests to entertain until the cessation of hostilities, and probably for many years after peace was restored. He lingered in camp just long enough to select the mounts and make up the packs before they rode out towards the great blue silhouette of the mountain on the western horizon. His spirits lifted with every mile that brought them closer to it.

They made camp that evening at the base of Lonsonyo, and he sat late beside the fading embers of the campfire, staring up at the dark massif against the starry splendour of the African night sky. He found himself studying the mountain in a way he never had before. For the first time he was seeing it as a potential battlefield over which his little *Butterfly* might soon be pitted against the menace of Graf Otto's mighty *Assegai*.

It had worried him that he would have to wait until Loikot's *chungaji* scouts spotted the airship's approach, before he could take off to intercept it. He would be at an enormous disadvantage. The *Assegai* would be at her cruising altitude of ten thousand feet so he would have to climb up and over the massif of Lonsonyo Mountain under full power from all his engines to meet her, which meant burning most of her fuel reserves as he pushed the *Butterfly* to the limit of her operational ceiling. And if the winds, humidity and air temperature were in the *Assegai*'s favour she might sweep on over his head and be gone before Leon could coax the *Butterfly* high enough.

He felt discouraged and depressed by the prospect of such an abysmal defeat and stared up angrily at the mountain. At that moment a ripple of distant sheet lightning far down the Rift Valley near Lake Natron backlit the heights boldly. The massif seemed like the glacis of an enemy castle, a great obstacle he must overcome.

Then some odd trick of the light and the play of lightning changed his perspective. He started to his feet, knocking his coffee mug flying. 'By God, what's wrong with me?' he shouted at the sky. 'It's been under my nose all along. Lonsonyo is not my obstacle but my springboard!' Now the ideas poured over him, like water from a ruptured dam wall.

'That open tableland in the rainforest that Eva and I discovered! I knew it was significant the moment I laid eyes on it. It's a natural landing strip on the highest point of Lonsonyo. With fifty strong men to help I could clear the undergrowth in a couple of days, enough to be able to land her up there and get her off again. I won't have to chase after the *Assegai*. I need only wait on the mountaintop and let her come to me. What is most important, I'll be able to open the game with the advantage of height. I'll be able to swoop down

on her instead of climbing up laboriously to intercept her.' He
was so excited that he slept only a few hours, and was on the
pathway to the summit long before sunrise the next morning.

Lusima Mama was waiting for them under a favourite tree
beside the path. She greeted her sons and made them sit one
on each side of her. 'Your flower is not with you, M'bogo.' It
was a statement, not a question. 'She has gone to that land
far to the north.'

'When will she return, Mama?' Leon asked.

She smiled. 'Do not seek to know that which is not for us
to know. She will come in the fullness of days.'

Leon shrugged helplessly. 'Then let us speak of that which
is for us to know. I have a favour to ask of you, Mama.'

'I have fifty men waiting for you near my hut. It is fortunate
that the Mkuba Mkuba has already cleared much of the
ground for you with his lightning bolt.' She smiled slyly at
him. 'But you do not believe that, do you, my son?'

Lusima accompanied the expedition to the open tableland
above the waterfall. She sat in the shade and watched her
men labour. Leon soon understood why she had come: under
her eye the team worked like a pack of demons and by noon
on the second day he was able to pace out the extent of the
ground they had opened up. At such high altitude the air was
thin and he would have to maintain a high approach speed to
avoid stalling his aircraft. It would be a near-run thing to get
the *Butterfly* down on such a short runway. In fact, it would
have been impossible if it were not for the slope and aspect of
the ground. The landing strip was on the very edge of the
cliffs. If he made his approach from the valley side, the strip
would be at an uphill angle, and once he touched down, the
slope would bring her to a rapid standstill. On the other hand,
if he took off down the slope the *Butterfly* would accelerate
and reach her flying speed equally swiftly. Then when he shot
off the top of the cliff he could hold her nose down in a
shallow dive and her airspeed would rocket up.

'Interesting times ahead for all of us,' he told himself. He
had not yet considered the nub of the problem. If everything

worked out as he hoped the *Assegai* would come down the Rift Valley from the north. She would not be flying higher than ten thousand feet above sea level: her crew would be in danger of oxygen starvation if she flew higher than that for any extended period.

There was no possibility that Graf Otto could bring the monster down the centre of the valley without being spotted by the network of bright-eyed *chungaji*. Leon would have ample warning of his approach, certainly enough time to get the *Butterfly* airborne and into her patrol station. 'But what happens then?' he asked himself. 'A gunfight between the two of us?'

He laughed at that ludicrous notion. From the illustrations he had seen of the airship, the *Assegai* would be armed with at least three or four Maxim machine-guns, which would be served by trained German airmen from a stable firing platform. Taking them on from the *Butterfly*, with his two Masai armed with service rifles, would be a novel means of committing suicide.

He had been able to beg two hand grenades from Hugh Delamere, and had a vague idea of flying above the *Assegai* and dropping one on top of her great domed hull. There would be two and a half million cubic feet of highly explosive hydrogen in her hull and the resulting fireball would be spectacular. As the grenades had only a six-second delay after they connected with their target, though, the *Butterfly* would be near the centre of it.

'There must be a better plan than frying myself,' he murmured ruefully. 'I just have to find it before I run out of time.' According to Eva's last cablegram from Switzerland, there were only five days to go before the *Assegai* was due to leave Weiskirchen. 'I haven't even had a chance to test the feasibility of the new landing strip. We must go to Percy's Camp tomorrow to fetch the *Butterfly* and bring her here.'

Leon decided to sleep that night at Lusima's hut and head down the mountain at first light the next day. He and Lusima sat side by side at the fire, sharing a bowl of cassava porridge for dinner. She was in an expansive mood and Leon was encouraged by this to speak of Eva. He was trying to milk from Lusima any details or suggestions that might be of value in the endeavour that lay ahead. He could see by the wicked twinkle in her dark eyes that she knew exactly what he had in mind, but he persisted and framed his questions as subtly as he could. They spoke of Eva and he reiterated his love for her.

'The little flower is worthy of that love,' Lusima agreed.

'Yet she has gone from me. And I despair that I will ever see her again.'

'You must never despair, M'bogo. Without hope we are nothing.'

'Mama, you spoke to us once of a great silver fish in the sky that brings fortune and love.'

'I grow old, my son, and more often these days I speak great stupidity.'

'Mama, that is the first and only stupidity I have ever heard you utter.' Leon smiled at her, and she smiled back. 'It comes to me that soon the fish you do not remember will take to the sky.'

'All things are possible, but what do I know of fish?'

'I thought in my own stupidity that, as my mother, you might be able to tell me how to catch this fish of fortune and love.'

She was silent for a long time and then she shook her head. 'I know nothing about the catching of fish. You should ask a fisherman about that. Perhaps one of the fishermen of Lake Natron might teach you.'

He stared at her in astonishment, then slapped his forehead. 'Fool!' he said. 'Oh, Mama, your son is a fool! Lake Natron! Of course! The fishing nets! That's what you were trying to tell me!'

Leaving Loikot and Ishmael on the mountain, Leon and Manyoro hurried to Percy's Camp. He wanted to keep the load on the plane for landing on the mountain to a minimum.

From Percy's Camp they took off almost immediately for Lake Natron. This time Leon took no chances with another landing on soft ground: he put the *Butterfly* down safely on the firm surface of the soda pan. He and Manyoro bargained with the chieftain of the fishing village and finally bought four lengths of old, damaged netting from him, each roughly two hundred paces long. As they had not been used recently they were dust-dry, but even so, the weight taxed the power of the *Butterfly*'s Meerbach engines. Leon had to make four separate flights to the makeshift landing strip on top of the mountain, carrying one net at a time, each landing a challenge to his skill as a pilot. He had to bring the *Butterfly* in fast to keep her just above stall speed and made a heavy touch-down that strained the landing gear to its limit.

By the afternoon of the second day they had all four nets laid out on the open ground. They sewed them together in pairs so that finally they had two separate nets, each about four hundred paces long.

There would be no opportunity for practice or experiment with packing and deploying the nets. They would go straight into action against the *Assegai*, and had only one chance of unfurling the nets successfully. Leon hoped that, with the first attack, he might be able to entangle the propellers of the airship's two rear engines and slow her down to the extent that he had time to return to Lonsonyo landing strip and load the second length for another attack.

One of the many critical aspects of the scheme was to pack the net so that it would unfurl from the bomb bay and stream out behind the *Butterfly* in an orderly fashion. Then, once Leon had entangled the airship's propellers in the mesh, he had to be able to release the net from its retaining hooks

before the *Butterfly* became snarled up in it. He had to be able
to break away cleanly. If he failed to get clear, his aircraft
would be dragged along tail-first behind the stricken airship.
Her wings and fuselage would be broken up by the unnatural
forces brought to bear upon them. There were so many
imponderables that it would all depend on guesswork, team-
work, quick reactions to any unexpected development and an
inordinate amount of good old-fashioned luck.

By the evening of the fourth day the *Butterfly* stood at the
head of the short strip of cleared ground with her nose pointed
down the slope, the cliff face falling away abruptly at the end
of the runway. Twenty porters waited in readiness to throw
their combined weight behind her and give her a push start
down the slope.

At dawn and dusk each day Loikot had stood on the
heights of Lonsonyo and exchanged shouts with his *chungaji*
companions across the length and breadth of Masailand. It
seemed that the eyes of every *morani* in the territory were
fastened on the northern sky: all hoped to be first to spot the
approach of the silver fish monster.

Leon and his crew sat under a crudely thatched sun-shelter
beside the fuselage of the *Butterfly*. When the call came they
could be at their stations in the cockpit within seconds. There
was nothing they could do now but wait.

It looked like a solid unbroken wall in the sky, stretching
across the eastern horizon and reaching from the dun
desert floor to the milky blue of the heavens. Eva was
alone in the control gondola of the *Assegai*. The airship was
on the ground, moored for the day, and she was standing her
watch like any of the officers. Every other member of the crew
was either off-duty and resting after the night flight or busy
servicing and tuning the main engines. Graf Otto was in the
nacelle that housed the forward port engine. Despite four
hours of determined effort he and his men were still unable to

restart it, and had realized the extent of the damage. They were stripping the crank case to get to the root of the problem.

Eva knew that sounding the alarm was not a decision that could be taken lightly. She hesitated a few minutes longer, but in the short time that the eastern horizon had been blotted out by the approaching yellow wall, the speed of its advance was startling. She could see that it was no longer solid but swirled and rolled upon itself, like a dense cloud of yellow smoke. Suddenly she knew what it was. She had read about it in books written by desert travellers. It was one of the most dangerous natural phenomena. She breathed the single word, 'Khamsin!' and darted across the bridge to the ship's main telegraph. She yanked down the handle and the jangling of the emergency bells drowned every other sound.

From the main cabin, crew members stumbled from their mattresses, still more than half asleep, and stared out at the approaching sandstorm. Some were stunned into silence by its size and ferocity, while others jabbered at each other in panic and confusion.

Graf Otto came racing up the companion ladder from the gondola of the damaged engine. He stared at the storm for only a second before he took control. Within minutes two of the three serviceable engines were running, and he signalled the docking team to release the mooring cable from the bows.

The third engine in the forward port gondola was silent. The engineer there was still having difficulty starting her. 'Take command, Lutz!' he shouted. 'I have to go down and get that engine running.' He ran out on to the open catwalk and disappeared down the ladder to the engine nacelle.

Lutz ran to his control panel and opened all eight gas valves. Hydrogen rushed into the *Assegai*'s gas chambers and she flung up her nose so violently that Eva and those men who had no handholds were thrown to the deck as she went into a nose-high climb with half a million cubic feet of buoyant gas hurtling her aloft.

The atmospheric pressure dropped so rapidly that the needle of the barometer spun giddily around the dial. Lutz, the ship's commander, who was suffering from an infected sinus, squealed with pain and clutched at his ears. A thin trickle of blood ran down his cheek as an eardrum ruptured. He doubled over and fell to his knees. There was no other officer on the bridge who could take over from him, so Eva dragged herself to her feet and, pulling herself along the handrail, she reached Lutz before he lost consciousness with the pain. 'What must I do?' she screamed.

'Vent!' he moaned. 'Blow the gas from all the chambers. Red handles!' She reached up, took hold of them and forced them down with all her strength. She heard the escaping gas howling from the main vents above. The airship shuddered and bucked, but her uncontrolled climb steadied, and the needle on the barometer slowed its wild gyration.

Graf Otto had come up the giraffe neck of the companion ladder from the forward engine gondola, where he had gone to start the engine. Now he was pinned on the open catwalk, clinging to the side-rail while the *Assegai*'s violent manoeuvres threatened to hurl him into space like a pebble from a slingshot. He was fifty feet from Eva and yelled at her urgently, 'Both starboard throttles, full ahead.'

She obeyed him instinctively and the engines thundered, driving the airship's nose around in a counter-turn. For a few moments she steadied sufficiently for Graf Otto to release his death grip on the rail and run lightly along the catwalk. He burst in through the main doors as the *Assegai* started to spin in a clockwise direction. He reached Eva's side and grabbed the controls. His movements were quick and co-ordinated to those of the *Assegai*. He gentled the great airship like a runaway horse, but before he had her steady she had climbed to fourteen thousand feet and was taking a terrible buffeting from the khamsin winds. However, the full force of the storm passed under the hull and left her at nine thousand feet, running southwards on an even keel. But she had been battered by the winds: the forward port engine was damaged beyond hope of repair, and a number of struts in the framework of the gas chambers had been broken. The shell bulged over these weak spots, but she was still making eighty knots and her cargo had been secured and lashed down.

Ahead they could just make out the shape of the Nile winding through the desert. Suddenly the radio squawked and Graf Otto started with surprise. This was the first contact they had heard since they had crossed the Mediterranean coastline.

'It's the naval radio at Walvis Bay on the south-west coast.' The operator looked up from his set. 'They're asking for a secure contact with Graf von Meerbach. They have an urgent top-secret message for you.'

Graf Otto handed the helm to Thomas Bueler, the first officer, and put on the earphones. He turned the switch to suppress the sound so that only he could hear the transmission. He listened intently, his expression darkening, and flushed with anger. At last he ended the contact and went to stand at the forward window, staring down at the mighty river passing below.

At last he seemed to reach a difficult decision and growled brusquely at Bueler, 'In ten minutes, assemble the entire ship's company in the control room. I want them seated in two ranks down the centre of the deck, facing forward. I am going to make an important announcement.' He stumped out and went to the tiny cubby-hole cabin that he and Eva shared.

When he emerged, Eva was filled with dread: he had changed his artificial hand. In place of the steel finger and thumb, he now wore the menacing spike-headed mace. The crew, too, were staring at the strange weapon, which he made no effort to conceal as he took up a position facing the two rows of seated men. He glared at them in silence until they were sweating and fidgeting with anxiety. Then he said, in a cold hard tone, 'Gentlemen, we have a traitor on board.' He let them think about that for a while. Then he went on, 'The enemy has been alerted to our mission. They have been informed of our course and movements. Berlin is ordering us to abort the operation.'

Suddenly he lifted his armoured fist and slammed it into the chart table. The panel shattered into splinters. 'I am not turning back,' he snarled. 'I know who this traitor is.' He prowled down the front rank of seated figures, and stopped behind Eva. She felt herself cringe inwardly and steeled herself. 'I am a man who does not readily forgive treachery. The traitor is about to learn that.' She wanted to scream and run out on to the catwalk, hurl herself over the side of the airship and die a clean, quick death rather than be mutilated and crushed by that steel fist. He touched the top of her head gently. 'Who is it? you are wondering,' he whispered.

She opened her mouth to shout defiance at him, dare him to do his worst. Then she felt him lift his hand from her head, and he walked on down the line. She felt hot, bitter bile rise in her throat, and it took all her strength to prevent herself vomiting with terror.

At the end of the line of men Graf Otto turned, and then he was coming back towards her. Her bowels felt as though they were filled with hot water and that she had to vent them. His footsteps stopped and she drew a quivering breath. It sounded as though he was directly behind her again.

She heard the blow and almost screamed. The sound was not as loud as the shattering of the chart table had been. It was a muffled wet thump and she clearly heard bone break. She whipped around as Hennie du Rand fell forward on his face. Graf Otto stood over him and swung the iron fist again and again, lifting the mace high, then putting all his weight and strength behind the blows. When he straightened up he was breathing hard and his face was speckled with droplets of blood.

'Throw the filthy dog overboard,' he ordered, in a milder tone, and he was smiling. 'It's always those you trust most who betray you. I repeat, gentlemen, there is no turning back. But we cannot allow our cargo to fall into the hands of the British. If we maintain our speed, by noon tomorrow we will have reached Arusha in German territory and be safely through the worst of it.'

He walked slowly from the cabin and Eva covered her eyes with both hands as two crewmen laid hold of Hennie's ankles and dragged his corpse out on to the catwalk. Between them they lifted him over the rail and let him drop into the Nile valley, far below. Eva found herself weeping silently but each teardrop seemed to burn her eyes, like the sting of a bee.

The moon was so near full that when Eva woke and went to the observation car it was low over the high ground of the escarpment, glowing like a huge gold coin. She watched it sink below the dark horizon, shrouded by garlands of cloud that were blowing in on the monsoon winds streaming from the Indian Ocean. Before it disappeared completely, the first rays of the rising sun sparkled on the silver dome of the airship, and gradually the details of the landscape reappeared out of the darkness. Then her heart was thumping against her ribs as she saw the familiar outline of Lonsonyo Mountain taking shape before her eyes. Every detail was etched on her memory. She recognized the red cliffs above Sheba's Pool and saw the foaming waters sparkle at the touch of the first sunbeams. It was as though Badger was with her again. In her mind's eye she saw every plane and angle of his naked torso as he stood under the cascading falls and laughed at her, teasing her, daring her to come to him.

Oh, my darling, she lamented silently, where are you now? Will I never see you again?

Then, miraculously he was before her, so close that if she reached out her hand she could have touched his beautiful sun-browned face. He was gazing directly into her eyes. It was only for the most fleeting moment, but she saw that he had recognized her, and then he was gone, as suddenly as he had come.

Leon was still asleep, buried in his blankets. He heard distant voices through the last shreds of sleep, the calling of the *chungaji* in the stillness of the dawn. Something in their tone had alerted him. He forced himself awake as Loikot shook him with a hand on each of his shoulders. 'M'bogo!' His voice rang with excitement. 'The silver fish is coming! The *chungaji* have seen it. It will be here before the sun is clear of the horizon.'

Leon leaped to his feet and was, in the instant, fully awake. 'Start up!' he shouted at Manyoro. 'Number-one port side.' He scrambled up on to the *Butterfly*'s lower wing, then swung himself over the cockpit coaming.

'Suck in!' he shouted, and primed the carburettor. The machine seemed as eager for the hunt as he was. The engines caught and fired on the first swing of the propeller. While he waited for them to run up to full operating temperature he peered up at the sky. From the clouds he saw that a stiff breeze was coming in from the ocean, blowing straight down the short, narrow runway. It was the perfect wind for take-off. It seemed as though the gods of the chase were already smiling on him.

Loikot and Ishmael climbed into the cockpit, and when Manyoro scrambled up behind them, it seemed as though there was not enough space for all of them. He eased open the throttles and the *Butterfly* rolled forward. The Masai porters on the wing-tips swung her around to line up on the runway and then, as he opened the throttles wide, they shoved with all their strength on the trailing edges of the wings. The *Butterfly* accelerated away swiftly, but not swiftly enough, for she was still under her flying speed as they came to the end of the runway and the cliff face dropped away. Leon's instinct for survival warned him to stand hard on the wheel brakes and save them from the plunge, but he went against it and kept all the throttles pressed hard up against the stops. The engines were howling in full power, and at that moment he felt a stronger blast of air hit his face. It was a freak, a stray unlooked-for gust. He felt it get under the *Butterfly*'s wings and give her a gentle lift. For a moment he thought even that was not enough. He felt one wing drop as she staggered on the edge of stalling and forced her nose down mercilessly. He felt her bite into the wind and suddenly they were flying. He kept her nose down as his airspeed rocketed to a hundred knots, then eased back on the control wheel. She climbed away gamely, but he was panting with fear. For a moment they had been on the verge of death.

He put the fear behind him and looked ahead. They all saw it at the same time: the enormous silver fish gleaming in the early sunlight. He thought he had been prepared for his first sight of her, but he discovered he was not. The sheer size of the *Assegai* astonished Leon. It was several hundred feet below the *Butterfly* and had almost passed their position. A few minutes more and they would have lost her for ever. But the *Butterfly* was in a perfect position for him to close with her. He was above and behind her, sitting perfectly in her blind spot. He pushed the nose down and went for her. As he closed with her swiftly she seemed to balloon in size until she filled his entire field of vision. He saw that one of the forward motors was already out of commission, the propeller standing upright as rigidly as a sentry on guard duty. The two rear engines were mounted in their gondolas just below and abaft the passenger and cargo cabin. He was so intrigued that he almost forgot to give his crew the order to deploy the entangling net.

He knew that this was one of the most critical moments of the plan. It would have been so easy to entangle his own tail skid or landing gear as the net spread out behind him. But the easterly monsoon wind pushed its heavy folds gently to one side so that they streamed out perfectly four hundred feet behind the *Butterfly*. He let her slide down the side of the airship's gas chamber, overtaking slowly until he was flying level with the observation cabin and command bridge.

It came as a shock to see live human beings behind the

glass windows. Somehow the airship had seemed to have a monstrous life of its own, entirely divorced from anything human. Yet there was Graf Otto von Meerbach only fifty feet away, glaring at him with an expression of outrage, his mouth working silently as he shouted obscenities that were lost in the thunder of the engines. Then he spun around and ran to man the machine-gun mounted in the angle of the bridge.

Leon froze with shock when he saw Eva standing behind the German. For an instant he was looking into her deep violet eyes as she stared back at him in bewilderment. Graf Otto was working the loading bolt and traversing the fat water-cooled jacket of the gun towards him. Leon roused himself and put the wing of the *Butterfly* hard over just as Graf Otto fired the first burst. The tracer bullets arced out towards him, but Leon cut sharply across the front of the airship's control bridge. The burst of tracer flew high and behind him.

The *Assegai*'s two rear engines were hanging down vulnerably below the keel. Leon glanced back at the long line of netting trailing behind the *Butterfly*, and then, judging the relative angles and speed of the two aircraft finely, he dragged the net across the spinning propeller blades of the airship's engines. They snatched up the folds and wound them almost instantly into tight balls that smothered them. It had happened so quickly that he was almost taken off guard.

'Let fly!' Leon screamed at Manyoro, who reacted swiftly, heaving with both hands on the release handle. The retaining hooks opened, allowing the heavy rope to drop away cleanly, an instant before it could pluck the *Butterfly* from the sky. The airship's huge fishtail rudder brushed their upper wing as it passed over them. And then the *Butterfly* was free and clear. Leon brought her around and climbed back into the position above and behind the *Assegai*, keeping in her blind spot. The burst of tracer from the Maxim machine-gun had come too close. He would not make that mistake again.

He watched smoke billow from the airship's rear engines. The netting and heavy drag lines were so deeply tangled in the propeller bosses and other moving parts that both had seized up and cut out. The *Assegai* was no longer responding to her helm. The single forward engine did not have the power to hold her against the cross-wind of the monsoon and she began to pay off sharply and drift straight for the rocky cliff face of Lonsonyo Mountain. The helmsman was running her with the throttle wide open and the strain was too much. Now the surviving engine started to blow blue smoke from under her cowling as it overheated.

Graf Otto ran across the control room, grabbed the helmsman by the shoulders and flung him aside. He crashed into the window head first and dropped to the deck, blood pouring from his broken nose. Graf Otto seized the wheel and looked up at the cliffs. They were only half a mile away, at least a thousand feet below the summit, and the only way to avoid colliding with them was to inflate the gas chambers to their utmost and take her up as fast as she would climb and try to skim over the top. He reached for the valve control and pulled it wide open. Instead of a rush of hydrogen squealing through the inlet pipes, there was a weak hiss, and although the airship shuddered, she rose only sluggishly.

'Hydrogen tanks are flat!' he screamed with frustration. 'We blew off all the gas in the desert, fighting against the khamsin. We'll never make it. We're going to run full into the cliff. We'll have to jump! Ritter, get out the parachutes. There are enough for all of us.'

Ritter led a rush for the storeroom behind the bridge and they started to fling the parachute packs through the door into a pile on the deck. There was a panic-driven scramble as the men fought over them. Graf Otto shouldered them out of his way and grabbed one in each hand. He ran back to Eva. 'Put this on.'

'I don't know how to do it,' she protested.

'Well, you have about two minutes to learn,' he told her grimly, and slipped the harness over her shoulders. 'As soon as you're clear of the airship you must count to seven, then pull this cord. The parachute will do the rest.' He pulled the straps of the harness tightly across her chest. 'As soon as you hit the ground, open these buckles and get rid of the chute.' He buckled on his own parachute and day pack, then dragged her to the doorway, which was already blocked with men fighting to get out.

'Otto, I can't do this,' Eva cried, but he did not argue with her. He seized her around the waist and carried her bodily, struggling, to the doorway. With powerful kicks he booted the two men ahead of him out of the way, and as soon as the doorway was open he threw Eva out. As she dropped away he shouted after her, 'Count to seven, then pull the cord.'

He watched her fall towards the top gallery of the rainforest. Just when it seemed she must crash into the branches her parachute burst open and jerked her so violently that her body swung on the shrouds like a puppet's. He did not wait to see her land but stepped out into space and plunged towards the trees.

Leon held the *Butterfly* in a tight turn above the cliffs and peered down at the human bodies spilling out of the hatchway in the airship's control cabin. He saw at least three parachutes fail to open and the men drop, arms and legs flailing, until they hit the treetops. Others more fortunate were carried away on the monsoon wind like thistledown and scattered across the mountainside. Then Eva was falling free, smaller and slimmer than any of the men. He bit his lip hard as he waited for her parachute to open, then shouted with relief as the white silk blossomed above her. She was already so low that, within seconds, she had been sucked into the dense green mass of the jungle.

The *Assegai* floated on, nose high and yawing aimlessly across the wind. She was rising slowly but he knew at a glance that she would never clear the top of the cliff. Her tail touched the trees and she came around abruptly. Like a stranded jellyfish she rolled on to her side and her cavernous gas chambers snagged in the upper branches of the trees. They collapsed and the airship deflated like a punctured balloon. Leon braced himself for the explosion of hydrogen that he was sure must follow – it needed but a spark from the damaged generators – but nothing happened. As the gas gushed out and was dispersed by the wind, the *Assegai* settled in a shapeless mass of canvas and wreckage on the jungle tops, breaking down even the largest branches under her massive weight.

Leon put the *Butterfly* into a tight turn and flew back only a few feet over the wreck. He tried to see down into the forest, hoping desperately for a glimpse of Eva, but he could see nothing of her. He circled back and made one more fly-past. This time he saw a body hanging lifelessly on the shrouds of a parachute, the silk tangled in the branches of a tall tree. He was so low now that he could recognize Graf Otto.

'He's dead,' Leon decided. 'Broken his rotten bloody neck at last.' Then the *Butterfly* was directly over him and her lower wing blocked Leon's line of sight. He did not see Graf Otto lift his head and look up at the aircraft.

Leon turned back and put the *Butterfly* into a climb for the landing strip, keeping low along the cliff face so that he did not waste a moment. He wanted to get back and find Eva. As he flew past the cascading white waterfall and looked down into Sheba's Pool at the foot, he checked his landmarks carefully. He was only a few minutes' flight from the wreck of the *Assegai*, but he knew it would be heavy going to cover the same ground on foot. The moment he landed and cut the engines he reached under the seat to pull out his gun case. With three quick movements he reassembled the stock and barrels and loaded the chambers of his big Holland. Then he swung his legs over the side of the cockpit and jumped down, shouting orders to the crowd of waiting *morani* who ran forward to meet him.

'Hurry! Get your spears. The memsahib is out there alone in the forest. She may be hurt. We have to find her fast.' He raced down the slope, hurdling low bushes. The warriors following him were hard put to keep him in sight through the trees.

S winging wildly on her parachute shrouds Eva stared down as the forest tops rushed up to meet her. She crashed through the uppermost branches, twigs breaking and crackling around her head. Each time she collided with another branch it slowed her a little more, until she hit the ground in a small clearing on the mountainside.

The slope was steep so she let herself roll head over heels until she came to rest in a patch of swamp. She remembered Graf Otto's advice and tugged frantically at the buckles of her harness until she could shrug herself free. Then she got gingerly to her feet and checked herself for injuries. There were a few scratches on her arms and legs and her left buttock was bruised, but then she remembered the terror of being thrown out of the airship and saw how lucky she had been.

She squared her shoulders and lifted her chin.

'Now, where will I find Badger? If only I had some idea of where he came from, but he popped up out of the blue.' She thought about it for no more than a few seconds before she answered her own question. 'Sheba's Pool, of course! It's the first place he will look for me.'

She knew the ground so well because she and Leon had wandered over it on their forays about the slopes during the enchanted months they had spent at Lusima's *manyatta*. Now a sudden glimpse of the cliff face through the jungle helped her to orientate her present position. 'The waterfall can't be more than a few miles to the south,' she told herself.

She started off, using the direction of the slope to guide her and keeping the line of the cliff on her right hand. But then she pulled up sharply. There was a commotion in the bushes ahead and a hideous spotted hyena bolted out of the thicket, a strip of tattered raw flesh dangling from its jaws. She had disturbed its meal of carrion.

She went forward cautiously and found the corpse of Thomas Bueler, the first officer, lying crumpled in the shrubbery. He was one of those whose parachute had failed to open. She recognized him by his uniform: most of his face was missing – the hyena had torn it away. She was about to hurry on down the path but then she saw that Bueler had a small rucksack fastened to the front of his harness – that was why the parachute had failed to open: it had snagged the shrouds of his chute. Perhaps it contained something that would help her to survive, alone and unarmed, on the mountain.

She knelt beside the corpse and forced herself not to look at its mutilated face as she opened the rucksack. She found a small first-aid kit, several packets of dried fruit and smoked meat, a tin of Vestas for fire-making and a 9mm Mauser pistol in its wooden holster with two spare clips of ammunition. All these things could be invaluable.

She disentangled the strap of the rucksack from the parachute harness and slung it over her shoulder, then jumped up and hurried along the game path. Half a mile further on she heard Otto's voice, calling plaintively for help from a little higher up the slope: 'Can anybody hear me? Ritter! Bueler! Come! I need your help.' She turned off the game trail she was following and moved cautiously towards the sound. When he called again, she looked up and found him. He was hanging high in the canopy. His shrouds had wrapped around a large branch, and he was dangling seventy feet above the ground, swinging himself back and forth, trying to get a grip on the branch from which he was suspended, but he could not muster sufficient momentum to reach it.

Eva looked around her carefully. None of the *Assegai* crew was in sight. They were alone in the forest. She was about to sneak away and continue her escape when he spotted her. 'Eva! Thank God you have come.' She stopped. 'Come, Eva, you must help me to get down. If I open my harness I will fall to my death. But I have a light rope in my pack.' He reached under its flap and pulled out a hank of jute twine. 'I am going to drop the end of it to you. You must pull me towards the branch so I can get a hold on it.' She stood perfectly still, staring up at him. Now that he knew she had survived the crash she could not leave him. He would follow her. He would never let her escape.

'Hurry, woman. Don't just stand there. Take the end of the line,' he shouted impatiently.

For the first time in their long relationship he was totally in her power. This was the man who had murdered her father, the one who had humiliated and tortured her mentally and physically. This was the moment for retribution. If she killed him now she could expunge all those memories. She would be clean and whole. Moving as slowly as a sleep-walker, she came towards him, at the same time reaching into Bueler's pack.

'Yes, Eva, that's good. I know I can always depend on you. Take the rope.' There was a wheedling tone in his voice that she had never heard before. She felt strength and resolution flowing through her body. The hilt of the Mauser fitted perfectly into her hand.

'I am the dark angel,' she whispered, as she stared up at the man hanging helplessly above her. 'I am the revenger.' She drew the pistol, and pulled back the slide. There was a sharp metallic click as she let it fly forward again, feeding a round into the chamber.

'What are you doing?' Graf Otto shouted in consternation. 'Put that gun down. Somebody will get hurt!' Slowly she lifted it and aimed up at him.

'Stop, Eva! In the name of God, what are you doing?' Now she heard fear in his voice.

'I am going to kill you,' she said softly.

'Are you mad? Have you lost your mind?'

'I have lost more than my mind. You have taken everything from me. Now I am taking it back.'

She fired.

She had not expected the report to be so loud and the recoil to be so vicious. She had aimed at his black heart, but the bullet had nicked his left arm above the elbow. Blood trickled down his earm and dripped from his fingertips.

'Don't do this, Eva. Please! I will do anything you say.' She fired again and this shot flew wider than the first. It did not touch him. She had not known how difficult it was to shoot a pistol accurately at that range. Graf Otto was wriggling in the harness, swinging and jerking from side to side. She fired again and again. He was screaming with terror. 'Stop! Stop, my darling! I will make it up to you, I promise. You will have anything in the world you want from me.' She drew a deep breath and tried to still the pounding of her heart as she levelled the pistol for the last time – but before she could squeeze off the shot a strong arm whipped around her from behind and a hand fastened on her wrist, pushing the gun down. The shot ploughed into the ground between the toe-caps of her boots.

'Good man, Ritter!' Graf Otto bellowed. 'Hold her fast! Wait until I can get my hands on the treacherous bitch.'

Ritter twisted the pistol out of Eva's hands, then bore her to the ground with a knee between her shoulder-blades. He held her hands behind her back while one of his crew secured them with half a dozen workmanlike knots. Ritter handed him the Mauser. 'Shoot her if she gives you an excuse to do so,' he ordered, then ran to bring Graf Otto down from the tree. He grabbed the end of the dangling line and pulled it across. Graf Otto took a firm hold on a branch, then swung himself up until he was lying across it. There, he unbuckled his harness and let it fall. As agile as a huge ginger ape, he swarmed down the main trunk to the ground. He paused for only a minute to catch his breath, then walked slowly to where Eva lay. 'Pick her up,' he ordered the crewman, 'and hold her firm.' He smiled at her and showed her the metal fist. 'This is for you, my darling!' He hit her. He had judged the strength of his blow carefully: he did not want her to die too quickly.

'Bitch!' he said, then took a handful of her hair and twisted it until she fell on to her knees. 'Treacherous bitch. Now I understand that it was you all along, not that pathetic Boer creature.' He pushed her face into the rain-soaked earth and put his boot on the back of her head. 'I don't know what is the best way for you to die. Should I drown you in mud? Should I strangle you slowly? Or should I pound your beautiful head to jelly? It is a difficult decision.' He lifted her face and stared into her eyes. The blood oozing from her nose mingled with the mud, streamed down her face and dripped off her chin. 'Not so beautiful any more. More like the dirty little whore you truly are.'

Eva threw back her head and spat at him.

He wiped his face on his sleeve and laughed at her. 'This will be great sport. I shall enjoy every moment.'

Ritter stepped forward and tried to intervene. 'No, sir. You cannot do this to her. She is a woman.'

'I will prove to you that I can, Commodore. Watch this.' He lifted the armoured hand again, but as he leaned towards Eva, a deafening thunderbolt numbed their eardrums. It was the distinctive report of a .470 Nitro Express rifle. Graf Otto was hurled backwards, arms flailing, as the heavy bullet tore into the centre of his chest and erupted from between his shoulder-blades in a bright fountain of blood and pulped tissue.

'There is another bullet for anyone who wishes to dispute the issue further. Hands high, please, gentlemen!' Leon said in German, as he stepped from the bushes with Manyoro, Loikot and twenty Masai *morani* armed with stabbing *assegais* at his back.

'Manyoro, tie these people like chickens going to market. Have the *morani* take them to the army fort at Lake Magadi and hand them over to the soldiers,' he said, then ran to where Eva knelt in the mud. He jerked his hunting knife from its sheath and cut the rope. Then he cupped her face in his hands and lifted it to his.

'My nose,' she whispered. He brushed a kiss across her muddied and bloody lips.

'It's broken, and you will have a lovely pair of black eyes, but it's nothing that Doc Thompson can't deal with as soon as I can get you back to Nairobi.' He lifted her and held her tightly to his chest as he started back up the mountainside to where the *Butterfly* waited on the landing strip. There, he laid her tenderly on the deck and covered her with a sheet of tarpaulin, for she was shivering with shock.

When he stood up he saw that Lusima was standing by the fuselage. 'I'm taking her to Nairobi,' he told Lusima, 'but there's a great service you can do for us.'

'I will do it, my son,' she said.

'The silver monster lies broken upon the mountainside. Manyoro will take you and your *morani* to it. This is what I want you to do for me.'

'I am listening to you, M'bogo.' He spoke urgently. When he had finished she nodded. 'All these things I will do. Now take your lovely broken flower to safety and cherish her until she is healed.'

I t was four years almost to the day before they returned to Sheba's Pool. They left Lusima, Manyoro, Ishmael and Loikot at the old campsite and rode up alone to the pool. Leon came to lift her down from the saddle and kissed her before he set her on her feet. 'Passing strange,' he said, 'but how is it that you grow younger and more beautiful every day?'

She laughed and touched the side of her nose. 'Except for a little kink and a bump here and there.' Even the medical magic of Dr Thompson had not been up to the challenge of straightening her nose completely.

'You call that a little bump?' he asked, as he laid his hand on her belly. 'What about this one?'

She looked down at it proudly. 'Just watch it grow.'

'I'm agog with anticipation, Mrs Courtney.' He took her hand and led her to her usual seat on the rocky ledge. They sat side by side and gazed down into the dark waters.

'I bet you've never heard the tale of the missing Meerbach millions,' Eva said.

'Of course I have.' His face was straight and serious. 'It's one of the great mysteries of Africa. On a par with the lost mines of King Solomon and the Kruger millions that the old Boer president spirited away ahead of Kitchener's army when he marched into Pretoria.'

'Do you think somebody will solve the mystery soon?'

'Perhaps today,' he replied. He stood up and began to unbutton his shirt.

'It's been lying here for almost four years. What if somebody has found it already?' she asked, and her light mood began to fade.

'That could never have happened,' he reassured her. 'Lusima Mama put a curse on the pool. Nobody would dare go in there.'

'But aren't you afraid?' she asked.

He smiled and touched the little carved-ivory charm that hung on a thong around his neck. 'Lusima gave me this. It will ward off the curse.'

'You're making that up, Badger!' she accused him.

'There's only one way I can prove it to you.' He hopped on one leg as he shed his trousers, then took a running dive from the ledge into the water.

She jumped to her feet and shouted after him, 'Come back! I'm afraid to know the answer. What if it's all gone, Badger?'

He trod water and grinned at her from the middle of the pool. 'You're a determined pessimist, my love. In a few minutes from now we'll know the worst or the very best.' He drew four deep breaths and ducked. For a few seconds his bare feet kicked above the surface of the water and then he was gone. She knew it would be some time before he surfaced and she let her mind travel back over the last four years. They had been filled with excitement and danger, but also with love and laughter. She had been with him most of the time he was on campaign with Delamere's light horse in the bush against that cunning rascal, von Lettow Vorbeck. Leon had taught her to fly the *Bumble Bee* and to act as his observer and navigator. The two of them had made a famous team. Once, when Leon was not with her, she had landed the aircraft under heavy fire from the Germans to rescue four wounded *askaris*. Lord Delamere had pulled every trick in the book to see to it that she was awarded the Military Medal.

'But now the war is fought and won, I will be grateful for a little less excitement and danger and a lot more love and laughter.'

She jumped up as Leon burst out of the water with a mighty splash. 'Tell me the bad news!' she yelled.

He did not reply but swam to the ledge below her and lifted his right hand out of the water. He was holding something and threw it at her feet. It was a small canvas bag and it was heavy, for the mouth burst open as it hit the ledge. Golden coins poured from it and sparkled in the sunlight, and she squealed with excitement and fell to her knees. She gathered them up in her cupped hands and looked down at him with an unspoken question in her eyes.

'Some of the cases have burst open, probably when Lusima's *morani* dropped them into the pool from the top of the waterfall, but it looks as though none or very little is missing.' He slithered out of the water like an otter and she dropped the handful of gold sovereigns and reached out to hug his cold, wet body.

'Don't we have to give it all back?' she whispered into his ear.

'Give it back to whom? Kaiser Bill? I think he went out of business recently.'

'I feel so guilty. It doesn't belong to us.'

'Why don't you look upon it as full and final payment from Otto von Meerbach for the patents he stole from your father?' he suggested.

She rocked back, held him at arms' length and stared at him bemusedly. She started to smile. 'Of course! When you look at it like that it's really quite different.' Then she laughed. 'I can find no fault with your reasoning, my darling Badger!'